The Baltic Gambit

The Baltic Gambit

An Alan Lewrie Naval Adventure

Dewey Lambdin

THOMAS DUNNE BOOKS

ST. MARTIN'S GRIFFIN

NEW YORK

THOMAS DUNNE BOOKS.
An imprint of St. Martin's Press.

THE BALTIC GAMBIT. Copyright © 2009 by Dewey Lambdin. All rights reserved. Printed in the United States of America. For information, address St. Martin's Press, 175 Fifth Avenue, New York, N.Y. 10010.

www.thomasdunnebooks.com
www.stmartins.com

Maps copyright © 2009 by Carolyn Chu

The Library of Congress has cataloged the hardcover edition as follows:

Lambdin, Dewey.
   The Baltic gambit : an Alan Lewrie naval adventure / Dewey
Lambdin. — 1st ed.
      p. cm.
   ISBN 978-0-312-34806-9
   1. Lewrie, Alan (Fictitious character)—Fiction. 2. Ship captains—
Fiction. 3. Great Britain—History, Naval—18th century—Fiction. I. Title.
PS3562.A435B35 2009
813'.54—dc22

                                                        2008040343

ISBN 978-0-312-60348-9 (trade paperback)

First St. Martin's Griffin Edition: March 2010

10 9 8 7 6 5 4 3 2 1

This one is for one of my greatest fans,
my mother,
EDDA ALVADA ELLISON LAMBDIN
August 22, 1916–May 24, 2007

She *might've* fudged a couple of years off her birth
year, though—*most* of the Ellison sisters did.

Bold Knaves thrive without one grain of Sense,
But good Men starve for want of Impudence.

-JOHN DRYDEN

Full-Rigged Ship: Starboard (right) side view

1. Mizen Topgallant
2. Mizen Topsail
3. Spanker
4. Main Royal
5. Main Topgallant
6. Mizen T'gallant Staysail
7. Main Topsail
8. Main Course
9. Main T'gailant Staysail
10. Middle Staysail
11. Main Topmast Staysail
12. Fore Royal
13. Fore Topgallant
14. Fore Topsail
15. Fore Course
16. Fore Topmast Staysail
17. Inner Jib
18. Outer Flying Jib
19. Spritsail

A. Taffrail & Lanterns
B. Stern & Quarter-galleries
C. Poop Deck/Great Cabins Under
D. Rudder & Transom Post
E. Quarterdeck
F. Mizen Chains & Stays
G. Main Chains & Stays
H. Boarding Battens/Entry Port
I. Cargo Loading Skids
J. Shrouds & Ratlines
K. Fore Chains & Stays
L. Waist
M. Gripe & Cutwater
N. Figurehead & Beakhead Rails
O. Bow Sprit
P. Jib Boom
Q. Foc's'le & Anchor Cat-heads
R. Cro'jack Yard (no sail fitted)
S. Top Platforms
T. Cross-Trees
U. Spanker Gaff

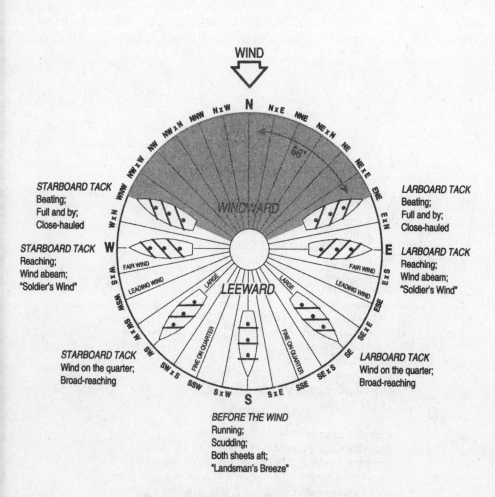

POINTS OF SAIL AND 32-POINT WIND-ROSE

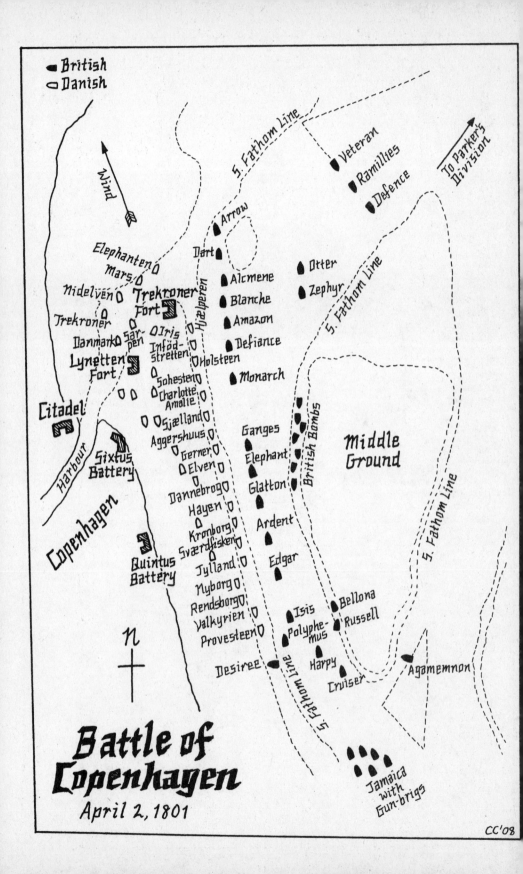

Battle of Copenhagen
April 2, 1801

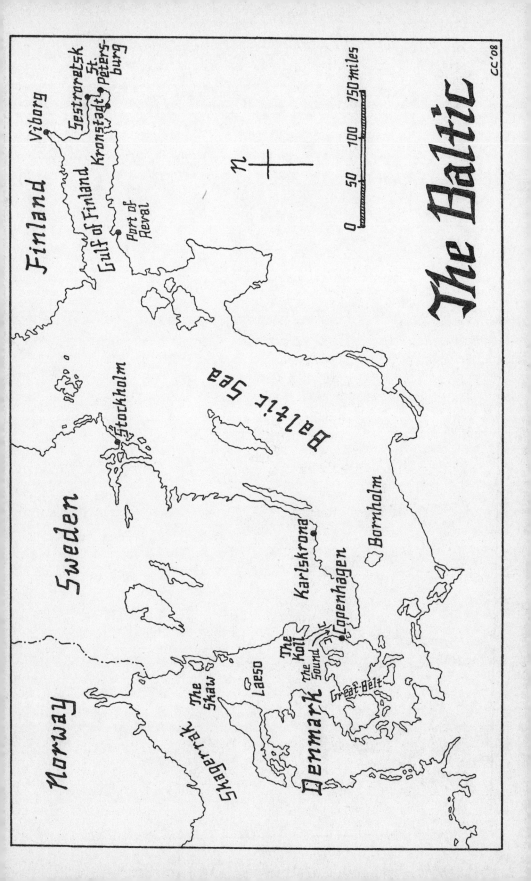

The Baltic

Norway
Sweden
Finland

Viborg
Sestroretsk
St. Peters-burg
Kronstadt
Gulf of Finland
Port of Reval

Stockholm

Baltic Sea

Bornholm

Karlskrona
Copenhagen
The Koll
Laeso
The Skaw
Skagerrak
The Sound
Great Belt
Denmark

N

0   50   100   150 miles

CC'08

PROLOGUE

Perge, Ira, perge et magna meditantem opprime,
congredere manibus ipsa dilacera tuis;

Then on, my wrath, on, and crush this plotter
of big things; close with him, thyself rend him in
pieces with thine own hands.

-LUCIUS ANNAEUS SENECA,
HERCULES FURENS, 75-76

CHAPTER ONE

A bloody awful day for 't," Sir Hugo St. George Willoughby commented as the hired coach-and-four clattered and swayed to a stop on the cobblestones before the steps leading up to the Old Bailey. With a wince and a sniff, he sampled the weather, sticking his head out of the right-hand side door window into the cold.

"Arr," his son, Captain Alan Lewrie, Royal Navy, idly replied. Lewrie, it must here be pointed out, was a *tad* hung over, after a sleepless night in his rooms at the Madeira Club, a sedate lodging for gentlemen not too far away from the Old Bailey, at the corner of Duke Street and Wigmore Street. His father, the old reprobate, leaned back to gather his walking stick and cloak, allowing Lewrie a view of the building. "Oh, Lord," Lewrie whispered.

Epiphany Sunday of the new year of 1801 had been on the fifth of January, and Hilary Term for King's Bench trials had, therefore, waited to open on Monday the sixth, with all the pomp, majesty, and circumstance of which England was capable, designed over the centuries to impress upon all Crown subjects, the innocent and the guilty alike, the terrible and implacable inevitability of Justice and Law.

Lewrie (whom no one could ever call innocent, exactly, but who had yet to learn if he was to be declared guilty) was definitely one of the impressed. Daunted, in point of fact. Shuddering in dread.

And did we mention hung over?

Lewrie looked beyond the horde of gawkers and spectators who spilled off the sidewalks onto the cobbled street, who had yet no inkling of whom the coach contained . . . up the wide steps that were clogged with even more spectators, from nobility to pick-pockets, prostitutes and the "flash" lads, the middling sort, and the idle poor, to the grim façade of the building. Up beyond the roof to the sky that was grey and gloomy, half coal smoke and half wintry overcast that boded even more snow later in the day, up beyond to the flagpole . . .

"Oh, Lord," Lewrie reiterated, squeezing his eyes shut to squint for a second, before taking a second peek at the flag. "Eyes must be going, I think," he muttered.

On January 1, the Act of Union 'twixt England, Scotland, Wales, and Ireland had come into force, with twenty-eight new Lords Temporal and four Lords Spiritual seated in Parliament, along with even more Members seated in the House of Commons. The old Union Flag had gotten updated with a so-called St. Patrick's Cross superimposed upon the old St. Andrew's Cross of the new Union Flag, which made it, to Lewrie at any rate, look rather . . . squiffy and un-focussed.

Maybe it's just me, Lewrie thought as a coachee opened the door and folded down the metal steps; *ev'rything* else *seems clear.* Though he had to shake his head and go "Brr!" before returning his eyes to the spectators.

"There 'e is! 'At's 'im! Huzzah!" several voices cried almost together as Lewrie alit on the street cobbles, and tried to shrug into the deep folds of his heavy wool boat-cloak, and clapped on his cocked hat. "Saint Alan, the Liberator, 'imself!"

Christ, I wish they'd lose that'un! Lewrie thought, wincing as his father jostled him as he got out behind him.

"Black Alan!" was hooted from others. "Three cheers, huzzah!"

Hell's Bells, that'un's not a whit better! he thought.

"Smile, damn ye," his father cautioned in a harsh whisper right near his ear. "Confidence, hmmm? Show for the damned Mob, what? As yer barrister said?" Sir Hugo prompted.

Lewrie forced himself to smile, took off his hat, and transferred it to his left hand, to leave his right one free . . . to fend off the pick-pockets, if for nothing else. The last time he'd appeared before King's Bench the summer before, one particularly skilled young lady of "the lifting lay," as his notorious old school friend Clotworthy Chute called it, had made off with his watch and fob and leather coin purse right as he'd threaded his way through throngs of well-wishers after his case had been held over for review! So it was understandable he kept his "top-lights" skinned for the charming "Three-Handed Jenny"!

Thursday the eighth of January, and bloody damned early in the morning to boot, was a hellish cold day for London. Had Lewrie his druthers, he'd have worn *two* boat-cloaks and a carriage blanket round his knees, but . . . his impending trial had become a Nine-Day Wonder, no thanks to the many tracts, cartoon prints, and "bought" newspaper articles put out by the Reverend William Wilberforce's Society for the Abolition of Slavery in the British Empire the last year, entire, so Lewrie could hardly disguise himself any longer, nor could he swaddle himself against the weather, either. Reluctantly, he flung back the boat-cloak to reveal his gilt-laced uniform coat, and the hundred-guinea presentation sword given him by the East India Company after a sea fight against a French frigate in the South Atlantic that saved a small convoy of "John Company" ships returning from India, in 1799.

And, despite his wariness of pick-pockets (and eyes darting for signs of "Three-Handed Jenny"), Lewrie was thronged by gentlemen and ladies wishing to take hands with him, by people fluttering portrait prints of the artist de Koster's charcoal life sketch (now available from Mr. Brydon's shop in Charing Cross) for him to sign with pencil in the margins.

Ye'd think I'm Nelson, fresh from the Battle of the Nile, not a slave-crimper! Lewrie ruefully told himself, and wondering if he'd attract the same sort of acclaim should he be found guilty and carted off to the gallows, a few days hence. And would he have to put on the same confident and affable show, to "Go Game" as a convicted high-wayman?

"God bless you, sir! Good on yer! Might you do me the honour of inscribing . . . ? Best of luck t'ye this day, sir! Me son served wi' ye in th' old *Jester* sloop, Cap 'm, un' . . . The Devil take those horrid Beaumans, and God uphold the right, I say, Captain Lewrie!" came from dozens as he slowly made his way up the broad steps to the welcoming doors, now standing wide open despite the cold, and visibly blasting waves of warmth from the interior. Calls for "Abolition of slavery, throughout the British Empire, now!" were followed by " 'Ere, oo's *at* git?" with the faint cry of "Thief, thief!" from the edge of the crowd, out by piles of shovelled-away snow, now gone grey from coal smoke grit and frozen half to ice. Thankfully, it was not directed at Lewrie, but at some clumsy pick-pocket, who was sprinting away as fast as his legs could carry him, with or without the object of his craft, pursued by a clutch of men.

Oh, there *were* some stout and prosperous-looking men, heavily and expensively overcoated against the chill, who stood far back at the edges of the crowd, round to either side of the top of the steps, who glowered at him; men engaged in the sugar trade, which utterly depended on slave labour for their crops . . . men in the tobacco, rice, rum, and cotton imports, and men in the West Indies and American shipping businesses, which maintained the infamous Triangle Trade of British gewgaws to Africa, slaves in exchange to the Americas and West Indies, then raw goods back to Great Britain. Any threat to slave economies would mean utter ruin to their fortunes. Sadly, among those silently jeering men were several senior officers of his own service; most-like muttering "that bloody bastard, Lewrie"—there were more than a few who'd formed that opinion of him during his twenty-year naval career!

Closer to, though, was a shivering clutch of "Saint Giles Blackbirds," Negro sailors off merchant ships docked, or frozen in, in the Pool of London. Freemen, or slaves who had been successful in running away to sea, thousands of miles from the warmth of their islands in the Caribbean, half starved on bad victuals, cheated of their due pay by skinflint captains, "crimped off" at the end of their voyages to the Impress Service without ha'pence of their wages by some captains even cleverer, they huddled in the slums of St. Giles a clan apart, waiting for an outbound vessel to sign them aboard once more; and, living hand to mouth and begrudging every meal at a two-penny ordinary, every pot of ale or beer in the meantime.

"You show 'em, sah! You whup dem slavah mens!" they dared cry out. "Ya git anuddah ship, sah, *ah'll* take yah Joinin' Bounty, sah! De Good Lord bless ya, Cap'm Lewrie!"

Lewrie turned aside to go to them, the crowd parting before him like the Red Sea had for Moses, and shook hands with as many as were in reach; though he felt like snarling to hear the simpering and cooing of the "Respectable," and superior, sort among the Abolitionists, who kept the objects of their Cause at arm's length, and patted themselves on the back for their Doing of Good Works . . . of the Drawing Room variety, and would never even *think* of going down to St. Giles . . . or of deeming those "Blackbirds" *real* people.

And what had led to this display of acclaim? A ship's crew in the West Indies ravaged by Yellow Jack in 1797; a disagreement between the Beauman family of Jamaica and his old friend Christopher Cashman, who had retired from the Army with his reaped wealth from hard field service in "John Company's" army in India, and who had, for a time, thought the life of a slave-owning sugar planter on Jamaica would be the sweet life. The bloody slave revolt on the ultra-rich sugar colony on French St. Domingue, which butchered Whites no matter their class or station, and which had drawn a British Army with an eye to seizing the whole thing . . . thankee that damned scheming fool, Henry Dundas, the Secretary of State for War, who would trade ten thousand British soldiers' lives for an enemy colony in the West Indies, and a cheer in Commons . . . had led the "patriotic" Beaumans to raise a regiment, and who better to lead it than former-Major Christopher Cashman, with that simpering twit Ledyard Beauman as Colonel of the Regiment over Leftenant-Colonel Cashman, with the rest of the officers' mess made up from Beauman kin and the younger sons of fellow planters. Most-like with an eye for new lands for themselves, and stout workers, once they were back in chains!

Outside Port-au-Prince, though, in the middle of a battle with the howling, fanatical army of the ex-slave general Toussaint L'Ouverture (no slouch, he, but damn' near a military genius!) Col. Ledyard Beauman, who'd gotten his martial experience from books and tabletop games with lead toy soldiers, had panicked, issued orders for retreat, and had galloped to the rear with his cousins and toadies, leaving Lewrie's friend Christopher Cashman to sort out the mess!

Back on Jamaica after the eventual evacuation of all British forces, the volunteer regiment shamed and dis-banded, the Beaumans had laid all the blame on Cashman, using their newspaper to vilify everyone but them, which had led to a duel of honour; which duel had turned to a farce, for Ledyard had been shivering drunk and fearful, and had turned and fired early, clipping the top of Cashman's shoulder. "Kit" had winced, but turned, and had taken careful, implacable aim, and Ledyard's cousin, George Sellers, his second, had thrown Ledyard a spare pistol, aiming his own at Cashman, and naturally Lewrie, as Cashman's second, and the judges on the field, to boot, had shot down the cousin, whilst Christopher had carefully plumped his own ball into Ledyard Beauman's belly, the sort of wound that would take several excruciating days to prove mortal.

With such a feud, which now included Lewrie, and death threats from the Beaumans, Cashman had begun selling up his lands, livestock, furnishings, and slaves for a fresh start in the United States, just about the time that Lewrie's precious HMS *Proteus* frigate had been hit with the Yellow Jack. As a cruel joke on the Beaumans, "Kit" Cashman had proposed a scheme for a dozen Beauman slaves off one of their plantations on Portland Bight (next to Cashman's) to run away and go aboard *Proteus* some dark night, which they had done, with HMS *Proteus* slipping close ashore like a thief in the night, and sailing back out as quietly as smoke went up a chimney.

Christopher Cashman landed in Wilmington, North Carolina, eventually, swearing he'd never own another slave (he'd manumitted almost all his household servants, and all the married couples, old'uns, and children), and Lewrie had gone on to cut a swath of destruction and mayhem through the King's enemies in the West Indies . . . 'til 1799, when the shoe finally dropped, and the Beaumans discovered just who had made away with their "property"!

Hugh Beauman, the elder of their Jamaican clan, with his icily beautiful new young wife, his Jamaican solicitor, and witnesses in tow, had come to England last spring, toting a preordained, bought-and-paid-for verdict of guilty, and a sentence of death by hanging. For a time, it had appeared that King's Bench would uphold the verdict and Lewrie would be doing a "Newgate Hornpipe," but for the intercession of Rev. William Wilberforce and his Abolition Society, who had taken the case as a "Holy Cause," gotten him a wily young barrister to defend him, and paid for his legal fees; shouted Abolition to the rafters of the House of Commons daily, and had flooded all London, all the British Isles, with tracts to keep the pot boiling, and the Cause advanced . . . embarrassing as all that notoriety was to Lewrie.

Now, here he was, about to enter a court of law to hear what Lord Justice Oglethorpe of King's Bench thought of that trial *in absentia*, and the conflicting evidence that Lewrie's barrister had presented in reply. Free of well-wishers and glad-handers at last, at the doors to the Old Bailey at last, Lewrie turned to the crowd and waved his hat, plastering a broad grin on his phyz that he most definitely did not feel, and went inside. No matter what transpired in the next few hours—and most trials in England barely lasted more than four)—at least he might be warm again.

CHAPTER TWO

*T*he outer halls of the building were just as thronged as those icy steps, though the "ton" of the crowd inside was considerably higher, and better known to Lewrie. There was his brother-in-law, Major Burgess Chiswick, the beautiful young lady to whom he was but lately affianced, Mistress Theodora Trencher, and her wealthy Abolitionist parents. His fond supporter and patron since '96 in the Adriatic, Sir Malcolm Shockley, of the Midlands coal and iron fortune, was there with the earnest young Sir Samuel Whitbread, he of the beer fortune, and one of the new "Progressives" in Commons with Sir Malcolm. There was his old schooldays chum, Lord Peter Rushton, and by his side stood "too clever by half" Clotworthy Chute, a trimmer and "Captain Sharp" who specialised in separating newcome heirs down to London from some of the wealth by playing guide to all things Fashionable. Despite that stern majesty of the Law, the both of them, and the lovely ladies by their side, hooted, huzzahed, and stuck their fingers in their mouths to make shrill whistling noises, cackling away like loons, and waving at him . . . which only encouraged even the haughtiest to follow suit.

"Bread and circuses," his father, Sir Hugo, griped *sotto voce* as a servant took his hat, cloak, and walking stick. "Bad as a Roman raree show, I swear. Necessary, I s'pose, but . . . what flummery."

"Bloody Hell!" Lewrie exclaimed, dignity and serene confidence bedamned, as he turned over his own hat and cloak, and caught sight of a bevy of Navy men waiting for him with bright eyes and smiles. "How the Devil did they dredge *you* up? Just damn my eyes!"

For there stood officers and men from old HMS *Proteus*, those who had turned over into his latest ship, the *Savage* frigate, and had been there off Portland Bight the night of his "crime"—Lt. Adair, his former Second Officer; Lt. D'arcy Gamble, Third into *Savage*, then a Midshipman; Sailing Master Mr. Winwood; Midshipman Grace, even Coote, the Purser; along with all seven surviving sailors of the dozen he'd absconded with! The only man missing was Anthony Langlie, then First Officer of *Proteus*, and now Commander Langlie, and in command of HMS *Orpheus*, a brig-sloop of his own.

"*Savage* put into Torbay to re-victual on the Second, sir," Lt. Adair gleefully explained as he pumped Lewrie's "paw" in joy, "and up pops an order from Lord Saint Vincent, aboard the flag, before we got the kedge anchor down. Captain Wolters wasn't keen on it, but, here we all are, sir, ready to testify on your behalf. No delay, really, with the weather foul in the Channel, and at least a fortnight's work to put the ship right."

"Gentlemen . . . lads, I'm damned glad t'see ye, *damned* glad . . . and not just for your testimony, hey?" Lewrie enthused, shaking hands with one and all. "Dry, read affidavits are one thing, but your tales in your own words'll be quite another, my barrister tells me. You've met my father, before? And, here comes Desmond, Furfy, Aspinall, and Jones Nelson. Old Boys' Week, ha ha!"

His Coxswain, Liam Desmond, and his big mate Patrick Furfy, Lewrie's longtime cabin servant and cook Aspinall, and the very big Black sailor (most recently his personal bodyguard) Jones Nelson had come into the hall, so it really did become a grand reunion.

Introductions had to be made all round, from Lord Peter, who had precedence, down to the burly Irishman, Furfy. Then there came Lewrie's barrister's clerk, one Mr. Sadler, who was forced to play his usual role of coughing into his fist and "aheming" to beat the band to herd Lewrie down the hallway to the proper courtroom. "Sir . . . sir. Captain Lewrie? Ahem. Mister MacDougall suggests we should be entering . . . ahem?"

"Right, right then," Lewrie finally had to allow. "My pardons, Mister Sadler, and we'll be going. Lead on, do you please."

⚓

The long and heavy table set aside for Defence Counsel was piled high with octavos bound in "law calf" the colour of pie crust, with a large easel standing off by the far wall, and something framed nearby, currently covered, and as big as a bed sheet.

"Joy of the morning, Captain Lewrie!" his young Puck of an attorney declared, spreading his arms wide, and swirling the black legal "stuff" robe he wore. Mr. Andrew MacDougall, Esquire, stood about four inches shy of six feet, plump, round, and moon-faced; no amount of dark cloth could make him appear sober; nor did the stiff white peruke with three tight horizontal side-curls and out-standing ribbon-bound queue that jutted from the nape of his neck over his own generous dark blond hair. MacDougall might have come extremely well recommended, but Lewrie still thought of him as the merest boy, who should still have been playing pranks at university.

Talented, aye, Lewrie allowed to himself; *successful with past cases, but . . . 'tis no skin off his arse does he fail. It's just one more court appearance . . . notorious enough t'make his name either way.*

And it rather irked Lewrie that the stout young whelp was all but ready to cut capers, or do a horn-pipe of glee.

"Good morning, Mister MacDougall," Lewrie felt fit to reply. "I trust we'll both be smiling when the day's done . . . ow! Damn!" for he had stubbed the toe of one of his gilt-trimmed Hessian boots against a large wood box placed under the table.

"I am completely certain that we shall, sir!" MacDougall replied. "Now, more than ever," he added, rocking on the balls of his feet and bestowing upon his "brief" a "sly-boots" smile.

"What?" Lewrie enquired with a scowl of some confusion. It was his life on the line; for a second he could conjure that the box under the table was reserved for his head after they lopped it off, hanging bedamned. "You know something I don't?"

"A most *wondrous* something, Captain Lewrie!" MacDougall all but chortled, his face dimpled and rosy with delight. "Word has come to me from Mister Twigg of the Foreign Office concerning your accuser, Hugh Beauman, sir. It seems that he, that frostily handsome young wife of his . . . his own attorney, and *all* his *witnesses* . . . have decamped!"

"So?" Lewrie said with another frown of confusion. "Last time they were in court, he turned into his own worst enemy with all o' his bellowin' and threats. His barrister most-like—"

"His *witnesses,* sir!" MacDougall reiterated, peering at Lewrie as if he were too simple to understand plain English. "Decamped. Gone like thieves in the night. No longer in London. No longer in *England,* d'ye see."

Christ, Twigg's killed 'em? Lewrie just had to imagine. There wasn't any reason that he could see for Hugh Beauman to withdraw his case, short of a dire threat from official circles in H.M. Government, or a gang of hooded assassins to hustle the bloody, bound corpses into the Thames. God knew how many thousands of pounds Hugh Beauman had already spent to discover who'd stolen his slaves, to bring the prosecution before a rigged Jamaican court and justice, pack the jury with his kin and employees, then spend over a year in England, supporting all of his henchmen (paying thousands more to amuse and please that icy blond wife of his, and her passion for shopping, too, by God!) waiting for a court date.

Lewrie had known the Beaumans since 1781, off and on, and, no matter they were as rich as the Walpoles, they were so "Country-Put," so "Chaw Bacon," they could make the crudest John Bull country squire gawk and sneer. Dog-slobberin', huntin', shootin', fishin', tenant-tramplin', slave-whoppin', arrogant, brute, and boorish as they come were the Beauman men (and God help their womenfolk) with thousands for Publick show, yet penny-pinchin' miserly in private. Overbearing and *loud,* un-grammatic and blasphemous (*well, so am I,* Lewrie admitted to himself!), and so used to getting their own way, all the time, that it was ludicrous to think that Hugh Beauman, the very worst of a very bad lot, would just fold his tents and steal away, after coming so close to getting his revenge!

Zachariah Twigg and his "unofficial" little private battalion of watchers, noters, spies, and bully-bucks (both male and female) served the Crown damned well, and God only knew how many foreign agents were crab-food, downriver. *Had it come to that stage?* Lewrie wondered; *So what? Good for him, but didn't he leave it just a bit late? Native chiefs, rebel rajahs . . . it ain't like Twigg t'hold off so long.*

Lewrie involuntarily looked about to see if anyone was watching before sketching a finger across his throat and shrugging a question best left unsaid in a court of law.

"Oh, Lord no, Captain Lewrie, nothing like that!" Mr. MacDougall wheezed with good cheer. "They have absconded . . . coached off to Yarmouth to board the Portugal packet . . . out of reach of a King's Bench warrant for perjury, and laying a false prosecution."

"Well, just damn my eyes!" Lewrie barked, too loudly, drawing the attention of every spectator now filling the benches in the court room. "Gone to Portugal, in this weather? They'll be lucky do they not drown . . . or get taken by a French man-o'-war. Humph! Couldn't happen to a worse set o' people. The wife, excepted . . . perhaps."

"Aye, that would have been a mortal pity," Mr. MacDougall said with a bemused nod. "It seems . . . " MacDougall added, drawing Lewrie towards the far wall of the richly panelled court room, near the mystifying covered easel, "that Hugh Beauman was made aware that, should his barrister, Sir George Norman, put him, or any of his witnesses, in the box to testify, they would lay themselves open to some *extremely* serious charges. Then, once I presented *my* case in refutation of all their lies . . . with all your officers and men, and your Black sailors to prove them liars . . . well, t'would be a genuine wonder did Beauman and his people not wind up in gaol awaiting their own trials. A risk that Mister Hugh Beauman evidently would not take."

"His attorney, Sir George, might've told him?" Lewrie asked.

"No . . . I rather doubt that, Captain Lewrie," MacDougall said as he tapped the side of his nose sagely, and tipped Lewrie a broad wink, lowering his voice even further. "Sir George Norman is, ah . . . still not cognisant of the flight of his principals. Though I'm certain all shall become plain to him soon enough, haw haw! And, given the fact that it is not customary for principals to place more than a retainer fee with the solicitor who engages a barrister, with the balance due *after* the completion of a barrister's duties . . ."

"Beauman left a huge debt when he scampered?" Lewrie gawped in delight, trying to keep his own voice down. "Sir George can't touch him in Portugal! Why, there's *thousands* owing!"

What my father did, when he went bust, Lewrie enjoyed recalling; *after he crimped me into the Navy, and Granny Lewrie refused to die and leave me ev'rything.* He took a second to look back at the spectators' benches and espied Sir Hugo, who was hovering rather droolishy and leeringly wolf-like over some "chickabiddy" woman in her late thirties.

"I do *so* look forward to seeing the expression on Sir George's face when *that* shoe drops, 'deed I do, Captain Lewrie," Mr. MacDougall whinnied like a panting pony.

"If they've decamped, this could just be dismissed, then . . . just like that?" Lewrie asked with a snap of his fingers.

"Well, not quite, sorry t'say." MacDougall sobered, leading him back towards the Defence table. "Our first outing last year was an evidentiary hearing, with Lord Justice Oglethorpe ruling that he would review both the trial transcript, and our affidavits. Even with those Beaumans gone . . . and Sir George left without a leg to stand on, with all previous testimony against you declared 'colourable,' there still remains the fact that, with your own witnesses giving the lie to the evidence in the trial transcript, you do lay yourself open to the charge of Illegal Conversion of another's property . . . assuming the jury will be of a mind to consider your Black sailors property. Once I learned of the Beaumans' departure, I *did* consider requesting an *en bane* proceeding, with Lord Justice Oglethorpe to rule upon your guilt or innocence, yet . . .'tis not the irrefutable *facts* of your defence t'will prevail today, but the irrational *emotions* of your Black sailors' testimony that will carry the day. Logic bedamned. 'Tis the heartstrings of the jurymen . . . the notoriety your cause has created among them beforehand . . . the sympathy for your Blacks, and for *you*, particularly, that the jurymen's *wives* have expressed over the last year, that will . . . hopefully . . . find you acquitted." Mac-Dougall all but promised in a sly, cagy way. "Be of sanguine takings, Captain Lewrie. You stand very good odds of walking out of court a competely free man. Aha!"

A side door at the back of the courtroom opened. A court official emerged in robe and wig, with a large ornamental mace in his hand, which he loudly thudded on the floor, crying "Oyez, oyez, oyez!" to silence the packed crowd, and order them to take seats.

Free to do what? Lewrie wondered as the procession of officials emerged, as Lord Justice Oglethorpe in his voluminous black silk robes and large bag-wig strode out as grand as a royal.

Even were he acquitted, Lewrie just knew that Lord Spencer at Admiralty would *never* give him another warship. He'd be assigned to the Yellow Squadron, that unofficial dust-bin for fools, incompetents, lunaticks, and dodderers. He'd stay ashore on half-pay, might even rise to Rear-Admiral of the Red, should he outlive his contemporaries—but "beached," waiting for seniors to die.

Lewrie knew his shortcomings; they were legion. He could not pretend to be a gentleman farmer; he'd tried that 'tween the wars and had been a miserably confused failure. He was too old to take up some new career, too gullible to stand for a seat in Parliament, too idle and slug-a-bed, if given the chance, to seek merchant service. He was too poor to play the market at the 'Change (and most-like would waste his last farthing on speculative idiocy and ignorance), too much of a stiff-necked "gentle-man" to stoop to anything that smacked of "Trade" and Commerce, no matter how lucrative (or risky) such turned out to be for other venturers. The prize-money he had reaped in the Med, in the West Indies, and South Atlantic was tied up in the Sinking Funds and Three Percents anyway, and sooner or later, the last of that'd come in, and there'd be nothing after.

Maybe Twigg needs a new cut-throat, he speculated as he took a seat at the Defence table, before the summons to the raised dock.

CHAPTER THREE

L ord Justice Oglethorpe was a stolid man, a phlegmatic and ponderous older fellow who, it was rumoured, could take an hour choosing an *entrée* from his club's daily menu, and so meditative at chess, cards, or backgammon that no one had asked him for a game since his teens.

"Your principals are not *present*, Sir George?" he enquired with a bland expression. "How odd."

"They are not, milud," Sir George Norman, usually a very smooth gentleman, responded, fidgeting a little, looking as if he wished that he could jerk his head about to hunt for them. Both his clerks had already been sent haring round the halls and into the street outside, in a desperate last-minute search for the Beauman party.

"And have you, sir, had cause to correspond with them prior to this instant?" Oglethorpe intoned, with his head cocked to one side.

"I have not, milud," Sir George had to admit, all but wringing his hands. "Not since a brief note from their lodgings in Islington, in receipt of my informing them of the date their case was to be held."

"How extremely odd," Oglethorpe commented with an uncharacteristic huff. "Mister MacDougall . . . I trust *your* witnesses are here."

"We are, in all respects, both ready, and eager, to proceed, my lord," MacDougall piped up as he bowed his head, taking a second for a smirk in Sir George Norman's direction.

A folder of pale "law calf" was opened, up on the *banc* surface, and papers rustled as Lord Justice Oglethorpe cleared his throat with several "ahems," waiting out the snickers and whispers of the court spectators.

"Ahem . . . in the matter of Beauman *versus* Lewrie . . . after an exhaustive review of the trial transcript from the High Court in Kingston, Jamaica . . . and comparing the witness statements sworn in that proceeding against the sworn affidavits provided by the defendant, I find such contradictions of the facts of the matter obtaining to warrant an entirely fresh proceeding, *de ovo*. Harumph!

"Further . . . the nature of the jury empanelled on Jamaica, with so many of the members either kin to the Beaumans, or kin to the Captain George Sellers, who perished along with Colonel Ledyard Beauman in an infamous duel of honour, *and,* the inclusion of men either *employed* by Mister Hugh Beauman or his kin, *or* intimately linked with the slave trade on Jamaica, smacks of collusion and prejudice . . . which as well requires a new proceeding, *de ovo.*

"Therefore . . . ahem! . . . I rule that Captain Lewrie's trial *in absentia* at Kingston, Jamaica, the verdict of guilty, *and* the sentence of death by hanging is null and void, and is set as—"

The last of his ruling was drowned out by hoots, whistles, and cheers from the spectators, and a boisterous round of clapping (along with the surreptitious exchange of pound notes as bets were paid off) that continued 'til Oglethorpe gavelled them to relative silence, and more carefully guarded pleased whispers, coughs, and the rustling of ladies' skirtings.

"At this juncture, ahem . . . ," Lord Justice Oglethorpe continued. "I should empanel a jury. I wonder, however, Sir George, whether such an action might be precipitate. If your principal is not here, and neither are any of the witnesses quoted in the transcript, I conjure you, sir . . . are you able to lay a case against Captain Lewrie, this day?"

"I . . . I . . . " Sir George Norman stammered, all his glibness and noble carriage punched from him. "Is the transcript of the previous trial eliminated, milud, I do not see how I would be able, no." Sir George could almost be heard groaning . . . or grinding his teeth.

"My lord!" MacDougall cried. "Will this odious charge hang over my principal's head the rest of his life, like the Sword of Damocles? Must Captain Lewrie's good name, his repute as a successful Commission Sea Officer in our Navy, be besmirched? His accusers are not present *today,* but . . . when *might* Mister Hugh Beauman come forth with a fresh proceeding, a new crop of witnesses, perhaps even an expanded list of *charges*, since the first set did not suit? A year, my lord? Two, or five, or ten?

"Captain Lewrie was, perjuriously, tried *in absentia* before," Mac-Dougall said with a sly look. "Once back on Jamaica, might Mister Hugh Beauman arrange a second? From wherever he has gone? No, I say, my lord! It must end here today. Justice must be done him!"

Oh Christ, it was almost over! Don't do . . . ! Lewrie fearfully thought; *I'd known Beauman scarpered, I'd've considered it myself!*

"I humbly urge you to empanel a jury of twelve men, good and true, my lord," MacDougall said with a hand on his breast. "Let them hear, and see, the facts of the matter, and determine Captain Lewrie's fate for good and all, my lord."

Some spectators cheered and huzzahed, though most made buzzing sounds of confusion and surprise; which noises covered Lewrie's groan. To the crowd in the courtroom, it *had* looked over and done with, and MacDougall's request seemed suicidal.

Mine arse on a band-box, Lewrie gawped to himself; *he wants to show off! Got all his set-pieces, and can't abide not usin' 'em!*

"Milud," Sir George Norman cried before the last of the hub-bub died down. "To proceed without my principal, my witnesses, and the use of the trial transcript, Mister Hugh *Beauman* might as well be tried *in absentia*! It would be so one-sided. . . ."

"Sauce for the goose, sauce for the gander!" MacDougall chirped.

"Ahem!" from the Lord Justice, and some more gavelling. "There is the risk to Captain Lewrie that at some time in the future, a trial *could* be demanded by the plaintiff. And, though your presentation to a jury may not go much beyond your opening statements to lay charges, Sir George, if counsel for the Defence has his affidavits, witnesses . . . whose Service may not allow them to be gathered together all in one place ever again . . . might even be unavailable to Captain Lewrie and some future attorney should the plaintiff in this matter decide to pursue his case on more salubrious grounds . . . well, they're here today. If you have no objections, Sir George, I am tempted to seat a jury and proceed. How say you, sir?"

Sir George Norman, K.C., could never admit that he'd been taken in by the seeming authority of the trial transcript from Jamaica; that the witnesses Hugh Beauman had imported might have been lying through their teeth; that he'd never looked into the makeup of the jury before MacDougall had brought it up.

There was also the honourarium to consider; his fee, which had been *partly* paid, and, with the Beaumans fled the country, looked like it might never be. *No skin off* my *arse!* he seemed to say to himself. He scowled in thought for a long moment, then bowed his head.

"If Mister MacDougall wishes to proceed, and the demands of the Navy would not allow his witnesses to be gathered together at a later time, then . . . I bow to your ruling, milud."

With *voir dire* objections and questioning, it took an hour for a jury to be seated; then came the opening statements. Sir George did his best, though with a "third party" distancing air. "My principal asserts that on such and such a date, Captain Alan Lewrie, with malice aforethought . . . witnesses at the scene of the crime asserted that . . . did conspire with Leftenant-Colonel Christopher Cashman, now fled the jurisdiction of King's Justice to America, to receive twelve Negroes slaves, from my principal's plantation on Portland Bight, the value of the slaves at the time twenty-five pounds apiece . . . "

MacDougall ostentatiously cleaned his fingernails with a pen-knife 'til Sir George was done, then sprang to his feet like a Jack-in-the-Box.

"My lord, gentlemen of the jury, I am not quite sure whether counsel for the plaintiff has just accused Captain Lewrie of outright theft, or of the lesser charge of illegal conversion! Either way, is it believable that the value of a human being's life, the value of his short and brutal labour, so back-breaking and hideous that most perish within five years, is only worth twenty-five *pounds?* And if so, why did not Hugh Beauman sue in the Court of Common Pleas for three hundred pounds?"

He then encapsulated for the jury the injustice done his client at the trial on Jamaica; to which Sir George Norman made no objections. . . . He might have been contemplating dinner, for his part was done. It was old news for the spectators, but visibly distasteful to the jury as they learned what a sham the trial *in absentia* had been, and the feud that had preceded it.

"Now let us proceed, gentlemen, to the root cause," MacDougall said, returning to the Defence table for a letter that his clerk, Mr. Sadler, handed him. "Here is a letter from former Leftenant-Colonel Christopher Cashman, with whom Captain Lewrie allegedly conspired. I wish you to be patient as I read this affidavit, sworn before a Justice of the Peace in Wilmington, North Carolina, in the United States, and witnessed and notarised . . . which affidavit has already been presented to the court and laid in evidence."

The affidavit laid out Cashman's career in both the British and East India Company armies, his return to the West Indies, his initial acceptance of slavery as a necessity to work his lands, his previous military service in conjunction with then Lieutenant Lewrie during the last year of the American Revolution, and their *rencontre* in the '90s, when he had been asked by the Beaumans to lead the volunteer regiment. The botched battle, Ledyard Beauman's cowardice, and the feud that followed, which led to the duel. Then . . .

"By this time, I was heartily sick of Jamaica, heartily sick of the Beaumans, and all their brute class, and, most especially, sick of the horrid institution of slavery, a view which I was pleasantly surprised to learn that my old friend Alan Lewrie wholeheartedly shared," MacDougall stressed, pacing urgently before the jury box as he read on. He'd sold *some* of his slaves off, the most troublesome and truculent, but freed the bulk of them. Then as he was selling up, after the duel, it had been *Cashman* who had suggested freeing some of Beauman's slaves as well.

" 'I took it upon myself to approach the field hands of Mister Hugh Beauman's plantation next to mine on Portland Bight, using one of my newly freed house servants as intermediary, hinting that those among them who wished to run and join the Royal Navy would be welcome aboard a frigate which would be off the coast in a few days. I then suggested to my fellow Abolitionist, Alan Lewrie, that, was his crew so decimated by Yellow Fever that he was in difficulties to keep her manned, there could be a round dozen eager volunteers available . . . ' "

Lyin' like a Turkey carpet! Lewrie flummoxed to himself in the dock; *Didn't happen* quite *like that. A damned* good *lie, though!*

" '. . . night that *Proteus* closed the coast, I rode down shoreward, to the edge of my property, which abutted the Beaumans' lands, and with a great deal of satisfaction, watched as the boats came ashore, a dozen young men embark into them, and was, for a time, fearful that the commotion from their parents and kinfolk, who had come down the beach with them to see them off, might awaken the overseers, for such lamentations of loss, yet joyful hosannahs of relief that some few of their fellows might gain their freedom, were hardly to be contained no matter the need for quiet and secrecy. At that moment I felt such a rush of pride that it was successfully carried off, without interruption, along with such a flood of emotion that brought tears to my eyes to see even a *few* young men escape the clutches of the Beaumans, and *take* their freedom from a life that is little better than a death sentence, that I swore at that moment that not only would I abjure from owning another human being in my life, but would work tirelessly to see slavery outlawed in all the nations of the earth, no matter what that stance personally cost me.'

"The words of a man who now *resides* in a nation which upholds slavery . . . in a state famed for its agriculture, and naval stores . . . all of which *require* Negro slave labour. In a town where such views are *anathema*, where, once the contents of Colonel Cashman's affidavit are known to his fellow citizens, he very likely faces social and financial ruin, sirs. Consider what courage that took for him to testify on Captain Lewrie's behalf," MacDougall posed to the jury.

"Milud," Sir George Norman said with a piteous smirk as he rose to his feet, "it would seem that my learned colleague has just admitted his principal's *guilt*!"

"To what specific crime, my lord, does Sir George refer?" Mr. Mac-Dougall quickly retorted, plucking the front of his black court robe. "Does he maintain that Captain Lewrie *instigated* and *premeditated* the crime of *Robbery*, in the face of Leftenant-Colonel Cashman's confessing affidavit? Or does he wish to now *reduce* his accusations to *Conversion* of Property? The waters must be un-muddied upon this head for the clarification of the jury, my lord. Let us be specific."

Has he lost his fuckin' mind? Lewrie could but goggle quietly.

Lord Justice Oglethorpe scratched his scalp under his bag-wig with a pencil, scowled, pursed his lips, then impatiently waved both barristers forward to the front of his bench, where ensued a lengthy, hushed conversation; one that must have pleased MacDougall right down to the ground, for, when Oglethorpe shooed them away, he had a bright smile plastered on his phyz, whilst Sir George Norman was shaking his head.

"Ahem . . . upon reception of the confession from Mister Christopher Cashman, counsel for the plaintiffs has amended his accusations to a charge of illegal Conversion. Silence! Silence in the . . . !" He had to cry and gavel for order as the spectators raised yet another great cheer.

"Now, let us see how the event occurred, that dark night off the coast of Portland Bight, three years ago," Mr. MacDougall said in the relative silence, after the crowd had settled down once more. He waved to his clerk, Mr. Sadler, and another assistant, who stood up the easel and hung the bed sheet–sized roll of cloth upon the cross-piece, allowing it to fall open.

Wonder what that *cost?* Lewrie thought, shifting in his chair in the dock to look at it. MacDougall had gone to a chart maker's for an up-to-date map of that section of coast, compared the new one to the old one that *Proteus*'s Sailing Master, Mr. Winwood, had used, and had an artist or sign painter do up a large-scale version in full colour; pale blue wash for ocean, rocky shoals in grey, sand bars in tan, and land in pale green, with forests and fields done in a darker green. A topographic map of the plantations in question surely must have come from Jamaica, as well, for the Beaumans', and Cashman's, plantings were delineated quite accurately, right down to the locations of the houses, barns, and slave quarters; all of them neatly labelled, as was the beach where the ship's boats had grounded; and all distances from specific points clearly marked, corresponding to a distance scale in the lower left corner.

"At this point, my lord, I call Lieutenant Adair to testify," Mac-Dougall intoned, going all solemn, now that he was at the meat of the matter.

MacDougall worked his way down through the Commission officers to Mr. Winwood, and the Purser, Mr. Coote, showing how the "crime" was committed. Sir George Norman sat mum at his table through it all, a befuddled and seemingly dis-interested air about him. Under English Common Law, he had no right to cross-examine witnesses, and, with no witnesses of his own to present in rebuttal, his continued presence was merely decorative.

Yet MacDougall did not stick to the distances, the times, or the particular actions that Lewrie's juniors had performed that night; to Lt. Adair, he posed the question of what he heard and saw on shore.

Had the other slaves been celebrating?

"They were, sir," Adair stated. "I was fearful that their cries might rouse the overseers." The form of it? "Tears, and hugging, and hand-shaking, sir. Joy and sadness, mixed. Soft singing, and such."

"And once into the boats and making your way back to *Proteus*, sir, did anything *odd* occur?" MacDougall asked.

"We heard barking, sir," Lt. Adair answered. "At first, I imagined that the overseers and their dogs were near the beach, but in a short time, we discovered that the barking came from seals, sir."

"Seals, Lieutenant Adair?" MacDougall said, striking a surprised pose, obviously with foreknowledge of what Adair would say. "In the West Indies? Are they not hunted out?"

"It was . . . eerie, sir," Adair declared. "Aye, seals are rare in those seas, but that night, they appeared all round us. Every man at the oars saw them, and commented on them. A dozen or more of them, swimming about our boats, just beyond the reach of the oars, right to the ship's side, sir, where the rest of the crew saw and heard them, as well."

"And what did you make of that, sir?" MacDougall crooned.

"God's blessing 'pon our action, sir," Lt. Adair solemnly said, then smiled. "Captain Lewrie and seals, well sir . . .'tis mysterious how often seals have appeared in warning or . . . almost *approval,* sir, just before Captain Lewrie went into a fight. For so is the rumour in the Fleet about him, d'ye see, sir. A minor miracle, some say."

Did the dozen slaves sign aboard willingly? Were they fed and clothed, kitted, and paid, the same as any English sailor? Were any of them troublemakers, drunkards, discipline problems; were any of the Black sailors stupid, were any of them cowards? MacDougall asked him.

Willingly, aye; treated the same as any volunteer; very little trouble from any of them; the usual binges on runs ashore, which were rare, same as British tars; illiterate, but not stupid, for many went on from Landsman to Ordinary Seaman, two had been rated Able in short time, and, there were certainly no cowards among them. The runaways were as brave as lions, every Man Jack, Lt. Adair could swear.

Lt. Gamble and Midshipman Grace reiterated Adair's high opinion of them, whilst Mr. Winwood told of their muster-aboard baths under a wash-deck pump and hose, which he likened to their baptism into a new life; how little they'd been told of Christianity, and the sacrifice and resurrection of the Saviour (which had many a lady in the courtroom dabbing her eyes with a handkerchief) and how he had taken it on himself to minister to their spiritual needs and education, seeing as how HMS *Proteus* did not, at that time, rate a Chaplain willing to ship to the Fever Isles of the West Indies.

"Are you conversant with slavery laws in the Crown colonies, Mister Winwood?" MacDougall finally asked.

"Somewhat, sir. More so now, than previous," Winwood intoned in his sober and ponderous manner; and frowned when his comment was taken as slightly humourous by the spectators.

"What charge may be laid against a slave who runs away from his master or mistress, Mister Winwood?" MacDougall pressed.

"Uhm . . . that, since he is not a free man, sir, only property, . . . not reckoned a man at all, really . . . that he is guilty of stealing himself, I believe," Winwood replied.

"Guilty of stealing *himself*?" MacDougall pretended consternation in a loud voice. "And the punishment would be what? An hundred lashes? Pilloried in the stocks? Branded? His hamstrings cut so he may only limp? A foot cut off with an axe?"

"I have heard-tell that one, or all, of those punishments are awarded, sir," Mr. Winwood agreed in grave sadness, shaking his head sorrow-fully. "A second unsuccessful attempt may result in death by the lash, or being hung."

"Do civilised people do such to cows that stray, horses that take the bitt 'tween their teeth and gallop?" MacDougall posed. "To a dog that piddles on the carpet? A cat which climbs a tree?"

"Indeed *not*, sir!" Winwood said.

"Yet many slaves do risk such punishments each year, do they not, Mister Winwood? Steal themselves and run . . . on Jamaica, to the so-called Cockpit Country . . . to the Blue Mountains, and the jungles, don't they? What do they call them, Mister Winwood?"

"They do, sir. They call them Maroons," Winwood answered.

"Do you believe that Captain Lewrie is a thief, Mister Winwood? One who received stolen property for his own use, sir?"

"No, sir. In this instance, I would call him a Christian gentleman," the Sailing Master somberly replied, turning to look the men of the jury in the eyes. "You might as well put me on trial, for what we did that night. . . . I only wish we'd had a ship of the line, 'stead of a frigate, in need of hands, and taken all of them away."

MacDougall paced back towards the Defence table, but paused in midstride and whipped about. "One last question of you, sir. . . . If, under Jamaican slave law, the Blacks in this matter stole themselves, who, then, used them for his own purposes, Mister Winwood . . . Captain Alan Lewrie, or King George the Third, in whose service twelve brave Black men willingly volunteered, and five of whom have perished?"

"Now, I must object, milud!" Sir George Norman cried, shooting to his feet, roused from his nodding stupor at last. "The witness is a War-rant Officer in the Navy, not a legal scholar, and cannot form a legal judgement, in the first instance, and . . . for honoured counsel for the Defence to suggest that his Majesty shares any guilt in this crime is abominable and shameful, in the second!"

"Withdrawn, my lord," MacDougall offered, hiding his amusement. "I have no more questions for this witness."

"The insult to the Crown, milud!" Sir George pressed.

"Mister MacDougall," Lord Justice Oglethorpe said with a dyspeptic scowl or warning, "you are known for frippery in court, but let me caution you to eschew any suggestion of *lèse-majesté* against our Sovereign."

"The question is withdrawn, my lord," MacDougall said, looking a trifle hurt, like a boy caught skylarking and called down for it. "An injudicious phrase, when the proper statement might have been the Royal Navy, or Great Britain, which prospered from the services of the sailors in question, rather than our King. I stand admonished, milord."

"Very well, then. You have more witnesses?" Oglethorped asked.

"I do, my lord."

"It is now nearly a quarter to twelve," the Lord Justice said, "so we shall adjourn for dinner. Proceedings shall resume this afternoon, at half past one."

"All rise!" the chief bailiff intoned.

Once Oglethorpe had left the courtroom, Lewrie came down from the raised and railed dock to join MacDougall, who was shedding his peruke and putting it in a small wood box, and shrugging out of his robes. "A deuced good morning, sir," MacDougall told him, all smiles and high spirits. "A splendid beginning. Imagine! A trial that will take all *day*, why, we'll be the talk of the town by supper, and atop the front pages of all the papers by tomorrow morning, ha ha! Hungry, are you, Captain Lewrie? There's a delightful chop-house not a five minutes' stroll from here."

"Aye, I s'pose," Lewrie allowed. "You think we did *well*?"

"Extremely well, sir," MacDougall was quick to assure him, with a Puckish grin.

"I thought just laying out how we . . . committed the deed, just like *that*," Lewrie fretted, "would doom us. Me."

"As I shall tell the jury this afternoon, Captain Lewrie, was the deed an act of criminality . . . or, was it a deed of liberation? I will fill the afternoon with the testimony of your Black sailors, and there will not be a dry eye in the courtroom, once I'm done. Not one stony heart unmoved. Ready, Mister Sadler? Shall we go, then, for I am famished."

Lewrie fingered a breeches pocket to assure himself that his coin purse was still present, and that it was suitably stuffed with a sufficiency of bank notes and coins, enough to bear the cost of dinner with such imposing trenchermen as MacDougall and Sadler. No matter the financial support of the Abolitionists, and other "Progressives," for his legal expenses (and all those visual aids), dealing with attorneys was a dear business.

"As a matter of fact, Captain Lewrie," MacDougall said as he stowed away his court wear, "I am so sanguine about the rest of the day that, this once, allow me to treat."

Lewrie's jaw, it here must be noted, dropped rather far.

CHAPTER FOUR

*T*he afternoon's testimony indeed turned out to be emotional and dramatic as Mr. MacDougall put all seven surviving Black sailors in the witness box, and led each of them first through their wretched lives as chattel slaves in the West Indies, and on the Beauman plantation in particular, then about their flight, their reception aboard Capt. Lewrie's frigate, and their experiences in the Royal Navy, since.

Shoddy clothing, if clothed at all; the poorest, meanest rations of condemned salt-beef or salt-pork, bug-infested rice, and but a few fresh greens or vegetables, with even so-called holiday victuals of a barely unremitted sameness, for even the rare duffs or puddings were, though cooked on a *sugar cane* plantation, sadly lacking in sweetness. How prime field hands, sleek when first they came from the slave ships and the vendue houses, wasted away to skin, gristle, and bones before three years were out . . . which was considered a bargain by unfeeling masters, considering the sad, low price placed on a human being they'd initially paid. There were always ships arriving with healthy slaves from Africa, the barracks and pens were continually full, and prices for people were nigh as low as those for cattle.

Crude huts for shelters, leaf-stuffed sacks for bedding on the dirt floors at night, exposed round the clock to insects and weather; up before the sun to the tolling of bells and the crack of whips, poor victuals choked down after being scooped by hand from communal pots, then back-breaking labour 'til the sun was all but set, with only one brief break in the shade for a miser's dinner.

And whips, and chains, and choke-collar boards round their necks for the slightest act of mis-behaviour, hot irons to brand recalcitrant shirkers; hot irons to sear the tongue from those who dared speak back without being asked a question, or for the merest suspicion of lying to an overseer, master, or mistress.

Poisonous snakes had been imported from Africa and India, turned loose in the surrounding forests to make sure that slaves wouldn't *dare* run off without risking a "five-stepper" death.

For the slow, the slow-witted, or lazy, for those who broke the poor tools they were given, for hiding a cane-cutting machete or knife, there was the whipping post, where the lashes were doled out capriciously; thirty for this sin, fifty for another, perhaps an hundred for the same offence at the whim of the overseer's imagination, with age or sex no assurance of leniency.

And slave women . . . the young, firm, and handsome were masters' prey, overseers' perquisites. In the fields, in the huts after dark, it was just rape, when drunken sons of slave-masters and their friends or cousins felt like it, and the mother, the father, the lover who objected in the slightest laid himself open to pure torture, and no one could lift a hand to rescue the young girls. After all, slave children quickened by White men fetched more when auctioned off, and made lighter skinned, less-African-featured house servants-to-be.

Did house servants have it slightly better? Of a certainty, but they paid a high price. Did slave women, mothers against their will, hope that their offspring might be "bright" enough to be spared field work? Of course. If girls, though, planters' sons *desired* them more.

Did anyone ever preach the Gospel to them? Only the snippets from Saint Paul's letters that urged, "Slaves, behave your masters."

"And, since signing articles aboard *Proteus*," MacDougall asked the wiry young George Rodney, who had been a spry topman and a sharpshooter, "did Captain Lewrie ever put you, or any of the other volunteers to any work in his great-cabins? To wait upon his table, buff his boots, do his laundry? Anything like that?"

"Nossuh, he nevah did. Wull, Jones Nelson be in 'is boat crew, but dat 'coz he big un' strong oarsman. Be a run-out tackleman on de twelve-poundah'r eighteen poundah'r, sah."

"So Captain Lewrie did not consider you his personal property?"

"Oh, *nossuh!*" Rodney firmly replied. "I'z a British sailah in de Royal Navy, sah. I'z a sailah o' King George."

"Captain Lewrie rated you a topman . . . one of the lads who goes aloft? Yes. Did you *want* to be one?"

"Oh, yassah. Topmen be kings o' de ship, sah."

"And he trained you, all of you, with pistols, muskets, swords, and boarding pikes?" MacDougall asked, as he had of all the rest, but Mr. Cooke, who was a bit too old and stout for close combat; for he was indeed well-named, and had been *Proteus*'s ship's cook.

"Lemme shoot Frenchmen wid his own Ferguson rifle-musket, me or his ol' Cox'n, Andrews, 'e did, sah," Rodney boasted. "Said de bot' o' us have de good eye."

"Yes, and have you killed a *lot* of Frenchmen?"

"Yassuh, I sho' have! 'Specially when we fight de French frigates two year ago," Rodney supplied. "Round dozen, right dere."

"You mentioned Coxswain Andrews," MacDougall went on. "Of what race was Coxswain Andrews?"

"He Black, like me, sah, well . . . fo' he run, I hear tell he wuz a house slave'r body slave," Rodney related, "so he wuz light-skinned. He be Cap'm Lewrie's Cox'n almos' since de 'Merican Revolution. But he got killed in de South Atlantic, two year ago."

"Was *he* a body servant to Captain Lewrie?" MacDougall shrewdly asked, looking at the jury, not his witness.

"Nossuh, he run de Cap'm's boat when he be called ashore, an' such," Rodney said. "Only fellah dat sees t' th' Cap'm is 'is cook an' cabin steward, Mistah Aspinall, ovah yondah," Rodney said, with a jab of his arm to the sailors behind the Defence table.

"And did Captain Lewrie ever have one of you fellows flogged for disobedience?" MacDougall asked.

"Can't recall dat evah happen, sah," Rodney said, frowning in reverie. "Cap'm Lewrie ain't big on floggin', 'cept fer when a man's been *real* bad. Didn't even flog Hood, Howe, Whitbread, Groome, and Bass, when dey git wobbly-drunk on Saint Helena, an' borrowed Mistah Wigmore's donkeys f'um de circus, an' raced 'em up de valley. Weren't no zebras, like dat Mistah Wigmore said, just painted up t'look like 'em. Dey git de donkeys drunk, too, at de las' tavern up de valley."

"And Captain Lewrie didn't flog anyone else on Saint Helena?" Mac-Dougall enquired. "Not even when they tore up the island governor's gardens? Stole a magnolia tree, and rose bushes?"

"Cap'm be plenty mad, aye, sah," Rodney tittered with delight, "but 'e didn' flog nobody, just put 'em on bread an' watuh, wid no rum ner 'baccy fer a week. Didn't even flog when me an' Groome run off t'see Africker. Well, Groome died when de Cape Buff'lo trample 'im, an' I got mauled by a she-lion, so I s'pose I wuzn't fit t'flog fo' a spell . . . it ain't like we wuz desertin', sah, 'cause de circus people hadta come back t'Cape Town wid dey new beasts fo' de shows, but Groome an' me jus' wanted t'see where we come f'um fo' a bit, sah. I'z clawed up and bit on right bad, an' I s'pose de Cap'm think I punished enough."

The spectators could not contain simpers and snickers when the lad named his compatriots, who, at Mr. Winwood's urging, had taken new, freemen's names after their mustering-in baths under the wash-deck pump, as if leaving pagan lives of sin behind and being "washed white as snow" by baptism; new souls with new identities, and not what some capricious slave-master had named them.

Hood, Howe, Rodney, Anson, and Nelson for naval heroes; Groome and Cooke for their old occupations, then Bass and Whitbread for the imported beverages their masters had drunk.

Sir Samuel Whitbread, Member of Parliament, seated in the middle of the courtroom's spectator area that afternoon, perhaps didn't find it *quite* so amusing, but . . .

What Rodney described were sailors' antics, the sorts of things that young men of any race might risk when in drink and high spirits; and the *adventures*! Trampled by Cape Buffalo, mauled and bitten by a lion on a hunting, trapping jaunt into the wilds of mysterious *Africa* with a *circus*? Battling pirates in the Caribbean, the French and Spanish, with lashings of prize-money to prove their mettle, and success, why, what *English* lad didn't wish to run away to sea and have such adventures!

Lewrie peeked at the gentlemen in the jury box and was heartened to see a fair number of them smiling, or shaking their heads in *kindly* wonder over such doings.

"And you were paid the same as any British sailor in your rate, Seaman Rodney?" MacDougall good-naturedly asked him.

"Ev'ry penny t'th' jot an' tittle, sah," Rodney answered. "Ol' Mistah Coote, de Pursah, an' Cap'm Lewrie'z fair men, sah. An' ev'ry prize we take, I git my share same'z anybody. We whup de Creole pirates two year ago in Looziana, I made t'ree years' wages right dere!"

"And now you're a free man, Seaman Rodney," MacDougall continued in a softer voice, "do you wish to remain a British sailor, and a free man?"

"Best life I evah know, sah. Aye, I ain't *nevah* let any one make me a slave again," Rodney declared, with some heat. "I learn t'read an' write 'board ship, so nobody gon' trap me makin' my mark on somethin' I don't understand . . . got cypherin', too, so nobody gon' cheat me outta money, neither. War be ovah, I 'spect I'll ship out on a merchantman, 'less I find me a good girl an' start a fam'ly."

"And, finally, Seaman Rodney . . . what do you think of Captain Lewrie?" MacDougall asked him.

"He be a *fine* man, sah," Rodney gushed, "a fightin' man, and a good 'un, an' I just thank God he free me, an' God bless him fo 'evah."

And MacDougall's summation was glorious, of course, focussing not so much on denying the theft of slaves as he did *praising* it for a courageous Christian act. With the Jamaica trial transcript out, he could not refer to it, except to ask the jury to consider why not one accuser was present in court, even though the Beaumans had pursued the matter with white-hot eagerness, and at the cost of thousands of pounds for several years; did they suddenly fear being taken up themselves for laying a false and vengeful prosecution?

"And lastly, gentlemen," MacDougall declaimed in histrionic fashion, his arms outstretched, "consider that the dozen slaves, not worth three hundred pounds as less-than-human hewers of wood and drawers of water, worked to death in a few short years, then easily replaced with fresh young muscles . . . the merest pittance of those who yearly perish . . . the most minute fraction of all those hundreds of thousands yearning to live free! . . . have shed their blood for you, given their lives for you, who sleep snug at night behind Britain's 'wooden walls'! Go aloft, serve the guns, endure the boredom of blockading, and bravely face all the perils of weather and the wrath of the sea on our men-o'-war all round the world, this very minute, this very hour! Ask how many *more* would wish to emulate these stalwart young *men*. Yes, I say *men*, not dumb beasts, *men* who feel pain and joy, suffer disappointment and revel in victory . . . who serve God, King, and Country, in whose breasts burn the fires of patriotism as strongly as yours.

"It would be unconscionable to deny England their services . . . just as it would be equally unconscionable to return these men to the vengeful cruelty of slavery, to their former master, Mister Hugh Beauman of Jamaica!" MacDougall declared.

"And that, sirs, would be the logical result if the instrument of their new-found freedoms was condemned for a selfless act of liberation," MacDougall told the jury. "Human bondage had been outlawed in our happy isle for nearly fifty years, yet, do you find that Captain Alan Lewrie is guilty of stealing human beings, you reduce these men to chattel status once more, tacitly *admit* that they were mere *property*! Property, I say, with as little right to determine their own destinies as a bed-stead, or a dining room *table*! To even reward Hugh Beauman a single shilling per head as a compromise settlement would be tantamount to calling these eager young volunteers in our Navy no more men than a dozen pair of *shoe buckles*!

"No, gentlemen, don't do it," MacDougall urged the jury. "Deem what Captain Lewrie did a courageous act, the leeward gun fired in the challenge to a foe . . . as our beloved Admiral Horatio Nelson urges all captains to fire no matter the odds, or risk . . . a first, tentative, but significant blow against the abominable practice of Negro slavery that I am sure all true Britons despise . . . a bold *geste* done not for personal aggrandisement, which, I am also certain all Britons *cheer*, with nought but admiration for Captain Lewrie's courage in striking any sort of blow to this despicable institution, and expose its putrescent evils for all the world to see.

"We sing, gentlemen," MacDougall said, lowering his arms, sounding weary and exhausted, of a sudden, which forced the twelve men of the jury to lean a bit forward. " 'Britons never, never, never shall be slaves.' Fine for us, for we were *born* free men, and are now engaged in a war, defending our ancient right to remain free of a conquering tyrant with bulldog tenacity and determination. Can we deny the right to others who are just as determined to *become* free? Can we condemn a heroic Paladin who freed the first few?

"Find these charges baseless and mean, gentlemen!" MacDougall cried, suddenly finding new energy. "Acquit Captain Lewrie and set him free upon our nation's foes, and, in doing so, condemn the brutes who would make scornful mock of freedom for any man, Black or White, slave or free! Acquit, acquit, acquit, and show the world what true Britons think of human bondage!"

The jury shuffled out to their deliberation chamber, and Lewrie had time to visit the "jakes" for a long-delayed pee. Making his way through the throngs of supporters in the hallways, who had not gained seats in the courtroom, was a maddening hindrance 'pon his bladder, and it was with an immense sense of relief that he could stroll back out after doing up his breeches buttons to face the gauntlet once again, now of much better, less impatient takings.

"Sir! Sir, come quick!" MacDougall's clerk, Mr. Sadler, urged, making a narrow aisle through the crowd and beckoning in some haste. "The jury is ready to render. Bless me, not above eight minutes, in total. Never seen the like!"

"Is that good or bad?" Lewrie asked, considering that, whilst in the "necessary," it might have been a good idea to throw on his boat-cloak, exchange hats with a civilian gentleman, and "take leg-bail" for parts unknown.

"Might be very good, sir. On the other hand . . . excuse us?"

I'd love t'meet a one-armed law clerk or lawyer, Lewrie told himself; *who* can't *say 'on the other hand.'*

MacDougall gave him a tentative smile as he re-entered the grim courtroom, and a shrug as Lewrie re-mounted to the railed dock, where he felt too unsettled to sit down. Lewrie paced the tiny enclosure, a fair approximation of a condemned man's cell, he could imagine, trying to appear stoic, with a slight touch of bemusement, as he looked over the refilling courtroom from his elevated vantage point.

Damme, there's a stunner! he irrelevantly thought, espying an especially attractive young lady in a lavender gown and matching hat; *Hope springs eternal . . . all that.* It cheered him that the handsome lass smiled at him and dipped him a brief bow of encouragement.

Bang! went the bailiff's mace, and the cry of "Oyez!" as Lord Justice Oglethorpe resumed his place in the *banc,* and court functionaries filed in and took their own places . . . as the twelve men of the jury re-entered the courtroom through a side door and took seats in their own railed-off box. There was much shuffling of feet, coughing into fists, the rustling of gowns and men's coats, the creaking of a new pair of boots, and the *bang!* of a stubbed toe against the pew-like benches of the spectators' gallery. Oddly, there was no whispering or chatting, this time; only an expectant hush worthy of the last act of a tragedy staged in Drury Lane.

"The jury has determined a verdict in the matter of Beauman *versus* Lewrie?" Lord Justice Oglethorpe enquired, once the last of the traditional forms had been acted out.

"We have, my lord," the elected foreman announced.

"Pray, do you declare it," Oglethorpe ordered.

"Ahem!" from the foreman.

"Free him, pray God!" some feminine voice was heard to utter.

"We, the jury, find, in the matter of Beauman *et al.* versus Captain Alan Lewrie, Royal Navy, that the defendant is not guilty."

"Halleluah!" a male spectator shouted, a second before womanly shrieks of relief and joy, and a general "hoo-raw" and chorus of "huzzahs!" mixed with a tidal wave of bright chattering and glad laughter. Sailors behind the Defence table raised "three cheers"!

Holy shit! Lewrie thought, dumbstruck, and nigh-shaking with unutterable relief himself; ready to break out in maniacal laughter as well! What a marvellous thing it was, to know that one would not be cashiered, that one would *not hang,* and . . . that one did not owe one's lawyer tuppence! *Not guilty! Well, not* innocent, *exactly, but it'll more than do,* Lewrie thought; *more . . . what did MacDougall call it? Jury nullification? Emotion ruled, not logic . . . and thank* God *for't!*

He goggled round the courtroom at the spectators, the powerful and dedicated to abolition, the enthusiastic, and the mere lookers-on who'd come to any notorious trial. Lewrie spotted wee Rev. Wilberforce and his coterie, all looking about to break into unaccustomed dances of glee (for such an earnest and usually dour crowd), and confessed to himself that he'd let them down badly that night, for it was better than fair odds that he'd be drunk as a lord . . . drunk as an *emperor* by God! . . . by midnight!

Lord Justice Oglethorpe was gavelling away, had been for several minutes in point of fact, before the crowd in the courtroom subdued to a level where in he could make himself heard.

"Captain Alan Lewrie," Oglethorpe solemnly intoned in a loud voice, looking as stolid as ever he might had the jury gone the other way. "A jury of your peers having found you not guilty of the crime with which you were charged, I now declare you a free man."

Which formal declaration only served to set the crowd off once more. Oglethorpe banged away for order, now looking "tetched" by the interruptions.

"Last year, when first you appeared before this court, Captain Lewrie, you put up a surety bond to guarantee your future appearance, which your presence today fulfilled," Oglethorpe announced, "in the amount of one hundred pounds. Such sum I now order returned to you. These proceedings I now declare at an end, and you are free to depart. Court is . . . dismissed!" he said, with one final bang of his gavel.

An hundred pounds? Lewrie thought as he exited the dock; *Orgy! A* fête champêtre, *a roast steer, and barrels and lashin's o' drink!*

"I *told* you!" MacDougall was chortling as he came to take hands with his "brief" and shake away vigourously. "I *told* you t'would be a complete exoneration! The jury found *slavery* guilty, as I planned."

"Nullification, d'ye mean? Wasn't it risky?" Lewrie asked, though in no mood to disagree with the verdict.

"Exactly so, sir," MacDougall crowed. "But no one ever went 'smash,' over-estimating the sway of emotions 'pon a jury, the pluck of the heart-strings, 'stead of the dry, paper rustlings of cold, hard logic. Congratulations to you, Captain Lewrie, 'pon your freedom, and for how far this case has advanced the noble cause of emancipation of all slaves in the British Empire. Mind, I'd not suggest you do such again, ha ha!"

"If I do, I'll engage only you, Mister MacDougall!" Lewrie teased. "Allow me to extend my hearty congratulations to you, as well, sir! For the notoriety of this will surely be the making of you . . . though, I dare say your name was *already* made. Congratulations, and my *utmost* thanks for being my attorney, Mister MacDougall. I am forever in your debt. Have I another son someday, I'll name him Andrew in honour of you."

Don't trowel it on that *thick!* Lewrie chid himself; *And Christ spare me fresh spit-ups and drool . . . legitimate or otherwise, but . . .*

"So, ye dodged the hangman, have ye? Huzzah!" Lewrie's father, Sir Hugo came forth to celebrate. "The Devil might have ye yet, but not this day, haw haw!"

Then there were his former officers and sailors to surround him, to clasp hands or knuckle brows, and, before the Sir Samuel Whitbreads and Sir Malcolm Shockleys, Lord Peter Rushtons, and fiery-eyed Abolitionists seized upon him, his Cox'n Desmond and his mate Furfy, Landsman Jones Nelson and the rest of his Black sailors hoisted him up and bore him in triumph from the courtroom; out through the double doors into the hallways to the massive entry halls (someone had enough wit to gather up his hat, sword, and boat-cloak) and outside to the steps overlooking the street, where people took up "Hail, the Conqu'ring Hero Comes" and "Three Cheers and a Tiger." Where, with his sheathed sword in one hand and his hat hastily clapped far back on his head, Lewrie felt free enough—*free!*—to wave with his right hand to all in sight, and "Huzzah!" right back at them.

Hope they get me to a carriage quick, though, he had to think; *Someone's got my cloak, and it's perishin' damn' cold!*

BOOK 1

Juno:
Tellus colenda est, paelices caelum tenent.

Juno:
I must dwell on earth, for harlots
hold the sky.

-Lucius Annaeus Seneca
Hercules Furens, 5-6

CHAPTER FIVE

I'm the wrong sort o' hero, Lewrie thought with a yawn as he tossed back the covers at the fashionable hour of 10 A.M., a gentlemanly time to rise just a few years back. He hurriedly slipped his feet into a pair of ankle-high bearskin slippers, slung a floor-length dressing robe about his body, and dashed for the ebbing fire in the grate of his room at the Madeira Club.

Proper heroes got a servant to intrude—damned quietly!—to lay fresh kindling and sea-coal in the fireplace, so they could sleep in well-earned peace 'til noon, and awake in a toasty-warm chamber, too! Lewrie was certain. Proper heroes were not lodged amidst the earnest and dedicated, either; the sounds of early risers stamping about, taking their ablutions, opening and slamming chest lids, opening and slamming doors on their way belowstairs to the dining room for a hellish-early breakfast—clattering their shoes and boots on the steps and greeting each other with cheery bleats, to boot!—had made Lewrie's attempts at sleep all but impossible, since before 8 A.M.

The right sort of British hero (someone like Horatio Nelson, say) would be roused to the accompaniment of a steaming cup of coffee, co-coa, or tea, with buttered toast and jam, or rusks, too; but Lewrie saw no signs of such luxuries, and doubted ringing for their fetching would result in their prompt delivery. The kitchens and dining room closed at nine, not to open again 'til dinnertime.

Nelson'd be roused by Emma Hamilton's tits, too, Lewrie sourly thought as he "whizzed" away into the chamberpot. He gave the cooling bed a fond look for a moment; now the morning stampede of Respectable gentlemen was done, the lodging house would be quiet enough for a nap 'til the dining room re-opened, but . . . he'd made a late night of it, was dearly in need of sustenance, and, at that moment, could have killed someone for a cup of coffee. After a shave and a perfunctory wash-up, he threw on his civilian suitings, pulled up his own boots, tied his own stock, and grabbed hat, boat-cloak, and walking stick, and headed for a warm and cozy coffee-house.

It wasn't that his recent fame (or notoriety, if one prefers) denied Lewrie of a hero's *panache*. It was the *sort* of people with whom one was invited out to dine. Oh, there were a few cheerful souls from Parliament, in Commons and Lords, eager to have him in, but, in the main, the bulk of the invitations he had received the last week were of the grim, dour, and "Respectable" stripe, to whom a witty comment, a double *entendre,* or a glass of wine above strict necessity would be simply appalling. Abolitionists, social reformers, anti-hunting and anti-gaming enthusiasts; those grimly intent upon the eradication of prostitution (in London, for God's sake!) and the reclamation of the "poor, soiled doves" engaged upon it; those who fretted and wrung their hands over the sad lack of morals, the absence of evangelising among England's sailors, soldiers, and Marines. Why, there had been people who'd *seemed* in possession of all their wits, at first, earnestly dedicated to the eradication of Demon Rum, Ruinous Gin, and Soul-Sucking Brandy, and so enthusiastic about their Noble Cause as to appear quite fanatical.

For the last week, Lewrie couldn't even leer at a promisingly bulging chest, admire a graceful neck, or ogle a fetching female face. Not if he wished to maintain the good will of those who'd paid all his legal fees, he couldn't! A praiseful comment on "The Mouth of the Nile" playing at the Covent Garden Theatre in honour of the 1798 battle and Adm. Nelson, or conversation, about the overly melodramatic "Pizarro" in Drury Lane, had been received with odd pursings of mouths, much as if Lewrie had lifted a cheek and shot off a "cheeser." To his earnest hosts and hostesses, the only good thing about "Pizarro" were the *moral* lessons of the drama. Lewrie wasn't sure what those were, exactly—slaughtering umpteen thousands of Inca pagans, spreading Christianity with fire and sword, and raking up mountains of gold and gems was a good thing? That being a *Spanish* conqueror resulted in final tragedy, as opposed to, say, Clive of India, who'd done pretty much the same thing, but was so thoroughly British that he came home smelling like Hungary Water in comparison? Or was it the new fashions and colours that "Pizarro" had sprung upon a drab London winter? Purple, yellow, puce, and scarlet, along with spangled hair nets and fifteenth-century hats as big and floppy at throw-pillows (or exaggerated French berets) for women? Anyway, it was only the stylish, the "flash," and the young sybarites who sported such togs; pointedly *not* his hostesses, who were as staid as throw-backs to Cromwell's Puritans.

The first night right after his acquittal, there had been his former officers to roister with, but they had departed the day after, back to HMS *Savage* at Torbay, taking burly Landsman Jones Nelson with them, for he sorely missed his fellow Black mates and felt lost without them. Next to go, not a day after, was *Aspinall!*

"Em, sir, ah . . . ," Aspinall had stammered, red-faced, that morning. "I wonder could I raise a point with ya, Captain Lewrie."

"Aye," Lewrie had said over his cocoa and jam (the last time he had had personal service in his rooms at the Madeira Club). "Say on."

" 'Tis me mother, sir," Aspinall had explained, all but wringing his hands. "The people she does for, they've been most generous, an' lenient with her, th' last few years, sir, but her ailments ain't gettin' better. My sister, Rose sir . . . she's in service with another household, an' can't see to her as she should, so . . . well, I've alla my prize-money, an' I've thought I could purchase a wee place f'r all of us . . . make her last years comfy, in a place of her *own*, d'ye see, sir? I woz wond'rin' . . . might ya write Admiralty for my Discharge on fam'ly grounds, sir?"

"You'd leave my employ as well?" Lewrie had said, stunned and feeling sudden loss; Aspinall had been with him damned-near forever, and where would he get a cabin servant, steward, and cook as good as Aspinall? Someone as understanding and "comfortable"?

"Fear I must, sir," Aspinall had gloomed. "Same thing, really. I'm that sorry t'let ya down, sir, an' I'll stay on 'til ya finds yer new man, but . . . "

"No no, Aspinall," Lewrie had assured him. "I'll look around. For a while, I may depend upon the staff at the Madeira. I'll write Admiralty at once. Humph. 'Tis good odds Hell'd freeze over before they wish to employ *me*, in future, so I doubt I'd need anyone with so many skills as you possess. But . . . whatever shall you do to earn a living, Aspinall? Prize-money's fine, but it won't last forever."

"Uhm nossir," Aspinall had related, a lot more cheerfully, "I know a man in th' publishin' business, int'rested in my journals, an' those songs I collected aboard ship . . . along with amusin' anecdotes 'mongst the lads, an' such. He thinks we can sell a lot of them to lads intent on volunteering'."

Aspinall and his publishing partner had been a bit more aspiring than that; was the first volume successful, there were plans for a guide to a world of useful sailors' knots, along with a companion book on the making of sennet-work "small stuff" into rings, bracelets, necklaces, and doilies, the sort of things that sailors wove for loved ones in their off-duty hours or "Make and Mend" Sundays. All lavishly illustrated, of course, for Aspinall had always been a dab-hand sketch artist, saving the cost of hiring one. There'd be a guide to the various parts of a ship, the standing, and most especially, the running rigging that controlled the sails . . . all an eager lubber needed to find his way through the mysterious world of the sea and its arcane language, for there would be a lexicon of all the former and current slang and jargon decyphered for the complete neophyte!

It had been with some measure of surprise, and a great deal of reluctance, for Lewrie to wish Aspinall and his family well, offer to write Admiralty that very day, obtain his Discharge and final reckoning of his pay, and, to be gracious, offer his name as a subscriber to all the future works; even pen a recommendation to introduce the first one . . . assuming the use of his name would not drive purchasers *away* from it.

Wife reclused from him, in high dudgeon, in Anglesgreen down in Surrey, and his daughter Charlotte clinging to Caroline's skirts, and her spites; Sewallis and Hugh both back at their public school now Hilary Term was begun and Christmas holidays were over, and busy with their lessons; his brother-in-law (the one who'd still talk to him) Burgess Chiswick was head-over-heels in love, newly affianced to the lovely (and rich!) Theodora Trencher, and also busy with his newly purchased

Majority in a foot regiment . . . the only people left to Lewrie from family, in-laws, or contemporaries in the Navy was his slyly Irish Cox'n, Liam Desmond, and Desmond's old comrade, the simple but strong Patrick Furfy—neither of whom could butler, valet, or even boil a pot of water, far as he knew of their civilian skills.

Both those worthies, much like his cats Toulon and Chalky, did seem more than happy to remain with him, for several very good reasons; firstly, they were not presently at sea, and could stay warm and dry for a change; secondly, the quality of their victuals beat Navy issue food all hollow; thirdly, there were thousands of pubs and taverns in which to slake their thirsts, and at Lewrie's expense; and, fourthly, said taverns were in *London*, where there were women by battalions for them to ogle, flirt up, and serve Jack Sauce, or manage to put the leg over, by finagling or the offer of a shilling or three.

And London was so full of theatres, music halls, exhibits and pleasure gardens, and street rarees that Desmond and Furfy likely felt they'd gained the sailors' paradise, "Fiddler's Green," where every lass was comely and obliging, the music never ceased, rum and ale flowed round the clock, and publicans never demanded the reckoning!

Stout fellows, in the main, the both of them, but . . . like his cats, they weren't good conversationalists . . . they weren't Aspinall.

CHAPTER SIX

*T*he Admiral Boscawen Coffee House, at the corner of Oxford Street and Orchard Street (site of the present day Selfridge's) was just the sort of warm and cozy place that Lewrie needed after a brisk stroll from the corner of Duke Street and Wigmore Street. There was a blue-aproned lad to take his hat, cloak, and walking stick, a man to see him to a table of his own, not *too* far from one of the two blazing hearths, and yet another young man to fetch him his first cup of coffee with cream and sugar. Before toast, butter, and jam could be fetched, there were piles of newspapers from which to choose, as well, and Lewrie, who had been rather busy at saving his arse the last week or so, was glad to find some back numbers so he could catch back up with the latest doings.

"Brown bread fer toast, only, sir . . . sorry t'say," the waiter apologised after laying a plate before Lewrie. "Th' Lord Mayor's gotta down on white bread, 'long with the Crown."

"It's been banned?" Lewrie had to gawp.

"Bad harvest, they say, sir," the waiter said with a shrug. "Th' war, an' all. Anything else, sir?"

"Not for the moment, no," Lewrie told him. At least there was still more than enough fresh butter, and a full pot of lime marmalade. Truth to tell, Lewrie rather liked brown bread, so the ban on fine white bread was not much bother. He was hungry enough, by then, to chew sawdust.

And the coffee was decently hot, for a rare wonder; which was one reason why he preferred the Admiral Boscawen.

In *The Times*, there was a reprint of the King's address to the closing session of Parliament on New Year's Eve, which had featured King George escorted from the Presence Chamber by both Admiral Hood and Nelson to the throne, and Lewrie stopped chewing long enough to read:

"The detention of property of my subjects in the ports of Russia contrary to the most solemn treaties, and the imprisonment of British sailors in that country, have excited in me sentiments in which you and all my subjects will, I am sure, participate . . . "

Far from English waters most of the previous year, off the foe's shores in the mouth of the Gironde River, and weeks from fresh papers from home, he'd missed most of the dust-up with the Danes.

British and Danish warships had tangled in the Mediterranean in the summer, the Danes insisting that their convoys and independent merchant ships were not subject to stopping for inspection for contraband that might aid the French. A Danish frigate, the *Freya*, had traded a few shots off the English coast later on, striking her colours to protect another small convoy.

Just before Christmas, the Danes, Swedes, Russians, and even the mostly land-locked Prussians, who had hardly a navy or merchant marine to speak of, had resurrected their former Armed Neutrality, which they had insisted upon (none too strenuously!) during the Seven Years' War *and* the American Revolution. Russia had gone even further, seizing nigh three hundred British merchantmen in their ports, and force-marching nearly a thousand British captains, mates, and sailors off to the wilds of Siberia, just as winter was coming on.

". . . if it shall become necessary to maintain against any combination the honour and independence of the British Empire, and those maritime rights and interests on which both our prosperity and our security must always essentially depend," the King had further declared, "I enter no doubt either of the success of those means which, in such an event, I shall be enabled to exert, or the determination of my Parliament and my people to afford me . . . "

A later edition of *The Times* told that "the public will learn with great satisfaction that Lord Nelson is about to be employed on a SECRET EXPEDITION and will hoist his flag in the next few days. His instructions will not be opened until he arrives at a certain latitude. We shall

only permit ourselves to observe that there is reason to believe his destination is to a distant quarter, where his Lordship's personal appearance
would preponderate over the influence of the intrigues of any Court in
Europe."

Secret? Lewrie scoffed to himself, with an audible snort; *Mine arse on
a band-box! Not* now *it ain't! Some news writer needs to be shot! It's the
Baltic for certain . . . even if he can't take his dear Emma,* which thought
make Lewrie smirk.

Those prim and newly righteous hosts and hostesses of his were
down on Horatio Nelson, just promoted to Vice-Admiral of the Blue on
New Year's Day. He'd been jumped from the eleventh of fifteen Rear-
Admirals of the Red over senior men, and even if his rash actions had
won the Battle of Cape Saint Vincent, even if he had destroyed a whole
French *fleet* at the Battle of the Nile, then captured *Malta,* that was
grumbled over, not cheered, for Nelson was not quite . . . Respectable.
Not enough for *them,* anyway.

Nelson was carrying on an affair (grand, to some; infamous to others) with Lady Emma Hamilton, doting over her like a calf-headed cully
in "cream-pot love" right out in public, *and* with her doddering old husband, Sir William Hamilton, by their side. Lewrie had heard he snubbed
his long-suffering wife, Fannie, leaving her to trail behind like a maid-
servant. At an Admiralty supper back in November, she had sat mum,
watching her husband spoon and gush over the bouncy, buxom Emma's
every word; she'd shelled some walnuts for him and put them in a glass,
which Nelson had so brusquely brushed aside that the glass had been
broken, and it couldn't have been blamed on his blinded eye.

Gentlemen of the aristocracy and squirearchy had been having mistresses and affairs time out of mind; it was almost considered the *proper*
thing, once male heirs were assured upon the wife . . . though an affair
was not usually so *overt,* with the husband tagging along, and a *fuming*
wife in tow! Most British gentlemen would hardly cock an eye over such;
the man was a fighter and won battles, by God!

The common people, and the Mob, loved him, and, with their usual
waggon-load of common sense, cheered him like Billy-Oh, and if a
naked romp with Emma Hamilton in the middle of the Strand took
place at noon, they'd chortle and snigger and call him a Hell of a fellow,
huzzah!

Maybe I should let folks know how Caroline and I stand, Lewrie idly
mused; *or, that I rantipoled the mort in Naples, long before* him! *Any odds*

ye wish, the suppers I'm invited to would be from a livelier set! 'Had Emma too, did ye? Why, ye could dine-out on that for years!'

His toast done, and with a fresh cup of coffee poured and milked and sugared to his taste, Lewrie read on through the pile of papers. An item in *The Morning Post* spoke of armaments being carried on in Swedish and Danish ports, a "rupture" with the new Northern League, and "it is daily expected that orders will be issued for capturing the vessels of those nations." Tit for tat; seize our merchantmen, we'll seize yours.

And, from *The Times* on the thirteenth of January, there was even more lunacy. "Yesterday, Lord Nelson took his leave of the Lords of the Admiralty, and this morning his Lordship will positively leave town to hoist his flag. . . . We have reason to believe to know his destination is NOT the Baltic."

"My God, they can't be *that* clumsy!" Lewrie muttered. "*Not* the Baltic? Who do they think they're fooling, I ask you?"

"Who, indeed, sir," a fellow in Navy uniform scoffed as he and two others took seats at the next table over; he was a Lieutenant, and with him was a Midshipman, and an older fellow in civilian clothes. "I beg pardon for intruding, but, how open may our press be, to speculate or publish rumours, of things that should remain secret, so freely. I saw in *The Times* on the sixth that Admiral Nelson was to be sent to the Dardanelles, to chastise the Russians there. What foolishness!"

"With Admiral Lord Keith already in the Med with a strong fleet?" Lewrie said, with one mocking brow up. "Nothing for Nelson there, if we wish t'swat the bear's nose. Lord Keith, allied with the Ottoman Turks since Napoleon invaded the Holy Lands, can kick the Russians in the fundament, while Nelson goes for their throat in the Baltic, soon as the ice melts. Good morning to you, Lieutenant, young man . . . sir?"

"God, your manners, George," the elder fellow chid him. "Allow me to name my nephew to you, sir, for you sound like a Navy man. This is George Follows. The younker here is my youngest son, Roger Oglesby . . . soon to go aboard his first ship, and I am William Oglesby."

"Captain Alan Lewrie, sirs," Lewrie said, rising to shake hands with them all.

"B . . . Black Alan Lewrie?" the Midshipman gushed.

"Guilty," Lewrie said with a chuckle, though he felt like wincing over that sobriquet. "Or, as the court recently decided, *not*, ha! A pleasure to make your acquaintance, Mister Oglesby, Mister Follows,

Midshipman Oglesby. Will you join me at my table, sirs? What ship?" he asked as they moved over to sit with him.

"Ehm . . . I'm to go aboard the *Trojan*, sir . . . seventy-four," Midshipman Oglesby shyly said. "With cousin George."

"I'm Fifth Officer into her, Captain Lewrie," Lt. Follows said, eyes alight with glee to be introduced to an officer with a reputation in the Fleet as a scrapper, who went after enemies with the ferocity of a howling Tom; hence the name Follows more-likely knew, the "Ram-Cat"; that, or as Lewrie sarcastically suspected, to run into a lucky thief in the flesh! "I convinced my captain that *Trojan* needed another gentleman-in-training . . . the more the merrier, hey?"

"We've spent the last two days purchasing the lad's sea-chest and such," the elder Oglesby told Lewrie, with a wink. "George, here, supervised, so Roger'd not go to sea with an hundredweight of useless fripperies. Tomorrow we'll all coach down to Portsmouth."

"And the very best of good fortune go with you, sirs," Lewrie wished them as the waiter arrived to take their orders. "Why, with any luck, *Trojan*'ll be in the thick of it by mid-March."

"And you, Captain Lewrie?" Lt. Follows enquired. "Will you be with us, do you imagine?" He sounded eager enough for a good fight.

"I had to give up command of *Savage* before Christmas," Lewrie was forced to admit, "the trial, and all, d'ye see, and . . . so far, I have not yet heard from Admiralty as to any new openings. One hopes for another frigate, even one *half* as fine, but . . ." He ended with a shrug, as if it was only a matter of time before he received a fresh active commission, though in his heart he was dead-certain that Hell would freeze over before Lord Spencer or Evan Nepean would consider him "Decent" enough to command another King's ship.

"Dev'lish-odd, this Russian business," the elder Oglesby said as he spooned sugar into his tea. "Thought we were allies not all that long ago. Now, this nonsense. That Tsar of theirs must be daft if he thinks he can take on England."

"Man's got a huge army already, and millions more peasants to conscript if he feels like it," Lt. Follows remarked as he stirred up his own tea. "Big as the French Army is reputed to be, with that *levée en masse* of theirs, I expect the Russians could field three times as many men. And wouldn't *that* be grand to see . . . the Tsar and Bonaparte going at each other hammer-and-tongs!"

"He can *parade* an army," Lewrie said, "but I doubt he's any experience with ships. Strong as the Russians are on land, I doubt anyone'd *try* to invade, so they really don't have much *need* of a fighting fleet, and don't expect their navy to have much of a role to play, if anyone did. What did the Russians do at sea back when they beat the Swedes, early last century? Galleys and gunboats rowed up coves and marshes . . . round the maze of islands? Up the rivers?"

"Well, they *did* send a strong squadron alongside us when we went at the Dutch, in '98," Mr. Oglesby pointed out. "Don't recall all *that* much action at sea, then."

"Another fleet from the Black Sea," Lt. Follows added, "sailed round the Aegean, and the Med. And their Black Sea fleet has gained a lot of experience 'gainst the Turks over the years. When Catherine the Great was still alive, *she* knew to maintain an efficient navy . . . even if about half the officers were really British, or Americans."

"Like John Paul Jones!" Midshipman-to-be Oglesby dared to contribute to an adult conversation.

"I've met some fellows who served with the Russians," Follows told them, "when they couldn't find a post in our Navy. Promotion is quicker in Russian service, and the rates of pay are more lucrative, though . . . I never heard them say much good of their ships, or their men."

"How so, sir?" Lewrie prompted, waving for a fresh coffee.

"The way they told it, Captain Lewrie, is . . . when the Russians need warships, they go level several forests and set up shipyards on the banks of the nearest river to the sea. They round up just *any* old sort of carpenters, and put them to work in *work-regiments*, using green wood with no more seasoning or drying than the timbers get coming down to the banks from the woods on waggons! And they conscript their men the same way. Turn Army regiments into sailors overnight . . . conscript serfs from the nearest estates and drill them like parade ground soldiers on *facsimiles* of masts and decks ashore whilst their ships are still building. Good for part of the year, but when their northern ports freeze up, they're crammed into infantry barracks ashore, in unutterable squalor 'til they're needed again, and it's a wonder half of them don't perish. And by the time they're ready to go aboard in the Spring, it's good odds their assigned ship has *already* rotted and must be replaced.

"I'd expect things are better in the Black Sea, where they may sail almost year-round," Lt. Follows allowed, "but their fleet in the Baltic may not be all that formidable."

"Never *heard* the like!" Lewrie scoffed. "That's an *insane* way to care for a ship's crew, or train it to excellence."

"Not our way, certainly, sir," Lt. Follows agreed. "I'm told their discipline is hellish"—He winced as he saw his uncle's deep frown—"brutal in the extreme. Russians are, so I've heard, a cruel and surly race, their peasants little better than dumb beasts rolling round in pigstys. Illiterate, in the main, and *horrid* drunkards. Do they get their hands on vodka, they go as mad as Red Indians, and just as dangerous to themselves as anyone who crosses their path. With such men, I'd imagine only the cat-o'-nine-tails can keep control."

"Hmm, like British tars with a shipload o' wine or rum?" Lewrie japed. "Give them just enough of a vodka ration t'keep 'em mellow, do they? Devilish tipple, that. Worse for you than gin."

Back in better days, not all that long ago during the Frost Fair on the frozen Thames, Lewrie had run across Eudoxia Durschenko in an off-moment from her role in Wigmore's Peripatetic Extravaganza and had tasted a sip of vodka . . . used as he was to imported Kentucky bourbon, he'd thought he'd poisoned himself! It was better ice-cold, she had told him, but he rather doubted it. At least it did not have the juniper berry taste of good old British "Blue Ruin"!

"Malta was the problem with the Tsar," Mr. Oglesby mused aloud. "We took it back from the French before the Russians could get there. Admiral Nelson hoisted the flag of the Kingdom of Naples and the Two Sicilies, 'stead of our flag, or the Russians', and the Tsar most-like was mad enough to fall down and chew the carpets over it. That King Ferdinand of Naples *was* the real owner, in a way, after all."

"And Lord Nelson spent a lot of time with King Ferdinand and his wife, our ambassador to his court, Sir William Hamilton," Lewrie said (leaving Emma Hamilton *unsaid!*). "They *did* influence him, for certain, but I was in Naples in '94 through '96, and dined with King Ferdinand several times. D'ye know he maintained a waterfront fish shop, where he did the cooking? An *odd* sort o' bird! . . . and a dab-hand cook, too! But I never heard that Naples claimed Malta. 'Twasn't Malta owned by the Knights of Saint John of Jerusalem since the Crusades?"

"Ah, but King Ferdinand is the *Grand Master* of the Knights, sir!" Mr. Oglesby slyly returned. "The real one, I suppose. Though I heard that the Tsar thought *he* was, since a few Knights in the Russian court flattered him up and held an election of their own, making *him* the Grand Master. Imagine what an uproar that could cause in Russia, their own Tsar, the upholder of the *Orthodox* Church, accepting an honourific that is usually awarded by a *Catholic* Pope, ha ha!"

"The Tsar had another grudge with us, too," Lt. Follows contributed. "During the Holland expedition, there were two prizes taken . . . not worth tuppence, really, a fifty-six gunner and a seventy gunner . . . were supposed to be Russian prizes, but we kept them."

"My Lord, is he *that* petty?" Lewrie said, amazed.

"It would appear so, Captain Lewrie," Mr. Oglesby said, nodding. "What's worse, when his mother, Catherine the Great, was still with us, in 1787, Turkey declared war on Russia, for the umpteenth time, and we . . . Great Britain and Prussia . . . egged the Swedes to invade Russian-owned Finland, so Tsar Paul . . . Crown Prince Paul, then . . . naturally despised us for meddling, and distrusts us to this very day. The only reason Russia became our ally in '98 was because he thought that Napoleon Bonaparte's invasion in Egypt's final aim was against *Russia*, not our possessions in India! Why else would he ally himself *with* his worst enemy, the Ottoman Turks, *against* the French?" Oglesby said with a mystified shrug. "Perhaps only the madness of kings may explain why the Tsar now is so enamoured of Bonaparte, and the French."

"Napoleon told the Tsar he'd surrender Malta to the Russians," Lt. Follows stuck in. "Only the Russians. And Napoleon had captured thousands of Russian soldiers when he conquered Switzerland. To make the deal sweeter, he returned them, in new uniforms, boots, and kits, with all their colours, as a gesture of good will."

"Hmmph," Lewrie commented. "I s'pose that would be enough for the Russians to say 'thankee kindly' and stand aloof from now on, but . . . to cozy up to the Frogs? Surely their aristocracy should be quaking in their boots, lest all that Jacobin French insanity take root in *their* country. '*Liberté, Égalité, Fraternité,*' and bloody revolution, would be the end of 'em. *Whish . . . chop!*" he said, miming the drop of the guillotine's blade with one hand, "I've an . . . acquaintance who's Russian, who's told me how they use their serfs so cruelly. Let the landless, powerless slave-peasants get a whiff of freedom and rise up, and it'd be the Terror all over again, *with* the slave revolt on Saint Domingue thrown in, to boot!"

"Factor in, Captain Lewrie, the atheism of the French Jacobites," Mr. Oglesby sagely pointed out, in full agreement with him. "Russia is a *deeply* religious country, though its Orthodox Church is even more of a mystery to me than Popery. I'd imagine their theologians and lords spiritual would consider the French the very imps of Hell, and their First Consul, Napoleon Bonaparte, the Anti-Christ revealed."

"Indeed, uncle," Lt. Follows chimed in. "One of the fellows who took service in their navy told me that the peasant conscript sailors 'board his ship took the authority of their priests as solemn as their officers', and that the only reason there weren't *more* revolts by serfs out in the countryside was deathly fear of condemnation and excommunication by the local priests. Even *nobles* walk wary round them. After a thousand years of servitude, with the threat of abandonment by their church, *and* the coming of the Cossacks to hack them to pieces should they turn on their masters, abject subservience and resignation to a life of misery is common.

"Mind, he said your average Russian sailor or soldier is a marvellous fighter, if decently led, and treated," Lt. Follows said on with a grin, "but, dull as oxen, in the main. Superstitious, un-educated, and easily controlled . . . so long as one doesn't act *too* much the tyrant."

"Push 'em into a corner, whip 'em for no reason?" Lewrie mused aloud. "You bully and beat a puppy, you end up with a wolf who'd tear your throat out. Sounds t'me as if all Russia is teeterin' on a thin razor's edge, with nothing but the fear of Hell and Cossack sabres to keep it from exploding."

"A grievous social system," Mr. Oglesby sadly commented, "much like our own West Indies colonies, or the American South, with so many restive slaves. I doubt any rich or titled, and *landed,* Russian dares sleep too sound of a night. Surely, the Tsar knows, as does his court nobles and church leaders, how dangerous this new friendship with the French can be."

"Well, you mentioned the madness of kings," Lewrie japed. "But as you say, surely those who have the Tsar's ear could advise him not to run the risk."

"Fellow's a Nero, a Caligula," Mr. Oglesby said with a sniff of disdain. "Emperor of All the Russias, reputed to be as mad as a hatter, and, unlike our parliamentary system, he's a total autocrat, as powerful as any Roman emperor, with nothing and no one able to rein him in. And, like a Caligula, the Tsar is *indeed* mad. Cruel, sadistic, and is rumoured to be . . . perverted. Cover your ears, Roger, there is evil coming," he told his youngest son, who had been sitting gape-jawed to be allowed to hear adults talking of such worldly things. "The man is said to have the morals of a wild beast, such that no woman, from the highest to the lowest palace servant, is safe. Some also say that no man is safe, either," Mr. Oglesby added with a grimace of distaste of such practices. "Does he take a dislike to someone . . . noble, valet, or stableman . . . because he didn't like the wine, the temperature of the soup, someone's new suit or dress, hair ribbons, or a beard not shaven that morning . . . well, off one goes to gaol, Siberia, or a dungeon full of instruments of torture.

"Russia has already had one ogre such as he . . . Ivan the Terrible," Mr. Oglesby intoned with a grim nod. "Thankfully, the Russians did away with him, though I cannot help but imagine that his death was but a temporary respite. An absolute monarch will, sooner or later, turn monstrous, if only to preserve his seat on the throne . . . which is *so* rewarding and pleasing."

"Well, with luck, perhaps his nobles will treat this Tsar Paul as they did their Ivan the Terrible," Lt. Follows said with a laugh. "Oh, I know . . . *lèse majesté* and all that," he partly retracted not a tick after, but still with a merry air, "yet . . . he's not *our* King . . . "

"Thank God," Midshipman Oglesby piped up.

". . . and perhaps the new'un might take years before he goes as mad as his predecessor, ha ha!" Lt. Follows suggested. "Unless insanity runs in the Romanov family."

"Peter the Great was sane," Mr. Oglesby pointed out, "though I can't recall why his heirs weren't suitable to rule, and Russia ended with a German girl on the throne. After the Dowager Tsarina died, and Catherine got rid of her useless idiot of a husband, no one could say that Catherine the Great ever evinced the *slightest* sign of madness. Her son, though . . . well," he said, finishing his latest cup of tea, and dragging out his pocket-watch. "Good Lord, lads, we were to meet the wife in the Strand by twelve. We must go, else she'll be wroth with us . . . me, more to the point. You will pardon us do we depart, Captain Lewrie?"

"It has been a pleasure to make your acquaintances, sirs, and a most enlightening conversation, for which I thankee," Lewrie said as they all rose and made their parting salutations.

After they'd bustled out the door in overcoats and boat-cloaks, Lewrie decided that he might as well pay his reckoning, too, and hunt up his own mid-day meal. Stultifying, and as earnest, as dinner conversation at the Madeira Club could be, with so many gentlemen who had made their fortunes in Trade sharing stock tips and complaints about workers, prices, and goods, the club *did* lay a good table, and could boast of a wine cellar that even Almack's, White's, or Bootle's might envy.

There was also the realisation that said table, said wine list, was included in his weekly fee, which his father had arranged for him, which was about a quarter less than the others were charged—in some instances, being kin to the old lecher had its advantages!

Was his pace quick enough, he could just make it back in time for a glass of something warming before the dining room door opened!

Though, as he maintained a brisk stride back up Orchard Street to Wigmore Street, Lewrie could not help recalling a late-night talk with that devious old rogue Zachariah Twigg nearly two years before, when his legal troubles were just beginning to come home to roost . . .

Twigg's grand scheme did not care a whit for the abolition of slavery, though many of the reformers thought him an ally against the "peculiar institution," did not care if thousands of planter families in the West Indies were impoverished should slavery be outlawed in the British Empire, along with the slave traders and shipping interests in West Country seaports. What Twigg intended was to cripple any threat to Great Britain from slave-driving nations, with his own country and its abolition of slavery the shining example; the United States of America, for one, whose economy, treasury, and power was based on agricultural exports, mostly reaped by slave labour. Create a rebellion as bloody as Saint Domingue, or Haiti, or whatever they were calling it, these days, and America might even fracture in twain, with one of the halves forced to ally itself with Great Britain against the other half, perhaps even see the error of its ways and rejoin the Empire someday!

No matter how much blood might be shed in servile revolts and civil war, no matter how many hundreds of thousands perished! And . . . hadn't Russia come up, that night? What had Twigg cold-bloodedly said? That, if Russia ever turned its insatiable appetite for conquest westward, and set its massive peasant conscript armies on the march, those "white slaves," the serfs, could be turned against the nobility and the landowners, against the Tsar himself, and all the Cossacks in the world could not put down the revolution, the civil wars 'tween the warlords that would ensue, in the Holy names of Abolition and Freedom!

Russia now seemed a foe. And what was Twigg up to in the face of that? It wasn't just the nip in the air that made Lewrie shiver!

CHAPTER SEVEN

$\mathcal{T}$here was a warming pea soup, served with a pleasant hock; then Dover sole with boiled potatoes and carrots; the salad course was nothing worth much, in the dead of winter, but the roast pigeons, accompanied by more potatoes, carrots, and peas, was succulent, and complemented by a promising Beaujolais. Cheese, sweet biscuit, and the port, some of the house's famed namesake, a Portuguese Madeira, finished off the meal, which, despite the victuals, was nothing but a litany of bad, sad, gloom, and the portent of utter ruin.

Some of Lewrie's fellow lodgers, while not *strictly* so deep in Trade that they kept a shop and handled money directly, had all taken "flyers" on the Exchange, had invested in stocks and bonds beyond the safe and sane Three Percents and the Sinking Fund as a repository for their "New-Made Men" profits, and the Northern League recently formed round the shores of the Baltic, their Armed Neutrality, and the threat of an expanded war, had many of them shivering like a dog that was trying to pass a peach pit . . . as an American naval officer had so vividly said to Lewrie a few years back.

"The Tsar is so demented he could be committed to Bedlam," said one who had invested heavily in naval stores.

"They don't have one," an Army officer in *mufti* rejoined.

"Well, they should," the civilian fellow reiterated. "And that King

Christian of Denmark's not a whit better. How else explain why the Danes joined Russia in this pact?"

"Same as the Swedes, old man," said another near the head of the long table. "It's fear of what Russia would do, did they *not* sign on."

"King Christian's in Bedlam, of a sorts, already," the Army officer snickered. "Called his royal apartments. Soon as the Danes ousted King George's sister, Caroline Matilda, and chopped the head off her lover . . . what the Devil was his name, their Prime Minister, then?"

"Struensee," a much older gentleman told them between bites of his meal, "Johann Friedrich Struensee, and one of the biggest fools of the age. I remember it well. A feather-brained German, besotted with Voltaire, Rousseau, and all those pagan French reformers. Turned all Denmark inside-out before they did for him and his cronies. Imagine, a commoner *German* running an entire country, and fathering bastards on a queen! He'd all but buried King Christian in a dungeon before he was deposed. Mind now, the Danish king *needed* to be put in a dungeon, for he was a vicious lunatick."

"So their Crown Prince, the Regent, is really Struensee's illegitimate 'git'?" a member asked. "Egad!"

"They say not, but *he* ain't insane like the old king, so . . . ," the old gentleman lasciviously hinted. "They shuffled off the little princess. . . . They were *sure* Struensee quickened her, and Crown Prince Frederick *was* the only male heir."

"The Swedes, though," Lewrie posed.

"Beaten to a pulp by Russia, their northern empire lost back in the seventeen-twenties," the Army fellow offered. "Swedish Pomerania gone, Polish provinces, and Finland, too. Fear, again, sir. Why they even attempted to fight the Russians again in '87 is beyond me."

"But what about Prussia signing on?" another asked.

"Fear of Russia, again," the Army officer said with a shrug. "Perhaps a fear of France, too, after Napoleon gave them a drubbing. Better to crouch in Russia's shadow than stand out in the open, alone. And, since, as Captain Lewrie here will tell you, the Prussians don't have much of a navy, nor much of a merchant marine, either, it's no skin off their nose. Ain't that right, sir?"

"Nothing to lose at sea if we retaliate, for certain," Lewrie agreed as he broke open a fresh hot roll and buttered it.

"All those ships confiscated, put out of business," the investor in naval stores bemoaned. "It's an outrage, a violation of a solemn treaty! And the embargo they threaten on their goods will cripple our navy. Pine mast stocks, tar, pitch, turpentine, and resin . . . hemp for sails and rope rigging. . . ."

"Well, there's Nova Scotia and the Maritime provinces, there's Wilmington, North Carolina," Lewrie suggested. "Much the same available in New England . . . Vermont, New Hampshire, and such?"

"Longer voyages, higher prices," the sad investor grumbled.

"Aye, trust the Yankee skin-flints to take quick advantage of us, and wring every penny they can from our lacks," another said.

"Do they not embargo us, as well," a very gloomy cynic down the table posed. "There's no love lost, 'twixt them and England since the Revolution ended, and despite that little 'not-quite-war' they had in '98, the United States still thinks the French hung the very moon!"

"Demned war's gone on long enough," someone said.

"Oh I say now!" several cried.

"We've not a single ally left, Bonaparte's driven Naples out of the war and beaten the Austrians so badly at Marengo and just last month at Hohenlinden, they've sued for peace, too," the doubter retorted. "Seven years of war worldwide, millions of pounds spent to prop up so-called allies . . . *none* of them *faithful* . . . the Treasury reduced to issuing paper *fiat* money, prices five times what they were in '93, and all these horrendous, crushing *taxes*. And what have we to show for it, I ask you, gentlemen? A few conquests in the West Indies, more lands for rich sugar planters, and nigh fifty thousand of our lads dead, mostly of tropical fevers. Consider the very bread we eat today, sirs . . . rye, or barley, not wheat, and—"

"Oh dear, there goes the price o' beer and ale!" a younger wag said, sniggering, which at least gave most of them a relieving laugh.

"Staple of your common Englishman, indeed, young sir," Doubting Thomas quickly said, "and, as you say, becoming dearer by the minute, as are all foodstuffs and goods. Yet, do our common Englishman's wages increase in like measure? They do not, and this war is pinching the very souls of the people."

"He's to stand for a seat in Commons, next by-election, or so I heard," the Army officer in civilian suitings whispered to Lewrie.

"God help us, then," Lewrie muttered back. "Ye'd think he was one of those who *cheered* the French revolution."

"I'm sure 'twill be a pretty speech, on the hustings," the Army man hissed behind his hand. "Bloody Liberals."

After dinner was done, Lewrie took himself upstairs to his rooms for a lie-down. He removed his coat, undid the buttons of his vest, and tugged off his boots. He plumped up the pillows and stretched out on the new-made bed, welcoming his cats, Toulon and Chalky, who awoke from a snooze on the bench before the fireplace and pounced up to join him with glad cries, arch-backed stretches, and playful expressions.

There was nothing for it but to indulge them, fetch some of their toys from the night-stand, and dangle them by their strings, letting the cats dash and pounce, capture and leap, 'til they were worn out and ready for naps of their own, with Toulon slung against the side of his leg, and Chalky softly purring on a pillow by his head.

Not in the Baltic, mine arse, Lewrie thought as he tried to go to sleep, yet mulling over all he had heard that morning. Nelson was the very fellow to daunt the Danes, Swedes, and Russians. Did he get a fleet into the Baltic before the ice melted at Copenhagen, Karlskrona, or Reval and Kronstadt—before this new Armed Neutrality could get their fleets to sea and combined—he could crush them as completely as he had the French in Aboukir Bay.

As odd a bird as Lewrie considered Horatio Nelson to be, he was a man who did nothing by halves. At the Battle of the Saintes in the West Indies in 1782, Admiral Rodney had been satisfied to capture only five French ships of the line, and let the rest slink off. Lewrie had been at the Battle of St. Kitts, and had watched the famous Adm. Hood *repulse* the French fleet, yet not go after them after they were cut up and damaged. Adm. Hotham in the Mediterranean in '95, whose laziness and caution had nigh-driven Lewrie berserk, thought he'd done very well to capture a mere *two*! Well, the wind had been scant, yet . . .

Cape St. Vincent and Camperdown; Lewrie wore the medals for both great battles, and had seen Adm. Sir John Jervis, "Old Jarvy," and Adm. Duncan in action. Despite their estimable repute as scrappers, Jervis had let the Spanish fleet return to port after taking only a few ships as prize (two of them Nelson's doing, that day) whilst at Camperdown, at least, Duncan had managed to overawe the Dutch and force them to go about and head for port, scotching their hope to link up with a French fleet in the Channel and invade England, firstly; then, *herded* the foe into the shoal waters of their own coast, strung out in a long line of battle, before driving right into them in several columns at right angles, and shattering them thoroughly, taking *most* of them as prizes in Nelson-fashion.

Or, Duncan-fashion, Lewrie thought with a snigger, recalling the wild-haired, towering Duncan, who'd take you on with his fists for the possession of a wheel-barrow, if his blood was up. *And, when* does *the bloody ice melt in the Baltic anyway?* he asked himself, wishing he had asked one of the "trading gentlemen" at-table an hour before. Truth to tell, Lewrie had never served in the Baltic, and, in point of fact, had only the foggiest notion where Sweden, Denmark, and Prussia *were,* much less the location of their naval bases. They all lay to the east, he was pretty sure, t'other side of the North Sea, with Russia the furthest east of them all, where one ran out of sea water.

Supper, then up early tomorrow, Lewrie ordered himself; *Drop by Admiralty . . . see in what odour I'm held. Then a bookstore or a map maker's. Another good nap after that, then . . . the theatre, again, or Ranelagh Gardens?*

There would be a grand expositon of new nautical art held there through the Spring, along with a magic lantern slide depiction of the Battle of the Nile, replete with stirring musical accompaniment and a narrator hidden behind a curtain. Lewrie had bought his children one of the smaller magic lanterns at Scott's Shop in the Strand for Christmas, along with Bissinger's chocolates and a new doll for his wee daughter Charlotte; one of the better ones that went for ten guineas. Hopefully, the boys hadn't burned down the house with the oil lamp yet, or broken all the glass slides.

"Supper scraps suit ye, lads?" Lewrie asked his cats.

Toulon cocked his rather large head up over his thigh for a second or two, gave out a guttural, close-mouthed *Mrr,* then lay back down. Chalky stretched out his forepaws to touch Lewrie's head and yawn, all white teeth and pink mouth, before dozing off again, too.

"That's what I thought," Lewrie muttered, closing his eyes once more.

CHAPTER EIGHT

L ewrie had found himself an atlas, so at least he knew *where* the possible enemies were; Sayer's & Bennett's had Baltic charts and larger-scale charts of their principal naval harbours, so he had a rough idea of how things lay. As for when the ice melted, though, all he'd gotten was a day-long series of shrugs.

Admiralty had been no better. The infamous Waiting Room was an arseholes-to-elbows chamber of hopefuls, so many of them that the fireplace was almost redundant when it came to heating that large room, as the lucky ones holding active commissions or warrants crowded in for a bit, were ushered abovestairs, then came clattering quickly down with a fresh set of instructions and making hasty departures . . . not without a smirk or two from some of the cockiest of the lucky at those cooling their heels in hopes of employment.

A hint of action, the chance of more older warships being fitted out and manned, brought out even the nigh-dead; oh, it was a grim mob that Lewrie beheld. There were grizzled Lieutenants in their fourties, Captains in need of crutches in their sixties, all of whom had been on half-pay since the end of the American Revolution, whose uniforms were ready for museum pieces, all sniffing the air like white-muzzled foxhounds who could barely *walk* anymore . . . bleating like ancient sheep, all rheumy-eyed, for just one more shot at sea.

Christ, is that what I have t'look forward to? Lewrie wondered to him-self, appalled. He had sent his name up to the First Secretary, Evan Ne-pean, 'round ten of the morning. Rather too quickly for belief a silky-smooth young snotty had called out his name and sought him out with a note of reply in hand. For one *brief* moment, Lewrie had felt a surge of hope. Even through the flunky's smug smirk.

> *The First Secretary regrets that pressing matters preclude an inter-view with you today, Cpt. Lewrie; or in the near future. At any rate, there are no openings in the Fleet at present for a Cpt. of your qualities. Given your single year on the Senior Cpt's List and lack of seniority, it may be some time before we may contemplate your active employment.*

Polite way o' sayin' it'll be a cold *day in Hell,* Lewrie thought as he quickly wadded up the note and jammed it into a side pocket of his uni-form coat, his face reddening in embarrassment and anger. And that smooth young *flunky* was still standing there before him, with a faint smirk on his face.

"Waitin' for a *tip?*" Lewrie harshly muttered. "Bugger off!"

With the eyes of an hundred or more of his contemporaries upon him, Lewrie gathered up his hat and boat-cloak and prepared to depart, his soul smarting . . . to be gawked at and whispered about behind hands by such a pack of superannuated dodderers and droolers, by failures and drunkards, by fools too lack-wit to pass their Lieutenants' exams, and incompetent twits and no-hopes. Worse yet! To imagine what false sym-pathy some felt. "Bugger him, more chance for me! Oh, poor fellow . . . the bastard! *Born* one, ye know, hee hee!" To be *pitied* by such a lot!

"Off to a new ship, are ye, sir?" the garrulous old tiler said as Lewrie stepped through the anteroom for the doors to the walled-off courtyard. "Well, I reckon ye'll give them damned Rooskies a good bash on th' noggin, hey, sir? Make way fer a fightin' captain, ye younkers," the old fellow barked at an incoming pack of Lieutenants and Midshipmen. "Part like the Red Sea fer Moses, there, an' git ye in. There's a mob o' others waitin', so don't git yer hopes too high. Standin' room only, an' don't tread on nobody's boot tips, neither, mind, har har."

Equally galling were the smiles and appreciative looks from the many civilians 'round the environs of Whitehall. England might be all alone against France, without allies, and threatened by a fresh set of enemies, the war's length and cost might be wearying, yet . . . the *Navy* would set things right, the Royal Navy; aye, the Navy and Nelson! The people who doffed their hats, the ladies who inclined their heads with grins, imagined Lewrie off to *save* them.

Why else was that naval fellow so grim-faced, and walking quite so quickly? Surely eager to board his ship and fillet anyone who *dared* challenge Great Britain! Why, the angry stamping of his boots denoted dread determination, egad! See how his hands flex so on the hilt of his sword, and all? Damn my eyes, wasn't he that Lewrie chap, by God? Then God help the Roosians! Maps, and books, just making ready . . .

Capt. Alan Lewrie, RN (sure to unemployed 'til the dawn of the *next* century!) *fumed* his way back to his rooms, blackly contemplating how he might trail Nepean home some dark night and throttle him for his haughty and brusque dismissal; how he'd go about challenging the *next* sniggerer or smirker to a duel, and how much pleasure he'd find in the skewering or shooting of the fool!

Damn my eyes, there's going t'be a battle, Lewrie furiously imagined; *two or three of 'em, if we can take 'em on separately . . . and I'll not have a part in 'em? Become one o' those . . . losers? No, I'll not ever! Mine arse on a band-box if I'll haunt the Admiralty, beggin' for scraps like a . . . stray cur! Christ on a crutch, I've put in twenty-one years, most of 'em at sea, and miserable, too. They don't want me any longer, well . . . just bugger 'em! Somethin' t'be said for warm and dry, for a change.*

Thirty-eight wasn't all *that* old, he could comfort himself to think; there were naval officers who had actually *given up* active commissions to sit in Parliament, go into business, enter government service . . . and make a pile of "tin" off the sops and graft that resulted!

Lewrie imagined that taking Holy Orders was pretty much out for his sort, even a lowly rector's position in a poor parish, with an absent vicar taking the lion's share of the benefice and tithes. Besides, no one would ever believe it of him!

Trade, and Business? Well, he *was* a skilled mariner, capable of being a merchant master—was "John Company" still grateful to him for saving that convoy in the South Atlantic last year? Captaining an East Indiaman would be pleasant, and hellish profitable, to boot.

Or he could live on his invested prize-money, his savings with Coutts' Bank, and his late grandmother's £150 annual remittance, keep rooms (at a family discount) at the Madeira Club, and become an idle wastrel about London. Where one could have a drink whenever . . .

"Drink, by God," Lewrie muttered under his frost-steaming breath. "I definitely need strong drink . . . now! Drink, and distraction."

As soon as he attained his lodgings, Lewrie made haste to strip off his uniform and pack it away in his sea-chest, stow his cocked hat in a japanned wooden box, and change into a tail-coat that was all the "crack"; single-breasted and cut to the waist, with wide lapels and M-shaped collars in a newly fashionable black, over a snug pair of long grey trousers, with plain and unadorned black boots on his feet, minus the gold lace trim and tassels he'd wear with his uniform. To become even more a civilian, his black neck-stock he replaced with a cravat woven in blue, gilt, and cream paisley.

Walking stick instead of sword; a thimble-shaped black beaver hat with a royal blue band and short, curled brims; a single-breasted overcoat with triple capes, and he was ready for a good, long, and very unmilitary dinner, a bottle or two of wine, with port and brandy to follow, and while away the rest of the day 'til it was time to toddle off to the theatre or Ranelagh Gardens.

With the aforementioned restful nap, of course.

CHAPTER NINE

*T*he next week passed in slothful idyll; late risings and lazy days, followed by heady afternoons roaming central London for delightful diversions, followed by even headier evenings. There were public subscription balls, drums and routs, concerts, and even a rare trip to a ballet or opera—all followed, of course, by light midnight cold collations washed down with champagne, and pre-dawn tumbles into bed at the Madeira Club. Not to mention the requisite hangovers.

And while such a rakehell (partially reformed) as Alan Lewrie might have so far tumbled into bed *alone,* it was a Devilish close-run thing, for London, the greatest city in the world no matter what Frogs boasted of their own Paris, possessed the most impressive collection of fetching young women of every stripe and grade.

Actresses, ballet dancers, orange-seller wenches in the aisles, "grass-widows" abandoned by straying or absent husbands still looking for affection, the *handsomest,* fetchingest young un-married girls down to search for a suitable husband, some of them coyly eager for a "ride" or two, away from their unaware parents. . . . For a stray male, London was a paradise. And that didn't even begin to count the shop girls and house servants out on a spree on their lone days off, or the ones of "the commercial persuasion," who ranged from costly courtesans and mistresses to the over-made, bright-eyed morts available for a "knee-trembler" in a dark doorway.

Sadly, though, sometimes being regarded as a "hero" played to one's detriment. People simply *would* regard Lewrie as "high-minded" or even "Respectable", after all the flattering coverage in newspapers and Abolitionist tracts, the past year. He'd be *introduced* to lovely un-married daughters by beaming Papas and Mamas, but was expected to be the courtly but gruff sea-dog that, it seemed, all England expected. Even though the trial was over, and he could be as beastly as he wished to be once more, still there was that damnably "honest" part to play, and God help him should he step outside it.

Well, there was Theoni Kavares Connor, the rich widow and mother of his bastard son. She seemed to turn up wherever Lewrie sported, at least twice a week, and made it quite plain that since he had so much time on his hands, with his wife estranged from him and safely off in the countryside (and how the Devil she'd discovered that? Lewrie had to wonder) they should partake of a passionate *rencontre,* and Lewrie was not quite sure why he *hadn't* leaped upon her slim, wee body, and those glorious tits of hers, yet . . . there it was. *Shiverin' guilt, most-like,* he told himself; *or lingerin' fear o' gettin' caught out.*

Equally maddening and mysterious was Eudoxia Durschenko. With Daniel Wigmore's so-called Peripatetic Extravaganza (read circus *cum* theatrical troupe) in winter quarters 'cross the river in Southwark, the girl was free to explore London, too, and, maddeningly, was simply everywhere Lewrie had gone! Did she have a spy network worthy of Zachariah Twigg's, or the Secret Branch of the Foreign Office?

Did he hire a prad to take an icy, but bracing, ride in a park, there Eudoxia Durschenko would be on her magnificent trained stallion, Moinya, from her circus act. Did Lewrie attend a subscription ball, she was there, too, dressed in the height of fashion. At Ranelagh Gardens, Covent Garden, theatres in Drury Lane, shopping in the Strand, gawking at rarees and street performers, and pursued by a clutch of rakehells and hopeful swains, especially at those midnight champagne suppers.

With her exotically dark, curly hair and high-cheeked, almond-eyed features and full lips, and those intriguing hazel-amber eyes of hers, Eudoxia Durschenko would have been the belle of the season, no matter her class or origin, and even the latest fashionable colours of puce, lavender, purple, and all set well upon her graceful form; even those sofa-pillow "Pizarro" hats looked cunning atop her head.

In point of fact, was he forced to choose between Eudoxia and Theoni Connor, Lewrie would have plumped for the exotic Russian girl, hands down . . . assuming he could wedge himself into her circle of admirers without looking like a *total* fool or moonstruck cully. Assuming Eudoxia's constant chaperone would let him.

Unfortunately, her father, Arslan Artimovich Durschenko, was at her elbow constantly. Fetching as she was, desirable as she was, her father had once intimated that Eudoxia was still a chaste young maid, and he was determined for her to *remain* virginal, even if he had to kill the first half-dozen young lechers who got within whiffing distance of her perfume!

It did not improve Eudoxia's romantic odds that her father was just possibly the scariest, and ugliest, patch-eyed old devil Lewrie had ever clapped his "top-lights" upon. The Durschenkos claimed Cossack origins, so both were expert riders, but Arslan Artimovich could swing a sabre with the best of them. His previous circus act, before the pan of a rifled musket blinded his right eye, had been that of a marksman with any sort of rifle, musket, or pistol, and the recurved Asian bow and arrows—from horseback, standing in the stirrups, standing on the horse's bare back, hanging like a Red Indian under its belly or its neck . . . the act that Eudoxia now so ably performed. After the accident, he'd turned lion-tamer and kept four of the beasts, grown from cubs to *huge*, rangy adults. Arslan Artimovich was also able to substitute at the knife-throwing act.

He was, in fine, so menacing and scary that Blackbeard and his *pirates* would have pissed their breeches in dread of him! It must be admitted that Arlsan Artimovich certainly gave Lewrie the "squirts"! He had to admit, though, that the risk of his life to her papa's vengeance, or his lions, just *might* be worth it.

"*Kapitan* Lewrie, *zdrazvotyeh* . . . how good to see you again!" Eudoxia had gushed the first night he'd "crossed hawses" with her in the lobby of a theatre. She had swept in from the cold, swathed in a sleek, long fur overcoat with hood. Soon as she had carefully removed the hood from her artfully styled hair, she had boldly crossed to him and offered her hand to be kissed, a regal yet eager smile plastered on her face, and her eyes alight with glee. "My bold *Kapitan* Lewrie! I was so reliev-ed you are ac . . . acquitted. My English improves, yes?"

Buzz-hum of talk as he took her hand in his: "That's 'Black' Alan Lewrie, don't ye know" . . . "Princess Eudoxia from Wigmore's circus, begad! What a stunner!"

"Indeed it does, Mistress Durschenko," Lewrie had purred over her lace-gloved hand. "It is my pleasure to see you again, as well. You are enjoying London?" he had asked, lingering a trifle longer in his bow as she dropped him a fine curtsy; her gown *was* low-cut, and revealed a *promising* pair of poonts!

"It amazes me, *Kapitan*," Eudoxia had declared. "Pooh. You do not use my name?"

"Eudoxia, aye," Lewrie had said with a sly smile, one that she matched, until they both heard a bear's deep warning growl, making him wonder if Jose was there with his dancing bears, Paolo and Fredo. But it was Arslan Artimovich.

"You remember Papa, *Kapitan*?" Eudoxia had said with a roll of her eyes and a minx-ish grin.

"Arslan Artimovich, sir," Lewrie had responded, letting go her hand (rather precipitously, in point of fact) and turning to bow greetings to her father. "Delighted to see you well, sir. Your servant."

"*Kapitan* Lewrie," the old cut-throat had rumbled, arms akimbo to spread the wings of his own fur coat, revealing a flashy blend of Eastern and Western garb; a fur cap on his grizzled locks, a double-breasted tail-coat made of royal blue wool over a cream-coloured Russian silk shirt that buttoned up the side of his neck; a scarlet waist sash (fortunately, no sign of daggers or pistols shoved into it, God be thanked!), buff-coloured snug trousers, and tall top-boots (minus spurs). "You still alive," Arslan Artimovich had added, sounding as if he was rather surprised . . . or was pointing out a *temporary* state, dependent upon Lewrie's behaviour. He smiled . . . evilly.

Lewrie had *tried* to continue a conversation with Eudoxia after that, just long enough to not seem ungentlemanly, or cowardly, for he had felt a *strong* urge to toddle off to greet some others. That was hard to do, though, for there came from the glowering Papa Durschenko a constant raspy whisper consisting of fondly recalled Russian phrases such as "*Peesa*," "*Sikkim Siyn*," "*Tarakan*," "*Nasyakomayeh*," and that old favourite, "*Gryaʒni sabaka*"!

What could one do when a lovely girl's father called you Prick,

Sonofabitch, Cockroach, Insect, and Dirty Dog? All in stone-heavy Cyrillic letters that sprayed the parquetry like blood from a cut throat!

"You know, o' course, that callin' an Englishman such things is cause for a duel," Lewrie drawled to Papa Durschenko.

"Then choice of weapon is mine," that worthy off-handedly replied with a menacing hiss and a broad grin of expectation.

"Papa! *Stoi*! Stop insulting *Kapitan* Lewrie!" Eudoxia scolded. "Is boorish. *Ne kulturny*," she said with her nose up. Evidently, she had come a long way from her childhood Cossack village, or her family's nomadic *yurt*, for all Lewrie knew of her early years. Eudoxia mightn't be a *grand* actress, but her "turns" with Dan Wigmore's theatrical troupe had taught her how to *play-act* well-born hauteur. Her top-lofty air put her papa in his place; all he could do was utter an inarticulate "Grr!" and, for a moment, share with Lewrie a frustrated look over his willful daughter's new ways.

There was a sudden commotion at the doors to the theatre lobby, with the crowd parting like the sea at a warship's cutwater, with men in royal livery leading the way, the grand fellow in the very front waving a long staff in the bored manner of palace courtiers. "His Royal Highness, George, Prince of Wales," the gaudily clad fellow in a powdered wig in-toned in an equally bored manner, and the clench-jawed, nasally tone of the uppermost Oxonian. Men bowed and ladies curtsied deeply, all heads lowered as the Prince swept in, one hand languidly waving to one and all, with a faint smile on his phyz, and a nod to some he recognised. Well, there was also a flirtatious glint, perhaps even a wink, to some of the prettier ladies, though the heir to the throne acted as if his heart wasn't really in it. 'Til he espied Eudoxia, that is.

"My dear," the Prince of Wales murmured, stopping before her.

"Ah . . . em?" from the stunned Eudoxia as he took her hand in his and brought it to his lips.

"Stunnin'," from the Prince. "Seen you ride and shoot, what? We were *most* impressed."

"*Spasiba*, em . . . thank you, your . . . highness," Eudoxia replied in a stutter, like to faint, yet reddening with pleasure.

"*Yob tvoyemant*" from her papa, and Lewrie discreetly took hold of his arm before he reached out to strangle the fellow.

"Fascinatin', hey?" the Prince of Wales asked of one of his simpering courtiers, cocking a brow significantly. Lewrie realised that his courtier looked to be making a mental note to himself, nodding to the Heir as if he caught his meaning. He'd be up 'til dawn, discovering where she lodged, when she rode in the park, and what her favourite colour was.

Royalty bestowed upon her a departing nod, a fond smile, then glided on to the stairs to his reserved box.

"*Doh!*" Eudoxia said under her breath, employing her fan for its real purpose. "God Above!"

"Who *is* pasty fellow?" Arslan Artimovich growled.

"The Prince of Wales . . . heir to the throne?" Lewrie explained. "One day, he'll be George the Fourth. A great'un for the ladies, it's said," Lewrie slyly added, hoping that Papa Durschenko would lose sleep worrying over a rakehell royal, instead of him.

Sure t'God, there's some nice jewelry headed her way, Lewrie thought with a well-repressed snicker; *If the King lets him, that is.*

"God damn kings and princes," Papa Durschenko darkly muttered.

"I wouldn't say that too loud, were I you," Lewrie warned him. "*Paneemahyu?*" he added, using one of his very few words of Russian. "Englishmen take a very dim view of people insulting their rulers . . . even *pasty*-faced princes. Calls himself 'Florizel,' don't ye know," he imparted in a whisper. "Wants t'be everyone's friend. Young women, especially."

Which information elicited another "Grr!" from Durschenko.

"Well, I'll take my leave of you, sir . . . Mistress Eudoxia," Lewrie said with a grin, emulating the Heir and taking her hand to be kissed. "I'm off to my seat, and I hope you enjoy the show. Perhaps we may run into each other for a cold collation and some champagne?"

"Grr!"

Leaving it at that, Lewrie had toddled off, leaving Eudoxia to her moment of glory, and the greater adulation from her many admirers, *despite* what her papa wished!

CHAPTER TEN

*T*he second week of Lewrie's enforced idleness passed much in the same fashion as the first, but with a lot less relish on Lewrie's part. His last *rencontre* with Theoni Kavares Connor had turned out to be rather embarrassing, in the vast rotunda of Ranelagh Gardens, of all places. She'd been importunate and a bit of a shrew, all but demanding that he pay court to her, and Lewrie, never one to appreciate being pressed in a corner, and with only the lamest of excuses as to why he had not yet dropped by, namely that his new stature as a Publick Hero would not *let* him act as he had in the past—"Respectability, and all that, Theoni," he had claimed, which sounded stage-y even to *his* ear!—hadn't set all that well with her.

Hissed like a bloody goose guardin' her eggs! Lewrie had told himself at the time; *And like t'peck my shins an' flog me!*

Theoni's seething, barely controlled anger, then her tears, had made a nasty scene for the crowd in the rotunda, and sent Lewrie on a less-than-dignified trot to get away from her. Thankfully, for the last three days, he hadn't run into her anywhere, after that.

He still slept in late, but he didn't stay *out* quite as late in the A.M.s as he had the first week. *Fear of her,* he concluded. So he haunted the Madeira Club's library, which contained rather a respectable collection of books, and the Common Room, with its cheery fireplace and comfortable leather sofas and chairs, was a grand place to read up on all the latest editions. Mind, none of them particularly salacious or *interesting*; all followed the modern concept of Edifying, Uplifting, and *Useful*, or completely unworthy to the nineteenth-century gentleman. *And* damn *Priestley, Bentham, and the whole lot of Reformers,* Lewrie stewed as he found most of them hard slogging.

He was all but nodding over a book as mystifying as any done by Milton when a club servant *ahemmed* into his fist and handed Lewrie a note.

"Ah? Hmm," Lewrie said as he opened it, fearing that Theoni'd run him to earth at last, and wondering why there was nothing on the outside of the folded-over paper to show who had sent it. "Christ!" he muttered once he had it open, for it was from Zachariah Twigg.

> *My dear Capt. Lewrie,*
>   *A matter has just yesterday arisen which, I am sure, will prove to be of the greatest interest to you. Should this note find you in your lodgings, and not absorbed in your amusements, do, pray, join me at my club, Almack's, for dinner at One of the clock. My man will await your prompt reply.*
>
>   *Yr Obdt. Servant*
>   *Twigg*

It was worse than Theoni finding him, worse than Eudoxia dashing into the Common Rooms nude, with her father and his lions in hot pursuit and out for Lewrie's blood. It was *Twigg*, damn his eyes!

When'd he ever call me "dear"? Lewrie cynically thought; *And he just* had *t'get at least one shot in, 'bout my "amusements." Oh, this could be hellish-bad. Who does he want me t'kill?* And Almack's; he couldn't remember if that particular club was Tory or Whig, and if it was, did it really say anything about Twigg's personal politics? At least Lewrie knew that Almack's set a splendid table, and Twigg would be footing the bill, so . . .

"Pen and paper, please," he told the club servant, "and I think there's a messenger laddie waitin'?"

"There is, sir. I'll fetch them directly," the servant said.

"So pleased to see you, again, Lewrie," Zachariah Twigg said in what could be mistaken for a pleasant tone, almost purring with social oils, as it were, as he extended a long-fingered, skeletal hand to be shaken. "So pleased you got off. And, have been granted some time to re-acquaint yourself to the joys of London life. Cold enough for you?"

"Thankee for your invitation, sir," Lewrie replied, civil enough on his own part, but still wondering whose throat those fingers had strangled lately. "Not as cold as it was last week, no, but still chilly."

He felt like gawking at his plush surroundings, for he had not been inside any of the grander gentlemen's clubs in London, except for the Cocoa Tree, or one of the others that featured the *hearty* sort of revelry and gambling open to non-members, and folk of both sexes after dark. He felt like a "Country-Put" yokel just down from somewhere *very* dreary, and shown into Westminster Cathedral, for Almack's was a grand establishment indeed, done in the finest, and subtly richest, taste.

"Something warming, perhaps, Captain Lewrie," Twigg suggested as they strolled into a large library with many sofas and chairs. "A brandy for me, Hudgins."

"Yes, sir. And for you, sir?" the distinguished-looking older servant asked in a fair approximation of a courtly Oxonian accent.

"Kentucky whisky," Lewrie requested, a brow cocked in fun, just to see if Almack's stocked such spirits.

"Would Evan Williams suit, sir?"

"That'd be splendid," Lewrie replied, impressed even further.

"A quiet corner, over there, ah," Twigg said, pointing out one grouping of furniture near the tall windows at the far end of the room. The tall and cadaverous Twigg led the way, swept the tails of his coat clear, and took a seat on one end of a sofa, while Lewrie settled for a wing-back chair nearby.

"Cold, that's the bugabear, Lewrie," Twigg said in a petulant, business-like rasp. "Enough cold to keep the Danes', Swedes', and Russian fleets laid up in-ordinary, and unable to sail. The Thames here in London is already thawing below London Bridge, and the rest of the river is open to shipping. The passages into the Baltic are free of ice, and time is of the essence."

He promisin' me a command? Lewrie thought with spurred hope, of a sudden; *That'd be of great int'rest t'me, like he wrote!*

"I've met some other officers who know some who've served in the Russian Navy, sir," Lewrie told him. "Frankly, they don't sound so formidable . . . conscript crews, and all, and limited sailing seasons in which t'work their people up to competence. In the Baltic, at least."

"Quite true, yet . . . with the Russians combined with the Danes . . . as doughty fighters as the Dutch, and the Swedes with a very competent navy, things could get rather dicey, should they put to sea together. Their numbers would be daunting."

"So were the Spanish at Cape Saint Vincent," Lewrie scoffed. "I think 'Old Jarvy,' and Nelson, put paid to them, despite their numbers."

"You know that Bonaparte is behind all this," Twigg said with a sniff and a thin-lipped look of asperity.

"Anything to take pressure off France, and force us to squander our own advantages far afield, aye," Lewrie contentedly answered as he was handed a crystal snifter half full of amber bourbon, as Twigg got his own snifter of brandy from a silver tray. Both took a moment to swirl their drinks, study the "legs" of evaporating alcohol which resulted, and sniffed deep, as over a fine wine. Only after their first sips did Twigg continue.

"It's rather more devious than that, Lewrie," Twigg pointed out. "Does this so-called Armed Neutrality no longer recognise our right to stop and search their ships for contraband or materials of war, denying the existence of a blockade unless there is a Royal Navy warship off *every* bloody little piss-pot of a port, and limiting their concept of contraband to weapons, shot, and powder, Napoleon gets everything that he needs *but* cannon, round-shot, and powder with which to rebuild his own navy, *and* equip an even *larger* army, to the detriment of every nation in Europe . . . including us. Do but consider all that is exported from the Baltic, Lewrie . . . "

Oh God, he's lecturin' his worst student! Lewrie thought with a silent groan; *Hark t'this, stupid! . . . have ye the wits t'do so!*

"Flax, and woven linen for sails," Twigg counted off with the fingers of his free hand, pontificating, as was his wont. "Pine timber for masts and spars, tar, pitch, rosin, and turpentine with which to maintain ships, not to mention fibres for ropes and cables."

Ye did *mention it, didn't ye,* Lewrie scoffed to himself.

"As well as the raw materials for gunpowder manufacture," Twigg said on, almost running out of fingers by then, "and the wool for uniforms, the leather from Russia's vast herds of cattle for boots, shoes, saddles, and harness, and soldiers' accoutrement pouches and belts . . . "

"Swedish iron ore, aye," Lewrie stuck in, hoping to trump him on *one* item, at least; or, hustle him along to his main point.

"Em?" Twigg said, looking puzzled, for a rare once, and peering at

Lewrie like he would at a talking cat. "Iron ore, yes. I must allow I had not thought of that, harumph."

Well, damme! Lewrie chortled in silence.

"All good reasons to squash this pestiferous League of the North as soon as possible," Twigg added, after another sip of his brandy.

"West to east, sir," Lewrie said, smiling, and crossing his legs with ankle upon knee. "The ice melts at Copenhagen first, and Karlskrona in Sweden, second. The Russian ports of Reval and Kronstadt thaw last, so . . . we should engage them in like order, as I'm sure that Admiral Nelson has already considered."

"You impress me, Lewrie," Twigg said in genuine wonder (or what passed for it, at least). "It would seem that you have not *squandered* your free time ashore in idle pleasures . . . not completely, hmm? You are, quite implausibly, still alive, despite running into the lovely Durschenko mort . . . her well-armed and tetchy father, more to the point."

"*She* seems t'be as well informed of my daily whereabouts as you seem t'be, Mister Twigg," Lewrie answered, shifting uneasily, changing one leg to cross for another. "She *knows* I'm married, since Cape Town, and went nose-high and disdainful of me for it, yet . . . " He shrugged.

"And the equally entrancing Widow Theoni Kavares Connor, she of the currant trade fortune," Twigg drawled with a simper. "Oh, yayss."

He took a deep sip of brandy, smiling, and, for such an imperious fellow, almost mellowing to a soft chuckle of amusement. "I'm told that she, rather uncannily, is present wherever you go, as well, Lewrie."

"As good an intelligence service as yours, I expect," Lewrie said, rather morosely, and took time to sip his drink.

"And, upon that head, I have news which shall astound you," Mr. Twigg mysteriously imparted in a harsh whisper, leaning closer. "Ah! Hudgins, my dear fellow . . . is our table ready?"

"It is, Mister Twigg," the dignified major-domo assured Twigg. "The one you requested, in the alcoves, for privacy. You gentlemen are ready to dine?"

"Yes, let us repair to our dinner," Twigg decided, rising with the sudden, leggy spring a very large and lean grasshopper might flex. "I would have requested you dine me in at the Madeira Club, Lewrie . . . though I doubt you would wish my discovery revealed on your home ground. Good as the kitchen is at the Madeira, as excellent as are its wine cellars, still . . . it has become a rather *dull* establishment."

A-bloody-men! Lewrie thought.

"Oh, good enough when first started," Twigg allowed, "when the squirearchy down to London were its principal lodgers—but Good God!—now it is all Trade and all these 'new-men,' those *self-made* fellows in God knows *what* enterprises . . . and rigourously humourless, to boot! Such a commercial and grasping yet suddenly *respectable* lot."

"Good for cleanin' up my father's odour in London Society, his partnering with Sir Malcolm Shockley, in it," Lewrie commented.

"And yours, for lodging there," Twigg could not help remarking.

Ouch, and ow, Lewrie could only complain in silence.

CHAPTER ELEVEN

$\mathscr{T}$wigg, like all know-it-alls who held information that one must know, or dearly wished to know, maddeningly kept his secrets through their repast; though Lewrie thought it a hellish-*good* repast, and well worth the wait. The sliding doors to their private alcove room swept open to reveal yet another splendid course; a chicken soup laced with tangy tarragon, followed by roast squabs with green beans in lieu of a springtime asparagus, though dressed with a cheesy Hollandaise sauce. A bottle of *pinot gris* came with the first two courses, and remained just long enough to accompany the mid-meal salad of hot-house brussel sprouts and lettuce with a drippy-bacon dressing. Then came the main *entrée*, the sliced prime rib of beef with peas and frittered potatoes, all sloshed down with a fresh bottle (or two) of claret, and thickly sliced slabs of bread, buttered and toasted with garlic. *White* bread, and the recent law bedamned.

Apple pie, a *sauterne* in counterpoint, then port, cheese, and sweet biscuits followed all that, and a silver pot of coffee was put upon the small sideboard to await their pleasure.

"Now, to the matter at hand," Mr. Twigg said at last, as those doors were swept shut at his gestured command, making Lewrie thank a Merciful God that the trivial chattering, entertaining as it had been, was over. "Your anonymous tormentor, Captain Lewrie . . . your wife's

tormentor, rather . . . my 'Irregulars' have smoaked out the identity of
the author of those scurrilous letters."

"Who is it?" Lewrie demanded, perking up.

"When you delivered to me two letters at your ward's marriage in
Portsmouth last year, or was it at my town home here in London? No
matter the exact location, recall I did remark that the author of them
was obviously a person of some means, possessed of a good, copper-
plate hand, and the purse with which to purchase very fine, heavy bond
paper."

Oh God, but he will *prose on!* Lewrie thought; *Preen, rather!*

"Unfortunately, such fine writing paper is available throughout London, and many of the larger cities and towns," Twigg said, frowning,
"so until the unknown author sent a letter to your wife, insinuating your
further adulterous doings, and was caught in the act, we had very little
to go on, other than the clues unknowingly included in each of them . . .
to wit, the proximity of certain suspected persons to you at the moment
when you indulged your proclivity for the fairer sex, ahem."

Coming, so is bloody Christmas! Lewrie silently fumed, wishing he
could lay hands on Twigg, take him by the lapels, and *shake* it out of
him . . . assuming Lewrie lived after doing it, it went without saying,
for, as he could attest, Zachariah Twigg, one of the Foreign Office's
master spies and cut-throats, was a *thoroughly* dangerous man.

"I could, however, reduce the number of suspects to those who could
have witnessed, or heard of, your doings," Twigg archly related, "and,
through the employment of my 'Irregulars,' discreetly surveill those in
England."

Twigg employed upwards of an hundred of his so-called Baker
Street Irregulars, for his town-house upon that thoroughfare was the
very centre of his spider's web, the lair from which he directed minor
spies to keep an eye on foreign embassies, even the friendly ones, and
foreign individuals who kept too lively a correspondence with people on
the Continent. Chamber-maids and street vendors, messenger lads,
cooks, sweeps, and beggars, as well as an host of "Sharps" from London's criminal element who could pick the right pocket, crack the right
window or door in the dead of night or the light of day; copyists who
could forge false information or duplicate hidden documents quickly, so
the house-breakers could put the originals back where they'd found
them with no one, any foreign spy, the wiser 'til some other of Twigg's
minions, recruited from the military (who could safeguard the innocent,

or corner the guilty) either leave them bleeding in some dark alley, or simply spirit them away as if they'd never been, never to be seen again.

"Sir Malcolm Shockley's wife, Lucy, who was once one of those Jamaican Beaumans, came to mind," Twigg simpered on, "for the first of these letters appeared soon after you ran into her in Venice in '96, whilst she was on her honeymoon tour of the Continent with Sir Malcolm . . . and sporting with that Commander William Fillebrowne, who took your former mistress on. Tsk-tsk," Twigg said with a twitch of his mouth. "A rather disreputable baggage, for all her beauty. As for Fillebrowne, well . . . he's the spiteful sort. He proved that by throwing his possession of Phoebe Aretino in your face so tauntingly, yet . . . he's been at sea since, and nowhere near any of your *recent* slips, so we could eliminate him."

"All this, and the King's business, too?" Lewrie sourly asked. "Two jobs for the price o' one, or something like that?"

"If you do *not* wish to know, Lewrie . . . ," Twigg warned.

"Say on, then," Lewrie surrendered with a long sigh.

"I was able to place a maid-servant in the Shockley residence, to keep an eye on her correspondence," Twigg proudly explained, "with an assistant coachman, as well, able to report quickly, *and,* the most likely to be given the task of carrying any such letters. Lady Lucy, I have determined, is *not* your tormentor."

"Well, that's a relief, I s'pose," Lewrie said, going for the coffee, cream, and sugar on the sideboard.

"Pour one for me, as well . . . *noir,* no sugar," Twigg ordered. "For a time, I considered that the letters might have been a *French* ploy, 'til I realised that no matter the wrath of Guillaume Choundas . . . the Americans exchanged him home in '99, did you know that? . . . there was no real advantage in it, not with you so junior and un-important in the greater scheme of things."

Demean me some more, *I ask you. Please!* Lewrie fumed.

"That Lombardian female spy they set upon you in Genoa, that Claudia Mastandrea, I therefore dismissed," Twigg said with a pleased sniff as he sipped his coffee, "as I did your former mistress, Phoebe Aretino, for, though she may have prospered greatly the last few years, and could buy expensive paper, she is not as literate, nor possessed of a fine handwriting, as our culprit."

"Leaving . . . !" Lewrie pressed.

"I even considered that your former ward, *la Vicomtesse* Sophie de Maubeuge, might have written them, if only to pique your wife and her interference in her early flirtations with that idiot neighbour of yours, Harry Embleton. To escape the dreariness of Anglesgreen for the delights of London . . . as she managed to do at last."

"Sophie? Never!" Lewrie was certain enough to declare.

"Indeed, the young lady in question is sweet-natured and kindly . . . intelligent and commonsensical," Twigg admitted.

"Leaving . . . ?" Lewrie posed again.

"Theoni Kavares Connor, Lewrie," Twigg said with a triumphant smile. "The mother of your bastard."

"What? Why, the *bitch*!" Lewrie exploded. "Not three days ago, she was . . . well, it could have been embarrassing."

"I know of it, and it was," Twigg archly declared, sniggering, quite enjoying watching Lewrie slowly twist in the wind. "Consider . . . the letters to your wife began in '96, just after you rescued her from those Adriatic pirates, then bedded her on your passage back to Gibraltar. Did you blab your *peccadillos*, did you boast your older conquests to her?"

"*Christ*, no!" Lewrie gawped. "Mean t'say, what gentlemen'd be *that* foolish?"

Twigg looked down the length of his long nose at Lewrie as if he suspected that Lewrie *was* that sort of gentleman.

Superior bastard! Lewrie fumed to himself.

"Right, she was grateful for her life, her son's life," Lewrie said to fill the embarrassing silence. "That, and pleasin' sport after Lights-Out, well . . . *and*, fleein' the Greek Isles for good to come to England a step ahead of the French? Not sure she'd keep the fortune in the currant trade her dead husband'd made, and fear of how his kin would receive her?"

"She fell in *love* with you, Lewrie," Twigg said, "for all those reasons, and your skill at 'rogering,' I'd imagine. Then, to discover that she would bear your child . . . and also discover what a rakehell you are, yet *still* wished to keep you . . . " He trailed off with a gleeful smirk, to take a sip of his coffee. "Amazing, how women find cads so intriguing, and do anything to delude themselves, and wish to *keep* their unworthy men. Had she any sense at all, given your history with the ladies . . . soon as she ferreted it out . . . that she didn't simply write you off as a bad penny. The boy, I expect . . . "

"As if she needed *me* t'support him," Lewrie scoffed. "She's as rich as the Walpoles . . . richer! And it's not as if she needed me for the Guinea Stamp. Her husband wasn't *that* long dead that she couldn't explain the boy's birthing as legitimate."

"So *many* bastards," Twigg pretended to be shocked. "One of them a Midshipman in the *American* Navy, of all things! Half yours, t'other half a Cherokee 'princess'? My word, sir! One *could* refer to your offspring round this world as the Lewriean Miscellany."

"How'd ye know o' that 'un?'" Lewrie asked, much humbled and pale.

"I have my ways, do I not?" Twigg smugly simpered.

"Mmm, d'ye mean there's *others* ye . . . ?"

"For me to know." Twigg almost laughed out loud for a rare once. "And for you to confront in future, Lewrie."

"Sure it was Theoni," Lewrie said; it was not a question, really. One thing he was sure of was that Twigg knew what he was talking about, when he finally got round to it.

"Watchers on the house, a street urchin for running messages in my employ always at hand to deliver her correspondence," Twigg said. "She don't write her own, ye know . . . no, she has a cultured personal maid-servant for that, who polishes things up, and owns the fine hand.

"Evidently," Twigg said, reaching inside his double-breasted tail-coat to a breast pocket, and withdrawing one of the poisonous *billets-doux*, "your lack of attentiveness to Mistress Theoni Connor of late, and your public sham of respectability for Society the last two years to satisfy Wilberforce and his crowd, prompted her to take desperate measures."

"Something about Eudoxia," Lewrie quickly determined. "She's the only young woman I've been within sniffin' distance, lately. Am I right? Damme, Theoni's little tantrum at Ranelagh Gardens t'other day . . . desperation?"

"Exactly, Lewrie," Twigg informed him. "For here is a fresh one addressed to your wife . . . one designed to even further infuriate your good . . . if put-upon . . . Caroline. The good-scribbling maid was caught red-handed with it, on her way to the posting house so the coach could deliver it to your house in Anglesgreen. We have her confession, are you interested."

"Theoni knows of this?" Lewrie asked. "Well, no wonder I've not run into her the last few days. Thought it was our spat, but . . . "

"Desperation, indeed, to see her schemes produce so little fruit over the years, and you off at sea, not exactly as diligent as earlier in answering her letters," Twigg elaborated. "We have a second, meant for Eudoxia Durschenko . . . the usual anonymous 'dear friend, you must know,' laying out what an unfaithful cully you are. To deflect her before the girl puts any *more* stock in you."

"Hah! Fat lot o' good that'd do!" Lewrie said with a wry laugh. "Eudoxia's known I'm married since Cape Town, as I said, and her papa *already* hates me worse than cold, boiled mutton! B'sides, did Theoni have it scribbled in proper English, I doubt either one of 'em could make heads or tails of it."

"Then why does she seem to run into you so *often*, Lewrie?" Mr. Twigg sarcastically posed to him. "And, why . . . when she does . . . does she evince such delight to do so, even with her *very* watchful father at her side . . . hmmm?"

"Well, er . . . em," Lewrie stammered, half intrigued by the sudden possibilities, and half appalled with the image of how dead he'd be should he run the risk. "Surely, she must see that it's daft. Not to be. Better she takes up with the Prince of Wales, *he's* int'rested."

"With 'Florizel'?" Twigg scoffed. "Now *there's* a slender reed. Poor fellow . . . all he wishes is to be liked, to be loved by one and all. Or, merely appreciated. Good a King as he is, George the Third has been saddled with a *sorry* set of offspring. Oh, there may be some gewgaws and presents from the Heir, but they'd come with social ruin."

"For actresses and circus performers, that might be good publicity," Lewrie cynically said, draining the last of his cool coffee and going to the sideboard for fresh.

"You should warn her off, no matter," Twigg told him, snapping his fingers and pointing to his own empty cup.

"Me? Why me?" Lewrie asked. *Talk to Eudoxia, or pour ye bloody coffee, either one!* he thought.

"For the good of the Crown, Lewrie," Twigg told him, impatient to have to explain things to Lewrie, and for more coffee. "I cannot, for doing so would make it an official matter. The people's love for the Royal Family is paramount to continuing the war effort, and another bloody scandal involving 'Prinnie,' as some are wont to call him, would harm that. Frankly, I serve on sufferance as a partially retired consultant, and to interfere in the Heir's doings would be the ruin of me."

"But since I'm already ruined, there's no loss?" Lewrie snapped.

"That is pretty much it, yayss," Twigg drawled, smiling cruelly.

"Mine arse on a band-box," Lewrie said with a resigned, defeated sigh. He poured Twigg his desired cup, too.

"Hash things out with Theoni . . . stop her business," Lewrie said as he sat back down, idly stirring sugar and cream into his own coffee. "Coach home and confront Caroline with the truth, too? God o' Mercy!"

"Well, it is not as if you have much of anything else better to do, Lewrie," Twigg purred, "what with how things stand with you at Admiralty, at present."

"Oh, thank you just *so* bloody much!" Lewrie barked.

"Do you *want* to be reconciled with your wife, Lewrie?" Mr. Twigg asked with a piercing, probing stare.

"Well, o' *course* I do!" Lewrie shot back.

Hold on, do I really? he had to wonder, though; *Aye, for our children, if nothing else. It's not as if I've any other women in my life . . . that I could dally with openly, anyway.* Nelson *can get away with his affair with Emma Hamilton, but . . .*

"Even if we don't," Lewrie told Twigg, "after all the tears that Theoni put her through . . . *I* put her through! . . . I owe Caroline a *semblance* of a marriage."

"She would never believe a word that crossed your lips," Twigg said, matter-of-factly for a change, with none of his usual top-lofty acid. "Leave that to me. After all, 'twas I who sicced you on Claudia Mastandrea in Genoa, for the good of the Crown. That still leaves your Corsican mistress, Phoebe Aretino, and Theoni Connor to deal with, but . . . one could be explained by long separation, and the other by wounds and laudanum, in the beginning. *And* the machinations of a scandalous and crafty, spiteful, and possessive home-wrecking bitch."

"You would do that?" Lewrie asked with his head cocked over; it just wasn't like Twigg to be charitable, or very much care about people who were (sometimes) useful to him.

"You've done me excellent service over the years, Lewrie," Twigg told him. "Perhaps I feel as if I owe it to you. I will coach to your home town with the evidence, including the maid's confessions, and the last letter . . . to Caroline, at any rate. No need to include the one written to Eudoxia directly, hmm?"

"Caroline will *still* think I'm trying to put the leg over her," Lewrie glumly confessed.

"Then amaze her, and . . . for a rare once . . . *don't*," Mr. Twigg shot back with a brief bark of amusement. "Her father would feed your chopped-up carcass to his lions, if you did, ye know."

"Of that I'm *quite* aware!" Lewrie replied in sour humour.

"Well, that should conclude our business," Twigg said, quickly finishing his coffee and tossing his napkin onto the table. "I must be off. Too damned many Danes, Swedes, and Russians in England, with the sudden urge to correspond with people in their home countries . . . especially those who reside, or trade, in our naval ports. Codes to be decyphered, whole letters to be lost, or . . . enhanced with false information," Twigg simpered.

"Throats to be slit," Lewrie posed, tongue-in-cheek as he rose.

"Well, only do we *must*," Twigg said with a vague wave of his hand and an evil little grin.

"I don't s'ppose you still have any influence with Admiralty, do you, Mister Twigg?" Lewrie said of a sudden. "Mean t'say, there's war in the offing, and . . . "

"Not all that much, no, Lewrie," Twigg had to admit, grudgingly, as they left the alcove dining room and crossed the main hall towards the coat cheque. "Not, at least, with the current administration over there, though there are rumours . . . "

"Hey?"

"Pitt is quite unhappy," Twigg told him as a manservant took their tickets and went to fetch their hats and greatcoats. "He managed the Act of Union with Ireland, and convinced the King to ennoble all those new Irish peers, yet . . . Pitt hinged his entire legislation on a promise of Catholic Emancipation, allowing Papists to serve in the Army, Navy, and hold public office . . . perhaps stand for seats in the Commons, as well. King George, however, as Defender of the Faith, as his full title tells us, was adamantly against that. Does Pitt step down . . . d'ye see my meaning?"

"A new Prime Minister, a new First Lord, aye!" Lewrie enthused for a brief moment, then deflated. "But probably someone who's heard of me, and despises me as much as Lord Spencer already does. Damn!"

"Nelson has already hoisted his flag in the *San Josef* over at Torbay, in Plymouth, Lewrie," Twigg further informed him as the servant returned with his hat, greatcoat, and long walking-stick, and another club servant came to help him dress. "You've served under him I believe. Perhaps *he* could intercede for you. And you did Vice-Admiral Sir Hyde Parker good service, and fattened his bank accounts, with your seizure of all that lovely Spanish silver a few years ago. You could write *him* and ask for employment."

"Sir Hyde? What's he to do with this?" Lewrie asked, puzzled.

"Why, Sir Hyde Parker is to command the whole Baltic expedition, Lewrie!" Twigg told him. "Don't you read the papers? Nelson is to be his second-in-command. Do all the preparatory work for him, I'd think, since Sir Hyde is, for the moment, deeply involved with his wedding."

"God Almighty, Parker?" Lewrie was forced to gawp.

"To wed, again?" Twigg snickered, completely missing the point of Lewrie's sudden discomforture. "And why not? Though his bride-to-be is the daughter of Admiral Sir Richard Onslow . . . Frances, I believe her name to be . . . and is barely eighteen."

"Christ, Mister Twigg . . . Sir Hyde's sixty, if he's a day!"

"Lucky devil," Twigg simpered as he drew on his gloves. "Sir Richard Onslow, to get a son-in-law so rich in prize-money. The girl to land such a secure future, and Sir Hyde the, ah . . . fresh dew of her youth."

"Mister Twigg," Lewrie muttered, stepping closer to impart his knowledge of that worthy, "surely they must *know* that Sir Hyde's not possessed of an *urgent* bone in his body! 'Twas his frigates that did his work for him, and specially commissioned lesser tenders. The Frogs and the Dons didn't have anything in the West Indies with which to challenge us, so Sir Hyde spent all his time sittin' on his . . . officiatin' from his *shore* office, and his flagship anchored 'til the Apocalypse. He *might've* cruised *Barfleur* over to Saint Domingue to talk with some of his junior officers now and again, but he hasn't sniffed gunpowder since the American Revolution!"

"Indeed," Twigg asked down his long nose, with a worried look on his skeletonously lean face. "Now that is rather discomfiting news to me, when speed *is* of the essence, anent the melting of the ice over yonder in the Baltic naval ports. Ah, but he *does* have Nelson, don't he, Lewrie? And with Nelson involved . . . a most impatient and urgent fellow, he . . . we cannot go very wrong. Well, I am off, Lewrie. I do hope my informations have lightened your burden somewhat."

"You have my eternal gratitude, sir, for all you've done," he had to respond, with a hand upon his breast, and a sketch of a bow.

"I'll hold you to that, Lewrie," Twigg said with an ominous look as he clapped his rather unfashionable old hat on his head. "One never knows when your, ah . . . inestimable talent for mayhem may prove useful again."

That promise-in-parting turned the excellent meal in Lewrie's innards to cold lead, for he already knew what neck-or-nothing, harum-scarum use Twigg could put a fellow to!

And, there was yet another cause for his dyspepsia . . . now he knew that it had been Theoni writing those letters all these years . . . what was he to *do* about her?

And how best to go about crushing the spiteful bitch!

CHAPTER TWELVE

*A*nother hellish-cold morning in London, though the sun was out, for a rare once, and the sky was fresh-washed and clear blue. Lewrie's breath steamed as he briskly strolled to the Admiral Boscawen Coffee House, deftly dodging the throngs of other pedestrians, the trotting teams of carriages, goods waggons, and carts, and the impudently rude London drivers and carters, who filled the morning with shouts of "By yer leave!" and "'Ave a care, there!" and "Make a way, make a way, ye bloody . . . !" with the choicer curses bitten off.

Admittedly, it *was* rather early for Lewrie to be astir, given his bred-in-the-bone penchant for laziness; it was barely a tick after 8 A.M., and even the usually unperturbable servants at the Madeira Club had been forced to goggle their eyes to see him up and dressed so early, and bound out the doors "close-hauled" at a rate of knots.

Once seated with a cup of coffee before him (closer to the fire than before) he slathered up a finger-thick slice of toast, spread the jam heavy, and chewed as he perused *The Morning Post,* one of London's saucier papers, and the one most filled with gossip and anonymous *innuendo.*

> Sir Hyde Parker's appointment to a command in the North Sea
> has converted his honeymoon into a sort of ague; a complaint
> always attended with a sudden transition from a *hot* to a *cold* fit.

A ragged earlier edition told him, followed by the newest of that morning, the thirty-first of January, to wit:

> Should the gallant Admiral who late entered the Temple of Hymen be sent to sea again, he will leave his sheet anchor behind him.

Which smirking line made Lewrie wonder if the writers at *The Morning Post* were referring to Nelson, as well; hadn't that worthy left Emma Hamilton behind to hoist his flag in the *San Josef*?

Wonder who writes *this drivel?* Lewrie pondered; *And how may I get in touch with one of 'em, an' put a flea in his ear?*

He supposed that *somebody*, perhaps a great *number* of somebodys, fed juicy and lurid tidbits of scandal and gossip to the paper, for *The Post*, and several other of the dailies, seemed to be marvellously well informed, with many of their racier items printed up the morning after the event, not days or weeks later, so they *must* have an host of tattlers and informers.

Informers, hmm . . . Lewrie thought. Zachariah Twigg possessed an army of informers, though he dreaded going to *that* well too often; he was already too "beholden" to that top-lofty old bastard. Lewrie also imagined that a clumsy call upon the offices of *The Post* would result in gales of laughter, *and* an item mocking his naïveté printed the very next day. Yet there must be *some* way to expose Theoni's scandalous letters.

"Where *does The Post* get all this drivel?" Lewrie said as the waiter poured him a fresh cup of coffee and took his order for fried eggs, a pork chop, and grated potatoes.

"There's thousands o' waggin' tongues, sir," the waiter replied with a snicker, "an' Grub Street's full o' scribblers livin' hand t' mouth, in need o' dirt. Don't work for the papers, direct, d'ye see. Might not *eat*, do they not git a morsel t'write up an' flog t' which ever paper'll take it. Most of 'em make their livin's off the tracts an' such. Hard-fry yer eggs, sir, or do ye prefer 'em softer?"

Grub Street, hmm . . . Lewrie mused as he stirred sugar and some rather dubious-looking "fresh cream" into his coffee; *didn't they do all those bloody tracts 'bout me for Wilberforce and his crowd? All those anti-slavery things?*

While he was no longer the subject of almost-daily printings, the campaign against slavery in the public mind, and the halls of Parliament, continued, with earnest hawkers on every street corner. All it might take would be for him to accept one of the damned things, see who had run it up, and call upon the printer . . . to offer his gratitude for all his efforts on his, and the Abolitionists', behalf, ha ha! If one of the scribblers could be named, he could approach *him*. A bit of hemming and hawing as to how one might expose a woman who had caused a British hero's wife so much pain . . . carefully leaving out the fact of said woman bearing said hero's illegitimate child, of course! . . . with an *authentic* anger, which he figured he could manage to convey.

Hmm, with a hint of a public scandal to come? Lewrie wondered; something right out in the open, like his scrambling from her sight at Ranelagh Gardens, he imagined with a wince of chagrin, to make it even juicier a story.

He took a sip of coffee and frowned as he considered how this plan might go awry. *Am I devious enough t'pull this off?* he thought; *Never have been,* before! Dim *bastard, most people think me. Yet . . . !*

CHAPTER THIRTEEN

*T*hink nothing of it, Captain Lewrie," Mr. Leaver, the rotund, ink-smudged proprietor of the printing business told him with a laugh. "You did us proud, this past year, with all the tracts and chapbooks ordered. Though, 'tis rare for the subject of our firm to come calling with *appreciation*, ha ha! More like, with an injunction, d'ye see."

"Reverend Wilberforce and his compatriots did us all proud, as I see it, Mister Leaver," Lewrie replied, "with all the financial support. And the well-written articles placed in the newspapers."

"Well, the texts were not our doing," Leaver told him as he poured them both companionable cups of warming tea. In the back half of the firm, past a high railing, printing presses creaked and clacked, like to drown out normal conversation, and everyone but Mr. Leaver seemed to be deeply stained and splattered black; the proprietor was nigh-immaculate by comparison.

"The same person who provided the, uhm . . . copy to you wrote the newspaper items, as well, I s'pose?" Lewrie idly wondered aloud; *trying* for idle, anyway. "I did notice a certain . . . similarity in tone."

God help me, does he ask for specifics, Lewrie thought, wishing he could cross fingers for luck against that eventuality.

"Not exactly sure, Captain Lewrie," Mr. Leaver allowed, ruminating with a faint frown. "I usually never met the writers. The text was de-livered by someone with the Abolitionist Society, and where they got it was anyone's guess. Now, there *was* Missuz Denby, who writes for the papers, who also came in with anti-slavery articles about you. She'll write for *anybody*. Sometimes the most scandalous flummery, ah-hmm."

"Gossip and such, like in *The Morning Post*?" Lewrie asked, with ris-ing hope, and striving to not *look* hopeful.

"Hmpfh!" was Mr. Leaver's opinion of such. "Missuz Denby *styles* herself the doyenne of the 'Quality's' doings . . . though she writes un-der the pseudonym of 'Tattler.' Poor thing. 'Twas her late husband, God rest him, was a printer like me, and a tract writer, and not a bad hand when it came to turning a phrase, I'll give him that, but . . . once he'd passed on, Missuz Denby lost the business, and has had to live by her wits, since. *Hardly* a business for a woman, hey? At least she gained enough from the sale of the presses and such to keep body and soul to-gether. Would have gone under in a year, had she not. Women simply do *not* have the proper head for business."

"I wonder how she manages to gather her information. I've seen her articles under 'Tattler,' and she seems remarkably well informed," Lewrie said, even if he'd never clapped "top-lights" on that by-line be-fore in his life.

"Attends *everything*," Mr. Leaver said with a shake of his head. "Brags that she's on cater-cousin terms with half the maids and footmen in London, and that rich and titled ladies slip her gossip all the time."

"Why, if she attends everything, I must have run across her," Lewrie pretended to gape in astonishment.

"Can't miss her, with all that red hair. Why, speak of the Devil, if that's not her heading into Chester's shop, just cross the street this very minute," Leaver declared.

Lewrie turned to espy a very chick-a-biddy dumpling of a woman, quite short, but done up in the latest fashionable colours of lavender and puce, and sporting one of those pillow-like "Pizarro" bonnets atop a towering old-fashioned mountain of vividly red hair.

"Good Christ!" Lewrie muttered.

"See what I mean?" Mr. Leaver said, chuckling.

"Well, thanks again for all your good services, sir, and I will take my leave," Lewrie announced, slurping up the last of his tea and doffing his hat on his way out the door with undisguised haste. He had a gossip-monger to deal with, and time was of the essence.

"Your pardons, Ma'am, but might you be Mistress Denby?" Lewrie en-quired with his hat to his breast, and bestowing upon her a gallant bow as he did so; to which the startled-looking woman replied with a quick, dropped curtsy. "The one who writes under the name of . . . ?"

"Well, damme!" Mrs. Denby yelped. "*You're* 'Black Alan' *Lewrie*, to the *life*! Oh, *sir!*" she gushed as she dipped him an even deeper, and longer-held, curtsy . . . even if she had to brace herself with her furled parasol. She rose at last, looking as if she had tears in her eyes behind the hexagonal spectacles perched on the end of her nose. "*Noble* Captain Lewrie! *Courageous* Captain Lewrie! Oh, but it is my *greatest* honour to meet you at *last*! I could but catch the *briefest* glimpse of you, 'til your re-cent *trial*, o' course. I *tried* my *best* to get close *enough* to you once 'twas *over*, to *receive* but a mere press of your *hand*, in passing. Damme! *Might* you grant me the favour of an *interview*? A round dozen papers would *bid* for it, *damme* do they not!"

"I was led to understand you wrote many of the Abolitionist chap-books and tracts, regarding my case . . . " Lewrie began to say.

"I felt it the *greatest* privilege of my *life*, sir!" Mrs. Denby loudly de-clared. "I *still* do . . . write their tracts decrying slavery, d'ye see my *meaning*, Captain Lewrie," she said with a nervous laugh, all but fan-ning herself.

"You did me a magnificent service, Mistress Denby, for which I am eternally grateful," Lewrie told her, clapping his hat back on his head at last. "I just spoke with Mister Leaver, over yonder, to give him my thanks, and enquired of him who wrote such moving things about me, He told me, and then, like a Jack-in-the-Box, up you pop, ha ha!"

"Fortuitous, *indeed*, Captain Lewrie," Mrs. Denby gladly replied. "And I am *quite* honoured . . . ever the *more* so! . . . that you took the *time* to thank me *personally!* Oh, *might* you agree to let me interview you!" she gushed. Had I *known* your *lodging* place, I'd have written a note, long *before*. . . . Even though certain *salacious* doings in *Society* have had me *quite* occupied, of late, I most *certainly could* make time to probe your innermost thoughts!" She was all but bouncing up and down on her toes.

Christ, but she can wear ya out, quick! Lewrie thought, wondering if turning his innermost thoughts loose on London was all that good an idea. *Wonder if* she *was Mister Denby's cause o' death! Enthusiasm!*

"I also was led to understand that you write for the papers as the 'Tattler,'" Lewrie said. "Are those the Society doings of which ye speak, Ma'am?"

"They are, *indeed*, Captain Lewrie!" Mrs. Denby admitted with a hearty cackle. "As to that . . . not only did I *write* in support of *Abolition*, and in firm support of *you*, I *spoke* . . . among all my contacts in the *fashionable* set, d'ye see, sir . . . *lauding* you to the *skies*, as enthusiastically as I *decried* the *abhorrent* institution of *slavery!*"

"You, ehm . . . have many contacts, I take it, Ma'am?"

"Oh, Captain *Lewrie!*" Mrs. Denby coyly confided (though a bit loud) and looking as if she would link arms with him. "Even servants at *St. James's, Marlbourough* House, *any* palace or estate you may *name*, confide in me . . . *as* do their masters and *mistresses*, when they wish to dish a *tasty* little rumour about their *rivals*, ha ha! Why, there isn't a drum, rout, exhibition, or public subscription ball that I do *not* attend, and . . . come *away* with fresh *meat* for *grilling!*" Mrs. Denby confided, snickering with wicked glee.

"Then I might have something right up your alley, Ma'am," he told her.

"*Oh*, Captain *Lewrie*! Call me Georgina, *do!*" she insisted with an even broader, hungrier grin. This time she did link arms with him. "Is it delicious? Is it *scandalous*? Filled with intrigues, romance, or *betrayal*? You have my *complete* curiosity, sir! And . . . ," she said with a sly look, "there is a *lovely* little coffee-house, *quite* near to hand, and there, in all *discreet* confidence, you *must* reveal it *all* to me!"

"Well, damme!" Georgina Denby said at last, thumping her plump little self back against the high wood divider of their corner booth. "What a *trollop*! What a . . . *foreign* baggage the wench is!" She took time to wipe her hands on a table napkin, for in her large bag she had stowed a steel-nib pen and a screw-top jar of ink. Steel-nibs weren't all that cheap, as Lewrie already knew, so he had to assume that hints and innuendos, and "dirt," paid *extremely* well. All through her interrogation (for that was what it had felt like once he'd broached the subject) she had been scribbling away in a large accounting ledger, filling several pages quickly, both front and back, with the details of Lewrie's "connexions" to Theoni Kavares Connor, and her damnably anonymous "Dear Friend" letters.

"Though you *do* admit that you *might* very *possibly* be the father of her *bastard*," Mrs. Denby added, in a pensive taking for the first time in the better part of an hour. "She has *yet* to take you to *court* with a '*belly* plea,' *so* . . . "

I wager she'd sing-song a soft whisper, Lewrie told himself.

"So?" he prompted, busying himself with pouring them both more tea.

"Damme, it's so *obvious*, Captain Lewrie!" Mrs. Denby chirped, back to her enthusiastic self. "She *wished* the child. You *saved* her *and* her firstborn, and she became *besotted* by you! I can *easily* see *why* . . . ," Mrs. Denby added with a flirtatious look. "An *heroic*, well-set-up man of all his *parts*, such as yourself? Still and all . . . it's *hardly* the way, *is* it, Captain Lewrie? Such *affairs* . . . with *children* born on the *wrong* side of the *blanket*. . . . A touch more cream, do you please, ah! . . . Why, the mort was angling to *land* you for her *own*, and *nothing*, and no *one*, was to get in the *way* of it!

"*Hardly* the *proper* way to solve such problems in *English* Society, is it?" she said with a disapproving sniff, and a sip of her tea. "The hussy *is* Greek . . . most-like *provincial*, and ignorant of *civilised* ways no matter *how* wealthy her *family* was in the Greek isles, *and* the trade in currants. *England*, and *London* Society, does not look with particular *favour* on those who do not observe the *niceties* . . . the foreigners!"

That Lewrie also well knew; any day of the week, in any street in the city, there were odd-looking foreign types being showered with rotten vegetables or fruit, clods of mud, or dung, and hooted and cat-called to their lodgings in a hurry by the infamous idle Mob. Before his trial his accuser, Hugh Beauman, had been hounded from one hotel to another, him and his ultra-fashionable wife, both, for looking too grand and pretentious! The only reason that Eudoxia's father, Arslan Artimovich Durschenko, wasn't pelted and insulted in his fur *shapka* hat, boots, sash, and odd Roosian shirt was that he looked too *dangerous* to mess with!

And in his wastrel youth (between schools after being sent down) Lewrie had hooted, jeered, and flung dung with the best of the Bucks-of-the-First-Head he'd run with. That was why ambassadors and exotic, pagan emissaries, from Ottoman Turkey, say, were escorted upon official business by royal Horse Guard cavalry!

"Well, for a foreigner, she's hellish-handsome," Lewrie dared mention. Auburn hair, almond-shaped eyes, with a slim waist despite bearing two children (or *damned* good corsets!) and the most promising set of poonts . . . "Beauty seems to forgive a lot in Society."

"*Medusa* . . . *Adam's* fling with Lilith in the Garden of *Eden* . . . Dido . . . ," Mrs. Denby replied, one hand waving in the air to conjure up infamous lovelies from the classics and the Bible, "*all* of *them* were fetching in the *extreme* . . . yet *deadly* and *un*-forgivable, like *Salome*, who lured King *Herod* to slay John the *Baptist*! No, Captain Lewrie . . . *proper* Society is *quite* brusque with those who *violate* the *rules* . . . unwritten, or *no*. Beautiful, or *not*!

"*I* see utter *ruin* ahead for *Mistress* Theoni Connor," Mrs. Denby prophesied, with a sly grin of anticipation to be involved in it. "She has *not* amassed a circle of supporters in London *Society*, even *with* all her *wealth* for *entrée*" she said with another dismissive sniff. "Hence, no *allies*. I *cannot* recall anyone of *importance* remarking upon any attempt by her to *insinuate* herself with them. I *assure* you, sir, the *amusement* such an attempt would have *provoked* among the 'Quality' with whom *I* associate would have reached me ears *already*, hmph! Why, the bitch will be *completely* destroyed, ha ha!"

Lewrie dared let a smile gather at that news.

"You've *attempted* to *'front* her, I wonder, Captain Lewrie?" she asked, bird-quick, peering at him.

"We had a run-in in Ranelagh Gardens a week back," he replied. "Not about this matter, no, for I still had no idea the letter-writer was her. She was pouty that I hadn't called on her since the trial. A Mister . . . well, someone very good at getting to the bottom of matters like this *did* nab her maid . . . the one with a good, copper-plate hand and an English education . . . who polished 'em up for her. After that, she's dropped out of sight . . . *my* sight, thank God."

"*Oh*, Captain *Lewrie*, you *must*!" Mrs. Denby enthusiastically told him; insisted on it, in truth. "A *public* scene without her very *doors*! Accusations *shouted* to the *roof-tops* does she refuse you *entrance* . . . in dread, *or* shame, no matter."

"Most-*like*, she'd let me *in*, to *explain*, or . . . ," Lewrie mused.

Damme, now she's got me sing-songin'! he silently groused.

"Well, 'twould be *best* were she not *in*, and you may *feign* that she *denied* you *entrance*," Mrs. Denby slyly suggested. "A note tucked into the *door* jamb, saying that you *must* speak with her, *and* most-like her *curiosity*, and the *chance* that you might have come round to *her* at last, will be piqued . . . resulting in another *very* public *denunciation* . . . which *I* and as many of the *better* sort shall *witness* . . . will be common gossip the morning *after* . . . along with my article in *The Post* and such *other* papers as I may *induce*, will take the *trick*, ha ha!"

"A public scene . . . in Montagu Mews," Lewrie pretended to ponder, as if loath to do anything *quite* so sordid.

"*Loud* enough to startle *both* the pigeons and the *horses*, sir," she said with a giggle. "To the roof-tops . . . to the *roof-tops*! I say. Then, you *must* send me a note by *runner*, telling me *where*, and *when*, the *actual* confrontation will *occur*. Why, I warrant within the *week*, the baggage will *remove* her vile self from London, *entire!*"

"Hmm . . . her late husband's kin live in Dublin," Lewrie said.

"Dublin!" Mrs. Denby barked with a shiver. "For the *shortest* moment, one could *almost* pity her *that!*"

A Greek, a foreigner, with a bastard son by another man in tow along with the late Michael Connor's real son, their only grand-son . . . *and* control over his shares of the family business to irk them even further . . . ! No, Lewrie couldn't quite imagine her reception in Dublin would be all that grand. Mind, he did have a *slight* desire to *witness* it!

"I'll see to . . . setting the scene, this very day, Ma'am," he told her.

"*Georgina*" Mrs. Denby chirpily insisted. "And *I* must be off, as *well*. You *will*, uhm . . . ?" she added, pointing to the slip of paper which bore the reckoning for their pot of tea and her sticky buns.

"But of course . . . Georgina," Lewrie said with smile, reaching for his wash-leather coin purse. He rose, handed her to her feet from the pew-like seat of the booth, and bowed her departure for the door.

More notoriety, he mused as he sorted out coins for the waiter; *That won't win me any less disapproval with Admiralty,* he reckoned to himself. *If I can't hope t'get another ship, well . . . I hope I enjoy this!*

CHAPTER FOURTEEN

*H*e was best known about London as Captain "Black Alan" Lewrie, Royal Navy, so it was not a night for what his brother-in-law, Burgess Chiswick, called civilian dress in Hindoo; *mufti*. No, it was his full-dress uniform with all the gilt lace and twin epaulets, his hundred-guinea East India Company sword, and both the Cape St. Vincent and Camperdown medals, and Covent Garden was the site of the confrontation-to-be.

Lewrie had already called upon Theoni's house in Montagu Mews, after determining that she and her maid were away, shopping in the Strand, and had raised quite a ruckus . . . after *seeming* to have knocked at the door and being denied entrance (during which he had slipped a card into the jamb), then descending the steps to the street to begin his rant . . . "to the roof-tops," as Mrs. Denby insisted.

"Hide from me, will you, Madam?" he had cried for a start, and feeling like the greatest fool; at the several good public schools of his youth, Lewrie had taken part in more than a few stage shows, to the detriment of his studies, and had usually been jeered for clumsy readings and stiff performances. "You wrote those scurrilous, lying notes to torment my wife, and I'll not *have* it! Admit me, or come out, you jade! You have poisoned my marriage with your lies and hurt my wife sore with your filth!"

Hold on, he'd thought; *Should it 've been 'sweet marriage,' or . . . ? Should've written this down first. Gad, this is lame!*

"How *dare* you! I'll have you in *court* for it!" he'd gone on, warming to his topic, as passersby, residents in the Mews, and street vendors had gathered. "Just 'cause I saved you and your son from those Serbian pirates in the Adriatic, . . . oh, your, letters to me were flatterin', but just 'cause I wrote you *back* didn't mean I *favoured* you . . . or felt *anything* for you! You're *deluded*! Jealous and spiteful! Get a man of your own, and leave me and my wife *be*!"

"Here, now, what's all this?" a dyspeptic neighbour asked him, coming out upon his own front steps from next door. "Hush up, you!"

"Not 'til Mistress Connor offers apologies!" Lewrie shot back.

"What, the Greek baggage?" the neighbour said with a sniff.

" 'E's arter some furrin mort, 'e is," a milk-seller wench told a girl with a trey of posies and nosegays.

"She's tormented my wife with lying letters for years," Lewrie accused to the neighbour, whose wife had now joined him. "*Daft* stuff, imaginin' she's in love with me, 'stead of bein' merely grateful, sir! Spun moonshine 'bout us together, sendin' anonymous letters to drive my wife and me apart, . . . as if I'd *ever* leave my Caroline for the likes of *her*! I found out just yesterday who's been sendin' 'em, and I mean t 'get satisfaction!"

"Well, get it somewhere else, damn ye," the neighbour grumbled. "Sue the uppity foreign bitch, and leave off botherin' this neighbourhood, or I'll call the 'Charlies' on ye. Begone, sir!"

"Mus' be a *mad* woman, lives 'ere," the teenaged flower vendor told a pieman and a passing couple of strollers. "Thinks she's got 'is feller fer 'er 'usband."

"An' 'im already married, tchah!" the milk-seller said with a spit on the cobbles. "Ready fer Bedlam, she is."

"Furriners," the pieman commented. "Too damned many of 'em in England, ye akses me. Oughter be run out o' 'ere."

"You'll hear from my attorney!" Lewrie shouted one last time, shaking a fist at the windows of Theoni's parlour before departing.

Covent Garden Theatre, the biggest and grandest of all the play-houses in the district, was, thankfully, no longer staging *Pizarro* and had fallen back on a popular Sheridan play, a recurring staple, though the styles and colours of the fashionable ladies showed that the fads inspired by that play would be around at least 'til midsummer. Lewrie milled round the ornate lobby with a glass of a rather thin Rhenish in one hand, barely tasting it in tiny sips that only moistened his lips as he scanned the arrivals for his prey. And, feeling as nervous as a pick-pocket in a room full of justices, wondering if Theoni would actually dare show her face in Publick, after Twigg had exposed her maid, and he had staged his petty dramatics before her doors.

Nervous as he felt, though, it was hard to keep his mind on the matter, for there were rather a *lot* of most-attractive women entering the theatre that night, more than a few fetching courtesans and ladies of the *demi-monde* strolling and trolling themselves before the gentlemen without partners, and even the girls who vended oranges and such . . . whose charms were as delightful as the high-priced courtesans, and whose morals were even lower than most *actresses* . . . seemed even more alluring than usual.

Lewrie bought himself a fresh glass of Rhenish, finding that he had drained the first without even noticing, and took an inventory of how long it had been since he had "put the leg over" *anything*.

Christ, has it been two bloody years? he gawped in wonder after he recalled his last amorous encounter; *'Tis a wonder I don't drool! Or squirt semen out my ears, from the pressure.*

His free hand involuntarily went to a left-hand pocket of his waistcoat. *Aha . . . two cundums stowed away. Just in case . . . hmm. 'Long as I go armoured, would a whore be all that bad?* he speculated.

Theoni would most-definitely be right-out, within the hour, he grimly determined, and even nuzzling Eudoxia's perfumed neck would be a death sentence. Caroline? The only reason his wife would ever let him under the covers with her again would be a ruse to whip out a very sharp knife and have his "wedding tackle" off, most-like! Even if she believed but half of what Mr. Twigg promised to tell her, there were a tad too many other women he could *not* explain away.

Must get a recent guidebook t 'London quim, he told himself, and began to regard the strolling women with sharper eyes.

"*Dear* Captain *Lewrie*!" a gay voice chirped in giddy sing-song. It was Mrs. Georgina Denby, damn her eyes, tricked out in a stylish satin gown of bright, shimmering blue, with rather more flesh exposed than Lewrie ever wished to see, earrings, necklace, and bracelet of a pale topaz set (if real, he speculated, gossip paid *hellish*-well!) and a pair of glasses perched on the tip of her nose. A reticule bag of pale blue satin hung from one elbow, and her hands held a small notebook and a pencil. "How *delightful* to *see* you, again, sir!"

"Ah, um . . . Mistress Denby . . . Georgina," Lewrie flummoxed and applied her first name at her coy prompting, The crowd in the lobby limited his movements, but he sketched her a bow. "You keep well?"

"*Excellently* well, Captain Lewrie!" she replied, dipping him a stumpy curtsy, then came quite close to mutter, "Has the bitch shown her face yet? Is this truly the appointed time and place?"

"S'posed t 'be, but . . . ," Lewrie said with a shrug.

"Frightened off, most likely," Mrs. Denby whispered, leering and rolling her eyes. "I must circulate. Only here as a witness, not a fellow *conspirator*, la la!"

"I trust you will enjoy the play tonight, Ma'am," Lewrie said in a more-normal voice, with another brief bow.

"Ah, *yes*, Captain Lewrie, I am *certain* I *shall*," Mrs. Denby replied in her normal gushing tones. "*Anything* by *Sheridan* always proves *immensely* droll and amusing. Ta ta!" With that, she tottered away to smile and nod among the fashionable, and "dirt-worthy."

And there she was! The doorman bowed Theoni Connor inside; a very nervous-looking Theoni, no matter the exquisite care she'd taken with her appearance. Her placid smile simply would not hold for more than a few fleeting seconds, and her eyes had the look of a harried deer as she paused just inside the lobby and peered about to spot him, carefully tossing back the hood of her cape from an artful, bejewelled "do," and unfastening it from her throat.

If I didn't despise her so much, I'd be tryin' t'bed her, Lewrie told himself, for Theoni had come to impress, with a costly set of diamonds on fingers, wrist, and throat, that impressively bouncy bosom of hers a tad more exposed than most women present, and wearing a new gown of champagne and ivory figured satin, with a white lace stole over her shoulders.

She saw him, *winced* for the briefest moment, then plastered a hopeful smile on her phyz and threaded her way through the crowd in his direction. Lewrie stood stock-still and scowled, and, as she neared, her smile went even sketchier.

"Alan, I . . . ," she said at last, with a nervous toss of her head.

"Madam," Lewrie intoned, still scowling. "I *know* what you did."

"Alan, if you would—"

"How *dare* you!" he barked, nigh to his quarterdeck voice. "Have you no shame?"

She squirmed as if looking for a hidey-hole, wringing her hands.

"There is *no* excuse for tormenting my wife with your anonymous letters, with your made-up lies, Madam," Lewrie harshly told her. "No excuse for besmirchin' me, and tryin' t'ruin my marriage with filth as you have. You'll write no more poison, hear me?"

This was as amusing as *any* Sheridan play, much like an *entr'acte* 'tween scenes on the stage inside, and the crowd of theatregoers in the lobby just ate it up, hushing breathlessly, then buzzing and whispering among themselves, all eyes on them.

"Damn you!" Theoni shot back, her artfully made face pale, and sounding breathless, like to swoon. "What of our son? What of all of our letters?"

"As for the letters, Madam," Lewrie replied, and one may trust that he'd thrashed that point out in his head beforehand, "after your rescue from pirates in the Adriatic, by my hand, you wrote me, and I wrote back, to be civil. As for your son, well . . . *you* have a son by *someone*, most-like your dead husband, is one *charitable*, for you were not *that* long a widow when I saved your life.

"Leave my wife alone, Madam," he quickly added, raising a hand to cut off her protest, as spots of colour dappled her cheeks. "We'll have no more of your imaginings. Get yourself a man of your own, and do not torment us further. I do not *know* you, Madam!" Lewrie said in a stern voice, turning away and giving her the "cut direct."

"Why, you . . . ! Lying . . . !" Theoni spat, then made the worst of all errors one could make in England . . . in her shock and outrage, she lapsed into what Lewrie took for modern Greek, hurling curses at him, and, falling back on her upbringing on Zante in the Ionian Islands, she added several insulting hand gestures, of the maledictory variety, too.

A couple of ushers and a manager forced their way to Lewrie, as another pair of ushers approached Theoni, as well. "Hear now, sir, we will have none of this. I'm afraid we'll have to ask you to leave the theatre, sir."

"My pardons to you, sir," Lewrie said in answer to that threat, in the mildest of takings, "but the scandalous way that . . . woman has abused my wife over the years . . . the identity of the anonymous writer I *just* discovered . . . rowed me beyond all temperance. I *hardly* expected the . . . her, to show her face in polite society. My pardons, again, for any disturbance, and of course I shall leave, for the sake of your other attendees."

"Well, that'd be good, sir," the manager allowed.

"Though I hope, sometime in future, to be allowed *back*?" Lewrie asked with a hopeful grin. "With *her* barred for life, I promise I'll be as quiet as a dormouse."

"We'll see, sir, and thankee for your consideration," the manager said with a relieved look, looking over towards the doors. Theoni wasn't taking it *quite* so well, was stamping a foot imperiously, and spitting-mad, still lapsing into Greek at times as she fumed.

"Foreigners," someone said with a sniff of disgust near Lewrie. "Simply *won't* behave proper, hey?" A buzz of agreement followed.

"*Courtesan*, most-like, my dear," a gentleman told his partner.

"Captain Alan Lewrie . . . that trial, don't ye know . . . got off, and good for him. . . . Imagine her bloody *gall*, m'dear, impugnin' a hero such as he . . . writin' his wife filthy letters, he said . . . alarmin' her for years, the bitch," was the general tone of the theatregoers. As Lewrie gathered up his boat-cloak, hat, and sword, and as he watched Theoni put up a brief struggle against ejection, the grin he wore upon his face could not help from slipping from muse-ful to gleeful.

Once sure that Theoni Kavares Connor had coached away in high dudgeon, and that the coast was clear, Lewrie took a stroll round the theatre district, popping into a cleaner-than-average tavern where a group of coaches awaited, and ordered himself a pint of porter in celebration. From a street stall, he had purchased a *Guide to Covent Garden Women*, and idly flipped through the pages. Surprisingly, his half-sister, Belinda, was *still* listed, though getting rather long in tooth by then, but the lavish description of her charms, and what she specialised *in*, was even lengthier, her "socket-fee" risen even higher.

Yet he had not come out with a full purse, and only two of his cundums, and once "in the saddle," two would not be enough. He knew he was too hungry to be sated by a mere two romps, and the last thing he needed, and what he had amazingly avoided during his long career as a rakehell, was the French Pox. What he imagined he could afford that night by way of Cyprian charms would be riskier than he wished, in that regard. There was also the very real risk of being lured into a jade's rooms, accosted by her "fancy man" and his accomplices, and being found days later, a naked corpse in the mud-flats of the Thames!

Yet . . . ! With the idea firmly embedded in his mind, Lewrie turned the pages to Brothels. London's many church bells began to chime the hour; it was a quarter past eight P.M., or so his pocket-watch said after he took a quick peek at it. Why, it wasn't even the *shank* of the evening! The theatres were barely into the middle of their first acts, of yet, and the chop-houses were still packed with diners.

" 'Nuther porter, sir?" the waitress enquired, slyly projecting a hip to the edge of his table. Even here, in a somewhat clean tavern, there'd be rooms abovestairs for rantipoling, and the servers augmented their earnings with sport. She wasn't to his taste, though, in his now-stimulated state, Lewrie began to wonder exactly what his taste *was* and where he'd draw the line.

"No, I'm off," Lewrie said, tucking the guidebook into a breast pocket of his uniform coat, and fumbling for his coin purse.

"Cor, wot a pity," the waitress leered, 'an yew with h'int'rest in a li'l sport."

"Ta," Lewrie said, hastily taking his leave. To the first hacking coach outside, he shouted "Madeira Club, Duke and Wigmore" to the coachee, and clambered in. Time was wasting!

CHAPTER FIFTEEN

*I*n *mufti* again, armed with a stout walking-stick that disguised a slim sword, and with bank notes squirrelled away in several pockets, he was pleased to discover himself back in his old haunts, where he had rented his first London lodgings; in Panton Street, where many foreign emissaries lived . . . or kept their mistresses. The house that his hired coach took him to he remembered as one which in his time, in 1784, had been the residence of a single family. Now, though . . .

> No finer establishment for the discerning gentleman in search of Corinthian delights in St. James's, in the utmost of security and serenity, the house of Mistress Batson may offer the most exquisite selection of jewels of the demi-monde . . .

Or so the guidebook said, and if Mistress Batson's lived up to a *tithe* of its advertisement, it would be worth it, Lewrie decided as he alit and paid the coachman.

There was a hulking sort of fellow loitering by the front stoop who gave him a chary look-over. "Come as a patron, sir?" he asked in a gruff warning voice.

"Aye," Lewrie simply replied.

"Then go right in, sir, and take joy."

Lewrie barely had to rap the large door-knocker once before the portal was opened by the hulking fellow's obvious twin, this one done up in a sober sort of livery. From a cold night street to a gust of warm air, from the stinks of London to inviting aromas of perfumes and Hungary Waters in a *mélange* of scents; from the din of carriages and dray waggons and the *humm-umm* of people to almost a hush. A violin played in company with a flute or recorder. There was a faint clink of glasses, a convivial buzz of conversation, and soft, teasing female laughter coming from somewhere beyond the entry foyer.

A stout older woman in the sack gown and over-done makeup of at least two decades past greeted him with a curtsy, to which he replied with a short bow, a "leg," and the doff of his hat.

"Welcome to Mother Batson's, sir," she said, looking him up and down, much like a tailor might. "You come for ease, I take it?"

"I do, indeed, Ma'am," Lewrie told her as another liveried servant took his hat, boat-cloak, and walking-stick, and gave him a claim chit.

"I see by your cloak you are a seafaring gentleman, sir," the older woman said.

"The Navy, Ma'am . . . just back from *years* at sea," Lewrie said.

"And God bless our 'wooden walls,'" she said back, smiling at last, "though . . . *years* at sea, my my. You sound insatiable."

"As we say of those who do not stand evening watches, Ma'am, I would like 'all night in,' and a morning departure," Lewrie told her. "When the sun's above the yardarm, and the streets are safer."

"Now that would require a guinea, sir." The older woman leered. "Come into our parlour, take seat, and have a glass of something, where you may find your heart's delight." She offered not an arm to steer him, but a palm to be crossed. Once a pound note, and a silver shilling, had been placed in that palm, she did take him by the arm and lead him into a much larger room.

Where the music was, where other men lolled at their ease with drinks in their hands and young women by their sides; where a waiter with a tray of glasses circulated, and offered him champagne.

"Bottle in the room will be extra, when you're ready" was said in a soft voice. Another pound note went to the manservant, who winked acknowledgement, then drifted away.

Lewrie took a look around and chose a short settee, a bit away from the others. Even as he settled himself, two men made their choice and were led by their Cyprians to the grand old staircase.

Damned if one of the men wasn't Sir George Norman, K.C., the one who had prosecuted him just weeks before, now minus his court periwig . . . and his rectitude! Sir George jolted to a halt and gawped at him, stupefied for a brief moment, before Lewrie raised his glass in salute and smiled; to which Sir George performed a slight shrug, and displayed a worldly-wise smile, before following his doxy to the stairs.

And damned if the fellow with him wasn't a Member of Commons, a fellow noted for being in the "progressive," reforming, and moralising faction. By the gay and bawdy interplay 'twixt Sir George, his choice of Poll, and the other couple, it didn't appear as if they'd be taking separate rooms, either!

"Do you have any preferences, sir?" the older woman in the towering wig enquired after she had seen the foursome up the stairs with fond wishes. She sat beside Lewrie on the short settee, hands in her lap as prim as a vicar's wife at high tea. "We boast of ladies to every taste. Dark and exotic from the West Indies or Africa, perhaps? Girls worthy of a *rajah*'s harem in India or the Far East? Old, stout . . . slim and young . . . dark or fair? Whatever is your fondest wish . . . short of a child, of course. . . . Here, you may find your heart's desire. And all skilled in every aspect of the pleasurable arts," she said with many a simper and sly grins.

"Well, hmm . . . " Lewrie paused, colouring a bit, for it had been years since he'd had to visit a commercial establishmen. *Christ, wasn't it Charleston, way back in the American Revolution? Or with Cashman in Port-au-Prince, in '98? Had no need o' brothels,* he told himself; *not with so many willin' sorts about.*

"Slim and fair'd be nice," Lewrie told the "Mother Abbess" at last, "as English as plum pudding . . . and, as sweet."

"Then I have the perfect one for you, sir," the woman said, rising to her feet and beckoning to a girl in the far corner near the musicians, who was by herself and nodding dreamily in time to the melody. "Tess, my dear . . . come and meet our guest, the naval gentleman."

The girl seemed almost to jerk from her pleasant musings, as if waking from sleep at dawn. She sprang to her feet with a shy and winsome smile before remembering her "lessons" in grace, then crossed the parlour to join them in a well-schooled glide. It was a good thing the parlour was well-warmed by two fireplaces, for she wore only a thin and silky chemise, cinched round the waist with a pale blue ribbon, with a darker blue dressing gown over that, un-sashed, so it peeked open with each step to show off her low-heeled shoes, her white silk stockings tied above the knees, and now and then showed off her slim ankles and thighs . . . though she did keep her hands close to the laced edges of the dressing gown as if wishing to fold it snugger and less revealing.

"Tess, this is, ah . . . no names are necessary, are they? But he is one of our naval heroes," Mrs. Batson (for surely it must be she) airily said by way of introduction. "Sir, this is Tess, new-come with us by way of Belfast. Not *quite* English, as you said, but now that we are all *British*, hmm?"

"Honoured t'meet you, Tess," Lewrie said, rising to greet her, to give her a short bow from the waist.

"Yer servant, sir," Tess replied, dipping him a graceful curtsy.

"Will ye join me in a glass of champagne, my dear?" Lewrie bade.

"The gentleman requests the rest of the night, Tess," the older woman said in a soft coo, to which Tess gave a grateful, relieved grin. "I leave you to your pleasures and amusements, Tess . . . sir. Do take joy," Mrs. Batson wished them, then glided away.

Lewrie took the girl's hand and led her to a seat on the settee, then sat down beside her. A second later, the manservant was back with a fresh tray of glasses of champagne for them both.

New-come to us, mine arse, Lewrie cynically thought; *Sweet and young she may look, but . . . they might've sold her virginity to one o' the highest bidders, the last six months runnin'!*

She was pretty, though; not painted up or tarted up with artifice, for she had no need for rouge or paints. Pretty in a *country* way, like a maid-servant to a rural squire's house, a goose-girl or milking maid one might meet in a village on market day.

She had a nice oval face with a high forehead, a quite cute nose, and a smallish mouth, with a bit of an overbite that gave her face the sweetest seeming innocence. Her eyes were dark-green-hazel, and her sandy-brown hair, with the faintest hint of strawberry red, was parted mis-sishly simple in the centre of her head, gathered loosely with ribbon at the nape of her neck, and fell in long, lazy curls, with a few wispy strands either side of her face.

"Well, I s'pose I could reveal that my first name's Alan, without spillin' any Crown secrets," he said, grinning, by way of beginning.

"And ye're really a Navy officer?"

"A Post-Captain," Lewrie confided.

"Whatever that is, sir," she said, with another shy grin.

"Warships are Rated," Lewrie casually explained to her. "Now, Admiral Nelson's new ship, the *San Josef*, which he made prize at the Battle of Cape Saint Vincent years ago, is a First Rate of ninety-eight or an hundred guns." He stretched his legs out a little and put one arm on the back of the settee, shifting to face her. "Anything below the Rates, a Lieutenant may command, or a Commander, but when you get to a frigate of the Sixth Rate, with more than twenty guns, that's what Admiralty calls an official 'Post' ship, and only a full Captain will command her. Hence . . . 'Post' Captain. I've had two frigates so far, *Proteus* was a Sixth Rate of thirty-two guns, and my last was *Savage,* a Fifth Rate of thirty-six guns."

"Oh, an are ye goin' t'th' Baltic with Admiral Nelson, then?" Tess enthused, shifting more to face him, too, "Will ye be beatin' th' BeJesus outta th' Roosians, and such?"

"Speakin' o' Crown secrets!" Lewrie scoffed, almost hooted, in point of fact. "Why, everyone in England—and ev'ry enemy spy!—must know that, by now. But, no . . . I'm without a ship, at present. I had t'give up *Savage* before Christmas. There were some . . . civilian things t'see to ashore, so another captain has her now. Damn his eyes."

"Ooh, I think I know who ye are!" Tess whispered excitedly, and squirmed a little bit closer still, almost jouncing on her bottom in sly glee. "Damme if ye're not that Alan *Lewrie* wot's been in all th' *papers,* are ye not!"

"Guilty . . . of that, at least," Lewrie confessed with a teasing touch of his finger to her lips, then to his own with a *shussh* sound.

Gettin' bags *o' use from that 'un,* he thought; *Guilty . . . or not! Dined out on it for weeks. Ha-bloody-ha.*

"Yer secret's safe with me, Captain . . . Alan," Tess teased, in return. "Mum's th' word." They clinked glasses and drained them and waved for refills as the girl wriggled even closer, under the arch of his arm, with her warm hip and thigh against him. "Don't know as I've ever . . . been *introduced* to a real hero before. Oh, officers an' such from *some* regiment or t'other, or so they claimed, but . . . " She checked herself with a pretty *moue,* a shrug, and a toss of her hair, as if talk of previous clients was discouraged by "Mother" Batson and those bully-bucks of hers. After all, the *illusion* was the thing.

"Soldiers, by God," Lewrie sneered. "Pack o' cod's-wallops, the lot of 'em. They *buy* their commissions, whilst Navy men have to *work* t'gain ours."

At least he assumed that Tess was talking about gentlemen officers, not the sweaty rank and file. Mrs. Batson's didn't look like the sort of establishment that would have private soldiers or Ordinary Seamen in, even on Boxing Day. More to the point, Lewrie *hoped* that Tess had dealt with "well-armoured" gentlemen in the past.

"You stick with naval gentlemen, they'll see ye right," Lewrie told her, with a grin and a bit of a rising leer.

"Uhm . . . like you, Captain Alan?" she asked, coyly inclining her head, bestowing upon him another of those shy and fetching smiles, her lips parted slightly.

"Care to discover the diff'rence, Tess?" he muttered, cocking a brow, and suddenly very aware of the heat and closeness of her body and the scent of her perfume, and her fresh-washed hair.

She took a deep sip of champagne, eyes turned away as if studying his proposal, seeming somewhere 'twixt solemn and wryly amused . . . then looked back at him, smiled shyly once more, and slowly nodded.

"Let us go up to your room, then, Tess," he said, winking.

"Aye, let's," she agreed.

CHAPTER SIXTEEN

*H*er room was three storeys above the street, beyond the grandness of the lower staircase, where marble was replaced by solid oak, and the carpeting was more worn. Tess lit them up with a single candle in one hand, and Lewrie's in her other. They went down a wide and gloomy hall, only lit here and there with a sole candle on a table, or one or two mounted in wall holders.

There was a final door at the right of the hallway, which Tess opened. Beyond it, instead of a good-sized bed-chamber, there was yet another passage, much narrower, which forced them shoulder-to-shoulder as she led him past a door to either side, then an equally narrow cap to the T, which presented a final pair of doors. The one on the right-hand side was slightly ajar, and Tess preceded him into the room beyond, tiptoeing and hesitant.

Ambush, here? Lewrie had to worry for a moment as he followed, quickly peering about for the sight of a bully-buck with a lead-loaded leather cosh, or a whacking-thick cudgel.

"More light, Captain Alan?" Tess asked. "Or, d'ye prefer th' dark?"

"At least one or two more candles . . . for now," he said, satisfied that he would not be bashed on the head and robbed. Yet. As she ignited more candles with her first one, Lewrie could see where he was.

There had to be four smaller rooms carved out of the original large

111

bed-chamber, he deduced, the new walls and passageway made up of plain deal partitions, though painted white with the impression of fine mouldings just painted on, like stage scenery. The wall to his right was substantial plaster, still wallpapered. The one ahead of him was also papered, with a set of dark and heavy drapes covering a window. . . . He crossed to it with difficulty, squeezing between a chest-of-drawers and the foot of the bed to pull the drapes apart and look out, down to Panton Street far below. He let the drapes fall back together, for it was cold, the panes frosted and semi-opaque. Come to think on it, the room was chilly, too, and he couldn't imagine what they'd done with the fireplace that should have warmed the larger, original room.

Now that he could see, Lewrie took in the bed, fairly close to the draped window, then to a taller old-style night-stand on the other side, where his requested bottle of champagne stood chilling in a pail filled with slushy snow, aside two fresh glasses. There was a folding screen set out from the deal partition they had passed through, on the floor beside it a storage chest, and, against the middle wall, by the chest-of-drawers, stood a wash-hand stand with a pitcher, towels, and two bowls.

"They charge extra for the candles, do they?" Lewrie asked her with a wry chuckle.

"Oh, nossir," Tess told him with a little laugh of her own as she finished lighting the requested candles. "Now, d'ye wish t'have a fireplace, those rooms there, an' there, t'ones we passed comin' in, well . . . th' established girls get those, 'less ye put in a request t' Mother Batson."

"Didn't know," Lewrie said with a shrug, peeling off his coat. "Where does one . . . ?"

"There's a row o' pegs, yonder, sir," Tess told him. She went to the row of pegs herself, quickly exchanging her lacy and revealing silk dressing gown for a heavier one of tan wool, wrapping it round her body with a shiver. Not so quickly that Lewrie couldn't get an appreciative eyeful of her figure, despite the looseness of her chemise. It only came to mid-thigh, and, silhouetted by a fresh candle, the sight made him grin. She was girlishly slim in arms, back, and hips, with very shapely slim legs, right down to an alluring gap 'tween her upper thighs. *Yum-bloody-yum!* he thought in sudden lust.

He went to the pegs, hung up his coat and waist-coat, stuffed his sporty paisley neck-stock into a pocket, and sat on the chest to tug at a boot.

"Lemme help ye with those, sir," Tess volunteered, kneeling to lend a hand. Lewrie stood in his stockinged feet and shivered. There was a set of small carpets on the floor, but they were old and threadworn, without a bit of give or insulation.

"Maybe I should bring a dressing robe along, next time," Lewrie said, hugging himself for warmth.

"I can only wish ye think enough o' me t'come a second time," Tess teased, still sitting on her heels below him. "There's a quilt t'wrap up in, do ye want." She rose to her knees and placed a hand on the buttons of his breeches, looking up somewhere 'twixt shyness and flirtatiousness as her fingers found his mounting erection. "Might I help ye further, . . . Captain Alan?"

Lewrie's hand to the waistband buttons, hers working up from the bottom of the row, and he was free in a trice, breeches and stockings discarded atop the chest, and the boots, and the room's chill a sensual thrill from the hem of his shirt to his groin.

"Ye have 'armour'?" she softly asked, her hands under his shirt, on the tops of his thighs. "They'll not let us, without. Do ye not, I've a few in the—"

"A round dozen," Lewrie told her in a throat-constricted mutter as Tess's hands slid up to his hips, bracketing his taut belly.

"Saints preserve us, but I hope ye'll spare me the use of *all* of 'em, arrah!" Tess said with a gasp of alarm, false or not, he could not tell. She dropped back to her heels, eyes wide.

"The Green Lantern's Best," Lewrie assured her, offering her a hand. "Let's get under the covers, then have another glass of champagne, me girl. *Vite vite,* as the Frogs say."

Out of her shoes, Tess was about four inches shorter than his five feet nine inches as she rose to her feet, and, with his hand in hers, quickly led him to the bed. He whipped the coverlet, blankets, and sheet back and they both jumped in, her heavy wool robe slung to the footboard, then the covers pulled up to her chin, the pile of pillows flounced up and braced behind their shoulders and heads. Lewrie reached for the bottle and the glasses, poured for both of them, then shifted to his side to face her, clinking his glass to hers once more.

She took a sip, then leaned back against the pillows, sighing contentedly. "Never had champagne 'fore I come t'London, I never," she told him, flashing her that rather sweet, shy smile again. "La, 'tis a grand thing, the 'bubbly.' "

" 'Deed it is," Lewrie happily agreed. "Why, a fellow captain I know, Benjamin Rodgers, couldn't go to sea at *all,* did he not have at least three dozen dozen bottles in his lazarette store. Goes through it like a country squire sucks up ale," he said with a hoot.

"An' here I thought goin' t'sea was all misery an' hard times," Tess said, shifting to her side to face him, one hand propping up her head. " 'Twas bad enough, just goin' by packet from Belfast t' Liverpool, and *sick*! I thought I'd die 'fore settin' foot on hard ground. Whush! Sure, and it'd take a power o' strong drink t'get *me* aboard a ship again. T'make such life even *passin'* tolerable."

"It ain't always that stormy, in the main," Lewrie told her. "More good days than bad, really. The worst part sometimes is days on end o' *boredom*. One week after t'other, exactly the same hum-drum and routine."

"And there's dancin' t'hornpipes, an' all?" Tess asked, smiling and much more at ease than their first moments. "Shinnin' up masts, an' such?" she added, with a sly leer in her eyes.

"Ye'd not ask me t'shin up a mast *tonight*, will ye, Captain Alan?" she asked with feigned dread.

"Seein' as how you're a landlubber, not a 'scaly fish,' I don't think I'll put ya to the main-mast truck quite yet, m'dear," he joshed with a grin and a throaty chuckle. He slipped closer, putting an arm behind her head, and she snuggled up to him, bringing welcome warmth and a heady mix of enticing aromas. "Perhaps I'll start ya out on the mizen . . . only as far as the cro'jack yard."

"Ye haveta learn another tongue t'be a sailor?" she asked with a shake of her head.

"We've our own language, for certain, Tess," he agreed.

"Ye'll not be too rough an' hungry, will ye, Captain Alan?" she asked in a soft voice. "Mean t'say . . . "

"I've simple, normal tastes, if that's your question," he assured her, feeling warm enough to undo his cuffs and slide out of his silk shirt. "Nor am I a brute. Mind though . . . it has been a long time. But, we have 'til dawn, or a little later, I'm assured. I *doubt* we'll go through the whole dozen. But . . . ya never can tell, am I inspired?" he said with a grin. "And you *are* inspiring."

They sipped at their champagne, he faster than she, and set his empty glass on the night-stand. He turned back, and she was waving her empty at him with a bolder grin of her own.

"Should I snuff some candles?" she asked as she slid down in the bed, sweeping her long hair to one side.

Only three single candles barely illuminated the small room; it was all amber and gently flickering shadows. Now they were silent, he could hear what was going on in the other cubicles; the rhythmic thud of mat-tresses and the squeaking of slats or ropes, urgent grunts, moans, and throaty soft laughter.

"Not right now," Lewrie said, sliding over to hold her close, to kiss her throat, her shoulders, and nuzzle below and behind of her ears. He moved up to her forehead, her cheeks, and her chin, testing whether she was the sort of whore who'd kiss for real, or turn her head away to feign passion. His lips found hers, and they were very soft and sweet as she al-lowed him . . . then, after a few light, teasing kisses, parted her lips and met him, measure for measure.

His free hand gently slid under her chemise to roam over her hip, and trail spider-soft down her thigh, then back up slowly, roving over the back of her leg 'til he could cup a firm, baby-bottom-soft buttock and stroke a circle; expanding wider to her waist. Tess shifted beside him, parting her thighs wide enough for him to put a leg between them, and feather his fingers from her waist to her belly, then down to her fluff. Her arms were round him, her kisses more urgent, and the musk of her breath intensifying. She slid a hand down to her waist-sash and undid the loose knot so he could tickle his hand up her back, above her waist, cross her rib cage, and slide the chemise up even higher.

"Let's have this off, sweetness," he growled, helping her lift it free over her head, and she flung it away, with no care for where it landed, then flung her arms round his neck, beginning to moan kittenish as he buried his face against her neck and hair.

"Oh, Captain Alan! Uhmm! Oh, yes, ooh!" Tess whispered, her fin-gers in his thick hair. "Ah, that's darlin'!"

It was *such* a sham, almost enough to put him off for a moment, yet he was determined, almost challenged, to take her beyond the play-acting, before the night was done. One last open-mouthed bout of kisses, and he slid down her body to her breasts.

Not all that large, yet soft and milky, and delightfully scented. His tongue rimmed her puffy pink *areolae* and nipples, smiling to himself as they went taut as he licked, flicked, and assayed a shuddery play-nip that made her moan a tad more authentically.

Lower down, bestowing attention on her sides, her ribs, and she went onto her back, slim thighs parted further to make room for him when he got to her stomach, her belly, her navel, and Tess's hips were slowly rolling and beginning to push up to him.

"Ooh, ooh, ah!" Tess uttered as he gained the deliciously soft tops of her inner thighs, and she lifted her knees, shifting again and widening her legs as his hot breath stirred her corn-silk-fine patch of fluff, kissing her belly above it, and feeling her stomach shudder.

If that ain't real, then it's one hell of a trick! he thought.

To the seat of pleasure at last, tongue and lips on her cleft, and she smelt so *clean*, for a moment, before the musk arose, as Tess went from dryness to dampness, then to slickness as he pressed his face to her.

There'd been a courtesan in his teens, then a Chinese whore in Canton, who had titteringly instructed him in how to pay attention to "the little man in the boat" . . . not just a brief visit, but a lengthy stay, . . . and the result he could conjure with what the Chinese girl had called "the hummingbird." And damned if he would go anywhere else 'til he'd lit a *proper* fire . . . an *honest* fire.

It seemed to be working, for Tess's fingers clawed in his hair, at his scalp, her hips jouncing up in time with his tongue, panting in rhythm, and mewling soft yelps and urgent whines.

"Oh, oh, oh Jesus, Joseph an' Mary, oh God, m'dear, *uhm!*" she whimpered, her hands now clamped round his head, knees almost to her chest, *shoving* him into her groin. "Oh, God in Heaven, ye *bastard* . . . ! Yes, yes, yess! Ahhhaa!" she wailed, arching her back, "Ah, ye darlin' man, oh *Jaysus!*" She froze of a sudden, loins pressed upward hard and her thighs gripping his head, her arms flung outside the blankets, to grip the pillows and the edge of the mattress, to claw the sheets. A moment more stiffness, and she collapsed with a shudder, croaking from a dry throat, gasping for air as he swarmed up her to take her in his arms, shift to lie on his side and stroke her all over.

"My *dear,*" Tess said with a shaky laugh once she'd gotten her breath back. "My God, but where'd ye learn that 'un? I never . . . "

"I *told* ye the Navy'd see ye right, dear Tess," he chuckled.

"Faith, if ye haven't. Whush!" She fanned herself with the bed covers. "But . . . isn't it time ye fetched one o' yer cundums an' had ye're own pleasure?" she whispered, beaming with fun.

"I do believe you're right, sweet 'un," Lewrie heartily agreed, Before he could turn over to fetch one, though, Tess swarmed over him to the drawer of the night-stand and pulled one out.

"Your turn," Tess whispered, a playful leer on her face for a moment. "My turn," she added, tossing back the covers and slipping down to his erection to tie the cundum on . . . but not before her lips tasted him, licked, and surrounded its top, her mouth and breath hot and wet and *maddening!*

"'Tis a fearful big thing ye own, Captain Alan," Tess said as she rolled away, opening herself to him. "But I *do* believe I'll manage . . . d'ye start out gentle."

In the candlelight, her eyes shone with mischief, and her mouth pouted so very prettily, her lips slightly apart. "Now, sir?"

CHAPTER SEVENTEEN

As the bells of London chimed the hour of one in the morning, a very pleased, and smug, Alan Lewrie allowed himself to imagine that he was not yet *that* old; that he did main-well for a fellow who'd reached his thirty-eighth year. His birthday had occurred a week before, to no particular notice from anyone else, friend or family.

"Hmm," he purred into Tess's hair as she lay half atop him, one slim thigh between his, and her belly sticky-damp against him. "Mmm!" was her matching purr as he stroked her back and kissed her cheek.

"Ye're feelin' sleepy yet, darlin'?" Tess asked, her head upon his chest.

"Is that a wish, Tess?" he asked, chuckling.

"Faith, it is *not*," she answered, propping her chin on him, to peer drowsily sweet into his eyes, with that fetching wee, shy grin of hers breaking out on her face. "I was only wond'rin' do ye feel a wee bit peckish. Should I ring for somethin' t'eat?"

"Besides your sweet self?" he teased.

"Sweet Jesus," she said, laughing softly, "sure and ye'll be th' end o' me, . . . an' starve me into th' bargain."

"Sounds good. I am hungry," Lewrie decided. "What might they have?"

"Well, each ev'nin', there's an invitation supper," Tess said, rolling away to grope at the foot of the bed for her heavy robe. "For the regular customers. More o' what they call a buffet than anythin' else . . . tonight was ham, roast beef, an' goose, an' there's sure t'be plenty left . . . enough for sandwiches."

"Aye, ring for something," Lewrie told her. "We might not need another whole bottle, but . . . we *could* stay awake long enough to finish one. Another bloody guinea."

"Sure t'be *part* of a bottle left by others, in the parlour," she speculated as she quickly dressed, and hopped out of bed to search for her shoes. "Be back in a tick."

"Wait," Lewrie said, getting up on one elbow and taking her by the hand. Tess was simply *delightful,* and, with her heavy robe still hanging open, he could not let her go without drinking in the sight of her. Her hair had long before come undone from its restraining ribbon, and hung long and fair to her waist in soft curves, and in the dim candlelight, her body was a study in amber wash.

"Best choice ever I made," Lewrie told her, " 'cause you're the *loveliest* girl I've clapped 'top-lights' on in years, Tess."

"Ah, go on with ye," she laughed, rewarding his words with one more shy grin and a cock of her head. "You keep the covers warm while I fetch us some vittles." She stepped out into the narrow passageway and Lewrie settled back with his hands behind his head, about ready to laugh out loud in glee to have stumbled upon such a sweet young thing . . . even if she was a whore.

He heard her shoes click down the passageway to the outer door, the door open and close, and listened to the sounds of the house, now that things had slowed down a bit. Damnably, there was still a wench in a nearby cubicle who must have aspired to the opera, who trilled and hallooed false passion, still. Cross the hallway, perhaps, muffled but still loud, there was a couple who cursed each other like salty bosuns, between animal-like grunts and whoops. When he and Tess were not busy, they'd giggled like schoolchildren to the sounds, speculating what the other whores and customers really looked like . . . and what particular act they were engaged in.

Sleepy? No, he didn't feel sleepy in the slightest, yet. There were seven more un-used cundums, and, with a cold collation and a new bottle of "bubbly" coming, he imagined he *might* attain a new record.

Tess was *that* intriguing, and enflaming.

And I'm too bloody hungry, he admitted to himself.

"Hallo," Lewrie muttered to himself as the amourous sounds of the house changed. There were shouts belowstairs, a thud or two, then the quick clopping of someone's shoes, the opening and slamming of the hall-way door, some closer clopping . . . which forced him to sit upright in bed.

There was a woman's shriek of alarm, another woman's voice raised in high dudgeon, men bellowing, and . . .

The door to the cubicle burst open, Tess with her hair flying as she dashed in with a champagne bottle in her hand! She slammed the door and clawed at a pocket of her heavy dressing robe. "Help me, Cap'm!" she cried. "The chest! The bloody chest!"

He sprang from the bed stark naked, padded to the door, and she tossed him the champagne bottle—half-full as promised, sloshing on his bare chest and stomach, as she dug in the other pocket, then sprang to the silk robe, then the night-stand.

"Shift th' damned chest! Block th' fackin' door, please Jesus, for I cannot find th' fackin' *key*!" she wailed. By then, all the customers and whores on both the second and third storeys were either yelling in fright or bellowing in anger.

"What the bloody Hell?" Lewrie demanded as he knelt to shift the large chest in front of the door.

"Fackin' mad man, oughter be in Bedlam, he should . . . !" Tess said in a gasping voice, then exulted as she found a rusty key. She tossed it to him, which he dropped, then scrambled for, and locked the flimsy door for her. He turned to face her.

"*What* bloody mad man?"

Tess was now holding the throat of her wool dressing robe shut with one hand, and in the other, she shakily held a shiny wee dagger.

Belowstairs—uncomfortably closer than before—there came sounds of a struggle, and a bellowed demand. "Tess! Vant Tess, and no other, hear me? Peasants! Serfs! How dare you? *Yob tvoyemat!*"

"Eeep!" was Lewrie's outburst upon hearing that Russian curse.

What's Durschenko doin' here? was his first panicky thought; *I ain't toppin' his* daughter, *so* . . . !

He picked up the champagne bottle from the floor, took a large swig that bubbled round his mouth and chin, then went to Tess's side.

"B'lieve I know a bit more about daggers than you, sweetlin'," Lewrie said, hand out to request it. " 'Less you've killed somebody in the past with it. Here, I'll trade you," he said, offering the bottle. For an off-hand weapon, he picked the empty champagne bottle from the night-stand.

"Now, who's this bloody lunatick that's callin' for ya," Lewrie asked over his shoulder, taking stance between Tess and the door. "His name ain't Durschenko, is it? Arslan Artimovich? Scrawny old Russian devil with an eyepatch?"

"No . . . no, he's a student," Tess said with a weak shudder to her voice. She'd climbed onto the bed and was huddling in the far corner near the drapes. "*Says* he was. Anatoli, he called himself. Russian, aye. Goin' t'Oxford, an' some sorta title . . . count or somethin'. He was took with me, but Jesus! He's a mean'un! I *told* Mother Batson I'd druther he come round no more . . . choose another girl, but . . . ! Ye'll not let him in an' git me, willya, Cap'm Alan, for th' love o' God?"

"Not if I can help it, no, Tess," Lewrie assured her, hefting his dagger and make-shift cosh.

It sounded, though, as if the struggle had reached a high-tide mark on the second-storey landing, safely a floor below. More curses in Russian, from two voices, some good old London accents from several more bully-bucks. "Sasha, *pamageetyeh! Doh! Viy mojetyeh mnyeh pamoch?*" from one, and "Oww!" and a grunt from another, preceded by some *lovely* meaty thuds from fists and cudgels. "Vill burn *house* down! Ow! Kill *all* you *pryazni* . . . oof!"

Of a sudden, it got *delightfully* quiet. While whores continued to fret and fuss, and gentlemen customers made idle threats, an ironic series of cheers could be heard; the grunts and heavy-footed shuffles as bodies were hauled downstairs, and victorious bully-bucks congratulated themselves on a duty well done.

"Think you're safe, now," Lewrie told Tess, turning around. She was *behind* the bed, 'tween the mattress and the wall, with the covers thrown over her to appear as a pile of blankets shoved off the bed . . . one frightened eye peeked from a tiny fold.

"He's gone?"

"Bashed senseless, by the sound of it," Lewrie said with a wry laugh, "him and another, both. Damme, I don't usually do my fightin' in the buff." He put the dagger back into the night-stand drawer, the empty bottle on the floor beside it, and hopped back into bed, pulling up the covers and shivering. "Well, don't I get a reward?" he asked with a laugh. Tess untangled herself from the pile of covers, spread them back out to cover all the mattress, and slid in from the off-side.

"Ye'da fought him for me?" Tess shakily exclaimed as she curled up to him under the covers, her wool robe itchy on his skin. "Ye'da risked yer life t'keep *me* safe?"

For a second he took that for false hero-worship, the fawning of a courtesan dependent on his purse, yet . . . she sounded truly amazed to have someone . . . anyone . . . stand up for her.

"Still have the 'bubbly'? Let me have a sip, there's a darlin'," Lewrie bade. He took a drink from the neck, then grinned at her. "Whoever the bastard was, you were terrified . . . *and,* he was spoilin' our time t'gether, so what *else* could I do for a pretty young lass? Doubt he'll be comin' *here* again, so . . . "

He would have handed the bottle back to her, but Tess threw her arms round his neck, thrust a thigh between his, and kissed him with a fierce passion. She jerked the knot of her sash loose and spread the dressing robe over him, pressing her fever-warm body to his . . . she whimpered and cooed and clung to him like a limpet.

And did he feel sudden moisture on his face . . . her face?

Oh, don't do that, he thought as he hugged her back, slipping his free hand under the covers and her robe to stroke her bare back and shoulders as she writhed against him; *A girl's tears'll* always *land me in trouble.*

"There, there, sweetlin'," he murmured into her hair. "It's all over, and no harm done."

"G . . . git one o' ye're cundums," she breathed, "an' make love t'me, this very minute!"

"Well . . . if it'll make ye feel better," he japed.

Damned if he wasn't ready to oblige her, in point of fact, for the threat of danger, then her warmth and softness, had made him as inspired as the first time, with an erection as stiff as a marling-spike. She sat up, "armoured" him quickly with trembling hands, then sat astride of him, her robe cocooning them both, and her long, curly hair brushing his chest.

"La, ye're th' grandest . . . bloody . . . man!" she moaned.

Minutes later there came a discreet rap on the door, which made Tess start and Lewrie scramble for the dagger. "Who's there?" the girl squeaked.

" 'Tis Bob, Tess," a man said in a gruff voice. "Wi' yer vittles. No fear, 'at Roosky bastard's long gone."

Lewrie had to help shift the heavy chest, and unlock the door so the waiter could come in with another salvaged bottle of champagne and a tray covered with a napkin, which when whisked away, revealed a pair of sandwiches, and a dish of pickles.

"Two pound, six, sir," Bob told Lewrie, who was looking for his coin purse, "an' we'll settle th' reckonin' in th' mornin'."

"Looks like you gave as good as you got," Lewrie told him, noting the waiter's bruises, and the beginnings of a black eye.

"Lots better'n he, sir!" Bob said with a boxer's grin. "Him an' his manservant, both. Poxy bastards'll look like raw beef fer a week."

"He'll not ever come back, pray Jesus?" Tess fearfully asked.

"Ain't sayin' 'e won't *try*, girl," Bob reassured her, clenching his fists together and cracking knuckles, "but we've leave t'dump 'is arse in th' Thames, if he do, Roosky titles'r no."

Lewrie dug some money from a pocket of his coat and slipped the man the reckoning, with another pound note atop it for his efforts, and tipped Bob the wink.

"Mmm, roast duck!" Tess enthused once Bob had left, and she had lifted the bread to look at her sandwich. "*Told* ye the house sets out a grand table." She sat in the middle of the bed, cross-legged with her robe spread over her lap, shifting with delight as she took a bite and chewed. Lewrie poured her a glass of champagne and slid under the bed covers, using the borrowed quilt to drape his shoulders and chest like a Red Indian. "Damme, this is good." Lewrie agreed, after a taste.

"Hot mustard and some sorta red jelly . . . apple, it may be, all stirred t'gether," Tess said, smiling with pleasure after chewing and swallowing, "like wot ye serve with venison'r grouse?"

"Mm-hmm!" Lewrie agreed again, with his mouth full. "So . . . who was this Anatoli character?" he asked, after a sip of champagne.

"A . . . customer," Tess told him, looking uncomfortable with the subject. "First he come, was round Christmas . . . end of Terms, he calls it . . . from Oxford? Once th' week'r so, 'til th' night he . . . and I . . . " She frowned and squirmed a bit. "He went with no one special, 'til he lit on me, damn his eyes. T'other girls said he was a rough 'un, so I was leery, d'ye see? But he *seemed* nice enough, th' first time'r two."

"But then he turned brute on ye?" Lewrie gently probed.

"Aye, that he did," Tess spat, "an' askin' for me only, fer all night . . . like you," she added, leaning over to nudge his shoulder with hers, and flashing a brief, adorable grin. "Mind, 'tis a lot easier on a girl, with but th' one feller t'deal with, an' a lot o' them older an' . . . Well, I gets a lot more rest with th' older fellers . . . not like *you*, Captain Alan, *that's* fer certain. No sleep in *you!*"

She reached out to brush his hair from his brow.

Uh-oh! Lewrie thought at her gesture; *Don't go* fond *on me!*

"*Him*, though . . . ," Tess said, turning pensive. "Ev'ry night, for a fortnight, an' him swearin' he'd buy me out, an' set me up an me own lodgin's for his own, brr! Mean t'say, 'tis a poor girl's fondest wish t'be set up good as a *lady*, but! Not with th' likes o' *him*, even was he rich as that *Tsar* o' his. Just *wouldn't* do it nat'ral, no, not him, an' wantin' me without 'protections' . . . in th' wrong . . !"

She made an angry *moue* and swiped at her own hair, tossing her mane with anger and impatience.

"That sorry I am t'bring it up, though ye *did* ask," Tess said, "for 'Mother' Batson says her gentlemen don't wanna hear 'bout t'other customers' doin's, or who went before 'em, 'cause half o' what we sell is . . . illusion, d'ye see? Affection, attention . . . grace an' beauty, an' all that shite. Oops!" she pealed out a laugh as she covered her mouth with a hand for a second. "B'lieve me, Cap'm Alan, this bus'ness can be powerful strange sometimes. See there, in th' corner."

Lewrie looked where she pointed; there was a bundle of birch rods, which he'd taken for an old broom, or kindling for a Franklin-pattern stove.

"There's some . . . real 'Quality' sorts . . . who can't get goin' without ye whip their bare bottoms, an' tell 'em what bad boys they be!"

"And some who wish t'whip *you?*" Lewrie scowled.

"Bedamned if they will!" Tess declared. " 'Mother' Batson don't hold with her girls gettin' hurt . . . scarred up, more-like."

"And this Anatoli liked t'be whipped?" Lewrie asked.

"Oh no, not him," Tess said, after a big bite of her sandwich and a swig of champagne. "He cared more for puttin' it in my mouth or my bum-hole, an' all th' time tryin' t'sneak his cundum off whilst I'm kneelin' on all fours like a bitch-hound. Might start *out* havin' me th' normal, Christian way, but that never lasted long. And, do I ever balk, he'd go all sulky an' teary, first . . . slip me more money, order up more wine an' gin . . . said if he couldn't get somethin' he called *vodka*, then gin'd suit, and Jesus but he could put it away like water! He got drunk enough, he'd get mad, give me th' back of his *hand* a time or two, but then . . . the daft bastard'd start weepin' again, and tells me how much he *loves* me, for th' love o' God! Onliest way t'shut him up was t'kneel on th' floor an' . . . ye know. Then he was cherry-merry, again . . . for a time.

"One night," Tess said, leaning close to confide in Lewrie, "he got th' window open, an' stood on th' ledge, stark nekkid an' drunk as a lord, fer *ev'ryone* t'see . . . swearin' if I didn't be his alone, then he'd jump, and . . . swear on the Bible, Cap'm Alan, 'twas all I could do not t'give him a push!"

"Maybe you should have," Lewrie said, laughing.

"T'other girls'd complained about him, an' after I told 'Mother' Batson about that, she told him he wasn't welcome no more, thank God," Tess said with a forlorn look for a moment. She took a pensive bite of her sandwich and slowly chewed.

"Not the sort t'take 'no' for an answer, though, I take it?" he asked.

"Bob an' them say they can spot him, lurkin' in th' street most nights," Tess said with a shiver, "him an' his 'man.' I haven't been able t'go out with 'Mother' Batson, since."

"They let you out?" Lewrie enquired, imagining the possibilities.

"This house don't keep no slaves, Cap'm Alan," Tess bragged. "If we need t'go shoppin', see a show or somethin', 'Mother' will take us, with a couple o' th' burly lads, o' course. We can't be stylish, elegant, nor fetchin' in th' same ol' clothes all th' time. We're closed of a Sunday, o' course, and wot 'Mother' calls 'dark' on Mondays, just like th' theatres. Used t'be an actress, 'Mother' was.

"Would ye like t'meet me away from here sometime?" Tess coyly teased. "Come t'yer lodgin's? 'Mother' *lets* us, does she trust us."

"I don't think the Madeira Club'd admit ladies, even were they proper wives," Lewrie said with a chuckle of amusement.

"That's where ye lodge, is it?" she whispered. "No matter, for there's so many hotels an' taverns with rooms t'let. I'd walk out with *you*, Cap'm Alan . . . even does that mad Roosky bastard follow us all th' way. I'd be safe with *you*.

"Fact o' th' matter . . . ," Tess cooed, leaning her head on his shoulder, putting an arm round his back. "There's gentlemen, an' there's *real* gentlemen, like you, an' do I have my druthers, I'd be with you fer tuppence, an' leave an earl fingerin' his purse. I like you, Alan Lewrie. An', 'fore God I like th' way ye bed me . . . like ye care, do I feel. . . ." Before he could begin to pooh-pooh that notion, Tess was kissing him again, this time lightly, fondly . . . almost dreamily. Even with bread crumbs on her lips, it was . . . sweet.

"We'll see about walkin' you out," Lewrie told her, putting on a wide, amusing grin, "once we know this Russky bastard's no more threat to you, hmm? I know some people," he hinted darkly. "For now, though . . . could I reserve you for all tomorrow night?"

"Ye could come early for th' supper, an' all!" Tess gaily said, all but clapping her hands; though Lewrie sensed a false note to her enthusiasm, as if she was secretly disappointed that he'd not squire her about in public, not right away, at least. She looked him over a bit, as if sizing up the heft of his purse, the status of his accounts. Perhaps she'd read the tracts or newspaper articles, which had touched on his long string of captures, and the scent of *much* prize-money. . . .

Don't care what she says, she ain't givin' it away for free! he cautioned himself; *She's most like schemin' for a place of her own, an' me her only patron, and I can't afford that . . . poor, hopeful thing.*

" 'Tis only three guineas, th' ev'nin'," she told him, her head cocked to see how he reacted to that, "with champagne an' vittles late at night, like now, extra, o' course."

"I'd call that a *toppin'* bargain!" Lewrie cheered, giving her a hug. "What time should I be here for the supper?"

"Starts at seven," Tess told him, looking relieved and pleased. "I'll be all prettied up for ye. More makeup than now."

"You don't need false artifice, Tess," he declared. "You're as handsome as any ever I did see, just the way you are."

"La, ye're th' gallant man." She chuckled. "Go on with yer fine self. 'Long as ye prefer me so, though . . . "

They finished their sandwiches, drained the last drops from the champagne bottle, and slipped back under the covers, her robe spread on the top of the blankets and coverlet. London's church bells rang two in the morning, and Lewrie yawned, his eyes beginning to feel gritty.

"Ye wish t'sleep now, Alan?" Tess asked, about half out of it herself. " 'Fore that . . . could ye lock th' door, again, an' slide th' chest t'block it? It'd make me feel safer," she asked in a wee voice.

He borrowed her too-small robe for a moment, went about the cold room snuffing candles, sliding the chest before the door and locking it with the key, then slipped back into bed with her. She came to him to drape across him as he embraced her; a hard squeeze from him, another from Tess, and a happy sigh in the dark after he'd snuffed the candle on the night-stand as she nuzzled and burrowed her head into the hollow of his shoulder.

Half-drunk, nigh fucked out . . . yet, Lewrie thought, head swimming. No, all he wanted then was to sleep for real, sleep warm with a warm girl next to him. A girl who was already breathing with her lips parted on his shoulder. *Give it a rest,* he chid himself; *give her one, too. There's always t'morrow mornin' . . . and t'morrow night.*

CHAPTER EIGHTEEN

What the bloody Hell am I gettin' myself into? he asked himself after breakfast at the Madeira Club, a somewhat hot bath and a change of clothes, a shave, and a half-hour tussle with Toulon and Chalky in his rooms; after they'd gotten over their sulks that he'd not spent the night in his own bed, he was beginning to feel human again.

Much refreshed, Lewrie trotted down to the Common Rooms to give the newspapers a gander, nodding good mornings to the other lodgers. He requested a cup of coffee, then picked among the pile of dailies that his fellow clubmembers had already read. He picked *The Morning Post* first, looking for Mrs. Denby's "Tattler" article, though it was hard to find.

Newspapers crammed items together much like a stew; onions next to broth, meat sunk beneath the oatmeal. The type font style and size was unvarying, with only the briefest separation 'tween the end of one and the beginning of the next, each headed by only the vaguest notices as to what each contained, with nothing standing out and shouting its importance; all, of course, intermixed with advertisements of the same sort, with only the rarest, and expensive, wood-cut illustration. One usually saw illustrations only in penny-tracts and pamphlets, not newspapers. One thing stood out, though . . .

"Jesus Christ!" Lewrie yelped as he got to the middle of the first page. Despite the ink smudges caused by previous readers' hands, he could make out that the government had fallen!

The Prime Minister, William Pitt (the Younger, he was called, as opposed to Pitt the Elder, now Earl of Chatham, his father who had preceded him in that office), had *resigned*! "Twigg was right," Lewrie muttered. "He really meant it."

The Morning Post speculated that a new government would be formed by Lord Addington, who would assume the office of Prime Minister at once. The King would request him to form a new cabinet which, *The Post* assured readers from their sources, would contain the Earl of Elgin as the new Lord Chancellor, Lord Hawkesbury as Foreign Secretary, and Lord Hobart would replace Sir Henry Dundas as Secretary of State for War.

"Admiralty . . . Admiralty," Lewrie hungrily growled in impatience. He scanned down the page, flitting from line to line—stumbling into an advertisement for ladies' hats before jumping to the top of the next column. " 'Old Jarvy,' by God!" he chortled as he found the speculated name. "I know him . . . and he don't *despise* me! Pray God he serves!"

Admiral the Earl St. Vincent, Sir John Jervis prior to his victory and elevation to the peerage, had been in command of the Mediterranean Fleet since 1797, then in command of Channel Fleet, since. Only one drawback stood in the way of "Old Jarvy's" acceptance of the office; he had been at sea for bloody years on end, in all weathers, and might be so broken in health—he was no "spring chicken," as Lewrie's North Carolina wife could colloquially say—that he'd rather come ashore to *retire*, not take on responsibility for the *whole* Royal Navy.

Lewrie almost gnawed a thumb-nail in fret, wondering whether he should write him that very morning, and send the letter to Portsmouth before Jervis even decided, or, whether to send it to Admiralty, hoping it would be the first thing the man opened and read upon taking charge. A letter to Portsmouth might cross Jervis's path, and miss him; one to Admiralty might get shuffled into the *bottom* of a vast pile of correspondence, if not outright tossed in the dustbin by a departing secretary, for the principal two secretaries to Admiralty kept their lucrative government posts at the pleasure of the First Lord, and the current head of the Navy, Lord Spencer, had no love for Lewrie; of that he was *damned* sure.

Get my best uniform sponged an' pressed, for later, Lewrie decided, realising that haste would serve no purpose; *And, get the cat-hairs off.*

He moved on to *The Times, The Chronicle, The Gazette,* and *The*

Marine Chronicle; the only copy of *The Courier* was last evening's and would have nothing to offer. All of them seemed to have spoken to the same anonymous sources in government, and cited the same names of new ministers expected to form the new government.

The Times speculated even further as to *why* Pitt had resigned. It was over Catholic Emancipation, of course. Public office, seats in Commons, military or naval commissions required adherence to the established Church of England; Catholics and Jews were barred from holding offices. Muslims, Jains, Hindoos, perhaps even some of the oddest of the Dissenter sects were barred, as well, for all Lewrie knew. People in the Army's ranks could rise to Sergeants-Major, people in the Navy could rise as high as Boatswain, or hold Admiralty *Warrant*, whatever their faith, but to hold *command* posts, well . . . ! Pitt and the King had come to logger-heads over it, and King George's stubborness had won. As Defender of the Faith, the King would brook no innovations in time of war against a heathen, pagan, anti-religious foe such as the Republican, Levelling French.

"Just as well," Lewrie grunted to himself. "No place in the gun-room for Whirlin' Dervishes, or even home-grown Druids . . . with or without paintin' themselves blue. Damme."

His hands, his fingertips were nigh-black with ink smudges, and his coffee was cold. "Uhm, Spears . . . a fresh, hot coffee, and a wet hand towel, if ye please."

He (gingerly) returned to *The Morning Post*, delving further into it, past the front page, in search of something labelled "Tattler."

"Aha!" he chortled when he found it, buried on page six. Court doings, scandals, upcoming Bills of Divorcement rumoured 'twixt unhappy spouses—mostly for adultery, which would make such salacious reading in the near future; there were publishers who would obtain the transcripts and print them up for sale as mild pornography for those who got their jollies from such accounts.

> Last night in Ranelagh Gardens there occurred a contretemps between one of our Naval Heroes, mentioned prominently in the news of late, and a wealthy lady of Greek extraction now residing in London, engaged in the overseas currant trade . . . "

Now there was a slur; Trade was *not* a gentlemanly endeavour and for a *woman* to run such a business was even worse a mortal error to Society's mores, even were she English-born, and to be *Greek,* well . . . !

Oh, Mrs. Denby had done him proud, Lewrie decided after finishing the article. Tears, a hint of a scandal, false charges of paternity, with prominent note taken of Lewrie's supposition that her late husband had quickened the child in question, and *those letters* sent in jealous spite . . . perhaps by a *mad* woman! Confrontation before her doors, loud protestations of condemnation for her actions . . . Theoni was, Lewrie smugly thought, ruined in London! Mrs. Denby had even interviewed last night's witnesses for anonymous comment after he'd gone, as if to spread jam—currant jam—on this particularly savoury duff. Outraged amusement was the carefully selected consensus opinion, with much sympathy for the "un-named Naval Hero" and his tortured wife, and nothing but loathing and revulsion for the perpetrator!

His fresh coffee came, and a wet hand towel with which he wiped his fingers. A moment later, another club servant approached with a note. Lewrie flicked it open, noting the initials TKC pressed into the wax seal. It was from Theoni, in her own hand for once, not the maid-servant who'd penned her poisonous letters, so the English syntax was a little hard to follow.

Beg for forgiveness . . . leave Caroline for her? he read in silent astonishment; *Good God, the woman might be* truly *mad! Think about "our" son, mine arse!*

"There be a reply, sir?" the servant softly asked, coughing into his fist. "There's a messenger waitin'."

"No, no reply," Lewrie snapped, crumpling the note in his fist.

He sipped his coffee slowly, a tad worried (it here must be noted) that Theoni might sue him for paternity; she certainly had the money to do so, and that would mean the rest of his life tied up in Chancery Court, where lawyers made bloody *millions* off the carcasses of their clients! Would she dare risk exposing herself, and the boy, to *public* certainty, instead of rumours and guesses about her identity?

Hadn't thought o' that, Lewrie ruefully mused; *But it* seemed *like a hellish-good idea, at the time. Christ shit on a . . .*

"Another note, sir," the same servant said with another cough.

"Bloody . . . !" Lewrie fumed, tearing this one open.

I did not imagine you to be quite so clever, sir, to expose your tormentor so quickly and adroitly. In celebration, might you dine with me at the chop-house in Savoy St. and The Strand at One O'clock? There are certain Considerations anent your actions that must be

discussed, as well as the amazing news of the Change in Govern-
ment. Please reply.

Twigg

"Meanin', he thought of lawsuits before I did, damn his blood," Lewrie muttered, scowling at the clock atop the mantel, then at the waiting servant. "The gentleman's runner is waitin'? Good. Tell him that I'll be pleased to accept the invitation to dine at the time and place proposed."

"Very good, sir."

By God, I do get tired o' runnin' t'Twigg t'save mine arse, he thought, squirming 'twixt dread, embarrassment; *Who knows* what *I'll end up owin' him? My first-born son? Patrons're s'posed t'be* nice *people!*

BOOK 2

Surge et adversa impetu
perfringe solito. Nunc tuum nulli imparem
animum malo resume, nunc magna tibi
virtute agendum est—

Up! And with thy
wonted force break through adversity. Now
get back thy courage which was ne'er unequal
to any hardship; now must thou greatly'
play the man.

–Lucius Annaeus Seneca
Hercules Furens, 1278-78

CHAPTER NINETEEN

*M*omentous news," Mr. Twigg simpered, dabbing his lips with his napkin as the soup course was removed. "I told you Pitt's administration would fall. It was only a matter of timing, do you see. And to resign over such a trifling matter, too."

"I'm sure Catholic Emancipation was close to his heart," Lewrie said. "God knows why. Perhaps he'd only sold the Act of Union to the Irish with such a promise. And what he'd promised to his own faction for *them* to back it . . . ," he added with a shrug.

"Which promises to his own faction he most certainly could never keep, either," Twigg interjected with a faint, thin-lipped smile. "They assuredly knew that Emancipation was a bootless endeavour from the very start, and shammed their support for it, knowing that the King's opposition to it would be its undoing. And Pitt's."

"Maybe he was just tired," Lewrie said.

"Or, looked to be at the end of his tether to his contemporaries . . . those hungry for his place, and higher positions," Twigg said with a sardonic cock of one brow. "The old and sick king-wolf *always* succumbs to the pack, in the end. Torn to shreds, his throat ripped out by the younger and stronger."

With his bemused smile Twigg looked as if he liked his simile, and would be partial to witnessing such an event. He'd always been a cold, bloodthirsty sort when necessary.

"Well, I am certain *your* odds have improved, Lewrie, with Jervis as First Lord of the Admiralty," Twigg breezed on as a waiter carried in some nicely browned squabs on rice.

"Depending on who serves him as First and Second Secretary, and how they feel about me," Lewrie pointed out.

"I do believe that Sir Evan Nepean will stay on," Twigg told him. "As will Marsden as Second."

"Then I'm still up t'my neck in the quag," Lewrie groused.

"Speaking of . . . ," Twigg said with a twinkle in his eye. "I suppose you've given your letters to the lady in question a thought."

"Hmm?" Lewrie replied, a glass of *sauvignon blanc* by his mouth.

"No, you haven't," Twigg said with a heavy, disappointed sigh. "Is Mistress Connor of a mind to get revenge in court . . . "

"Chancery, most-like," Lewrie gloomed.

"Ahem! As I said, is she of a mind, and, has she saved all your letters to her over the years . . . as I strongly suspect she has . . . then they could prove to be damning evidence that the affair was mutual, and that you *are* the father of her bastard. Protestations of lust, love . . . "

"I ain't *that* stupid!" Lewrie shot back. "Learned that from my father. Never put anything in writing ye don't wish made known later. *Especially* when it comes to women! False-promise, broken troths, belly pleas, and all that? Far as I can recall, I was chatty and pleasant, but I *never* made any sort of claim the boy was mine."

"Well, I *might've* asked of his health and progress, just as I did about her first-born," Lewrie added. "Family friend or *god*-father to the git, nothing more than that."

"And did you save hers?" Twigg pressed, scowling.

"Not a bit of it!" Lewrie told him. "Gone t'cat litter long ago."

"Well, that's something, I suppose," Twigg said, leaning back in his chair and swirling his wine glass idly. "One could not expect you to be *that* huge a calf-headed cully, no matter how desirable the lady. Or how eminently bed-able."

"Should I take that as a back-handed compliment?" Lewrie asked.

"*I'd* not," Twigg replied.

"Hmm," Lewrie gravelled at the back-handed *insult*. "Oh, by the by . . . last night I ran across something interesting you might wish to look into. About some daft, drunken Russian here in London."

"A Russian, d'ye say. Hmm," Twigg mused between bites.

"Some 'nabob' who calls himself a count. Anatoli, or something like that," Lewrie breezed on, between bites of his own squab and rice. "Damned fool took a strong liking to a whore at 'Mother' Batson's house and broke in past her pugs t'get to her. Must've run out of 'tin' for the 'socket-fee.' Beastly sort, I heard. Just *won't* do it regular . . . goes for the 'windward passage,' un-armoured, too, can he get away with it. Got himself and his manservant thrashed to blood puddings, by the sound of it. Mean t'say . . . what's a mad Russian count doin', runnin' free in London, and us about to send a fleet t'smash 'em?"

"So you *heard*," Twigg said, putting down his knife and fork and looking down that long nose of his most skeptically. "By word of mouth or by ear at the scene?"

"Well . . . " Lewrie flummoxed.

"You simply *can't* keep your breeches buttoned, can you, Lewrie?" Twigg resignedly asked.

"It's a *damned* good *house*," Lewrie pointed out. "Even my prosecuting attorney was there . . . the top-lofty bastard. *And* an M.P. close to the Progressives and the abolitionists, to boot. I'd gotten there early enough, I might've run cross a *bishop* in their parlour! Or the Prince of Wales."

"Oh, I am certain it comes *highly* recommended," Twigg sneered. He did, though, reach into a breast pocket for a slip of paper and a pencil, and scribbled something down.

" 'Mother' Batson's . . . or Anatoli?" Lewrie dared to jape. "As for recommendations, might I give you the girl's name, too?"

"You are *too* amusing, Lewrie," Twigg retorted with a faint snarl.

"I do my humble best," Lewrie said, lifting his wine glass in a mock toast. "Damme, but this is good. My barrister and I dined here before Christmas . . . so long as I footed the bill . . . and their food is excellent."

"Ahem," Twigg grumped, as if to shush him; or stop his gob long enough to get a word in. "Did you *see* this Anatoli? Could you describe him, or point him out later?"

"No, I only heard him battlin' his way up the stairs, him and his man . . . Sasha, or Pasha, or something like that," Lewrie told him. "I was on the third floor, and they only got to the second before 'Mother' Batson's bully-bucks stopped 'em. He's a young fellow, though. He was attending Oxford, as late as the last term, 'til he came down to London and never went back. He's lucky he didn't end up a naked corpse found floatin' in the Thames. Bad *cess* on the house, I s'pose . . . murderin' a *ti-tled* shit . . . even a *Russian* titled shit . . . and havin' it traced back to you."

"Thrashed rather badly, was he?" Twigg asked after a long period of brooding silence, his brows knit together.

"I'd expect," Lewrie said with another shrug and another sip of his wine.

"And where *is* this house of ill repute?" Twigg asked him, with his paper and pencil out, again.

"In Panton Street . . . where all the foreign emissaries live, and keep their mistresses," Lewrie informed him with a sly wink. "I'd have thought you'd have the whole street full of informers."

"Perhaps not as scrupulously as we might," Twigg said in a softer, more conspiratorial voice. "Usually, one watcher, at least, would have noted the disturbance in Panton Street and would have reported it. Though . . . did it occur past midnight, perhaps his report has not yet been read.

"Sure this fellow was a Russian, Lewrie?" Twigg asked, his head cocked over like a robin listening for a worm . . . and looking dubious, as he usually did when Lewrie was involved.

"The girl swore he was, and I definitely heard Russian," Lewrie told him. "*Pamajeetyeh* . . . that's 'help,' and, uhm . . . *viy mojetyeh mnyeh pamoch*? That's 'can I get some help?'" Lewrie carefully pronounced, syllable by syllable. "Along with the usual *pryaznis* and *gryaznis* and *yob tvoyemats* . . . the usual insults," he said with a tight grin of possibly knowing something that Mr. Twigg didn't. "'Fuck your mother,' 'you dirty this, you filthy that,' and 'peasant.'"

"Ah, but your association with Mistress Eudoxia Durschenko, and her *equally* charming father, have broadened your linguistic skills," Twigg simpered back, with an evil little grin to match his. It didn't last, of course, and vanished in an eyeblink. Twigg took a sip of his wine and turned his attention to his plate.

"So . . . what are you to do, now that Admiral the Earl Saint Vincent will take over Admiralty?" Twigg asked, changing from calculating to cheerful in another eyeblink, his eyes glued to his knife and fork.

Hallo, what's this? Lewrie was forced to wonder; *I know him too damned well. Since when's he ever played the "Merry Andrew" with me? Not without an ulterior motive, he ain't!*

"Assumin' he'll accept," Lewrie said pessimistically.

"I assure you he will," Twigg said, and to foozle Lewrie even further, he actually tipped him a "chummy" wink!

There's a dead Roosky in the near future, Lewrie determined; *or I'm a Turk in a turban. Did I stumble on a foreign spy for him? Soon t'be found with his throat slit in Saint Giles?*

"He's been at sea so long, he wants a shore position? Is that your thinking?" Lewrie asked, playing along.

"That, and the lure of enough power over the Navy to weed out all the graft and corruption in the victualling, arming, and upkeep of the Fleet . . . its sailors most importantly," Twigg breezily said, with knife and fork poised at mid-chest. "Jervis has fumed about it for years. Given a chance to shake the Navy's administration like a rag rug, from top to bottom . . . *and,* ashore as you said, in relative comfort for the first time in years, well . . . consider it a done thing."

Twigg bestowed upon Lewrie a *very* chummy smile, the sort that made his skin crawl, and foreign opponents shiver in sudden dread.

"Thank God for that, then," Lewrie said with a glad sigh. One thing about Twigg; when he gave you a promise, you could bank on it. And as Lewrie felt some sense of assurance regarding his career's revival, he also felt a swell of relief that Twigg had nothing more to do with his chances with Lord St. Vincent . . . and that he wouldn't end up *working* for the skeletal old murderer.

"You said you know him well, Lewrie?" Twigg casually enquired.

"We've *met* a time or two," Lewrie had to admit. "Not as close as cater-cousins, no, but I *think* I'm still in good odour with him."

"A word of advice, then, sir," Twigg said, resuming that lofty and smugly superior air of a man so well connected that his very word was Gospel to the less well informed . . . like Lewrie. "Saint Vincent is a very early riser, I am told, with great disdain for the slug-a-beds and lay-abouts. Were I you, once he's officially installed at Admiralty, I'd be knocking at the doors at the crack of dawn . . . scrubbed up and shiny as a bright new penny. A *sober* new penny."

"Bright-eyed and bushy-tailed," Lewrie added, and took delight to see Twigg puzzled. "A Colonial North Carolina expression. American."

"However you wish to phrase, it, yayss," Twigg drawled, leaning back in only *mild* scorn for the abusing of the King's English. "Now I have smoaked out your tormentor, and you have exposed Mistress Theoni Kavares Connor to the complete scorn of London Society . . . have you informed your good wife, of yet?"

"Well, it only happened last night, and . . . "

"And you were celebrating with a fetching young wench, yayss," Twigg scoffed. "No matter . . . as I promised, news of this, welcome though it may be, would best be delivered by me first. I shall coach to Anglesgreen before the week is out, and, once returned, inform you as to how my revelation was received. Time enough after that to write her," Twigg lifted his wine glass in Lewrie's direction, delivering yet *another* of those cheerful smiles.

"My thanks again to you, Mister Twigg," Lewrie said, bowing from the waist in his chair and lifting his own glass; prompted to share a glass no matter his reservations. "A glass with you, sir!"

"I am certain there shall come a time, in future, when you may find a way to repay me for my, ah . . . humble services, sir," Mr. Twigg slyly told him. "Let us not be niggardly . . . top us up a brimming measure, and I shall be delighted to have a glass with you!"

Lewrie filled their glasses; they clinked them together softly, then both tipped them back to drain them off in one go.

"Are you not equally certain that you will do me a service . . . someday . . . Captain Lewrie?" Twigg chirped, almost mischievously.

"Oh, of that I'm *mortal*-certain, Mister Twigg," Lewrie replied with a sinking feeling that his indebtedness to the old schemer just *kept* piling up, to a point that would *really* put his life on the line, for good and all!

After departing the chop-house, Lewrie ambled back to his club lodgings, stopping at the Admiral Boscawen for coffee to counteract all the toasts and shared glasses that Twigg had proposed. He was in dire need of another good nap, and a thought for supper on the town . . . somewhere.

I really shouldn't, he chid himself; *Surely, there's a whackin' good book t'read, a new play t'see, or . . . oh Hell,* he chid himself.

He went back to the brothel, of course.

CHAPTER TWENTY

*T*h' top o' th' mornin', Captain," the surly old long-time tiler at Admiralty chirped as Lewrie scurried through the archway passage in the curtain wall, underneath the winged horse statues, and quickly approached the doors. "May I say, ye're an early sort, right enough."

"Morning," Lewrie said with a nod.

"Mornin'! More like th' middle o' th' bleedin' night, sir!" the old fart barked, and wheezed out a laugh. "But, that's th' way it is round 'ere these days, an' God help th' late sleepers. Th' Waitin' Room's nigh half-full a'ready, but go on in, Captain sir, an' th' best o' luck t'ye," the tiler said, swinging a heavy oak door open for him, and tipping his hat. "Mind now, sir . . . th' jakes ain't been sweetened this early, an' they's no tea comin' 'til close t'nine."

Lewrie checked his hat and boat-cloak and mittens with the closet clerk, then shot his cuffs, re-settled his sword belt and waist-coat, and warily entered the infamous Waiting Room, *striving* for an air of sublime confidence before his contemporaries.

What a shower *o' no-hopes!* he thought as he sought a chair or a space on a hard wooden bench. The weather that morning—ten minutes shy of 7 A.M.—was brisk and wet, with a faint misty rain, and it was still cold, though not as cold as the week before. In England, it might as well be called the first harbinger of Spring, the first robin, or first crocus shoot, in comparison.

No wonder so many of the officers and Midshipmen were sniffling, hacking, and blowing their noses into handkerchiefs. There was little conversation, for the very good reason that they were all there to win an active commission, and everyone else was competition for full employment. It also seemed that few of them had served together before, either—complete strangers to each other, as they were to Lewrie. There was no one he knew in the Waiting Room.

The bad'uns are "Yellow Squadroned," and the good'uns are at sea, he sarcastically thought. A harried civilian clerk came trotting by, and Lewrie snagged his attention just long enough to hand him his note.

"A few minutes with the First Secretary . . . or the Earl, should he be in this early," Lewrie said with a false air of cheery hope.

"Oh, he is, believe me, sir!" the clerk replied with a put-upon and harried expression, before accepting the note and dashing up the stairs.

Lewrie was, in Colonial parlance, indeed "bright-eyed and bushy-tailed." Sober and clear-eyed, after but a single bottle of wine with supper, and a bedtime brandy; bathed, shaved, buffed, and polished fit to blind the unwary, from the toes of his boots to the gilt lace on his coat collar . . . and with the medals for Cape St. Vincent and Camperdown clinking on his upper chest. He had even eschewed Tess's companionship for two whole nights running, and had gotten a blissfully restful full night's sleep.

He found a seat at the end of a wooden bench, carefully sat down and crossed his legs, giving the dim-looking Midshipman seated at the other end of the bench a cheery nod, and picked up the discarded copy of *The Marine Chronicle* that lay between them. The Midshipman gulped and nodded back, rather vacantly, and snorted back an impressive dottle of snot that trailed from his larboard nostril. The lad looked to be a *born* mouth-breather, to Lewrie's lights.

By ten, his air of confidence was wearing a little thin. Others came and went; some lucky few were called abovestairs, but the bulk of them were sent on their way with sympathetic whispers from one clerk, or curt and thin-lipped dismissals from another. The tea-vendor's cart had finally made its appearance in the courtyard, but the "necessary" available for the denizens of the Waiting Room had *yet* to be emptied, and it stank like a corpse's armpit; the sort of reek that *lingered* on anyone who risked it; the sort of foul odour that turned fresh-pressed neck-stocks limp and put famished buzzards off their feed.

"Em . . . ," the more pleasant clerk shyly called, making them all shuffle their feet and look up expectantly. The vacant Midshipman at the other end of Lewrie's bench snorted back his last hour's cable of mucus and gulped aloud. "Captain Lewrie, sir? Are you present?"

"Here, my man," Lewrie announced, springing to his feet; with the fingers of his off-hand crossed for luck.

"The First Lord will see you, sir, if you'll come this way."

"Thankee kindly," Lewrie said, absolutely delighted with that glad news; yet . . . wondering what sort of reception awaited him once he'd gotten into the Earl St. Vincent's presence.

"My lord," Lewrie said, with a bow once he'd been shown into a grand private office.

"Captain Lewrie," Admiral Jervis said, rising from his chair and waving Lewrie to a chair before his massive desk. Lewrie wondered if Lord St. Vincent would stand throughout the length of the interview, or doff his wig above his head, for he had a most peculiar habit of removing his hat and holding it high in a constant salute, whether he addressed a bosun's mate or a fellow admiral. "I remember you, sir."

The good *parts, I bloody hope,* Lewrie thought.

"I am grateful that you recall me, my lord . . . and for taking some wee bit of your precious time to see me," Lewrie responded as he sat down. Yes, Admiral Jervis *would* stand. Lewrie began to rise.

"You and Nelson at Cape Saint Vincent," the Earl St. Vincent said, shoving a hand in his direction to order him to stay seated. "I think you insisted that your ship was *pushed* to break away and follow Nelson's? Even so, it was a bold gesture . . . one which checked the Dons' course long enough for the fleet to wear about. I hear you are still bold, Captain Lewrie . . . though no longer in need of pushing?"

Admiral the Earl St. Vincent, K.B., actually cracked a smile!

He had aged, of course, and gotten stouter. He wore his own hair, now nearly white and receded from a broad brow, still curly and unruly. A broad and long, almost doleful face, with the advancing wattles reflecting his age, and a round little chin, with the characteristic long, almost aquiline nose that seemed to persist among the titled, yet . . . with heavy-lidded eyes with bags under them that, at the moment, glittered with amusement.

"On my own bottom, my lord," Lewrie replied with a modest grin. "I find I'm much like Goodyer's Pig . . . never well but when in mischief."

"Notorious, more-like," Jervis commented, turning sombre. "An account of your recent trial and acquittal made its way to me. And of course, you are here, like so many others, to seek active commission."

"Ehm . . . aye, my lord," Lewrie sobered. "Though I would think it false modesty to imagine myself as a two-a-penny other."

One of "Old Jarvy's" thick eyebrows went up at that statement.

Damme, what a foolish thing t'say! Lewrie chid himself; *Now he thinks me a braggin' coxcomb!*

"I do *not* compare myself to a Troubridge, a Pellew, or Nelson, my lord," Lewrie quickly amended.

"Lord spare us another Nelson," Admiral Jervis growled.

"But I do believe that my record as a frigate captain speaks for itself," Lewrie went on. "It has been he . . . deuced hard to read of the preparations against the Baltic powers, and for the first time since the start of the war in seventeen ninety-three, to not have any role to play in the coming battles."

And what's he got against Nelson? Lewrie wondered; *His affair with Emma Hamilton? The scandal? Pray God he don't know the half of* me!

"Old Jarvy" just stared at him, though that brow was lowered to a placid, patient expression. The silence was squirmily painful. So, despite his fear of seeming to beg, Lewrie just had to fill the void.

"Command of a warship, in time of war, just may be the onliest thing I'm really good at, my lord," Lewrie confessed. "If there is any place where my services could prove useful in the coming weeks for the good of the Navy, well . . . "

"What do you think of H.M. Dockyards, Captain Lewrie?" the Earl St. Vincent said of a sudden, resting his thick fingers on the top of his desk.

"They're a pack of bloody thieves, my lord," Lewrie said, "with corruption from biscuit to artillery. Hangin' every tenth man, like the Romans decimated a cowardly legion, would screw the others honest."

"Hanging?" the Earl St. Vincent abruptly said, seeming to lean back. "Perhaps that might be a *touch* too draconian."

Oh, shit! I forgot! Lewrie chid himself, squirming despite his attempt to look calm. After the Spithead and Nore Mutinies of 1797 it was to Jervis's fleet in the Mediterranean and off the coast of Spain that the most vehement former mutinous ships, and their guiltiest men, had been assigned. Jervis had had to play the hangman, to see that the sentences of the courts-martial were carried out . . . out of sight and out of mind, as if the whole rebellious affair had been no more than a single night's drunken riot in the public mind; not the small bundle of kindling that could have ignited a nationwide revolution as bloody as that which had ravaged France in 1789.

"Three hundred lashes, then, my lord?" Lewrie substituted.

"What would you say to the notion of the dockyards threatening to stop work, is their pay not *doubled*, Lewrie?" the Earl gravelled.

"Doubled? I—"

"And, that a delegation is bound to London to press those demands upon me?" Admiral Jervis rumbled on.

"At the very least, I'd sack the lot of 'em, my lord," Lewrie told him, angered that, at such a critical time, the already well-paid dockyard workers would threaten a walk-out and cripple the fleet still hurriedly fitting out for battles in the East.

"My thoughts, exactly, sir," the Earl St. Vincent fumed, with a grim smile on his face that Zachariah Twigg might envy. "Them, and any who abetted them . . . the organisers and conspirators, to boot!"

"Damned un-patriotic of 'em, I must say, my lord," Lewrie said.

"And damn Sir Andrew Snape Hamond, into the bargain, for all of his laxness, that this matter should ever arise," Admiral Jervis fumed on. "I should bring Troubridge in to replace him, could I do so. To work *round* him at the very least."

Admiral Sir Andrew Snape Hamond had been Controller of the Navy since '94, in charge of all the various Navy Boards that supervised the dockyards and contractors supplying the Fleet. Lewrie had *heard* that Hamond had spoken up for him after *Proteus* had returned from the South Atlantic, getting him his larger frigate, HMS *Savage*, so quickly after, yet . . .

Glad Hamond ain't my real *patron, or I'd not have a* single *hope of another ship,* Lewrie thought.

"You know something of the work of the dockyards, Lewrie?" the Earl enquired. "Their management, or accounting?"

"Only to be at the receiving end of their . . . 'largesse,' " Lewrie admitted with a bleak smile, and the smile was forced, for he felt a sick feeling that whatever employment "Old Jarvy" might offer wouldn't be an active commission into a frigate, but a pen-and-ink shore post, about which he knew next-to-absolutely-nothing, and was sure he would be an utter disaster at. *Cobblers, stick t'your lasts,* Lewrie thought; *even if it's a damned narrow one. Civilian clerks'd be cheaper . . . or copyists under Nepean and Marsden.*

"Who was that young rogue who wrote the Board," the Earl mused with the slightest hint of frosty humour, "complaining of how little paint his ship had been allotted? 'Which *side* of the ship do you wish me to paint, sirs?' he asked, ha!"

"I can't recall, my lord," Lewrie replied, "though everyone I know wished he'd *been* that bold."

"No matter, then," the Earl said with a sigh. "I will enquire, Captain Lewrie. You *have* made for yourself an enviable reputation in the Navy . . . at sea, at least, hmm? In these parlous times, for you to be pent ashore on half-pay I consider a waste. I make no promises for the immediate future, mind, but . . . "

"I am grateful for your good opinion, my lord, and for keeping me in mind," Lewrie said, knowing a prompting departure line when he heard one. He got to his feet and delivered a bow. "I will take no more of your time, sir, and thankee, again, for seeing me."

Even as he reached for the door knob, there came a knocking and the bustling entrance of the dismissive, hard-faced under-clerk with a sheaf of papers, and an urgent "Out of my way" look on his phyz to claim the First Lord's attention.

Oh well, at least he saw me, Lewrie thought as he steeled himself to clomp down those stairs to the Waiting Room with a confident and self-assured air; perhaps a faint smirk in parting for the others who cooled their heels with even less hope of employment than he.

Now, what the Hell do I do with the rest of the day? he asked himself; *The week, and the* next?

CHAPTER TWENTY-ONE

*A*lan Lewrie discovered that, populous as London was, it *might* be possible for him to have spread himself a rather bit *too* wide about the town, when, in need of stationery, ink, and sealing wax, and upon shopping in the Strand one February morning, he ran into more people than he cared to know . . . at one time, and in the same one place, at least.

"Alan, me old!" Lord Peter Rushton, an old school chum, expelled at the same time from Harrow as he, came striding along the sidewalk in the opposite direction, with that ever-present *amanuensis* of his, that *seemingly* honest "Captain Sharp" Clotworthy Chute . . . another old chum from Harrow who specialised in fleecing the naïve and unwary newcomes.

"My lord," Lewrie cried back with a grin, doffing his hat and making a sketchy "leg" in answer. "How goes it in Lord's? Hallo to you, too, Clotworthy. How goes the 'gullible heir' trade?"

"Ninety-five percent dreadful-boresome, and only now and then int'restin'," Lord Peter, who now sat in the House of Lord's (napped there, mostly, during the intolerably long debates), said back.

"Main-well, old son" was Clotworthy's puckish reply as he rubbed his mittened hands together, grinning like an apple-cheeked cherub. "Main-well, altogether. I see you're still 'anchored,' as it were? So sorry. Though the London Season's been a joy, I'd imagine."

"I met with the Earl Saint Vincent last week, and it *sounded* promisin', but . . . ," Lewrie said with a shrug.

"Em, Alan . . . ," Lord Peter said with a leer. "Now you're done with that Greek creature, might you mind did I, ah . . . ?"

"Saw her, did ye?" Lewrie teased.

"At the theatre, before you saw her off," Rushton said, leaning closer. "Great God, what *tits* she has!"

"What'd your *wife* say t'that, hey?" Lewrie asked, a brow cocked.

"Same as yours, I'd imagine," Lord Peter haw-hawed. "Act'lly, I and she *prefer* sep'rate residences, now there's two male heirs afoot. Christ, who'da thought such a sweet chick'd turn so termagant so *quick*. Clotworthy here's the right idea . . . he don't purchase, he only *rents* for a time. Damme, have you turned hermit on us, Alan? We haven't seen hide nor hair of you since the trial was over. Where've you been keeping yourself?"

"*Know* ya don't gamble, but we thought you'd turn up at some of the better public clubs," Clotworthy seemed to complain.

"Well, there's the Abolitionist crowd," Lewrie began to explain. "Call a dog like me a good name, and it's risky to lose . . . "

"*Kapitan* Lewrie! *Zdrazvotyeh!* Hello to you!"

"Erp?" was Lewrie's comment as he turned about to see Eudoxia Durschenko alighting from a hired coach a few yards up the Strand, a fur-swathed vision of a winter princess, her lustrous dark hair spilling over the collar of a white ermine coat that reached to her ankles, yet open to reveal a rich dark-red gown.

"Bugger Theoni Connor, I'll take *her*," Lord Peter muttered in awe.

"Mistress Durschenko," Lewrie said, doffing his hat and bowing greetings as she strode up to them, the proper "graceful glide" bedamned. "How delightful to meet you again."

"You do not ride in park in the mornings?" Eudoxia said with a fetching pout as she dropped him a curtsy at last. "Do not tell me it is too cold for English gentlemen," she said with a teasing laugh.

"Some Navy business, of late," Lewrie explained. "Gentlemen, allow me to name to you Mistress Eudoxia Durschenko, of the world famous Wigmore's Peripatetic Extravaganza. Mistress Durschenko . . . this fellow is Viscount Draywick, Lord Peter Rushton . . . and our old school friend, Mister Clotworthy Chute."

"Ahem!" came a disapproving cough, and there was Eudoxia's papa, the lanky, one-eyed old devil, Arslan Artimovich Durschenko, again.

Lewrie doffed his hat to the old fart, forcing a smile; which courtesy Arslan answered with a sniff of disgust. Knowing the man's distaste for royalty of any country, Lewrie took a little savage joy in introducing him, too.

"Ah! You are the magnificent bareback rider, and archer, from the circus!" Lord Peter exclaimed. "Saw your performance *several* times before Christmas, haw haw! Said at the time, Mistress Durschenko was the most amazing of them all, didn't I, Clotworthy?"

"'Deed ya did, my lord," Clotworthy assured her. "Delighted to make your acquaintance, the both of you. And you're the lion-tamer chap, are ya not, sir?"

"*Da*" was her father's laconic answer.

"We are in winter quarters now, in Southwark," Eudoxia said in pleasure, "but still do dramas and comedies. Circus begin in Spring."

"Well, shall we all have tea?" Lord Peter suggested, simply oozing innocent charm.

"I be delighted," from Eudoxia.

"*Nyet,*" from her papa, looking like he wished to spit.

"I should toddle along," from Lewrie, locking eyes with him.

"Nonsense," from Lord Peter.

"Capital idea!" Clotworthy exclaimed.

"Pooh, *Kapitan* Lewrie!" Eudoxia coaxed. "Is *perfect* raw day for hot tea. We see so little of you," she added with a lovely *moue*.

"As have we," from Lord Peter. "Seen so little of him, haw! I insist, Alan old son. Come along!"

"Well . . . "

"Grr," from Papa Durschenko, and the sound of irregular yellow teeth grinding.

"Now, isn't this lovely," Lord Peter Rushton enthused once they were all seated round a large table near the fireplace of a fashionable tea- and coffee-house a block down from their mutual encounter. Unlike most coffee-houses that catered strictly to men and their newspapers, this one canted more to sticky buns, pies, puddings, duffs, trifles, and jam cakes. It was warm, dry, filled with several delicious aromas of baking goodies . . . and positively awash in ladies and children out and about their shopping.

"Uhmm, tea is good!" Eudoxia commented, amazing everyone by

stirring a large spoonful of jam into her cup. "Is very Russian, far sweet in tea," she perkily explained, "sugar not always av . . . available, so use honey or jam. In Russia, tea brewed in big *samovar*, and served in glasses with metal holders. *Very* strong, very hot."

"How fascinating," Lord Peter remarked, causing even Clotworthy Chute to discreetly roll his eyes. "So tell me——"

"Brave *Kapitan* Lewrie soon go to Russia, he brings back proper tea glasses, yes?" Eudoxia asked, turning to Lewrie.

"Don't know as I'll take part," Lewrie had to admit, shrugging as if it really didn't matter to him. "I still need appointment to a ship."

"Oh, pooh, you will get," Eudoxia assured him, blithely confident, and at her most captivating. "You go fight the Tsar, though, you will need warm furs. *Ochyen kalodni*! *Very* cold, the winter. And not warm 'til *late* in Spring. Not have furs, could catch your death."

"Freeze solid as *tree, da*!" Papa Durschenko added with a nasty grin, happily contemplating such a fate.

"Should we order some cakes?" Lord Peter suggested. "My treat."

"Would that make up for all the 'tatties' you cadged off me at school, my lord?" Lewrie teased. Both Rushton and Chute ever had been "skint," no matter their families' reputed wealth, while at Harrow, so Lewrie had learned to be leery of their appetites. Even after inheriting the title, rents, and acres once his elder brother had been carried off by an unfortunate *mayonnaise*-based "made dish" gone bad, that the proper heir's fiancée had cobbled together, there hadn't been all *that* much real income . . . not after Lord Peter, and Clotworthy, had squandered a respectable pile of "tin" on their ill-timed Grand Tour of the Continent (right in the middle of the war!), and Lewrie had heard some rumours that Lady Draywick, Peter's wife, was the daughter of an incredibly wealthy wool merchant with Army contracts, one of those "new-made" commoner families with aspirations to the peerage. These days, though, wealth made in Trade was everywhere, and, like most marriages, it was a canny arrangement for both sides.

"I doubt a *year* o' suppers would make recompence, hey, Clotworthy?" Peter guffawed. "Here, waiter."

The bell suspended over the door tinkled, and another party entered the coffee-house. Lewrie looked up and blanched.

Christ! he thought; *Ye gonna walk out, why pick* this *place, and why right bloody* now!

Mrs. Batson, the "Mother Abbess," in company with a brace of her whores, with Bob the bully-buck waiter and former boxer playing a role as escort and package bearer, came bustling in, chirping gay as magpies . . . and one of them was Tess!

A million people in London, they tell me, and yet . . . ! he gawped.

He had not, in point of fact, visited Mrs. Batson's brothel in almost a week, hadn't seen Tess in much more than a dressing gown and some slinky stuff . . . or the altogether! . . . and the transformation was nighblinding. Her hair had been styled by a dresser into springy ringlets to frame her face, the centre part now gone, replaced with girlish bangs upon her forehead, and its colour enhanced more toward strawberry blond, with a wee bonnet perched atop her upswept hair.

A puff-sleeved and high-waisted gown, with a very low-cut *décolletage*, very stylish and striking, with a modest muslin overskirt and an embroidered silk stole . . . to a casual observer, Tess was gowned as fine as an heiress, yet as *respectable* as a bishop's daughter. They'd done something with her toilet, too, the wee-est hint of rouge or paint, the faintest enhancement of her lips. . . . Why, she was *delectably* pretty!

She nodded to him, could not restrain a fond, excited, yet shy, smile as a servant took their outer coats and led them to a table.

"Ah-hmm," Lord Peter faintly croaked.

"Hmm," Clotworthy commented over the rim of his tea cup, as if making an appreciative "yummy."

"Aah . . . ," Lewrie let slip, discreetly nodding and smiling back.

"*Kraseevi*," even Papa Durschenko whispered.

"Papa!" Eudoxia chid him. "At your age! *Da*, she *is* beautiful, but *much* too young for you."

"*Nyeh malyenkee byelakoori, dyevachka*," Arslan Artimovich growled back good-naturedly. "*Bolshoi krasni galava*," he said, winking and lifting his hands as if hefting something. Lewrie took a second look, and deduced, though he knew very little Russian, that the old devil was more taken by a slightly older red-head, with an impressively hefty set of "cat-heads" and a seductive leer on her face.

"Papa!" Eudoxia tittered, a trifle embarrassed.

Bolshoi, that's "big," Lewrie puzzled out; *and I know* krasni *is "red", . . .* galava *must mean red-head, together?* Nyeh *is "not" . . . what?*

"*Mal-yenk-ee byel . . .* ?" he asked Eudoxia.

"Means 'little blonde,' " Eudoxia explained as the waiter returned to take their orders.

"Only nat'ral," Lord Peter tut-tutted, hoisting his tea cup in salute to her father.

"You think little blonde is pretty?" Eudoxia asked with a sweet smile on her face, yet with one brow arched.

"Well, I s'pose," Lewrie said, with a shrug. "If one likes that sort." He tried *very* hard not to squirm under her knowing gaze.

"Poor thing is *ryebyonak*," Eudoxia said with a sniff, turning to take a quick squint at the other table. "Little more than child . . . *shesnatsat eelee syemnatsat*, uhm . . . sixteen or seventeen?"

"Grack!" Lewrie commented, strangling on a sip of tea, and nigh to spewing a mouthful on the cheery tablecloth. "Indeed? Sorry. Must have gone down the wrong hawse pipe."

"Girls look like, ah . . . ," Eudoxia told him, leaning close so she could whisper close to Lewrie's ear. "*Prostitukas*. Girls of evening?"

"Really!" Lewrie exclaimed, pretending to be shocked.

"London is *fill* with . . . such," Eudoxia said, struggling for the proper word allowed in public. "We go to pleasure gardens, theatres . . . walk down street, they are everywhere in *bolshoi* number."

"Godless city," Papa Durschenko said with distaste; though his eyes were glued to the Rubenesque red-head's bosom. "Godless country. Not like Russia."

"In a respectable coffee-house?" Lord Peter feigned outrage, as well. "What *is* the world comin' to?"

From such a source, such primness was so unimaginable that Lewrie almost brayed out loud; though he did note that Lord Peter's attention was torn 'twixt Eudoxia and Tess in equal measure. He was all but fingering his crutch, could he have got away with it before children!

"Furs, d'ye say," Lewrie piped up, swivelling to face Eudoxia. "I note you and your father are very well garbed. Did you bring them from Russia, or did you find them here in London?"

"Oh, furs from Russia very old, now," she said, smiling again. "Circus and comedies so suc . . . successful, we find new. A furrier in Hudson Bay Company, in Haymarket, has *beautiful* furs! I help you shop for them, yes *Kapitan* Alan?"

"*Gryaʒni tarakan*," her father growled. Lewrie knew that'un by heart; "filthy cockroach!" he meant. The one-eyed devil glared daggers, and one hand was suspiciously near his waistband.

"I couldn't impose," Lewrie quickly said.

"Such an expressive language, Russian," Lord Peter dithered on. "Tell me, sir . . . what did you just say?"

"Have to practice acts . . . rehearse, I tell her," Papa Durschenko lied, his grin so feral that Peter leaned back a bit in his chair. "No time for shopping."

"All that in two words, hah," Clotworthy said with a shake of his head. "Impressive."

"Russian short and direct," Arslan Artimovich replied.

"Dangerous fellow, her father?" Lord Peter Rushton asked Lewrie, once they'd taken their leave and had repaired to a tavern that served much-needed restorative drink.

"Cut yer throat for tuppence," Lewrie assured him, between sips of a calming brandy. "Determined the girl *dies* a virgin, I think, and most-like'll be in the bed-chamber on her weddin' night, t'see does it go his way . . . or else."

"So you *haven't*, um . . . ?" Rushton asked, amazed.

"Wouldn't even chance it, 'less he croaks first," Lewrie admitted.

"Oh, rum go," Clotworthy said with a sigh. "Still, . . . the girl *does* seem took by you, Alan. Even if there's no future in it."

"Might prove a challenge," Lord Peter mused.

"Don't even *think* it, Peter!" Clotworthy cautioned. If anyone in London was familiar with the truly dangerous, it was Chute, and the old devil had put the wind up *him*. "Go for the chamin' little whore, instead . . . the *other'un* so took with Alan, here."

"You rogue, sir!" Rushton hooted. "Yes, I noted she had eyes for you. No *wonder* we ain't seen him since the trial. A *delectable* young beauty. Wherever did ya find her, Alan?"

Lewrie didn't *want* to tell him, of a sudden, even if Tess was only a whore. Oft as he'd sworn that he'd have made a topping pimp . . .

"Come come, now . . . don't make me depend on Clotworthy to ferret her out," Rushton pressed with an expectant leer. "Which brothel's she in, and what's her fee?"

"Dare ye risk bein' seen in a brothel, Peter?" Lewrie countered. "The wife, and all . . . your seat in Lord's, and reputation?"

"Oh, tosh!" Rushton laughed. "Easier for me than you, old son. Damme, I'm a *peer*! Ev'ryone knows how things stand 'twixt me and the wife. It's *expected* of my sort. Did whoring or keeping a mistress on the side make the *slightest* diff'rence, there wouldn't be the *tenth* of a quorum left in Lord's . . . only those who've outlived their cocks, and I sometimes wonder 'bout *them*!

"Seriously, Alan," Peter continued, all atwinkle, "it ain't like we haven't shared and shared alike before. Where can I sample her, and what does she cost?"

" 'Mother' Batson's . . . a new place in Panton Street," Lewrie reluctantly told him, knowing that Clotworthy Chute *could* smoak her out by suppertime, anyway. "Her name's Tess. New-come from Belfast. Didn't know she was *that* young, d'ye see . . . sixteen or seventeen, Eudoxia thought. Two or three guineas'll do."

She's just a passin' fancy, Lewrie thought, squirming; *So why does it irk me t'pass her on?*

"A bloody bargain, is she a good ride," Rushton snickered.

Rich as Peter Rushton, Lord Draywick, was from what was left from his inheritance, and his marriage into a Trade fortune, there was the possibility that he might find Tess a very pleasing diversion, even go so far as to buy her out and set her up as his mistress; "under his protection," the saying went. Certainly *he* could not afford to do that, or even go to "Mother" Batson's all that often.

Might be best for her, Lewrie considered; *A place of her own, with a maid, and a cook. Rich gowns, and jewelry. Some place warmer than that drab little cubicle she has now. Only the one customer to deal with, too. As much security as she could expect . . . 'til Peter gets tired of her. Might be best, all round. Might be Tess's fondest wish! And, since when did I care a toss for a whore's welfare, her bloody feelings?*

"I *thought* that bloody bell-wether in charge of her baa-lambs hellish-resembled Emma Batson," Clotworthy exclaimed as if he'd solved a mystery. "Famous in her youth, she was, and probably has her first shilling. A clever old baggage, with a head for her business as good as any 'fancy man,' I can tell you. Tess, is she? Tess who?"

"Don't know, really," Lewrie said, shrugging.

"Well, last names hardly matter, do they?" Lord Peter sniggered, his nose in his brandy glass. "First names, either, 'Dearie' and 'my Joe,' and 'darling' serve just as well. Sixteen or seventeen? Hmm!"

"She's hellish-sweet, and . . . endearing," Lewrie said, his eyes fixed on the far wall as he took a sip of his own drink. "A new-come, as I said." He almost shook himself to reject that line of thinking. "There's a supper every evening, for select patrons and the girls of their choice. It ain't a quick place . . . even though there's another parlour for the walk-ins. Set a quite nice table, really, and . . . ya meet the *finest* set o' gentle-men," Lewrie added with a bark of sardonic amusement.

"Damn my eyes, are you *sweet* on her, Alan?" Lord Peter Rushton exclaimed, feigning mock horror. "I do believe you *are*. Just like ya were at school . . . the chamber-maids who did for our rooms? Or that tavern wench at the Crown and Cushion, where we always went? Do you recall her, Clotworthy? Betsy, or Judy, or something?"

"Indeed I do, Peter old son," Clotworthy seconded with a dreamy expression on his phyz. "*Damned* impressive set of poonts, she had, as I remember. And a *most* obligin' mort. Alan here was so besotted with her, he'd have run off with her . . . had she not been makin' such a good livin' makin' half the students, and a fair number of the faculty, as happy as clams, haw haw! Made *me* happy, I can tell you, and only one shilling a throw. Oh, those were fine days. *Nights,* rather!"

"Ten minutes in the tavern's pantry," Lord Peter hooted, "with her skirts thrown up, and sitting on an ale barrel . . . for six pence! Oh, but Alan was always that way. Mad for quim, then in 'cream-pot' *love* for them."

Damme, I guess I always was! Lewrie confessed to himself.

"Poor fellow never figured out that *likin'* 'em ain't necessary, just 'cause he got the leg over," Clotworthy said, shaking his head in amusement. "Just throw down yer money, enjoy 'em, and be done, haw haw."

Damme, but I don't think I like *these shits* half *as much as I used to,* Lewrie thought with an uneasy feeling, a tightening of his innards; *Right, I've* always *been a calf-head cully when it comes to the women . . . whores or proper, no matter. Fine enough friends when we all were lads, but . . . have I changed? Did they change? Or,* never *have.*

"So, a good ride is she, this Tess creature, Alan?" Clotworthy gog-gled at him with a knowing leer.

Lewrie squinted with sudden anger for a second, before tamping it down firmly. "Well, you'd be the best judge of that," he said instead, slowly drawling his answer. *Damme, am I* jealous? he wondered.

"Does she play the shy virgin?" Peter queried. "Or is she game for any place, time, fashion, or orifice, hey? An acrobat, is she?"

Dammit! Lewrie silently fumed, taking time to answer by sipping on his drink; *They're like schoolboys, still . . .* civilian *schoolboys! A gentleman doesn't* tell *such*! *Have I got so old I can't feel chummy with fellow rakehells any longer? Or, have I gotten* wiser?

"That's for you to find out, Peter," Lewrie told him, faking a sly grin, after he had finished the last dollop of brandy in his glass. "Now, did I have *your* purse, I'd buy her out and set her up, for she's that pleasing to *me*."

"You'd play Pygmalion with her, Alan?" Rushton japed, not noticing his old friend's reticence; it didn't matter a whit to him.

"*On* her, most-like," Clotworthy interjected.

"Next time you call at 'Mother' Batson's, you'll put in a good word for me with the 'Abbess'?" Lord Peter asked. "With the girl, as well? Is her establishment as fine as you say, and sets such a fine table, I might become a regular caller. Panton Street's convenient to Whitehall, and my town-house. Let her know a wealthy patron's coming, hey?" he said with a wink and a leer at his double *entendre*.

"Well, of course, Peter . . . what are friends for?" Lewrie said, trying not to grit his teeth or slap the lecher silly; hypocritical as such an act might be, and ruefully chiding himself for being perhaps but a *shadow* compared to his old compatriots' lascivious natures.

"Then, a glass with you, sir," Peter insisted, snapping fingers for the waiter to come top them up. Lewrie would have risen and left, but for that offer, which could not be rejected, or be thought of as a "sneaker." Despite his distaste, he stayed on.

"Ah, but we're a merry band of rogues," Clotworthy said with a cheery smile. "Remember our old motto, Peter . . . Alan? What Wilkes said of life . . . 'a few good fucks, and then we die,' ha ha!"

"Damme, but I believe I started the day lookin' for stationery," Lewrie said, perking up as he changed the subject. "Yet here I sit, with not a single sheet, nor a ha'porth of ink yet. And there is that furrier in the Haymarket to discover . . . just in case Admiralty's run short of Post-Captains before the fleet sails for the Baltic."

"You'll not dine with us, Alan?" Clotworthy Chute exclaimed in seeming disappointment. Perhaps he'd fancied that Lewrie would foot the bill, as he had at Harrow with ale, porter, and "tatties."

"Some other time, Clotworthy," Lewrie demurred. "I think I'll finish this last glass, then toddle along. I believe we should *all* consider our drinks celebratory . . . that we survived an encounter with Mistress Durschenko's *charmin'* father, hmm?"

"Do you think we'll really have to go fight the Russians, Danes, and Swedes, Alan?" Clotworthy asked. "Mean t'say . . . "

"Aye, and the sooner the better," Lewrie assured him. "Time is not on our side, not with the weather warmin', and their navies' ports thawin' out. Do they put to sea, and combine, well . . . "

"Beat 'em like a drum, no matter," Peter scoffed with a sublime confidence that bordered on indifference; he even allowed himself one idle yawn. "We've Nelson, after all."

"And Alan . . . can he tear himself from betwixt his doxy's legs," Clotworthy chuckled over the rim of his glass.

"We'll see, won't we?" Lewrie asked, finally finishing off his brandy, and more than ready to depart. "One way or t'other."

"By yer *leave*, sir!" an impatient porter snarled at him, trying to make way on the crowded sidewalk with several wrapped packets.

"By yer *own* bloody leave, damn yer eyes!" Lewrie snapped back, more than ready to fight *someone*, raising his walking-stick in threat.

"Pardons . . . pardons." The weedy little brute shied away, more sauce than sinew, and scurried off.

"Bloody Hell!" Lewrie growled under his breath. "What a pack of cods-heads."

Are they *what I'd've become, if I'd stayed ashore in London . . . any-where in England?* he fumed to himself as he strode along for his lodgings; *Then, thank God for the Navy!*

Alan Lewrie had always cynically, cheerfully admitted that he would never be buried a bishop, that the most he had aspired to would be to be considered a "Buck-of-the-First-Head," a merry denizen of the "cock and hen" clubs in the more sordid parts of London; sleep in late, roister and rantipole 'til dawn, and begin it all over, had he had his druthers.

Such as he seemed to be doing now.

Yet . . . not only had it become tiresome . . . boresome! . . . but it was beginning to pall, the ambrosia turned to ashes in his mouth. The morning's encounter with Peter and Clotworthy made him squint with revulsion.

Christ, am I havin' an Epiphany? he wondered.

He shook that notion off with a shiver and a barely audible *Brr.*

Idle hands, the Devil's workshop, he recalled; *and I've been* damned *idle, since before Christmas. Or, t'other'un . . . 'lie down with dogs and ye rise with fleas.' Oh God, ye don't hear from me much, but . . . I really need t'get back t'sea! Doesn't have t'be a frigate . . . a* cutter *would do, a one-masted revenue sloop! Hell, even the Impress Service, just so long as I'm employed at* some-thing! *I'm not a huge sinner after all . . . compared to some I could name. Right . . . I'm a fool for women, and I always get in trouble ashore. There may be women aboard warships, despite what the Admiralty wishes, but . . . none that tempt* my *eye, the plug-uglies. Most of 'em foul an' rough as bosuns . . .*

He accepted the fact that Peter and Clotworthy were right in one re-gard; he never had been a callous, unscrupulous abuser of women's af-fections. He'd *always* gone soft on them. In point of fact, two of his duels, in his early days, had been in defence of a girl's good name or ho-nour, so . . . didn't that count for something? Mean t'*say* . . . !

Write off the odd convenient quarter-hour romp here and there, and what have you? he thought, scanning back over his conquests as he dodged a brace of strolling ladies and a street urchin bullying a wee dog; *A string of fond* relationships, *that's what, by . . . sorry. Long-time, mutually pleasin'* love *affairs! Don't make me a bad person, not like Peter, or Clot-worthy, or . . .*

He practically stormed up the steps to the doors of the Madeira Club, thrusting the doors back so forcefully that the day porter at the desk jumped in fright, scrambling to come round to gather up his cloak, hat, walking-stick, and mittens. "Still raw out, sir? A fine mist falling, still? I'll have your cloak and hat sponged, then send them up to your rooms, sir."

"Er, thankee," Lewrie mumbled, realising that he'd stomped back to the club so fiercely that he'd worked up a sweat under his clothes. "Any letters for me?"

"Uhm . . . nossir, none so far today."

"Very well, then. Do any come, I'll be in the Common Room."

"Very good, Captain Lewrie."

Lewrie dabbed at his temples and cheeks with a handkerchief to make himself presentable, once he'd found a nice, quiet corner, and a thickly padded leather wing-back chair near the fireplace. A servant took his re-quest for hot coffee, and padded away, leaving him to stew on the morn-ing's doings.

"What the Devil do I do?" he muttered as he stirred sugar and milk into his cup. "It can't go on like this. Not for long, or I'll be 'skint' by Easter." His accounts at Coutts's Bank, some prize-money that had dribbled in from Mediterranean captures way back in '96, was sufficient for keeping a gentleman of his station in *moderate* comfort, with enough to keep up his rented farm and home in Anglesgreen, both the boys at their school, his daughter Charlotte's first tutor, and his wife, with her typical thriftiness, in fine style. Dabbling with the whores, though, sweet as one of them was . . .

Lord Peter *could afford* such squandering, both of his purse and his repute, but *he* was the *beau ideal* of the Abolitionists, of the Respectable; of the dour Hannah More, Rev. Wilberforce, and all of their grim adherents, and he could not risk running into any *more* of them in "Mother" Batson's parlour. "Saint Alan, the Liberator!"

He would *have* to see Tess just one more time, he realised with what the French would call *tristesse*, a sweet-sad sorrow, flooding him. There really was no future in it, even were he as rich as the fabled Walpoles. Sadly, he also realised that if he *could* afford for her to be his long-time kept mistress, he'd tire of her someday, too, and abandon her to her uncertain fate. Better he spoke of Lord Peter to her, and hope that Tess struck him the right way.

After all, he *did* try to plant the seed of the idea in Peter's mind, of buying her out and setting her up under his protection; that would be best, in the long run. And go back to living the life of a "salty, tar-splotched" nautical monk!

CHAPTER TWENTY-TWO

*G*ood morning, Captain Lewrie," the day porter greeted him as he entered the club the next morning, giving him a chary, cutty-eyed look as
he took his things to hang up. "Breakfast will be served the top of the
hour, sir . . . there's to be pork chops *and* smoked mullet, fresh up from
Sheerness."

"Umph" was Lewrie's sleepy comment. "Thankee."

"Coffee or tea in the Common Room, sir," the porter advised, to a
man who looked badly in need of either.

"Morning, all," Lewrie nodded to his fellow lodgers gathered by the
table of pots, cups, and saucers. "Mister Giles, Major Baird . . . Mister
Pilkington . . . Showalter."

Pilkington was the club's Cassandra, sure that Trade would end, and
the economy go smash, due to this Baltic business; Showalter was still
angling for a seat in Commons, next by-election on his home hustings,
and courting monied supporters like a street-walker; Mr. Giles was *hellish*-
devout, and big in the leather-goods trade and tanneries, whilst Major
Baird, their "chicken-nabob" come back from India with a fortune of at
least £50,000, was still searching for a suitably proper wife . . . or oral
sex in the loge boxes at the theatres.

Yet *all* eyed him as charily as they would a naked drunk at the altar of
the local parish church. *Know too damned much about my business,*

Lewrie thought with a wince and a sigh; *and where I was, damn 'em.* There were some askance glances, some whispers and mutterings, making Lewrie wonder were his breeches buttons done up proper, or was a used cundum dangling from a coat pocket.

Frankly, it had been a *damned* sad night. Tess had noticed his moodiness and tetchiness, and had tried to jolly him out of it . . . 'til she'd learned the reason for his detachment.

She'd sat up in bed, a quilt and the coverlet wrapped round her, and her arms about her knees, with a pensive look on her pretty face.

"Ye'll not come t'me no longer, Alan me dear?" she'd said with a hitch in her voice, and a swipe at her eyes with a fist. "Sure, am I too expensive? Is that it?"

"No, Tess, it's not the money . . . though I'm not a rich man, not really," he'd tried to explain, practically curled up around her, with all the pillows under his shoulders and head.

"That dark-haired girl ye were with, then? D'ye wish ya were with her, the more?"

"Not if I wish t'live!" he'd said with a wry laugh, explaining Eudoxia Durschenko . . . and her fierce father. "There's no one else I wish t'be with . . . ye know I'm married, no matter how badly *that* has turned out. She and I . . . 'tis distant, now. *Might* improve . . . ?"

"Dear man, 'tis rare, the single man who *comes* here," Tess said with a wry look and a toss of her hair, a stab at a smile before she turned pensive again. "I know how men are . . . how *well* I know, and how the world is. I just hoped . . . " She broke off and lowered her head to her knees, shielding her face with the spill of her hair.

"That I could take you under my protection?" Lewrie softly asked, reaching out to stroke her head. In answer, she looked up for a second and jerkily nodded yes, before burying her face again.

"There's a fellow, though . . . ," Lewrie had posed. "The slim man with me in the coffee-house? Peter Rushton, Lord Draywick. He's rich as Croesus, and . . . he asked about you. I don't know." Lewrie sighed and shrugged lamely. "*Really* rich. Mad t'find where you were. Devil take me, but . . . I told him. He's very amusing."

"He ain't *you*!" she'd whispered, her urge to cry out muffled, and a bit sniffly, as if she wept.

"But he could get you out of here, Tess . . . with grand lodgings of your own. But the *one* fool t'deal with, not . . . ," Lewrie told her.

"Hmph!" was her comment on that.

"Did I have it in my power . . . was I free t'do so, *I'd* get you out of here," he swore. "And . . . not just t'have you to myself."

"Ye really care that much about me?" she'd asked, lifting her head, brushing back her hair, and swiping her eyes free of tears once again. "Aye, I *do* wish *someone* would, sure. 'Tis not the life they promised back in Belfast."

"Some procurer?" Lewrie had asked.

"I got in a speck o' trouble," Tess said, sitting upright, and smoothing the coverlet over her thighs. "We weren't *shanty*-poor, like most in Ireland . . . but, poor enough for all th' children t'know they must make their own way, soon as they could." Another wry smile, or a rueful quick twist of her mouth that could pass for one. "Mum an' Da was just scrapin' by, an' without th' rest of us workin' and sendin' 'em sixpence th' month, they'd haveta sell their loom an' go on th' road, beggin'. Got me a place, a good'un, I thought, tattin' lace . . . I'm clever with me hands, d'ye see, an' quick. And Mum an' Da taught me readin' an' cypherin', so I had me numbers, an' that's why I thought th' feller who run th' shop moved me up. I was makin' ten shillin's a *month,* an' sixpence sent home was no bother a'tall! An' that with me room an' board all found. 'Til th' feller who run it, well . . . ye can guess why he paid me so well."

"How old were you, then?" Lewrie had asked, dreading her answer.

"Fifteen," Tess said with a slight sniff and a shrug. "Before, I was workin' th' looms with Mum an' Da, but where we'd get enough to eat, all of us t'gither, was th' problem, so I had t'go out on me own. Like th' poor pig farmer'd say when th' corn runs short . . . 'root, hog, or die,' d'ye see," she said with a mirthless little laugh.

"How long ago was that?" He had his fingers crossed.

"Two year ago," Tess told him. "Th' feller *promised* more pay, an' he come through with a bit of it, an' . . . he wasn't *that* bad a man. 'Twas his *son* was th' real devil, him an' his friend, brought in t'manage, who took advantage of th' fetchin' girls in th' shop, an' when his father lost int'rest in me for a new-come, that was when it got bad on me, an' I schemed t'git outta there. That's when I got in th' trouble."

So she's seventeen, *round the age when a lot of poorer girls get married,* Lewrie thought with a sense of relief. He put an arm out to her, and she gratefully slid into his embrace, cuddled up next to him. "What sort of trouble?" he asked.

"What sorta trouble ya *think* a girl gets into, with two randy lads takin' turns with her, 'bout ev'ry night?" Tess scoffed, sounding bitter, and a bit amazed by his seeming naïveté. "I caught a baby an' was gonna be turned out with nothin' but me wages paid 'til the end of the week, so . . . I dipped into th' cash-box, an' I run t'Belfast where I didn't think they'd find me."

"The babe?" Lewrie pressed, stroking her back.

"No one'd hire a pregnant girl, an' th' parish churches were no help, either," Tess continued, ignoring his question. "Just wanted me t'move along t'th' next'un, so I wouldn't be a burden on their Poor's Rate. Finally . . .'bout the time *all* me money's gone, an' I hadn't et in nigh a week, I met this flash feller, who promised he'd take care o' me . . . did I let him fetch me t'London, where he promised me th' Moon, do I go on doin' what I'd been a'doin' fer tuppence. 'Til I begun to show too much, that is," she frankly admitted, with a wry *moue*. "Got me a mid-wife, he did, but I never saw it, th' day after. He *swore* he put it in th' mercy box in th' door of a parish church, but . . . next thing I know, he's sold me t'Missuz Batson."

"*Sold* you?" Lewrie gawped.

"Feller'd spent a lot on me keepin', an' th' birthin' an' all," Tess pointed out. "Then there's what *she* spent on me, all the dresses an' such t'get me started . . . hairdressers an' makeup, an' teachin' me t'speak right an' be charmin'?" Tess had said with a grin, as if it was the accepted way of the world. "Don't rightly know how *much* she paid him, but she *says* I've worked it off, an' only have *her* now t'repay.

"I've even laid a little by for meself," she'd naïvely boasted, "an' sent a little t'Mum an' Da, like before. *And* sent them bastards at th' lace-works all o' what I stole, so they can't have me took up, can they? Mean t'say, I've made rec . . . recompense. 'Twas more than ten shillin's, an' they *hang* people who steal that much. In th' main, I'm doin' alright." Tess had decided.

"For now, but . . .'tis a hard life," Lewrie had commiserated.

"Nary so bad as most," Tess had said with a little chuckle as she'd snuggled closer to him. "Did I come t'London, just another poor girl, I'd'a ended a maid'r tavern girl, not makin' ten pound a year, an' *maybe* gettin' room, board, an' one gown an' pair o' shoes at Boxin' Day . . . an' *still* be took advantage of, for nothin' . . . a shillin' at best!" Tess had said with a derisive snort. "No, Mother Batson's is a good place, for now. Soon as I pay back what she spent on me, I'm to get a third o' me earnin's all for meself, she says! Then I can come an' go as I please, maybe get a place o' me own . . . without dependin' on a feller like yer Lord Draywick, nor *any* man."

"And do what?" Lewrie had asked her.

"Why, th' same as I do *now*," Tess had declared, looking up at him askance, as if he was daft, giggling a bit. " 'Til I've raked me up a pile o' 'tin' t'invest in th' Three Percents. Who knows? I could remove t'another town an' open a ladies' shop o' some sort, and turn respectable as *anythin'*. Find me a decent feller . . . a clerk or a farmer, an' might even marry. Someplace where no one'll know what I did, before."

"So . . . even though you don't *like* the life, and do want to get out of here . . . you'll stay with it?" Lewrie further asked, confused by her initial sadness, then her blunt acceptance.

"What else is a poor lass t'do, Captain Alan? Tess had countered. "It's not *that* hard a life, though it's a hard world," she'd said in conclusion, then had groped under the covers to stroke his nudity. "Well, if I can't convince ye t'take me under yer protection, there's th' rest o' th' night left us. If you're *int'rested*, o' course . . . ," she'd coyly whispered. "Do I not see ya again, I'd wish a last grand night t'remember ya by, ya darlin', impressive man . . . "

"Oh, darlin', ye're own self," Lewrie had responded, passion rekindled in an eyeblink, hands caressing, lips kissing from her neck to . . .

"Seen the papers, Captain Lewrie?" ex-Major Baird enquired as he sidled up to get a refill of hot tea. "Thought they might be of interest to you."

"Uhm?" Lewrie replied, snatched from his sad reverie.

"The dockyards . . . the Navy dockyard workers," Baird chortled. "They had the nerve to send a delegation to town, demanding their pay be *doubled,* and Lord Saint Vincent sacked the lot of them, yesterday."

"Well, damn my eyes!" Lewrie exclaimed (rather a bit too loudly for the "Respectable" waiting for breakfast). "He *said* something like that would be his reaction. Good for 'Old Jarvy'!"

"Sent out orders for anyone who contributed to their trip, and anyone who joined in what he termed illegal combinations to be sacked, as well. The *gall* of the greedy . . . to threaten to walk out, just as our Navy is faced with another threat. Well, they got what they deserved."

"Hear, hear!" Lewrie heartily agreed.

"Ahem . . . gentlemen," the head butler intoned at the doors to the dining room, "breakfast is served."

"You spoke with Lord Saint Vincent?" ex-Major Baird enquired as they queued up to file in and take seats.

"A few days ago . . . looking for a ship," Lewrie told him, taking a bit of joy to be known among the powerful. "I was at the battle back in '97. Followed Nelson when he countered the Spanish van, and met Admiral Jervis, after. At least he remembered me, but nought was promised. We'll see. Ah, mullet kippers!"

He was famished, for he and Tess had fallen asleep just a bit after midnight, and had not sent down for their usual cold collation. A pork chop, a couple of kippers, two slices of fatty and crisp bacon, with two fried eggs and a heap of fried diced potatoes, and even the brown bread was cut two fingers thick, and nicely, crunchily toasted, wanting only slavers of butter and currant jam.

Didn't even linger for coffee or tea when I left, Lewrie thought with a guilty wince at his cowardice. All that had needed to be said had been said; had he found a way to slip out before she woke, he just might have, but . . .

"Excuse me, sirs . . . uhm, Captain Lewrie," the day porter said in a soft voice, leaning close to his chair, "you've a letter from Admiralty, Captain Lewrie, and there's a messenger awaiting your reply."

Ho . . . ly shit! Lewrie thought with a start, and a sudden flood of warmth; *And just thankee Jesus!*

"You gentlemen will excuse me?" Lewrie said, tossing aside his napkin and sliding his chair back. Frankly, it felt rather good for the other lodgers to goggle at him and speculate in muted whispers as he stepped out into the central hall, and broke the wax seal upon the creamy bond paper, and read it.

> *Sir,*
>
>   *You are required and directed to report to Admiralty as soon as possible following receipt of this letter, here to declare your immediate availabilty to take upon yourself the charge and command of His Majesty's Frigate, Thermopylae, now lying at Great Yarmouth. A brief written response pursuant to your acceptance of this posting, returned to us by Admiralty Messenger, should precede you. I am, sir,*
>
>   *Sir Evan Nepean,*
>   *1st Secty to Admiralty*

"You're bloody-damned *right* I will!" Lewrie whooped with glee, practically bounding for the front desk, and the spare pen and ink. A quick scribbled "Yes!" and a glance towards the young messenger who stood with his hand out, and Lewrie was headed for the cellar stairs, where he hoped Liam Desmond and Patrick Furfy were loafing.

"There ye are, my lads!" he cried, spotting them both chummily seated near the warm cooking fireplace and griddle stoves, devouring their own breakfasts with gusto. Furfy froze with a length of kipper in his mouth. "Round up all my chests from the storage down here, and the garret, and see I've all the keys handy. We've got a ship!"

"Huzzah!" Desmond shouted. "D'ye hear, Pat? We're goin' back t'sea, and about time, too!"

"I'll go dress, and be back in a few hours," Lewrie quickly told them. "Before nightfall, there'll be a power o' shoppin' to do, so you two look lively now!"

"Wot's 'er *name*, sir?" Furfy called to his captain's back as Lewrie hustled back up the cellar stairs.

"*Thermopylae!*" Lewrie shouted over his shoulder. "A frigate!"

"Wot'sorta name's Therm . . . whativer, Liam?" Furfy asked his compatriot once Captain Lewrie had gone.

"Why, ye great, ignorant spalpeen," Desmond chid him as he cut two slices of bread for a last fatty-bacon sandwich, "'twas a famous battle from long ago, or a famous admiral o' some sort o' th' Greeks or Romans. Iver hear th' English name a ship fer anythin' *else*? Get a move on, Pat . . . lash up an' stow, me lad, for sure as God made th' green apples fer a good purge, we're off t'th' Baltic with all o' th' others!"

"Gonna fight th' heathen Roosians, arrah!"

CHAPTER TWENTY-THREE

*B*y mid-day the next morning, Lewrie and his small party were on the road east—London to Chelmsford, Chelmsford to Ipswich, and east to the coastal road to Great Yarmouth, where the fleet was gathering for the Baltic expedition. It was an expensive and long trip in a hired carriage, with a carting waggon following close behind which bore all of Lewrie's stored furnishings, wine, and hastily bought supplies for God knew how long a time at sea.

Wine by the case, whisky by the barricoe, brandy by the gallons; those damned furs, which, at such short notice, Lewrie could only purchase some used items, and those reeking of badly cured hides and camphor. Whatever they were actually pelts *of*, he had no idea at the moment. There were dried sausages and smoked fish for the cats . . . the requisite keg of dry beach sand he could find for their necessary box he could buy later . . . his crated-up plate and pewter service, his glasses and china, the collapsible settee and chairs, a tea-caddy freshly filled with coned suger, tea leaves, along with sacks of chocolate and coffee beans, the grinder, the pots, pans, grills, and utensils, and all the myriad of easily forgotten things that made life at least tolerable at sea. Boot-black and metal polish, spare uniforms and slop-trousers, dress and undress rigs, shirts and stockings, underdrawers and neck-stocks for every occasion from a howling winter gale to a presentation ball before foreign dignitaries, Lewrie *thought* he'd managed to gather the important things.

There had also been Desmond's and Furfy's sea-chests and kits to re-stock, bills to be paid through his solicitor, money drafts for day-to-day voyaging expenses to be drawn, the quarterly sums to be set aside for his wife, Caroline, and his children, and the farm . . .

And, letters to write! He'd gotten finger-cramp before he was done, informing his father, Sir Hugo, Sir Malcolm Shockley, Lord Peter, Caroline, Hugh, Sewallis, and Charlotte, that he'd gotten a new ship, and to address future letters in care of Admiralty . . . and, last of all, a note to Eudoxia Durschenko, then . . . one to Tess, the poor chit.

And still he fretted as the coach rocked and jangled and thudded into the early evening that there might be something important that he'd forgotten, and might be unavailable in Great Yarmouth shops.

"Uhm, sir . . . ," Liam Desmond spoke up at last, after the boredom of watching the flat and depressing countryside of Essex rolling by in the gathering twilight. "What sorta frigate is this . . . Therm-diddle?"

"*Thermopylae?*" Lewrie grunted, dragging himself back from a reverie of his night with Tess. "Ah, she's a Fifth Rate of thirty-eight guns . . . eighteen pounders," he explained, repeating what little he'd been told by Mr. Nepean. "They took her lines off the French *Hebe,* but she's British-built, a little longer than the old ones . . . one hundred fifty feet on the range of the deck. So many of them coming into service, they're callin' her one of the *Leda* class. I've heard that they're good, stable gun platforms, and handle extemely well. Over a thousand tons burthen."

"Wot's it *mean,* though, sir, Therm . . . how ye say it?" Furfy pressed.

"A very long time ago, the Persians tried to invade Greece with a million-man army, and a fleet of five hundred ships," Lewrie replied. "The Greeks acted like the House of Commons on a bad day, and couldn't agree to cooperate. . . . They were all a bunch of city-states, not a real country then, so . . . the Spartans under King Leonidas set out to stop 'em. He picked a narrow pass right by the sea . . . high cliffs above, and a straight drop from the road, a place with a hot spring like at the resort of Bath that the Greeks called Thermopylae, which means a hot spring. And there they fought, for nigh on a week, with the Persians crammed into a narrow front, no more than twenty men wide, dyin' by the thousands 'cause they couldn't drive through the Spartans and their spears, shields, and swords. The Persian king, Xerxes, lost a tenth part of his soldiers. That gave time enough for the Athenians to beat the Persians in great sea-battles that destroyed most of the Persian fleet, and let the Greeks sort themselves out and raise their own army. Leonidas and the Spartans saved Greece . . . kept it from turning into a mess as bad as the Ottoman Empire, and saved the basis of our civilisation."

"Spartans, now!" Furfy enthused. "Ain't there a *Spartiate* in the Navy, arready? Lotsa ships named for Greeks an' Romans, both. I think there was even a *Leonidas,* too, weren't there, Liam?"

"Think I heard th' name, Pat," Desmond told his friend. "So, sir . . . once th' Spartans saved th' day, did they make this Leonidas king over all?"

"Uh, no . . . ," Lewrie had to confess. "A traitor showed the Persians a way round the mountains that was un-guarded, and took 'em from both ends, so . . . the Spartans died to a man."

"Oh" was Furfy's shuddery comment. He looked as if he wished to cross himself, or spit for protection against bad *geas.*

"They died *gloriously,* mind," Lewrie added. "Famous to this day, same as Helen of Troy, Hector, and Achilles in *The Iliad*. Like Horatius at the bridge, and—"

"Oh, like Horatio Nelson, then!" Furfy said, perking up.

"Ain't it a pity, Pat, that there'll niver be frigates or ships o' th' line named after Irish heroes an' such," Lewrie's Cox'n said. "Like Brian Boru, or the Battle o' Clontarf."

"Cuchulain, or Conary Mör, the high king, aye," Furfy supplied, his eyes alight, "or places like Tara."

"Conall o' th' Victories, or Finn Mac Cooal," Desmond added, in a wistful, respectful voice.

Lewrie, who knew next to nothing of Irish myths, kept his mouth shut, and even managed not to snicker, scowl, or raise a single brow, though he thought the both of them were off on a pagan religious jaunt. *Just like the Irish,* he thought; *Swannin' off into fables.*

"Pardon me more, Cap'm, but, is this *Thermopylae* still fittin' out?" Desmond asked him further. "Mean t'say . . . if she's fresh from th' gravin' docks, it might be weeks afore she's ready for sea."

"No, Desmond, she's aswim already, in full commission," Lewrie informed him. "And ready in all respects . . . but for the health of her captain. He's come down with the winter agues so badly, they told me, that he had to write and ask for relief, else his ship and his officers and men would miss out on things, and he thought that a worse thing than stepping aside, himself. A Captain Joseph Speaks, I think he is. Never heard of him my-self, even though I imagine he's a lot senior to me, and was 'made Post' years before I was. Have either of you?"

No, they hadn't, either. Furfy went back to staring out his windows at the countryside, whilst Desmond frowned in thought. Lewrie was about to shut his eyes and try to nap, despite the jolting of the coach, when Desmond spoke up in a soft voice.

"Cap'm, sir . . . it might be tetchy, yer takin' over. This Cap'm Speaks most-likes been posted a year or more, an' all his people would be usedta him, by now. Here's me, yer Cox'n, replacin' *his*, an' sore th' fel-low'll be, t'lose his 'call' an' his position, t'be certain."

"Well, there is that," Lewrie uneasily allowed. From his first *ad hoc* appointment to command of a converted bomb ketch in the Far East, to the *Shrike* brig when old Lt. Lilycrop had been invalided off, to the *Alacrity*, the *Jester* sloop, and the frigates *Proteus* and *Savage*, he had ei-ther commissioned them with new crews, or been the first appointed to them. *Shrike*, well . . . he'd already been her First Lieutenant when he had supplanted Lilycrop, so he'd been familiar with her crew, but . . . this would be the first time in his career that he would be stepping into some-one else's shoes, off-loading one man's cabin furnishings and putting his own in place . . . and facing an utterly strange new set of faces and names and attitudes; a ship's company that most-likely had rubbed together for a year or two already, and might look upon him as an interloper. Much like his last First Officer in *Savage*, Lieutenant Urquhart, had probably felt, being appointed into a ship whose crew had turned over entire after three years as shipmates in *Proteus*!

And he would be going aboard without the usual entourage that a Royal Navy captain should have, too. Instead of his own cook, clerk, and steward, his own favoured boat crew; he had a mere two, his Cox'n Liam Desmond, and the hapless Patrick Furfy. Most captains rated at least half a dozen trustworthy people from previous commissions together, some-times as many as fifteen for admirals, if one counted an extra clerk, and several more snot-nosed "gentleman volunteers" too young to qualify as Midshipmen yet, but could serve as cabin servants.

Such a coterie of long-time favourites *would* be upsetting to the men holding small "place" aboard a ship already in commission. Anyone who did not hold proper Admiralty Warrant could be demoted and re-placed in a twinkling, and that would further foment the distrust, and dread, of the coming of a new captain, who might prove to be as big a tyrant as Pigott had been in HMS *Hermione,* where they'd finally mutinied, and murdered, and sailed her into an enemy port!

Better the Devil ye know, Lewrie mused; *Oh, damn . . . servants.*

There was another snag. Lewrie had depended upon the staff of the Madeira Club after Aspinall had quit to enter his new career as an author. To replace all the skills Aspinall had possessed, he'd need at least *three* men; a cook, a manservant, and cabin steward, combined. And, most-like a cabin servant to aid the steward! As quick as his appointment had come, though, there hadn't been time to interview people and hire a few . . . not if he'd had two weeks' notice!

Lewrie could only hope that within his new frigate's crew, from among the people Captain Speaks had left behind, he might discover some who at least knew their left hand from their right, could boil water or brew coffee, set plates without breaking half of them, or scribble correspondence that was actually legible.

And stay out of his wine and spirits locker!

CHAPTER TWENTY-FOUR

"Ahem?" Mr. Midshipman Tillyard announced, rapping on the door frame that led to the officers' gun-room. "Sirs?"

"Come," Lt. Farley, the Second Officer, lazily called out.

Officers did not stand harbour watches; that was left to the Midshipmen and the petty officers. Midshipman Tillyard stepped into the frowsty warm gun-room, hat under his arm, and beheld his superiors at their leisure. Lt. Farley and Lt. Fox, his very good friend, were at the long table down the centre of the space in their shirtsleeves, a backgammon board between them, with Lt. Fox in mid-throw of the dice. The Marine Officer, Lt. Eades, in full kit despite the officially sanctioned idleness, was reading. The Sailing Master, Mr. Lyle, was poring over a chart, as usual, and the Ship's Surgeon, Mr. Harward, was playing a wager-less game of *vingt et un* with the Purser, Mr. Pridemore.

"Beg pardons, sirs, but there's a sailing barge bearing down on us, and there's a Post-Captain aboard her," Mr. Tillyard announced. "I think our new captain is come at last."

"Yipes!" Lt. Farley barked. "Who has the deck?"

"Sealey, sir," Tillyard told him.

"Bloody Hell, that'll never do!" Fox said with a snort, rising from the game, and a very promising cast of the dice, to throw on his waist-coat and coat.

"Sir?" Lt. Farley said, rapping upon the louvred door set into the deal partition to the First Officer's small cabin.

"I heard, Mister Farley, thank you," the First Officer replied, departing his cramped private space, shrugging into his own coat.

"Sarn't Crick!" Marine Lt. Eades was calling out, already out on the gun-deck beyond. "Side-party to the starboard entry-port!"

"Respects to Midshipman Sealey, and he's to summon all hands on deck, Mister Tillyard. How much time do we have?" the First Officer ordered as they all dressed properly and began the trot up the ladderway to the quarterdeck and gangways.

"She's still about a cable off, sir," Tillyard replied, "bound direct for us, but under reduced sail."

"Not trying to catch us napping, then," the First Officer said with a firm nod. "Perhaps our new captain is giving us time to welcome him properly."

"Aye, sir," Tillyard hesitantly agreed.

The First Lieutenant took a quick inventory once he was by the open entry-port; every yard squared to mathematical perfection, every brace and halliard, all the running-rigging, properly coiled and hung on the pin-rails, or flemished down on the decks. The sails were gasketed and furled as snug as sausages, the guns were stowed at proper right angles to the bulwarks, muzzles bowsed to the bottoms of the gun-port sills, their tackle and blocks taut and neatly stowed. There was nothing out of place, nothing to be faulted for.

Despite that, the fellow crossed the fingers of his right hand behind his leg, and almost muttered a prayer. Another glance about, and he was satisfied that they were ready in all respects.

"Boat ahoy!" Midshipman Sealey shouted overside through a brass speaking-trumpet.

"Aye aye!" a bargeman in the bows of the approaching boat yelled back, holding up one hand to show four fingers, as well, in warning that a Post-Captain was aboard, and in need of the requisite number of men in the side-party to receive him. The senior officer in the barge had also thrown back his boat-cloak to display the gilt epaulets on his shoulders. As the barge dropped her lug-sail and turned to ghost parallel to the main-chains and boarding battens, HMS *Thermopylae*'s First Officer's eyes crinkled at the corners, his full mouth tautening in a faint grin.

"Well damn my eyes," he muttered.

Officers presented drawn swords, Marines in full kit stamped and slapped Brown Bess muskets in salute, so hard that small white puffs of pipeclay arose from crossbelts and taut musket slings. The Bosun, Mr. Dimmock, and his Mate, Mr. Pulley, trilled away in long duet tune upon their silver calls as the dog's vane of the new-come officer's cocked hat peeked above the lip of the entry-port as he nimbly scampered up.

The new captain attained the deck, performing a last jerk upon the tautly strung man-ropes, a little hop for the last step before he doffed his hat in return salute, his eyes roaming down the line of officers "toed up" to the tarry seam of a freshly holystoned deck plank . . . and his mouth fell open in surprise.

"Arthur Ballard?" Lewrie gawped. "I was *wond'rin'* where you'd got to."

"Welcome aboard, Captain Lewrie, sir," Lewrie's former First Lieutenant into the converted bomb ketch, HMS *Alacrity*, in the Bahamas, replied, performing a brief bow from the waist.

"Well, just damn my eyes," Lewrie said with a pleased chuckle. "It's been what . . . twelve years now?"

"Aye, sir, about that," Ballard (pronounced Buh-LARD) answered in his typical sombre gravity; a gravity that camoflauged a dry wit.

"S'pose I should read myself in, then we'll have some time to catch up," Lewrie allowed, reaching into his best-dress uniform coat for his stamped and sealed commission document. Swords were sheathed, muskets lowered, hats plumped back on heads as Lewrie walked to the cross-deck hammock nettings at the forrud edge of the quarterdeck to face his new crew, gathered along both sail-tending gangways, and in the frigate's waist below the boat-tier beams and gangways.

"Ship's comp'ny . . . off hats," Lt. Ballard ordered.

" 'By the Commissioners for executing the office of Lord High Admiral of Great Britain and Ireland, and all His Majesty's Plantations, and *et cetera* . . . to Captain Alan Lewrie, hereby appointed to His Majesty's Ship, *Thermopylae*,' " he read to them in his "quarterdeck voice," so that even a half-deafened old gunner in the bows could hear him, "by virtue of the Power and Authority to us given, we do hereby constitute and appoint you Captain of His Majesty's Ship, *Thermopylae* . . . willing and requiring you forthwith to go on board and take upon you the Charge and Command of Captain in her accordingly. Strictly charging all the Officers and Company belonging to said Ship subordinate to you to behave themselves jointly and severally in their respective Employments with all due Respect and Obedience unto you their said Captain and you

likewise to observe and execute such Orders and Directions you shall receive from time to time from your superior officers for His Majesty's
Service.

" 'Hereof nor you nor any one of you may fail as you will answer the
contrary at your peril. And for so doing this shall be your Warrant.
Given under our hands and the Seal of the Office of Admiralty, this
twenty-third day of February, Eighteen Oh One, in the Fourty First
year of His Majesty's Reign,' " he concluded, carefully rolling up the
precious document into a slim tube, to stow inside his coat 'til he had
time to store it safely away in his great-cabins. Lewrie looked down on
the men who were now officially his crew, and noted that some of them
were smiling, whispering back and forth behind their hands or their hats.
As in most ships of the Royal Navy, there were some men from almost
every nation, even some from enemy states, and, of course, there was always a sprinkling of Free Blacks; Lewrie spotted at least half a dozen,
and they were all beaming fit to bust. The others, though . . .

What, they've seen me tuppin' Tess? he puzzled to himself; *Some other
"mutton"?*

"I know that the sudden change in captains can be wrenching to a
crew which has gotten used to the old one's ways," Lewrie said on in a
slightly softer voice, though with a stern expression plastered on his face
to appear "captainly" to the ship's people, despite wanting to grin, cut
capers, snap his fingers, and do a little horn-pipe of glee to be back
aboard a ship . . . any ship. "I am certain Captain Speaks's Order Book,
his postings to positions of trust, and his methods were carefully
thought out and crafted for the overall good of the ship and her people."

Don't know . . . he could've *been a ravin' crank*! Lewrie thought.

"So . . . 'til I've gotten myself sorted out and familiar with his stric-
tures, his ways will continue in force," Lewrie assured them. "In a few
weeks, perhaps sooner, the warships gathering here in this port, the ships
readying in other harbours, will sail for the Baltic . . . by now that's no
secret, is it? I fully expect that *Thermopylae* will be in the thick of things,
and am determined that she, and all of you, will acquit yourselves in the
finest traditions of our Navy. Mister Ballard?" he said, turning to face his
First Officer. "Carry on, sir."

"Ship's company . . . on hats, and dismiss!" Ballard ordered.

Lt. Ballard then introduced Lewrie to his officers and holders of Warrant, allowing Lewrie to make quick sketch-judgements about them.

Lt. Farley, the Second Officer, was a slim fellow with curly dark blond hair and a lean face; behind his grave expression, he looked to be a bit of a tongue-in-cheek wag. Likewise the Third Officer, Lt. Fox, who might as well have been his partner in crime. Lt. Eades the Marine was about the same age as the Commission Officers, in his late twenties, but a stiffer, more sobre sort, perhaps a stickler for discipline with his Marines. The Sailing Master, Mr. Lyle, was in his late fourties, a fellow from Felixstowe just down the coast, thick-set and round-faced. Unlike most East Anglians, though, he seemed most affable.

The Purser, Herbert Pridemore, was even stouter, proof of the adage that all "Nip Cheeses" fed better than the crew. The Surgeon, Frederick Harward, seemed almost amused, which was rare in the Fleet, and young for his posting.

"I'll request that you find me a large keg of sand, sir," Lewrie bade the Purser.

"Sand, sir?" Pridemore asked, puzzled. "For the gun crews, sir?"

"For my cats, Mister Pridemore," Lewrie said with a smirk, "so they can relieve themselves. My compliments to the Ship's Carpenter, as well, Mister Ballard, and I'll have him make me a box, about so . . . " he said, sketching the size in mid-air with his hands. "For their necessary."

"Aye, sir," Ballard replied, with one brow cocked significantly. "Surely old Pitt can no longer be with you."

"No, he's gone to Fiddler's Green long ago," Lewrie said, "but Toulon and Chalky are still young'uns."

"The 'Ram-Cat,' " Lewrie heard someone whisper in glee. One of the Midshipmen, of course; no one else'd dare.

Lewrie was then introduced to his six Mids, from the eldest down to the youngest. Midshipman Sealey was old for the rank, in his early twenties, and looked to Lewrie's lights to be none too bright, else he would have passed the oral exams by now. There was a lad in his late teens named Furlow, who appeared *bags* sharper. There was a Midshipman Privette, about sixteen, as hawk-nosed and dark-haired as a Cornishman, who looked tarry-handed. There was also Mr. Tillyard, who stood out of order with the younkers, who looked to be a wag, then a brace of fourteen-year-olds named Pannabaker and Plumb; one could barely gawk and stammer, whilst Plumb doffed his hat, gave a jerky waist-bow, and could not resist asking, "Are your cats the reason you're called the 'Ram-Cat,' sir?" in a cheeky manner.

"That's for me t'know, and for you t'find out, Mister Plumb," Lewrie said with a sly grin before turning to Ballard again. "Soon as

I'm settled in, Mister Ballard, I'd wish to meet the Bosun and his Mate, the Master's Mates, Quartermasters, the Master Gunner, and all department heads. Might as well get the names and faces settled in my mind, quick as possible."

"Very good, sir," Ballard replied. "Might you care to see your quarters now, Captain? We've sent the most of Captain Speaks's things ashore already. There are some, ah . . . remaining, for the nonce."

"Yes, let's," Lewrie agreed. "Oh . . . Mister Ballard, my Cox'n, Liam Desmond, and his friend Patrick Furfy, from my old boat crew."

"Lads," Ballard said with a nod. "Mister Dimmock? Work-party to see the captain's goods aboard."

"Aye aye, sir!"

The Marine sentry by the doors to the great-cabins presented arms and stamped boots as Lewrie entered, ducking under the deck beams. The great-cabins might have once been nice, Lewrie decided. There was the usual black-and-white chequer canvas nailed to the deck, and there were the 18-pounder guns bowsed to the port sills, which took up a lot of the space. The lower half of the inner hull planking was painted the usual blood-red, and the planking above was pale tan, as were the deal partitions that would come down, fold, and be stacked below when the frigate cleared for action. A chart-space had been constructed at the forward starboard side, its fiddled shelves now bare, and the tall desk with its slanted top empty. To larboard, Lewrie could see where a side-board, a dining table and chairs, had been placed. Much the same brighter marks or scuffs on the canvas deck covering showed where desk and chairs made the day-cabin, where a settee and more collapsing chairs had been grouped round a wine-cabinet to larboard. There was a narrow hanging-cot still slung in the sleeping-space, handily near to the larboard quarter gallery and its "necessary closet," and . . .

"Hello, you old bastard! Hello!" something squawked.

Furfy had fetched in the wicker cage which held the cats, both of whom stood on their hind legs, front paws working on the wicker and their tails swishing. Little jaws chattered as they let out shuddery urgent trills of hunting-killing lust.

"I meant to mention that, sir," Lt. Ballard dryly pointed out. "Captain Speaks's African Grey parrot. He's had it for years, and it's developed quite a vocabulary. Bought it at Cape Town when he—"

"Flog the bugger! Flog the bugger!" the parrot cried, once it had espied the cats.

"—was just a Lieutenant in the eighties," Ballard continued. "Captain Speaks's wife detests the bloody thing, and refuses to have it at the Wrestler's Arms . . . the hotel where they're lodging for him to recover."

"I'd think the hotel would *agree* with her," Lewrie commented.

"I'm a saucy rascal! Tweep!" the parrot cried. "Hello!"

"Go to the Devil, why don't you?" Lewrie muttered.

"Oh, don't *encourage* it, sir," Ballard cautioned. "That only makes it worse."

"What the Hell are we t'do with it, then, Arthur?" Lewrie asked.

"God only knows, sir. The gun-room don't want it, though there are the Midshipmen . . . ," Ballard replied, "but the Master's Mates and Surgeon's Mates who bunk with them might object. Strenuously."

Captain Speaks had obviously doted on the bloody bird, for its cage was big enough for a frisky mastiff, with many rods and ladders, and even a spread of inch-thick tree limbs for exercise, with a ball on a twine, a small mirror, a bowl of seeds, a water dish, and a dry cuttlefish on which it could hone its beak; the whole thing was made of dulled brass rods soldered together, with a bright green painted canopy.

"Won't last a Dog Watch, once my things are in, and the cats are free to roam," Lewrie predicted, removing his boat-cloak and hat, and looking for a row of pegs on which to hang them. "Good God, that's a Franklin stove!" he exclaimed as he spotted the squat metal monster in the semi-enclosed sleeping-space.

"We've spent the last year running the Baltic convoys," Ballard explained, "and prowling the Dutch and German coasts, right into the Heligoland Bight. There are French and Dutch privateers working out of Christiana and Amsterdam. Captain Speaks bought several of them, for the gun-room, and the people's quarters on the gun-deck. They've come in handy to take the chill off . . . when we can obtain coal. And that only during the day, when the wind and sea allow. The Victualling Board does not see the need to provide heat belowdecks in winter, and told us that supplying coal was our own business. Captain Speaks was thoughtful, but not so rich that he could purchase enough, all by himself, and it's been rare that the officers and hands could chip in and afford a decent store, either, sir."

"Meaning that I should, is that it, Arthur?" Lewrie asked.

"I would not presume to speculate, sir," Ballard replied. "But I admit some coal would be welcome, so long as we're firmly anchored. The harbour, and the North Sea, have been awfully raw this winter."

Lewrie could agree with that. If the weather had seemed to moderate in London, the further east he'd come, closer to the sea, the wind had blown colder and colder, wetter and downright icy. Even here, belowdecks and out of the wind, he still felt an urge to shiver now and then. "Well, we'll see, depending," he allowed. He pulled out his pocket-watch and checked the time; half-past eight in the morning. To prove it, One Bell of the Forenoon Watch chimed, far forward at the belfry. And a glad sound that half-hour bell was to Lewrie, for time to be rung . . . aboard a *ship* once again.

"I'd expect I'll be hard at it, past dinner, to get all my dunnage and bumf set up properly," Lewrie announced. "But I would like you to sup with me tonight, Arthur. Shall we say seven?"

"Of course, sir," Ballard responded with a solemn half-bow.

"Oh, shit," Lewrie said. "I've no cook or steward, or personal victuals . . . live or not."

" 'Scuse me, Cap'm," Furfy said as several sailors entered with chests and furniture. "Settee t'starb'd, same as ye like, sir?"

"Aye, Furfy, thankee," Lewrie told him. "Any recommendations, Mister Ballard?" he asked, now that others were present, and the use of first names might be taken the wrong way by the hands.

"Well, sir . . . Captain Speaks took his manservant ashore with him, to help nurse him through his illness," Ballard explained. "His wife insisted one of the cabin servants go, too. His cook is still aboard, though, a fellow named Nettles. He's very good. Used to be at an Ipswich hotel before the Captain discovered him and hired him away. You've one cabin servant left, a lad named Whitsell, though he isn't much. Only twelve, after all. You didn't bring the usual *entourage*, sir? I'd have expected to see Will Cony with you."

"He's a Bosun into a Sixth Rate now," Lewrie told his old compatriot. "Married to a woman in Anglesgreen. He and Maggie have two boys now. No, when I had to give up command of *Savage*, I could only take away three or four people, and one finally went back aboard her, and t'other, my prime man, had family need of Discharge. Since then, I lodged at a gentlemen's club where I had no need to hire anyone on, and . . . quick as a wink, orders came to report aboard, instanter."

"Aye, I heard, sir," Ballard said, with a veiled look, as if he disapproved but would not say so, about Lewrie's recent *contretemps*. "I do have a suggestion, sir, if I may?" he added, tilting his head to the chart-space, where there was more privacy. Once there, and with the first load of furnishings delivered and the work-party departing for a second load, Ballard continued. "There's a young fellow who's been aboard about a year, sir, who's more suited to steward duties than ever he would be as a sailor. Last up the shrouds, last down, and damn all useless aloft. Too puny for pulley-hauley, as well. The Bosun and mast-captains, gun-captains, all despair of him. He's named Pettus. A Pressed man, no matter he was never a seaman."

"How well I know that fraud," Lewrie said with a wry sigh.

"Indeed, sir. He *claims* he was a manservant to a bishop's residence, at Brighton, before he was rounded up," Ballard said. "Do you wish to see him, sir?"

"Round Seven Bells, aye," Lewrie decided. "I should have enough of my cabins set up, by then. Beggars can't be choosers, I s'pose. Ye have things t'see to, Arthur? Then I'll not keep you, if you do."

"Very well, sir," Ballard replied, delivering another grave half-bow, and departing.

"Hello, you old bastard!" the parrot squawked, bobbing its head.

"Stop yer gob, ye bloody . . . pigeon," Lewrie snapped.

"Give *me* the punch *ladle*, I'll *fath*-om *the* bowl!" the bird responded, singing the old drinking tune right on key.

"Roast parrot on a bed of rice!" Lewrie shot back.

"Damn my eyes, damn my eyes!" the bird sing-songed.

"I'll sic the cats on you if you don't shut up," Lewrie warned.

"I'm a *good* parrot, I am . . . tweep!"

"Christ on a crutch," Lewrie muttered, "but you're a nuisance."

"*Bloody* nuisance!" the parrot uttered, making Lewrie whirl about to gawp in wonder. *How smart* was *the damned thing?* he wondered; *And what'll he blab* next, *if I say anything unguarded in here?*

CHAPTER TWENTY-FIVE

*L*andsman Pettus t'see th' Captain . . . SAH!" the Marine sentry cried, banging the brass-bound butt of his musket on the deck.

"Enter," Lewrie commanded, looking up from his desk, where he and Captain Speaks's former clerk, a former solicitor's clerk with the unfortunately chosen name of George Georges, were going over the ship's myriad of forms and accounts, to assure that Lewrie was not accepting responsibility for a "pig in a poke."

In came a young fellow in his early twenties, tall enough to have to duck under the overhead deck beams . . . barely. It was more a hunched-shoulder diffidence or wariness, Lewrie thought, noting how the fellow appeared on the lookout for a cuff, or a touch-up from the Bosun's starter.

"You wished to see me, Captain sir?" Pettus said, looking fearful of committing some wrong without knowing.

"That'll be all for a little while, Georges," Lewrie told his new clerk. "Get some air on the gangway 'til I send for you again."

"Aye, sir."

"Flog the bugger!" the parrot squawked. "Trice him up!"

"I do not have a steward, Pettus," Lewrie said, rising from the desk in the day-cabin. "I came away at short notice, and your former captain's man is ashore with him, and I'm loath to call him back aboard, as long as

Captain Speaks is so ill and in need of him. Mister Ballard suggested your name."

"Aye, sir?" Pettus said with a note of hope to his voice. He'd made an attempt to be as presentable as he would be at Sunday Divisions. His face was shaved, his thick thatch of light brown hair was combed, and his slop-trousers were mostly free of slush and tar smuts. He wore a chequered blue shirt, a printed red calico neckerchief, and a short sailor's taped jacket that was a bit too short in the sleeves, and with some brass buttons replaced with plain black horn ones. His flat, tarred hat was in his hands before his waist, being turned round about in involuntary nervousness. Pettus *looked* lean and spry enough to make a topman, yet . . .

"You've served a gentleman before, I'm told?" Lewrie asked.

"I *have*, sir, aye!" Pettus eagerly replied, breaking out in an open grin. "In Brighton, sir, I was a footman to the diocese's bishop, him and his family. Not his *personal* man, sir, but I was with them for six years . . . since I was fourteen, and first got my position. I did for his younger son, for a year or so, as well as waiting at-table. . . . There was a lot of entertaining, sir, so I know my way about. It was a grand place, sir."

"Wardrobe? Laundry? Keep track of plates, and utensils and all that?"

"There were others who did that, sir," Pettus admitted, seeming as if his hopes were suddenly dashed, then quickly spoke up once more. "I *did* keep the son's wardrobe, sir, so he'd always have clean linen and pressed stocks, that everything was fresh and presentable, from the laundry maid. Blacked and buffed shoes, polished silver and such, for all the suppers, too! And, helped the scullery maids with the dishes, sir, before and after."

"Read and write?" Lewrie asked, sitting on the edge of his desk.

"Yes, sir!" Pettus said, "I mean . . . aye, sir. My dad taught at a local school, 'til he died, and I had to find a position. Higher mathematics I never mastered, but I can keep a running account book, as good as anything. I've a *little* Latin, a *dab* of French, sir."

"Why did you lose your position, then, Pettus?" Lewrie queried. "And, how the Devil did the Press get you?"

"Well, uhm, sir . . ." Pettus deflated, going all cutty-eyed as a bag of nails. "'Twas a *proper* house, the bishop's manse, sir. Run on *very* moral lines, as I expect you can imagine. Even did the son that I did for have a secret wild streak."

"Most vicars' sons do, as I remember," Lewrie said, thinking of several boys from Church families at his several public schools. *Wild was a* mild *word for 'em*, he thought with a private grin; *And God bless a vicar's daughter, too!*

"He was *mad* for drink, sir, and *someone* had to go along to keep an eye on him, keep him out of trouble when he got cup-shot," Pettus explained, the tarred hat going round and round more agitatedly. "And then there was a new maid-of-all-work that was hired on one summer for the season. I was . . . well, she was pretty as a bunch of flowers, sir, and she and I . . . struck up a liking. A *strong* liking. Just sixteen, she was, sir, and I'd a mind that, did I put enough aside, after a few years, the both of us might marry, sir, but . . ."

Oh dear, Lewrie thought; *You poor, deluded young bastard.*

"Well, sir . . . she and I went a bit ahead of ourselves, on our days off," Pettus mournfully related. "If you get my meaning, sir? We ah . . . found some private places a good walk from town, or the glebe, and, ah . . . made love, sir, like we were already married. The son . . . found out about us. Saw us, when he went riding near where we . . . and the next time I had to go along to guard his drinking bouts, he *japed* me something awful about her. And it didn't stop *outside* the house, sir. He started abusing me at *home,* too, making the worst slurs against Nan . . . the girl, sir, 'til I couldn't take it any more. One last insult, the middle of the day, *at table* before his family, and I . . .

"I dumped the soup tureen on him, sir," Pettus confessed in a meek voice, shrugging and looking down at his shoes. "Creamy pea soup, enough for twelve," he added with a rueful laugh.

"I'm a *saucy* rascal!" the parrot commented.

"Well, that's *one* way t'make an exit," Lewrie said, picturing that scene with some relish. It would have been the sort of thing *he* would have done.

"The only problem, though, sir, was that he blabbed all about the girl, *too,* and got us both sacked," Pettus said, returning to his misery. "Bishop's wife said she wouldn't stand for fornication in her house, and swore no *respectable* place would have either of us, not if we depended on *her* for a recommendation. Nan . . . she had to leave the parish, and try her luck in Chichester, and I haven't gotten one word from her since."

"And the Impress Service?" Lewrie asked.

"I had a little money laid by, so I could take *cheap* lodgings whilst I looked for new work, sir," Pettus said. "I do think I got it in my head to go looking for Mister Edw— . . . the son, sir, and give him a proper thrashing for what he'd done, but . . . I was never much of a man for drink, sir, but I knew taverns and public houses would be where I could find him, and . . . I got as drunk as a lord by the time I'd made all the rounds, sir. It was a warm night, so I'd taken off my coat and hat *somewhere*, and on the way to one of the really *low* taverns, I ran into the Press party, and . . . in trousers and waist-coat, with no neck-stock, either, they took my garb for 'short clothing,' cried that I was a *sailor*, and jumped me. Woke up in the Press tender on the way to Portsmouth . . . into the receiving ship, and then aboard *Thermopylae*, sir."

"Just damned bad luck, all round, Pettus," Lewrie decided aloud. "Do you still drink? Steal?"

"Never stole anything in my life, sir!" Pettus declared, almost angrily at the suggestion. "As for drink, well . . . ," he simmered down. "After being pressed, the rum issue *is* welcome. 'Tis all I can do to choke it down, sir, and give 'sippers' and 'gulpers' to the other lads, most of the time. That way, they don't . . . bully me quite so badly. I admit it makes life aboard ship more bearable, sir, but I'm *not* a sot. Your spirits would be safe with me, if that's what you're wondering."

"You understand that, serving me here in the cabins, you would hear things discussed that should not be blabbed to the other sailors," Lewrie went on. "Mum's the word about where we're going, what the officers and I talk about."

"Mum's the word, sir, aye," Pettus solemnly assured him.

"My last man, I allowed to berth in his pantry, yonder," Lewrie said, pointing his chin towards the dog's-box of a stores cabin that he had had the Carpenter, Mr. Lumsden, erect from spare partitions, in addition to the captain's store room below on the orlop, and the lazarette stowage beneath the padded transom settee, right aft. "You would be responsible for the safekeeping of all my goods, strictly under lock and key 'til I need something. Feel like 'striking' as my steward and 'man,' Pettus?"

"I *would*, sir!" Pettus exclaimed, all but wagging his tail like a puppy in eagerness. "You'll see, sir. I won't let you down."

"You'll have to tolerate the cats," Lewrie said with a smile as he decided to give Pettus a try. "Toulon, there, he's the black-and-white'un. Chalky's the other."

"And, er . . . Captain Speaks's parrot, too, sir?" Pettus asked.

"Bloody nuisance!" the bird chose to squawk.

"I *may* be fattenin' him up for supper," Lewrie said, scowling in the bird's direction. "Shift your dunnage, once you've eat, and as soon as you do, my Cox'n, Desmond, will show you where my coffee beans and grinder are. *And* the pot."

"Uhm, sir," Pettus shyly said. "None of my business, sir, but . . . Mister Perry, Captain Speaks's Cox'n, ah . . ."

"I'll deal with that, but thankee for mentioning it to me," he said. "Close to the Captain, is he, Pettus?"

"Been with him as long as the parrot, I heard tell, sir," Pettus replied.

"Maybe *he* could take the beast," Lewrie said with a snort. "Or, wish t'go ashore to tend to Captain Speaks. That'll be all, for now, Pettus. Report back by Two Bells of the next Watch."

"Aye aye, sir!"

Well, that's one *problem solved,* Lewrie thought, congratulating himself and considering sending to the galley for a plate of whatever the crew would be eating; *As for Perry* . . .

"Keel-haul the bastard!" the bird screeched. "Tha-wheep!"

CHAPTER TWENTY-SIX

". . . 'til we strike Soundings in the Channel of Old England . . . from Ushant to Scilly is twen-ty five leagues . . . tha-wheep!" the parrot sang within his cloth-covered cage, right aft—as far from the dining-coach as he could be placed.

"Bloody . . . !" Lewrie muttered under his breath.

"Let me out, for God's sake . . . *awrk*!"

"You must admit, sir, he's quite the remarkable vocabulary for a dumb beast," Lt. Ballard commented with a wry smirk. "One might conjure that it's intelligent. Or that the Hindoo concept of reincarnation is valid . . . that an 'old soul' came back as a bird."

"T'be dredged in flour and pan-fried, does he keep that up," Lewrie threatened, turning his head to scowl at the cage. Toulon and Chalky were seated below the cage, watching it sway gently, chittering and working their paws on the deck, their tails jerking. Turning back to Lt. Ballard, he asked, "Are you sure Captain Speaks's wife is dead-set against having it ashore?"

"Adamantly, sir," Ballard said with a grave expression and a pursing of his full lips.

"Well, I'm just as adamant that the bloody bird goes," Lewrie grumbled as he cut himself a bite of ham. "Cold as it will be where we're going, it'd be a wonder does the damned thing not freeze t'death. I s'pose the coal-burning stoves were Captain Speaks's way of keeping it tropic-warm?"

"The cage *was* hung quite close to a stove, aye, sir," Lt. Ballard replied as he delicately lifted a forkful of mashed potatoes and green peas to his mouth. "It is a wonder, indeed, that the bird has not succumbed to the cold and damp already . . . or, the loss of its master."

"Gravely ill, is Speaks?" Lewrie asked, motioning for the cabin boy, a snot-nosed twelve-year-old named Whitsell, to refill the glasses.

"Mister Harward, the Surgeon, said it was pneumonia in both his lungs, sir, quite grave . . . aggravated by Captain Speaks's recurring bouts of malaria, contracted long ago in the East Indies and African waters," Ballard informed him, taking a small sip of his fresh glass of wine. "He has hopes a shore physician may bring him through, though."

"Which will take a long time for recovery," Lewrie speculated aloud, assured that his posting would not be temporary. Speaks would not be popping up like a Jack-in-a-Box to reclaim his command anytime soon. "And pray God he does recover," he added, hoping he didn't sound too impious. "For now, though . . . much like old times, hey, Arthur?"

"Of course, sir," Ballard replied.

His old First Officer into *Alacrity* 'tween the wars had changed very little. Arthur Ballard was a square-built fellow, about an inch shorter than Lewrie's five feet nine, as fit and strong as a pugilist. His face was square, with a broad but regular nose, ending in a pronounced chin cleft. His hair was still as dark and wiry as Lewrie remembered, still cut close to his head, which had become the fashion of late; his brows were heavy and dark, as well, shading intelligent eyes of dark brown hue. Well, perhaps the frown lines either side of his mouth were deeper, and the crinkles round his eyes were more pronounced, and, perhaps, he had filled out and gained a little more weight than he had in the '80s in the Bahamas, but he was the same watchful, sobre, and contained fellow he always had been. It was only his mouth that betrayed another nature, for his lips were full and almost sensual, the bottom lip slightly protruding whenever his face was in repose.

Ballard had joined the Navy as a cabin servant at age nine, and had risen to Third Officer of a frigate in 1785 before she'd paid off, and he'd come aboard *Alacrity* as her Second, and only, Commission Sea Officer. What he'd done since 1789, when *Alacrity* had paid off, Lewrie would discover, mostly over suppers such as this one. They had written a few times to each other, then civilian matters had taken precedence, and they had lost contact shortly after the outbreak of the War of the First Coalition in February of 1793.

Still a touch shabby, Lewrie noted of Ballard's uniform; *as he always was. Lived on his Navy pay, with no extras from his family, as I recall.* For even if an invitation to dine with the new Captain was a formal affair, no matter their long acquaintance, Arthur Ballard's best-dress coat was a bit worn, the gilt lace going dull, and his shirt a bit dingy.

"Perry," Lewrie said after a bite of bread roll and a sip from his wine glass. "I expect he feels lost without Captain Speaks aboard. And to lose his place as Cox'n to my man, Desmond. Might he be able to 'strike' for Quartermaster's Mate, or some other post, Arthur?"

"The poor fellow is mostly un-lettered, sir," Ballard said with a sad shake of his head, "and lacks the mathematical skills required. He can barely add or subtract consistently."

"Best he goes ashore, then, to tend to his Captain," Lewrie decided. "Unless Speaks's wife objects to him, too?"

"I believe both Captain Speaks and his wife regard Cox'n Perry as a 'good work' to perform, sir," Ballard replied with a sly grin on his face. "Much as a parish church employs the village dullard as their Christian duty. He's faithful and utterly loyal to them, so . . . sending Perry ashore would be best, sir. He's a capital seaman, but we've more than enough of those aboard already."

"*And*, he takes the parrot with him," Lewrie added.

"Why, I do believe that Perry is immensely fond of the parrot, as fond as he is of Captain Speaks," Ballard rejoined, bestowing a brief seated bow and nod for Lewrie's decision. "I'll tell him he's free to go, before the Forenoon Watch begins tomorrow, if that will be suitable for you, sir?"

"Damned right it'll be," Lewrie said, casting a wary glance over his shoulder towards the cage. Stocky black-and-white Toulon was still seated, mouth agape in anticipation of a bite of parrot, but the spryer Chalky had just completed a flipping-over leap of some prodigious height that had jostled the cage enough to quiet the bird. "Come, lads. Ham for supper! You can eat the bird later."

"Old William Pitt," Ballard said in reverie of Lewrie's original pet, a very surly and stand-off-ish yellow ram-cat inherited from HMS *Shrike*. "I would have thought, mean as he was, that he'd have put you right off *all* cats, sir."

"They grow on you," Lewrie fondly said as the cats trotted over the table and leaped atop it. "And they're wonderful and amusing companions. Thankfully, *these* two scamps are *scads* more affectionate than old Pitt, too. Just what a captain needs to relieve the loneliness of command, right, catlin's?" he said, ruffling their fur and stroking them "bow-to-stern" as Pettus set out two saucers heaped with tiny bits of ham and peas and shredded rolls in gravy.

Odd, Lewrie idly thought, as the cats seemed wary of eating too close to Ballard, though they'd usually make pests of themselves with any table guest, with those who disliked cats the most of all. He had to tempt them to settle onto their haunches and dig into their tucker. Lewrie looked over at Ballard, who was craning his neck over his shoulder, peering at the forward bulkhead above the side-board for a moment.

"I know it's not the done thing, Arthur, but . . . let's say this is more a working supper," Lewrie suggested, returning to his victuals. "We may be at sea within the week, and I'd like you to discover all ye may t'me about *Thermopylae,* and her people."

"Of course, sir," Ballard said with another bow of his head, and a dab at his lips with his napkin. "All told, we've been in commission for about a year and a half, do you see . . ."

The Second and Third Lieutenants, Farley and Fox, were as thick as thieves, having served together as Midshipmen long before, and were immensely competent, though both were possessed of a merry, prankster streak. The Sailing Master, Mr. Lyle, quite unlike most of his post, was also a cheerful soul, though quite exacting when on duty. Surgeon Harward was a bachelor in his mid-thirties, a bookish fellow intrigued by natural philosophy and science, who kept pretty much to himself even in the officers' mess. His Surgeon's Mates, Fortnum and Potter, were better-skilled and more conscientous than the run-of-the-mill "cunny-thumbed" surgeon's mates one usually encountered; due to Harward's demanding standards, and their continual tutelage under his watchful eyes.

Their Purser, Herbert Pridemore, *seemed* more honest than the usual "Nip Cheese," a married man with three children to support, though, so it was early days as to just *how* honest his measures and books were.

The Marine Officer, Lt. James Eades, was a bit of a Martinet, a strict disciplinarian, though most thought him "firm but fair." Young for his rank (he was only twenty-two), Eades was simmering-hot for glory, combat, and honour, almost as bad as an *Army* officer, and how he'd gotten his place without the benefits of a well-to-do family was still a mystery.

Eades didn't have the innate gentlemanly manners of the class of fellows who attained commissioned rank; he could, when irate, curse like a Bosun, and was rather loud and prone to drink in the gun-room.

The Midshipmen . . . Sealey was the oldest at twenty-one, but he had failed his first oral examination for his lieutenancy, though he was good at his job. Furlow was eighteen, and very clever and sharp. Privette, the next youngest at sixteen, was just as competent, but a very dull sort. Oh, there was Tillyard, who was nineteen, and he was, Lt. Ballard tossed off as if it was no matter, or should not be, distant kin to him, but was shaping well as an officer-to-be. "I will not lavish him with undue praise to gain him favour with you, sir. Merely announce that we are cater-cousins," Ballard stiffly admitted.

The youngest lads, Mr. Pannabaker and Mr. Plumb, were fourteen, and, as was to be expected, had their good days and their bad days as petty officers, given their youth and middling amount of experience. Both could be slyly cheeky and pranskter-ish, though not of late.

"They are both Captain Speaks's *nephews*, sir," Ballard related. "He's *three* sisters, all with large families, and second sons in need of careers. Normally, they're lively and impish younkers, but without their uncle aboard, do you see . . . they are quite downcast."

"Cossetted, were they?" Lewrie asked.

"A bit, I must admit, sir," Ballard gravely said. "Good lads in the main, and the hands like them. *And,* obey them chearly," Ballard pointed out. "They are no shrinking violets, or fools. With a firm rein on their sillier moments, and a sharp eye on their performance of their duties, they both show great promise."

As for those who held Admiralty Warrant, both the Bosun Mr. Dimmock, and the Bosun's Mate, Mr. Pulley, were tough older "tarpaulin men," and nothing escaped their attention. The Master Gunner, Mr. Tunstall, the Gunner's Mate, Mr. Shallcross, and the Yeoman of the Powder, Bohanon, were equally capable, and that went for the Carpenter, Mr. Lumsden, the Quartermasters and their Mates, the Cooper, the Armourer, and the Sailmaker, Mr. Cable, and his Mate, Durham, to boot. The captains of the masts, the quarter-gunners, . . . almost everyone aboard, Ballard could find no real fault with.

Oh, among the Able Seamen, the Ordinary Seamen, and Landsmen, there were the usual drunks, the unwillingly pressed men and scrapings from the county Assizes courts and gaols, due to the Quota Acts, which swept up the dregs that the Army had not gotten to first, but . . . all told,

Thermopylae was crewed by as competent a ship's complement as one could expect in wartime. Growl they sometimes might, but go they would, and, if well-led, they'd do their duty, and more.

"I've only had time to flip through the punishment book," Lewrie admitted as they sat and savoured hot coffee and brandy on the settee and chairs, once the table had been cleared. "I didn't see all that many defaulters' names, nor did I note that many lashes awarded. Was Captain Speaks a Tartar, or merely 'firm but fair,' Arthur?"

"The Captain was, uhm . . . firm but fair, I would adjudge him, sir," Ballard cautiously stated, for the Navy frowned on criticising senior officers, even ashore, and in strictest privacy among juniors. "He cared deeply for the welfare of the ship's people, and was quite popular with them . . . though he in *no* wise ever cossetted or played a 'Popularity Dick.' He was . . . *is* a consummate sailorman, strict when necessary, yet a rather easy-going fellow most of the time," Ballard further explained, sounding almost prim in his choice of words. "They recognised his care for them, sir, and responded with, dare I say it, outright affection."

"Ouch!" Lewrie barked with a small laugh. "I've always thought of myself as an easy-going sort, too, but, damme! These are going to be a *tight* pair o' shoes t'fill. Well, perhaps as we rub together, the hands and I, we'll sort it out. Right, Toulon?"

After supper, and a brief romp with a couple of bottle corks, the cats had come to the settee, where Lewrie sat half-sprawled with a leg up on the cushions, Toulon to snuggle against his chest, and the other to drape himself across his thigh. Except for a brief sniff at his boot-shod legs, with their ears flat, both Toulon and Chalky had quite ignored Arthur Ballard, which was quite unlike their gregarious and curious natures, which again struck Lewrie as . . . odd. He was as good a fellow as any— Knolles of the *Jester*, Langlie of both HMS *Proteus* and *Savage*—and the arrival of supper guests from a First Officer to Midshipmen to a Marine messenger "passing the word" from a Watch officer was cause for glad, familiar greetings.

"And we'll be ready for sea, when, d'ye reckon, Arthur?" Lewrie lazily enquired, stifling a yawn. It had been a long and busy day, and his new-built bed-cot hanging aft, his usual "wide-enough-for-two" was calling. Pettus had filled some tin cylinders with boiling-hot water in *lieu* of ember-filled warming pans, and had even spread one of those furs atop the coverlet, so his bed would be toasty-warm.

"All but last-minute stores are aboard now, sir," Ballard said, head cocked over as he calculated. "Once Admiral Sir Hyde Parker issues sailing orders, I expect a full day for livestock, gun-room delicacies and such, to be fetched off . . . perhaps the coal as well, sir? After that, *Thermopylae* would be ready to sail, in all respects."

"Good," Lewrie said with a nod. "The Admiral is already here in Great Yarmouth?"

"I do not believe he is, as yet, sir," Ballard told him.

"Nelson?" Lewrie asked, faintly scowling.

"His flagship has not yet come round from Plymouth, sir, though he is expected daily." Ballard further informed him.

"Damme, time's wasting," Lewrie grumbled. "The ice in the foe's harbours could be melting as quick as our last snow. Is there anyone senior to talk to?"

"There is Captain Riou, sir," Ballard said. "He is the senior frigate captain present, and is expected to be named Commodore over all the Fifth and Sixth Rates in the expedition. He's in the *Amazon*."

"The fellow who sailed *Guardian* back to Cape Town after hitting the iceberg?" Lewrie said in some surprise.

"The very one, sir," Ballard agreed in his usual grave way.

That had been a tale! In 1789, *Guardian*, a partially dis-armed old 44-gun frigate, on her way to New South Wales with convicts, seeds, and £70,000 of stores aboard, had struck an iceberg in the fog east of Cape Town, and had come near to sinking. Despairing that she'd go down despite everyone, sailor or convict, manning the pumps round the clock, Riou had sent off all five ship's boats to try to make it back to Cape Town, 1,200 miles off. One boat had foundered in heavy seas, drowning all aboard, but the other four had managed to row away. One boat had been rescued by a French merchantman; the others had vanished without a trace. Then, *weeks* later, Riou, with less than thirty brave men still aboard to plug, fother patches, and pump incessantly, sailed *Guardian* into port, saving ship, stores, seeds, and lives!

"I look forward to meetin' him, then," Lewrie said, allowing a yawn at last. "I'll have another peek at the old Order Book whilst I eat breakfast, and will let you know if there's anything I wish changed, Arthur. Other than that, it sounds as if I've landed aboard a fine ship, with a fine crew."

"You have, sir," Ballard said with a touch of pride.

"And the very fellow I'd request for my First," Lewrie added, lifting his cup of brandy-laced coffee in salute, and smiling widely.

"I will endeavour to please, sir, as I did once before. Well, it's lacking One Bell to Lights Out, and the Master At Arms, Mister Mackie, is a humourless stickler. Would there be anything else, sir? If not, I will take my leave, and let you get a good night's sleep."

"None I can think of, Arthur," Lewrie said, rising. "Do let me know the price of coal hereabouts . . . and just how often the stoves could be used on your previous winter cruises. I'll consider it."

"Good night, then, sir," Ballard said with a departing bow.

"Good night to you, as well, Mister Ballard," Lewrie replied in kind. "Perhaps our *last* sound sleep before things get exciting, hey?"

"Indeed, sir," Ballard said. He turned and walked forward to the door, glancing once more . . . at the dining-coach partition.

"Will you be needing anything else, sir?" his new man, Pettus, asked as he gathered up the last cups, saucers, spoons, and glasses from the starboard-side seating area.

"No more tonight, Pettus," Lewrie told him, yawning again. "I think you and Whitsell can doss down for the night. Oh. The cook, Nettles."

"Aye, sir?"

"Relay to him my thanks for a handsome supper," Lewrie said. "I quite enjoyed it. Is that his customary talent, I expect I'll dine as well as I would at a fine hotel."

"He's probably in the galley with the ship's cook, Sauder, sir," Pettus said with a shy grin. "Keeping warm and nattering over a glass of rum, sir. I mean to say, uhm . . . not that he's a *drunkard* exactly, sir, but . . . ," Pettus stammered, thinking he'd blabbed too much.

"He's accommodated himself to life aboard a warship," Lewrie said with a chuckle. "Warrants and petty officers will always have a flask stowed away, and will take an un-regulated nip now and then. It's no matter, long as he can cook so well. I'll turn in. You and Whitsell finish up, and turn in yourselves. I can undress myself."

Still savouring the last lingering tastes of ham, potatoes and peas, fresh butter and succulent *white* bread rolls, a spicy vegetable and bean soup, a fish course of smoked mullet, *and* a cherry jumble, he went aft to his wash-hand stand, scrubbed his teeth with powder pumice and a stiff-bristled brush, rinsed, and began to undress. Quickly, for the temperature was dropping, and a cabin aboard a ship at anchor was an icebox . . . a *damp* icebox.

Lewrie usually slept nude, in better climes, but was thankful to note that Pettus had dug out a long flannel nightshirt for him, and had hung it on a row of pegs near the bed-cot. He kept his knee-high cotton stockings on, too, as he hefted himself over the railing of the bed-box and under the covers, where he found several patches of heat left by the tin warmers. Up to his chin went the blankets, a thick quilt his wife had made him long before, the heavy painted coverlet, and that fur rug, which reeked equally of camphor and . . . was it bear musk? North American bison?

No matter, for Toulon and Chalky were entranced by the scent, and padded all over it, sniffing and pawing, pausing to glare at him with their jaws half-open and their eyes slit in exotic pleasure.

"Do *not* pee on it, hear me?" Lewrie cautioned them.

"*Mrr,*" Toulon said in ectasy; "*Mrrf,*" Chalky added, sneezing.

"Good night, sir," Pettus softly said from beyond the partition to the bed-space as he snuffed the last candles.

"Night," Lewrie replied.

"*Good* night, ladies . . . *good* night, ladies. *Good* night, *ladies,* we're going t'leave you now," the parrot contibuted.

"Oh, *do* shut the bloody hell *up!*" Lewrie snapped.

"Whee-hoo!" the bird whistled back. "*Good* night, awrk."

Thankfully after that last utterance, the parrot quieted down, with only a few mutters and wing-flutters, and, after a few more long minutes of snuffling and exploration, Toulon and Chalky settled down, as well, curled up together in a wad behind his knees, silently grooming each other, by the feel of it through the thick covers. In darkness, and curled up in the fetal position to hug the last of the heat from the warming tins, and his own body, Lewrie could not quite go to sleep 'til he had puzzled out Arthur Ballard's odd behaviour. Not one time had he presumed upon their old friendship to call him "Alan," but "sir," even in private. Oh, back then in *Alacrity,* Lewrie and he were within six months of the same age, about six months as to the dates of their lieutenancies, and both of the same rank, with Dame Fortune tipping Lewrie the nod to command the saucy little converted bomb-ketch . . . a small vessel with a small crew, and they the only Commission Officers aboard her.

He didn't mention the trial, not once, Lewrie realised with a start; *Didn't ask anything personal, either. Damme, does he disapprove o' me doin's? The scandal?* Lewrie let out a little snort as he considered that Ballard might read London papers, and could have put two and two together about him and Theoni, too, no matter how salaciously veiled Mrs. Denby's article was! *Christ!* Lewrie thought, stiffening as he recalled how he'd caught Ballard looking about for the portrait of Caroline that usually was hung on the dining-coach partition or the forrud bulkhead over the side-board. *Arthur'd always been fond of her, and they got along like a house afire, the few times we were ashore in the Bahamas,* he remembered. As grave and dignified as Ballard carried himself, so much care he took with his every utterance, it was only the rare shore suppers in a chop-house, or at their rented cottage out by East Bay, when Ballard had ever let his guard down, and had japed and laughed like a normal fellow; only then did he un-bend and . . . *smile* a lot!

And the cats' odd reaction to him . . . God above, even that Frog agent, that fellow Brasseur, or whatever he'd called himself, who had come aboard *Savage* during the close blockade of the Gironde pretending to be a simple local fisherman, and had lied about the shore defences like a French newspaper . . . "lied like a bulletin from Paris" was the French expression . . . why, Toulon and Chalky had been *mad* for him when he came aft for a glass of rum and Lewrie's gold.

O' course, he was covered in scales, and reeked *o'fish,* Lewrie told himself; *yet, even so . . .'tis rare they run into a man they* shun. *Now, why is that?*

As if to answer his quandary, Toulon and Chalky shifted a bit, both uttering wee sleep-whimpers as they pressed closer to each other, and him.

Arthur don't like me, *for some reason!* Lewrie thought, almost with an audible grunt; *Can't be professional, can it? No, not him, so it must be personal. Oh, he'll do his* duty, *right enough, but I doubt his* heart's *quite in it, this time round. I'm his new captain, not his old'un, so maybe* that's *a wrench for him, same as for Speaks's nephews, or his Cox'n. Or his bloody parrot!*

Lewrie punched his pillows into a deeper pile and dragged a few last inches of covers, and fur, half over his head, leaving just enough of a gap so he could breathe, and tried willing himself to a peaceful rest. *Puzzle it out in the morning,* he thought.

CHAPTER TWENTY-SEVEN

*D*elighted to welcome you aboard, Captain Lewrie," Capt. Edward Riou said with what sounded like genuine enthusiasm, once Lewrie had taken the salute of HMS *Amazon*'s side-party. "Doubly welcome is your *Thermopylae*, of equal weight of metal to *Amazon*. You will take coffee or tea, sir, for 'tis an unbearably chilly morning."

"That'd be toppin' fine, Captain Riou, thankee kindly," Lewrie replied, shivering under his heavy wool boat-cloak.

Edward Riou was a very pleasant gentleman, though, by the way he carried himself so urgently, with every gesture and movement of his hands spare but efficient, Lewrie could quickly assume that Riou was a most active and hard-charging fellow. Once below in the great-cabins, and free of hats and cloaks, Riou appeared strong yet spare, with wavy hair thick upon his pate, and curling over his ears and neck, an intelligent high brow, thicker, darker eyebrows, and large, expressive eyes. His face was a long oval, split by a very long nose, a thoughtful sort of pose to his mouth, and a determined chin. He was scads senior to Lewrie, but showed him every sign of the nicest sort of condescension.

"There's a comfortable chair, sir," Riou offered. "Do take a seat, and we'll see you warmed up in a trice. You've replaced Captain Speaks, I take it?" Riou said, playing the perfect pleasant host.

"I have, sir, poor fellow," Lewrie told him. Riou sat down in a chair opposite, and his cabin steward was there with a tray bearing a coin-silver coffee pot, sugar, creamer, and Meissen china cups and saucers. "Cannot *stand* tepid coffee myself, so have a care, Captain Lewrie."

"My own preference, indeed, sir," Lewrie replied, grinning as he felt the heat through the cup. "Aah . . . splendid brew," he added after his first tentative sip. "Nigh to boiling, too. I do apologise if I interfere with your preparations for sea, sir, but, with neither of our admirals present yet, I thought it prudent to speak with the most-senior officer in port."

"Well, there *is* Rear-Admiral Graves, reputed to be on his way to us, but . . . for the nonce, I suppose I'll have to do," Riou said with an easy grin. "With the fleet divided into the usual three divisions . . . Van, Main Body, and Rear . . . I hear he's to be third in command, after Sir Hyde and Nelson. Pending the arrival of someone else, mind. It's all still a bit up in the air."

"Sir Hyde is not present, I'm told, sir?" Lewrie asked.

"Oh, he is, but he has not yet gone aboard *Ardent,* where he's hoisted his flag . . . temporarily," Capt. Riou said with a disappointed twitch of his mouth. "The rumour is that he's to have the *London* when she gets here, and will not go aboard *Ardent* only to have to shift all his dunnage later. He, ah . . . has taken lodgings ashore, at the hotel . . . the Wrestler's Arms," Riou added with a faint frown.

"Oh," Lewrie said with gawp of surprise. "I'd thought things were already afoot, all but ready to sail, sir. Time of the essence . . . all that? Ice melting?"

"One would think," Riou agreed, his frown a touch deeper than before, and rolling his delicate cup 'tween both hands for warmth. "It *is* a quickly gathered expedition, though . . . robbing Peter to pay Paul, as it were, taking vessels from Channel Fleet, recalling others from the French blockade, and juggling ships and officers like a circus act. Such things take time," he said, sounding as if he was putting the best face he could on what seemed a serious lack of urgency.

"Pray God, sir, not too *much* time," Lewrie said. "We should be at 'em. But then . . . people have accused me before of bein' too rash a *frigate* captain, who can't see the larger intent."

"Then you are a man after mine own heart, Captain Lewrie, and I do believe a 'drap' of rum in your coffee would not go amiss?" Riou offered with a conspiratorial, sly grin.

⚓

Lewrie had only stayed aboard *Amazon* for a bit less than an hour, being treated to a quick tour by a proud Capt. Riou to show off how fine was his frigate. *Amazon* was indeed "ship-shape and Bristol Fashion" in every respect.

"Damme, but I like that fellow!" Lewrie exclaimed once he'd sat down in the stern-sheets of his boat, and his Cox'n, Desmond, had gotten it underway for the town piers. "Captain Riou is one Hell of a fellow."

Now, if only Parker turns out t'be half the man Riou is, Lewrie thought; *Come t'think on't, I can't recall ever really* meeting' *him.*

He'd been under Admiral Parker's command in the West Indies for almost three years, and had exchanged reports and orders, but the closest he'd ever gotten to the man was to call upon his shore headquarters out on the point of Kingston Harbour . . . dealing with that drink-addled Staff Captain known as "the Wine Keg," later with Capt. Nicely, who had taken his place once the former had died "in the barrel," and . . . he'd heard Sir Hyde Parker *snoring* in his chambers just above the entrance hall. Lewrie had made the man a pile of "tin" with his capture of that new-minted Spanish silver at Barataria Bay, but then Parker's favourites, like Otway and others, who had been allowed to cruise independently and reap prizes like a dealer raked in cards from the baize of a gaming table had made him umpteen thousands more. He wondered if the man would even recall his name!

"More ships comin' in yonder, sir," Desmond pointed out towards the Sou'east, to the treacherous entrance through the series of shoal-banks offshore that guarded Great Yarmouth from the full onslaught of the North Sea. A brace of ships of the line, Third Rate 74s, led the procession, followed by a small frigate or sloop of war, and a brace of bomb vessels or gunboats; at that distance it was hard to tell how their masts were spaced.

"They keep a'comin' in like that, sor, 'twill be that soon th' whole shebang gits underway, aye, Liam?" Patrick Furfy, the starboard stroke oar, muttered to his mate.

"Eyes in th' boat, Pat," Desmond whispered back, "an' mind yer Ps an' Qs." As Cox'n, he was supposed to keep good order, though stern discipline, and a "hard face," came un-naturally to the fellow.

"Shebang?" Lewrie asked. "What sorta word is that? I've heard of Irish *shebeens* . . . all fleas and whisky . . . but what's a shebang, Furfy?"

"Lock, stock, an' barrel, like, sor," Furfy replied with a grunt of effort, paying more mind to the pace of the stroke. "Th' whole thing."

"You listen to Furfy long enough, you lads'll learn a thing or two," Lewrie told his boat crew, all of whom but for Desmond and Furfy were strangers to him, so far.

"Ye listen t'Pat Furfy, ye'll learn all th' *wrong* things!" Liam Desmond countered, which raised a small laugh from them all. "Easy all, now . . . bow man, ready with yer gaff an' painter," Desmond ordered as the boat ghosted towards the foot of the slimy stone stairs at a quay. "Toss yer oars, larboard," he added, putting his tiller over.

A moment later, and Lewrie was able to step over the gunwale to the wet steps, and trot up to the top of the quay. "Won't be but half an hour with Sir Hyde, Desmond. Hot cider on me if a vendor comes by, but keep 'em close," he ordered.

"Aye aye, sor," his Cox'n replied, knuckling his forehead in salute.

A foul wind was whipping over the harbour, out of the East-Nor'east, not quite a "dead muzzler" yet, to pen the gathered warships in port. It was a cold Scandinavian wind, though, that whipped his cloak and plastered it to his back, threatening to snatch away his best hat as he set a brisk pace towards the Wrestler's Arms hotel. Head down, and a hand on his hat, he almost rammed a pair of gentlemen who trudged against the wind in the opposite direction, giving ground and swivelling his shoulder clear without half looking at them.

"Captain Lewrie, sir? My stars, it *is* you!"

"Huh?" was Lewrie's witty rejoinder as he turned about. "Damn my eyes . . . Mister Mountjoy?"

"To the life, sir!" his former clerk in HMS *Jester* cried, looking both relieved and pleased. "Speak of coincidence, sir, but I was just in search of a boat to come out to you."

"Whyever, Mister Mountjoy?" Lewrie asked with a frown, recalling that Thomas Mountjoy, the younger brother of his London solicitor, was now employed by the Foreign Office—not by the silk-drawers, laced handkerchiefs, Oxonian drawlers who implemented and delivered British diplomacy, but by the *other* "department"; the one that employed Zachariah Twigg and James Peel. Spies, lurkers, and cut-throats, did the need arise, and dealing with their sort was never a very healthy thing to do.

"Well, first off, sir, Mister Keane, here, who coached down from London with me, is an Admiralty messenger," Mountjoy said, turning to indicate the young fellow with him. Lewrie cocked a brow in wonder.

"Admiralty Orders, Captain Lewrie," Keane said, tapping a thick canvas despatch bag slung over his shoulder, "just confirmed with Vice-Admiral Sir Hyde Parker, sir."

"Well, let me see 'em, then," Lewrie requested, holding out a hand.

"Well, erm . . . they might best be opened and read aboard *ship*, sir," Keane said, coughing into his fist, not from caution; it sounded wet, phlegmy, and ominous. "*Sealed* orders, sir, well . . . *one* set sealed, t'other, uhm . . . *private*." Keane might have said more, but for a fresh bout of hacking, which bent him half over.

"I suppose you've saved me a call upon our Admiral Parker, Mister Mountjoy?" Lewrie asked, beginning to get one of those fey feelings that association with Twigg usually engendered. "Customary, after all."

"Sir Hyde, sir, is, ah . . . quite busy, and barely had the time to see *us*, do you see," Mountjoy explained with a twist of his mouth. With a confidence that Lewrie had not seen in him when he'd served as his clerk, Mountjoy actually *winked*, and further said, "I do believe Sir Hyde and his bride are . . . otherwise engaged, Captain Lewrie."

"Draggin' his '*sheet*-anchor,' like the papers said?" Lewrie surmised.

"Lady Frances is become known as his 'little batter pudding,' I do believe, sir," Mountjoy replied with a salacious grin.

"Well, I can see why Mister Keane came down from London, Mister Mountjoy, but . . . why is *your* presence required, as well?" Lewrie just had to ask, though dreading the answer.

"Well, there is another niggling little matter, sir," Mountjoy confessed, looking more like his old, hesitant self for a moment. "If I may accompany you aboard your ship, I can enlighten you further," he said, tapping his lips with a mittened finger, which request for privacy—for secrecy!—almost set Lewrie's innards squirming into a Gordian knot.

"Mine arse on a . . . ," Lewrie grumbled, knowing that he'd been had—again!—and carping would not even make him feel better about it, much less get him out of whatever deviltry the new government had come up with. "Anything more for me from Admiralty, Mister Keane?" he asked instead, turning to that wheezing worthy.

"Nothing more, sir. If you would take possession of the orders, and affix your name in receipt of them, ah . . . here," Keane said, opening his canvas bag to produce a ribbon-bound and wax-sealed bundle of paper, a short receipt form, and a stub of pencil. "Save me a row out to your ship in this weather, do you see, and grateful for it, ha ha!"

Lewrie shoved the orders under his boat-cloak, into a side pocket of his uniform coat, then looked for a flat surface. "Turn round, Mister Keane, would ye be so kind," he said, employing the man's back as a writing desk on which to press the form and pencil his name down. "There ye are, then, Mister Keane, and take care of that cough."

"I fully intend to, sir, and thankee for your solicitous—" Keane tried to say, interrupted by another bout of fluid coughs. He had the good courtesy to turn himself away, alee of both Mountjoy and Lewrie 'til he was done.

"A hot mustard salve," Mountjoy hopefully suggested, "followed by candled tea cups applied, to draw out the humours, perhaps."

"A scalding bath, followed by a *bowl* of stiff-laced punch, sir" was Lewrie's sage advice. "Drunk in a bed piled with covers, and hourly changes o' warmin' pans. It don't work, ye can't feel any worse in the morning, Mister Keane."

"I thankee again for your solicitation, sirs, and take my leave to follow your advice," Keane said, bowing from the waist. "Godspeed," he concluded, before turning to lope for the nearest warm tavern.

"So . . . what the Devil is it, *this* time, Mister Mountjoy?" Alan Lewrie sourly demanded as he led his former clerk towards his waiting boat.

"It is more in the nature of a *diplomatic* mission, sir," Thomas Mountjoy told him, frighteningly cryptic and tight-lipped.

"Meanin' some diplomat's throat must be slit, I s'pose," Lewrie sarcastically rejoined. "Does Twigg have somethin' t'do with this?"

"He *did* participate in the initial consultations, yes," Mountjoy answered, though loath to say too much in the open. Lewrie increased his pace, if only to warm up, forcing Mountjoy to toddle along off his larboard quarter to keep up. "Mister Twigg was not instrumental in the choice of ship, or captain, however, sir. Does that mollify you."

"By God it does *not!*" Lewrie groused. "I should've *known* gettin' an active commission so quick'd have a catch to it. I'd get leery even if Twigg was only walkin' *by* Admiralty, or Whitehall, and wasn't at the bottom of it . . . whatever it is."

"Once completely laid before you, sir, you'll see that it really *is* quite straightforward," Mountjoy attempted to console.

"Well, they all *begin* that way, don't they, Mister Mountjoy?" Lewrie shot back, past gut-churning dread to a good fume. "Christ on a *crutch*, sir . . . will that foul old schemer *ever* be shot o' me? Or, me of him?"

"Perhaps when he passes from this mortal coil, at last, Captain Lewrie," Mountjoy said with an enigmatic smile. "Yet, when he finally does . . . God help England," he stated with a touch of awe and respect for his patron.

CHAPTER TWENTY-EIGHT

A Franklin *stove?*" Mountjoy enthused once Pettus had taken his overcoat, hat, and cane, and had seen to his captain's things as well. Mountjoy rubbed his chilled hands over the stove, savouring the heat.

"And thank God coal's cheap in England," Lewrie said, enjoying his early-morning splurge with the Purser in much the same fashion. He cocked an ear and looked about. "The parrot's gone!"

"Aye, sir," Pettus told him after he'd hung up their things on the row of pegs. "Mister Ballard sent him ashore with Perry, just at the change of the watch. Coffee, sir?"

"Nigh-boilin', aye," Lewrie gladly agreed, turning to lift the back of his coat to the stove. "Won't do in a sea-way, but our Surgeon, Mister Harward, says it's best for the ship's people, are they kept a *bit* warm. *Thermopylae*'s been prowling the North Sea and Baltic all winter, and there are a number of hands come down with consumption. More a matter of too many men cooped up below with hatches and companionways shut, he told me, Mister Mountjoy."

"Though, one might imagine that the body heat they generate, along with the warmth of the galley fires trapped below, would provide some heat," Mountjoy speculated, facing about to thaw his own bottom. "Hallo, you've made an addition! Hallo, Toulon, you old rascal. And who's the new one, sir?"

"That's Chalky," Lewrie told him as the cats tricky-trotted to greet the new arrival. "Came off a French brig we made prize in the West Indies. Well, the Americans took her, but Chalky came aboard as a gift."

"The Quasi-War 'twixt the United States and France, yes, sir," Mountjoy replied, kneeling and wiggling his fingers to attract Lewrie's cabin-mates. "My mentor, James Peel, wrote me of it, and your part."

Peel tell you my American bastard gave me the cat? Lewrie wondered, for Mountjoy's tone bordered on the cryptic again, as if he was smirking.

"Too bad Guillaume Choundas got away," Mountjoy commented, once Toulon had taken a tentative sniff, and had decided that Mountjoy was vaguely familiar.

"The American navy defeated his ship, so they had custody of th' shit," Lewrie explained, heading for the settee. "I *tried* to lay our claim on him, but . . ."

"Well sir, with the disagreement with France settled, the Yankees no longer had reason to hold him on his parole," Mountjoy said. "I think he's back in France . . . though in none too good odour with their new First Consul, Napoleon Bonaparte. Our sources say that Choundas is pensioned off from their navy, and no longer much of a threat. Lurking round Paris, looking for active employment, Mister Twigg said.

"It was most diplomatic of you, the way you acceded to the American claims, sir," Mountjoy said, looking up from his kneeling position on the floor, where Toulon was now rubbing him and purring as he was stroked. "The manner in which you cooperated with the United States Navy gained their trust, and kept our tacit support of them from public purview, as well."

"So I *can* be diplomatic, can I?" Lewrie scoffed. "Meanin' this should be a walk in the park?"

"Something like that, sir . . . oww!" Mountjoy meant to say in compliment . . . before Chalky, feeling left out, nipped him for attention.

"Should've warned ye 'bout Chalky, he's the jealous sort," Lewrie said. "Well damme, Mister Mountjoy, here it is almost Old Boys' Week. First my old First Officer, Arthur Ballard, turns up as *Thermopylae*'s First Lieutenant, and now you. Makes one wonder, do ye hang about in Yarmouth long enough, ye run into everyone ye ever knew. Ah, coffee!" he exclaimed as Pettus appeared with the black-iron pot, and cups. As soon as Mountjoy took seat in a chair across from him, *before* the cats could claim a lap, Pettus poured the coffee for them, then sat the pot atop the Franklin stove, tautly lashed down in the middle of the great-cabins, and firmly embedded in a tin-lined wood box filled with sand.

"Diplomatic, ye say," Lewrie said after a warming sip, once he had laced his drink with fresh-grated sugar, and some cream drawn from the frigate's nanny goat, kept in the forecastle manger up forward.

"Uhm . . . ," Mountjoy cautioned, casting a glance at Pettus.

"One of those 'mum's the word' moments, Pettus," Lewrie said to his new servant. "You and Whitsell take a turn on deck for a bit. Now," he said, once they'd departed. "Just who is it does Twigg wish me to murder? Or, would shovin' 'em over the side in the dark of night do?"

"In your orders from Admiralty, sir," Mountjoy uneasily began, glancing about for hidden witnesses, or for ears pressed to the windows of the coach-top overhead, "which you shall open and read shortly, you are directed to sail for the Baltic, preceding the fleet, and reconnoiter the ports of Copenhagen, Karlskrona, Kronstadt, and Reval to determine the thickness and condition of the ice which, at present, prevents the ships opposing us from sailing, and combining."

"All by our lonesome little *selves*, Mister Mountjoy?" Lewrie had to gawp and goggle. "Just who the bloody Hell dreamt *that* up?"

"I believe it was a suggestion from Admiral Nelson, sent to Captain Thomas Troubridge, who is now seconded to a seat on the Board at Admiralty, and relayed to Lord Saint Vincent, the First Lord, sir," Mr. Mountjoy related in a low, conspiratorial tone. "Whilst neither I, nor anyone at the Foreign Office, are privy to the thought behind the plan, I gather that the consensus was that, should a *lone* British frigate enter the Baltic, her presence would not be cause for much alarm among the powers in the Armed League of the North, do you see. Even with a war in the offing, it is only natural that, in the pursuit of a diplomatic solution to our *contretemps* with the Danes, Swedes, and Russians, messages from His Majesty's Government would still be delivered to our ambassadors 'til the very last moment, and their delivery by a fast frigate, not a packet brig, would elicit no undue response."

He's grown a lot since last I saw him, Lewrie thought, remembering the hen-headed, utterly landlubberly callow young cully who had stumbled over every ring bolt and coiled line, who, after one taste of adventure and mayhem ashore in pursuit of that French counterpart to Twigg—Gillaume Choundas—and their escape from the utter rout of the Austrian army, had been gulled into taking a more active part for

King and Country than scribbling in ledgers and account books, to take employment, and training, under Twigg's, and Jemmy Peel's, arcane tutelage.

"Though, Mister Mountjoy, the presence of a British frigate to *recall* our ambassadors before the shootin' starts'd make 'em scramble t'snap us up," Lewrie cynically pointed out.

"Well, that would be an act outside the diplomatic niceties, sir," Mountjoy took delight in countering quickly, "as beyond the pale of conduct between civilised nations as would our arrest and imprisonment of their embassies and legations. It just isn't *done*, sir.

"Besides," Mountjoy continued, legs now crossed in clubman fashion, one ankle resting on the other knee, with Chalky up in his lap, and his cup and saucer balanced on the bent knee, as serene as a man taking high tea with his doting mother. "With the navies of the Armed Neutrality iced up in port, the odds of encountering any of their ships already brought out of ordinary, manned, and got to sea . . . perhaps by chopping open channels through a *mile* of three-foot-thick ice . . . are rather low, sir," he said with a charming grin. "Why, it'd take *thousands* of workers to get *one* ship out. A task better suited to the Egyptians piling up the Pyramids . . . or the Chinese erecting, well . . . whatever it was the Chinese built, with a round *million* coolies, what?"

"There is that." Lewrie cautiously allowed him the point, loath though he was to admit it. *Thermopylae* might run a greater risk from punching her hull open on a stray floe or berg, of foundering on some badly charted shoal or small island . . . of which the Baltic boasted an appalling plenty. Ice, once the sun rose, just naturally created fog, like London spewed coal smoke. "Slow as the fleet for the Baltic is gatherin', it might be different in a few weeks, but do we sail today, or before the end of the week . . . ," he mused, shrugging. "Oh!

"That's the straightforward, *naval* mission, Mister Mountjoy," Lewrie said, once the other shoe figuratively dropped. "Go in, scout, then sail back out and meet Parker and Nelson somewhere in the Skagerrak, or the Kattegat, and report what we've seen. But ye said there is a *diplomatic* side to my orders? Are there letters to be delivered to foreign capitals?"

"Not . . . letters, sir, exactly," Mountjoy said, going all cutty-eyed and putting Lewrie back on his guard in a trice. "At least, not letters from Foreign Office that *you* will personally deliver, no. We have entrusted the plan for a possible peaceful solution to people who possess more influence

with the Tsar and his court than our ambassador, John Proby, Lord
Carysfort, at the moment. Well, actually . . . ," Mister Mountjoy went on,
squirming in a way that just naturally forced Lewrie to cross his own legs
to protect his "nutmegs" against an imaginary boot.

"At this moment, His Majesty's Government does not *have* an ambassador resident in Saint Petersburg," Mountjoy confessed. "Lord Carysfort is our ambassador to *Berlin*, and the Prussians, but . . . he's used to
dealing with the Russians, even at long distance, by post."

"I'm to pick up Lord Carysfort and take him to Russia?" Lewrie
asked. "Save him a long *troika* ride through the snow, is it? Spare him
from the packs of wolves?" he added, the sarcasm in full flow.

"Ah, no sir. You are to embark a pair of eminent Russian nobles,
who are to deliver His Majesty's offer for a peaceful solution to the Tsar
themselves," Mountjoy explained. "Tsar Paul's recent affection for
Napoleon, and France, his eager acceptance of support for his spurious
claim to the island of Malta, *and* his acceptance of the title of Commander of the Knights of Saint John . . . a *Catholic* honour awarded by a
very small, *heretical* batch of courtiers . . . well, it goes against the grain
for nobles steeped in the Russian Orthodox Church, sir. And what
France, and Bonaparte, stand for . . . Liberty, Fraternity, and *Equality* . . .
are *anathema* to the structure of Russian society, *sure* to cause bloody
revolution, the overthrow of aristocratic authority, rebellion of their
millions of serfs nationwide, perhaps a wholesale slaughter of the rich,
landed, and titled as vicious as the French Revolution, and The Terror
which it engendered. There is *great* concern that the Tsar's recent capricious actions, and the Armed Neutrality, might present the Russian Empire with war on two fronts, and with our Navy allied with the Ottoman
Turks in the Black Sea, they might lose all their conquests of the last
hundred years, entire, sir. There is the possibility that, should the unofficial embassy you carry to Russia succeed in contacting key members of
the Court, and swaying them to stand up to the Tsar . . ."

"But the Tsar is *daft*, Mister Mountjoy," Lewrie took great glee in
quickly pointing out, "as mad as a hatter . . . as a March Hare! And anyone who gainsays him'd have t'be even crazier than *he* is. Or, have a desire t'have his *head* chopped off. I can't see anyone *sane* opposing the
Tsar. Might as well insult a Genghis Khan with a *toothache* or a bad
breakfast, and 'whop' goes your head."

"Well, it may be slim odds, sir, but there's always the hope," Mountjoy
said, "and if the mission fails, then at least we *tried*. Lord Hawkesbury,

our new Foreign Secretary, has determined that the avoidance of a costly new war in addition to the present one against France, is best in the long run."

"Hmm," Lewrie mused, puzzling that one out. Toulon climbed into his lap and kneaded for "pets," which Lewrie gave, distractedly. "The only snag, Mister Mountjoy, is, is the ice so thick that the Russians can't yet get *out*, how the Devil am I to get *in* with my passengers?"

"If Saint Petersburg, Kronstadt, Reval, or any major ports are un-available, it is my understanding that any small fishing port will do, sir," Mountjoy told him. "Sleds could be summoned over the ice if even the small harbours are unreachable, and the embassy may proceed by land. Anyplace will suit, just so long as they are landed as close to Saint Petersburg as possible."

"And you'll be going along on this neck-or-nothing jaunt, Mister Mountjoy?" Lewrie asked. "To speed 'em on their way?"

"In point of fact, *no*, sir," Mountjoy answered, close to squirming again. "The presence of a British subject in company with the embassy would poison its chances of success, immediately," he was quick to explain, and for a second Lewrie could almost (but not quite) take that as believable. Yet . . .

"You'll sail with us, 'til landfall, at least, won't you?" he skeptically enquired.

"Sorry, sir," Mountjoy said with a stab at a dis-arming smile and a hapless shrug of disappointment to be missing a grand adventure. "I was instructed to escort them down from London, explain the matter to you, then return. Deliver them into your capable hands, then dash back to my superiors."

"Oh Christ," Lewrie gawped. "I smell a rat, Mountjoy. A great big, toothy, Twigg-scented rat."

"Rather . . . 'something rotten in Denmark,' sir? To quote the Bard," Mountjoy breezily replied, attempting a chuckle. "No, Mister Twigg, as I said, was *consulted* in this matter, only to the extent of advising Lord Hawkesbury as to who might best be approached in Saint Petersburg, and, who might best serve as the emissaries. Frankly, I'd he *delighted* to go along, sir. Working for our *particular* branch of the Foreign Office is not *quite* as exciting as Mister Peel made it out to be, when first he and Mister Twigg recruited me. I spend the most of my time office-bound in London, with only the occasional adventure."

"Uh-huh!" Lewrie scoffed at that. "Mean t'say my 'live-lumber' is already here in Yarmouth?"

"They are, sir," Mountjoy said, "warming their fundaments in a hotel for the moment. Another fellow coached down with Mister Keane and me . . . a Captain Hardcastle, a merchant master very familiar with the Baltic, and the ice conditions. All told, there will be six men to make room for. Admiralty was also to send down a Lieutenant Ricks, who took service with the Russian navy for several years, also in the Baltic. I'm told he wintered over with them at least two of his years, so he should prove most informative about how soon in the Spring they get their ships re-masted, re-armed, and brought out of ordinary."

"Six men?" Lewrie asked, wondering where Lt. Ballard would find room for them all. There would be some disgruntled officers in the gunroom if turfed out to accommodate foreigners.

"Two servants, sir," Mountjoy explained. "Only one manservant per emissary. They wished to have *three* apiece, but we finally convinced them they'd be going by *frigate,* not a yacht."

"Do they fetch a lot o' dunnage with 'em?" Lewrie pressed for more information; would the aristocrats be separated from their servants, even for the night, or must *Thermopylae* shift all her stores on the orlop at the last moment, too?

"We also convinced them to limit themselves to but *one* waggon-load of goods, sir . . . in addition to their trunks and bags," Mountjoy told him. "Rather a *lot* of it consists of wine and other spirits. I'd advise you, sir," Mountjoy said, leaning forward, "to *not* match them drink for drink, especially do they offer their national spirit, which is called *vodka.* It's powerfully intoxicating, and will sneak up and swat you 'tween the eyes before you even notice."

"Well, I survived *slivovitz* and Serbian pirates' plum brandy so I *might* essay at least a taste," Lewrie allowed, resigned to the fact that nothing outside Damnation to Hell lasts forever. He supposed he could tolerate a half-dozen lubbers for a month or so, even if he had to subdivide his great-cabins to accommodate some of them.

"Speak English, do they?" Lewrie quipped.

"Passably, sir," Mountjoy said with a grin, relieved, perhaps, that Lewrie was not kicking furniture or ranting over the sudden revelation of his orders . . . or Mr. Twigg's slight connexions to them. "You will have Captain Hardcastle and Lieutenant Ricks, both fluent in Russian, to carry you over the stickier translations. Of course, all Russian nobility . . . the Tsar's Court, especially . . . speak French in *lieu* of their own tongue. After several days of listening to the two gentlemen slang away in Russian, I can see why. A beastly language."

"Tell me about it," Lewrie commiserated, recalling Eudoxia and her father when they spatted with each other.

"Then, of course, sir, there is your own partial mastery of Russian," Mountjoy said with a smile and a nod.

"*What* mastery, Mister Mountjoy?" Lewrie said in surprise.

"I, uh . . . we were led to believe you had a *smatter,* sir, so . . ."

"I can tell when I'm bein' cursed. Beyond, that, not a bloody word," Lewrie took some joy in telling him.

"Oh, my," Mountjoy muttered.

BOOK 3

Movenda iam sunt bella; clarescit dies
ortuque Titan lucidus creceo subit.

Now must my war be set in motion; the sky is
brightening and the shining sun steals up in saffron dawn.

-LUCIUS ANNAEUS SENECA
HERCULES FURENS, 123-24

CHAPTER TWENTY-NINE

*O*h, springing joy," Lewrie dourly said as a hired barge came alongside *Thermopylae*'s starboard, cleared to make way for their passengers and goods, about ten in the morning of the day after Mountjoy had brought his news aboard. The two Russian nobles had found their coaching journey from London too exhausting, though Mountjoy had said that they'd been in no urgent rush, and had made stops every two hours for warm-ups, late-morning starts each day, and early-afternoon halts at only the best coaching inns or hotels from London onwards.

After reaching Great Yarmouth, they'd lodged themselves in the Wrestler's Arms, the same hotel where Vice-Admiral Sir Hyde Parker and his "little batter pudding" still enjoyed their honeymoon; where the gravely ill Capt. Speaks, his wife, retainers, physician, and parrot, strove for his recovery, and where there were several large fireplaces and deep-piled soft beds. They had sent word aboard that they would rest for a night, then join *Thermopylae* at first light, this morning.

Evidently, first light to a pair of Russian nobles meant closer to "Clear Decks And Up Spirits" at Seven Bells of the Forenoon, almost nigh to Noon Sights, than "Crack of Dawn," "First Sparrow Fart," even Eight Bells of the Morning Watch, at 8 A.M.

Forewarned, Lt. Ballard had concentrated upon the loading of any last-minute purchases by the Purser, the Master Gunner, Sailmaker or

Armourer, the Cooper or Carpenter, for the officer's and Midshipmen's messes, and the Captain's Cook.

Lt. Ballard surreptitiously pulled out his pocket-watch to take a squint at it, then heaved a small, fretful sigh before stowing it away again.

"Doesn't make a diff'rence, Mister Ballard," Lewrie told him. "The wind's still foul for us t'make an offing." He looked up to the long, snaking commissioning pendant at the truck of the main-mast . . . the winds had come more Sutherly, but not by all that much, as yet. "Whistle up the side-party, and All Hands, now they're almost alongside. Perhaps by sundown."

"Aye aye, sir."

"Beg pardon, Captain Lewrie," Capt. Hardcastle, their merchant master, intruded. Not willing to spend Admiralty funds on an expensive shore lodging when he could pocket the difference and sleep for free aboard *Thermopylae*, and drink and sup on Navy largesse, he had reported aboard just after noon of the day before. "In my experience, the wind will shift quick, by dawn tomorrow. Go back to stiff Westerlies. Let us get out slick as anything."

"Not having served in the North Sea before, sir, I thankee for that news, Captain Hardcastle," Lewrie told the fellow, who looked as if he'd spent most of his life being battered by stiff winter winds and heaving, green-white seas. Hardcastle was ruddy, chapped, skinny yet wiry as a teenaged topman, though going rapidly bald. Lewrie had dined him in the night before, and the man ate like a teenaged topman, too.

Lt. Eades appeared in his finest uniform, with a party of his Marines, accompanied by Sgt. Crick and Corporals Thomas and Frye. The frigate's officers and Midshipmen were there, as well, turned out in Sunday Divisions Inspection best. Pulley, the Bosun's Mate, sounded a call for All Hands to bring the crew up from where they'd been sheltering belowdecks from the wind and the cold.

"Humph!" Lewrie said with a suspicious sniff as he got an eyeful of the goods stowed down the centreline of the approachings barge. "A powerful lot of it for one waggon-load, Mister Mountjoy. Do they buy their wine by the tun, or do they fetch off their own *water* kegs?"

"I'm not quite sure, sir." Mountjoy, who had been scuttling to and from shore to hasten their arrival since the aforementioned Crack of Dawn, sounded as if the nobles' cargo had multiplied overnight. "I *think* something was said of last-minute shopping, but . . ."

"So," Lewrie demanded. "Which of 'em's which, then?"

There were only four civilian passengers in the barge, besides the three sailors managing her, all looking up at the railings of the frigate with varying interest; or the studied lack of it. There was a tall and thick-set older fellow in a lustrous and expensive-looking coat of some sleek fur that reached to his ankles, with the collar up round his neck below a fashionable narrow-brimmed thimble of a beaver hat. Was it his own hair that was so white, or did he sport a short peruke? He appeared sublimely indifferent to the proceedings.

"The older gentleman is Count Dmitri Rybakov, sir," Mountjoy prompted from Lewrie's right elbow, in a loud whisper as if in awe of foreign nobility. "The heavy-set chap in the *shapka* fur hat beside him is most-like his servant. The other one, standing by the stays, is Count Anatoli Levotchkin, and *his* servant. Now where's Lieutenant Ricks? He was to leave London but a day behind us."

"Um-hmm," Lewrie responded, more interested in the perfect turn-out of his side-party and officers for a moment, to make sure nothing was amiss. It would not do his suddenly resuscitated career any good for a titled foreigner to lodge a complaint of *lèse-majesté* upon him. Count Rybakov, so bored-looking, simply struck Lewrie as the very sort of arrogant pain-in-the-arse who'd take offence over the slightest bit of suspected dishonour or disrespect.

He then turned his attention to the younger man whom Mountjoy had pointed out to him. If Count Rybakov looked about fifty years old, the younger noble could pass for his son. Levotchkin appeared to be in his early twenties, if not in his late teens. He also wore a sleek, long double-breasted fur overcoat, though with the wide collar and lapels down, and had one of those fur hats—a *shapka*—on his head with the ear-flaps turned up. The "Baldy" beside him, his supposed manservant, was a hulking, pugilist-big and rough-looking brute, who not only wore no hat at all despite the cold, but wore a shaggier and cheaper hide coat lined with sheep wool open to the elements. Whilst the other men wore buckled shoes or top-boots that peeked from below the hems of their long coats, this fellow wore fur-lined mid-calf boots with his trousers stuffed into them.

"Looks like those two had a bad night of it, somewhere," Lewrie japed under his breath, taking note of a few fading bruises on both the young noble's, and his servant's, faces.

"I understand they were set upon by a gang of thieves a couple of weeks ago, in London, sir," Mountjoy supplied, *sotto voce* now that the barge was snugly alongside.

No! Lewrie goggled; Can't *be! Can it? What're the odds that that's* Tess's *'Count Anatoli'?*

"What were they doin' in England, anyway, before this scheme got dropped on 'em, Mister Mountjoy?" Lewrie asked, turning away from the barge to look at the fellow from the Foreign Office.

"Oh, Count Rybakov had come to purchase blooded race horses and hunters, sir," Mountjoy was happy to relate, to reveal his knowledge. "English and Irish thoroughbreds. Simply *mad* for them. And I think Count Levotchkin was doing a term or two at Oxford."

Christ, he very likely is Tess's *'Count'!* Lewrie realised as he tried to portray idle curiosity; *Now ain't this goin' t'be int'restin'!*

". . . liked London Society so much that he stayed on nigh a year, sir," Mountjoy was blathering on, cheerful as a magpie, "after he sent his new horses on to his Russian estates. He got invited to country houses for fox-hunting and steeplechasing last Autumn. The Pytchley or the Quorn, I forget which, but he took a hedge badly during one of the 'cub-hunts' before the season started proper, and had to heal up. By then, he was back in London, just in time for the winter balls and such. *Everybody* likes him immensely, even the Prince of Wales. He's a lively dancer, too, especially at the *contre-danses*."

"Who? Levotchkin?" Lewrie asked, taking another squint at the stiff-faced young twit clinging to the larboard stays of the barge's single mast.

"Oh *no*, sir, Count Rybakov!" Mountjoy corrected him. "I don't know that much about Count Levotchkin . . . just met him before we took coaches here . . . seems a serious sort of sprog, to me, he does."

"Well, does Rybakov dance well, I'll have the ship's band tune up, and let him try his hand at a horn-pipe," Lewrie wryly said.

"Does *Thermopylae* actually have a band?" Mountjoy asked.

"No . . . but I've still my penny-whistle," Lewrie told him with his tongue firmly planted in his cheek.

"Lord spare us," Mountjoy said in a whispered sigh; echoed by Lt. Ballard, who had overheard, and had been a victim aboard *Alacrity* when Lewrie had first tried his hand at music. His talent had not improved appreciably when Mountjoy had been aboard HMS *Jester*, either.

With his servant's help, the elder noble clumsily mounted the gunn'l of the barge, trying to balance for a breath or two, using his gold-knobbed ebony walking-stick as a prop, before stepping out for the main-mast channel platform. A slight harbour scend raised up the barge just in time to make it an easy step. Rybakov was quick to seize hold of one of the thick dead-eyed main stays; as if catching his breath at his daring before essaying anything more strenuous, he looked up for the first time, glowering at the difficulty of battens and man-ropes.

"Should we have lowered a bosun's chair, d'ye think?" Mountjoy whispered. "I know you always say it's undignified, but . . ."

"Might not have a clue," Capt. Hardcastle opined. "Might've got aboard a merchantman right off the pier, by gangway, sir."

Lewrie stepped to the bulwarks, and leaned out the open entry-port. "Might you require a chair-sling, sir?"

"How the Devil . . . ?" Count Rybakov fumed back, waving one hand at the boarding battens, "*tiy idysodar charochko,*" he added under his breath. "Aah!" he spat right after, discovering that his expensively gloved right hand was sticky with tar.

"The boarding battens are like rungs on a ladder, sir," Lewrie helpfully explained. "The ropes strung through their outer ends, one holds onto as one ascends. Really, we can rig a sling . . ."

"*Chort!*" Count Rybakov snarled; whether he meant "Damn" or did he intend "Shit," it was no matter. It was a quite useful word. He flung his walking-stick up at Lewrie, who, startled, barely managed to snag it as it twirled, else it would have gone into the waters between the hulls of the frigate and the barge, then stepped off the chain platform to the battens, took hold of the man-ropes with both hands, and made a slow way upwards; right foot up first, then he brought the left to meet it before moving up to the next batten. Once clear of the chain platform, the younger Count Levotchkin sprang up atop the gunn'l of the barge with ease, hopped across to the platform, then waited for the older man to clear the battens. He grinned, as if it was funny.

Lewrie couldn't make out what Rybakov was saying under his breath, but he could guess. Each deep exhalation sounded furious in *some* language. *He's goin' to complain, I just know it,* Lewrie thought; *A stern letter to the Foreign Office, Admiralty, askin' for my head.*

As the crown of Count Rybakov's stylish hat peeked above the lip of the entry-port, the Bosun and his Mate began to shrill a long duet call. Lt. Ballard cried for the crew to doff hats, and Lt. Eades barked for his Marines to bring their muskets to the Present, with loud and uniform slaps of hands on wood, and short boots stamping on oak decks.

Lewrie doffed his cocked hat with his right hand in salute, and tucked the walking-stick behind his left leg. "Welcome aboard *Thermopylae,* my lord," Lewrie said with a hopeful smile.

"Errr," Count Rybakov grumbled back, sounding very much like a pirate rolling off an angry "Arr!" as he stripped off his thin gloves. Without caring where they went, he tossed them over his shoulder, then stuck out his right hand. For an eyeblink, Lewrie thought he wished to shake hands, but realised that Rybakov only wanted his walking-stick back.

By then, the younger noble had scampered up the battens to the deck, as the Bosun and his Mate continued their long, intricate call worthy of an Admiral being piped aboard.

"Welcome aboard His Majesty's Ship *Thermopylae,* my lord," Lewrie repeated for him, doffing his hat once more. Count Levotchkin glared a very stern, chin-high look at one and all, slowly swivelling his head from bow to stern, and up and down the waiting row of officers and Midshipmen, who were "toeing the line" of a deck seam with their hats off and lifted high in salute. The young sprog had *seemed* excited when he had stood by the barge's stays, looking up, almost in wonder and expectation, but now, he had put his "aristocratic phyz" on, as if ordinary people and experiences were beneath him, and made no impression.

"Count Rybakov . . . Count Levotchkin, allow me to present to you Captain Alan Lewrie of his Britannic Majesty's Navy," Mountjoy quickly intervened to make the formal introductions, "an officer famed for his skill and courage. Captain Lewrie, I name to you Count Dmitri Rybakov and Count Anatoli Levotchkin."

"Your humble servant, my lords," Lewrie chimed in, bowing from the waist and making a "leg" with his hat swept to his chest. "May I present you to my officers, my lords? After all, we shall all be together for some time on our voyage."

"Are any of them noble?" Count Levotchkin asked, giving them all a dubious up-and-down scanning, much like a tailor to the Crown might to a pack of new-come *parvenus.*

"Uhm, I don't believe . . . ?" Lewrie said, looking to Lt. Ballard for help in that regard. Ballard gave his head a brief shake of no. "No one, sorry."

"Then it is of no matter," Count Levotchkin said with a snobbish sniff. "Where are our quarters? It is cold."

"British sea-dogs," Count Rybakov said more jovially, smiling broadly. "England's 'wooden walls,' yes? *I* would like to meet your officers, *Kapitan* Lewrie. Introduce me to them."

"Of course, my lord," Lewrie said, with a bit of relief that he was going to be friendlier than his colleague. *Maybe he* won't *write complainin' letters, after all*, he thought; *hoped*, rather.

Rybakov shot a stern glare in Levotchkin's direction before he went down the line of officers and Midshipmen with Lewrie, exchanging greetings. Thankfully, Lewrie could call all of them by name by then, right down to the youngest Mids, Pannabaker and Plumb. Levotchkin was forced to trail the elder man, bestowing short jerks of his head when each was named to him, obedient, but letting all know that he was very bored with the proceedings.

"Yes, our quarters, *Kapitan* Lewrie," Count Rybakov said after the last introductions were done, and the manservants had clambered up to the gangway with the lighter luggage.

"This way, my lords," Lewrie bade. "Mister Ballard, you'll see their dunnage hoisted aboard? I will depend on your servants to show my First Officer which items are required for your everyday existence, and which of the bulkier items may be stowed below on the orlop, sir?"

"Yes, my man, Fyodor, and Sasha, know our wants," Rybakov agreed.

Sasha! Lewrie twigged to the name; *Isn't that the fellow Tess's Count called to for help, the night Mother Batson's bucks beat 'em all t'puddin'? God, this'll be* really *int'restin'!*

"Aah . . . warmth!" Count Rybakov enthused, making a bee line to the Franklin stove to warm his hands, and unbuttoning his long overcoat.

"Take yer things, sir?" Pettus offered. Rybakov looked him over for a moment, as if sizing him up as *worthy* enough, before handing him his hat and walking-stick, and letting him remove that heavy fur coat. Once rid of his outer wear, Count Rybakov displayed a full head of hair atop his head, light grey, or dingy white, not a peruke, and worn in a modern style. His suit was dark green, waist-length in front with the long tails behind that were all the "crack" in London that season, with snug matching breeches below, and white silk stockings and stout shoes with gilt buckles. There was a waist-coat of jacquard stripes in white and salmon to add a jaunty note to a sombre overall hue, as did his neck-stock, of dark red moire silk. Forgetting his aristocratic airs, Count Rybakov turned about and lifted the tails of his coat to warm his bum, the same as any man, sighing and smiling with pleasure to have a thawed backside.

"A glass of something warming, as well, my lord?" Lewrie asked. "Or might you take tea or coffee, first?' Count Levotchkin?"

Damn the young sprog! He had flung off his own fur hat and his coat, and was prowling through Lewrie's wine-cabinet without leave.

"I'm sure you'll find *something* warming in there, sir," Lewrie said, allowing his sarcasm a looser rein for a moment. Levotchkin had tossed his hat atop the dining table, and had simply let his coat hit the deck in a furry heap for someone else to pick up later. Whitsell, the cabin boy tried to pick it up, but it was damnably heavy.

Without recognising that Lewrie had even spoken, Count Anatoli took a bottle of Kentucky whisky from the racks, unstoppered the decanter, and took first a sniff, then a short swig straight from the bottle. With a shrug that signifed that it *might* do, Levotchkin helped himself to a glass and poured it full, before crossing the cabins for a slouch on the starboard-side settee, with one top-booted foot atop the large brass tray-topped low table that Lewrie had fetched back from his time in India, 'tween the wars in the '80s.

"*Kulturny, plyemyaneek,*" Count Rybakov chid him in Russian.

Culture, Lewrie translated from his very limited stock of words and phrases, in his head; *T'other's . . . cousin? Nephew? One of 'em, so they're related somehow. Put some* manners *on, he's saying.*

"Kentucky Bourbon whisky, Count Levotchkin," Lewrie told him. "I am sorry we don't run much to *vodka,* nor gin, either. Rum's our stock-in-trade . . . that, and small beer, or wine."

"Tea, yes, *Kapitan,*" Count Rybakov exclaimed, using his enthusiasm to deflect his kinsman's bad manners. "Fyodor, ah . . . the glasses for tea. We Russians prefer it so hot, the tea glass must be surrounded by a metal holder."

"I'm familiar with 'em, my lord," Lewrie replied, though still fuming over the younger noble making so free with his spirits. "Sorry we don't have a *samovar* aboard to brew tea the way you like."

"Lots of sugar, Fyodor," Rybakov reminded his servant, who was digging through a small chest. "You have lemon, *Kapitan?*"

"For now, sir, aye. A limited supply, sad t'say. Hard to get in England, in mid-winter," Lewrie told him. "Tea, pipin' hot, Pettus. For you, Count Levotchkin?"

"*Nyet,* "the young man snapped.

"If you'll take a seat, sir," Lewrie bade the older man, an arm swept in the direction of the settee and chairs. And, cocking a brow over the sheer amount of luggage coming in a solid stream through the forward door and piled by his sailors where the dining coach had been, across from the chart-space. "I've taken the liberty of re-arranging the great-cabins to accommodate you on-passage, my lord," he said once he'd sat down himself. "I've shifted my sleeping space and my desk forrud, nearer the quarterdeck, and given you and Count Levotchkin my old space, there . . . aft on the starboard side, with a hanging bed-cot each. The, ah . . . necessary is on the larboard side, yonder, and we must share . . . sorry. There *might* be room left for your servants to sleep in hammocks, do you require them to be at hand at all hours."

The new arrangements had looked cramped before; with all the chests and trunks and leather *portmanteaus* coming aboard, Lewrie began to wonder if there'd be room in which to swing a cat, did Fyodor and that *huge* Sasha sleep aft, along with Pettus and Whitsell.

Speaking of . . . Toulon and Chalky, intrigued yet frightened of all the bustle, darted with their bellies scraping the deck to their one secure place, Lewrie's lap.

"You will sleep here, with us?" Count Levotchkin asked, as if the very idea was insulting. "With those filthy little beasts? Pah!"

"He is *Kapitan* of the ship, Anatoli," Rybakov gently reminded Levotchkin. "We are his *guests*. The *Kapitan* must sleep near the helm, and his watch officers, so he may respond to the slightest change, or emergency. It will only be a few weeks, after all," Rybakov said with a grin. "And cats are not as noisy as that damned parrot who shrieked the night through at our hotel last evening. Surely, the pet of some sailor . . . or a fiend."

"It is not dignified," Count Levotchkin groused, removing his nose from his glass of whisky just long enough to say.

"*Would* you require your servants to bunk here, my lord?" Lewrie asked again.

"No," said Rybakov. "*Da*," said Levotchkin. "*Nyet*," Rybakov insisted, glaring the sulky young man to surrender the point. "They are not necessary after we retire, *Kapitan* Lewrie," he stated, settling the matter. "And we both understand the constraints placed upon us and our usual comforts when travelling by ship . . . by a warship, not one built for their passengers' pleasures . . . do we not, Anatoli." It was not a question, but a pointed warning, to which the young man had to nod agreement . . . though his face and ears went a bit redder as he swallowed his bile.

Mr. Mountjoy entered the great-cabins, sidling past two sailors lugging yet another bloody-great leather round-topped trunk, and made his bows to the nobles, before leaning down to Lewrie.

"It would seem that Lieutenant Ricks will not be available, sir."

"Why not, Mister Mountjoy?" Lewrie said with a frown.

"He, ah . . . was taken up for debts the morning our party left London, sir," Mountjoy mournfully said, "and is now most-like held in the Fleet prison 'til he's repaid his creditors."

"Well, damme," Lewrie groused. "Can't Admiralty pay 'em for him, so he's available?"

"They are his *personal* debts, sir," Mountjoy explained, "and not any sums he might have run up in active *British* commission. Recall, he was on half-pay to Admiralty, the last three years, and was in Russian service 'til late last Autumn, so . . ."

"And, I s'pose there's no one else available?" Lewrie asked, and answered his own question. "No, of course there isn't . . . not in time t'do *us* any good. Might take a week t'whistle up another'un, and he'll take the best part of the *next* week t'come join us here in Yarmouth."

"Well, sir, with the Russian Baltic fleet iced up in harbour," Mountjoy pointed out, looking for the best face on things, "there may not be all that great a *need* for immediate expertise on their navy."

"We must delay our sailing?" Count Rybakov asked, a tad agitated upon hearing of it.

"I think not, my lord," Lewrie told him, puffing out his cheeks and lips in frustration, though putting the best face on it himself. "Mister Mountjoy is correct . . . does the ice keep your Baltic fleet in port a month or so longer, it's slim odds we'll run into any of them at sea, before we land you at the nearest ice-free port to Saint Petersburg, so Lieutenant Rick's presence would make no difference to us. I expect, soon as the wind's come Westerly, to set sail. Perhaps as soon as tomorrow, dawn."

"I am gratified to hear it, *Kapitan* Lewrie," Count Rybakov said with relief. "Our diplomatic mission, and the hope of a reconciliation between our two great nations, before a war can be set in motion, from which *no one* can prosper but the odious French tyrant, Bonaparte, must not be hindered."

No wonder everybody likes him, Lewrie thought.

"Most gratifying to the Foreign Office, as well," Mountjoy said with an open, relieved grin.

"By dawn, we could be on our way, Anatoli," Rybakov cheerfully said. "Does that not sound pleasing?"

"*Da* . . . yes, it does," Count Anatoli agreed, sitting up a little straighter, showing his first sign of any emotion other than bored-to-tears. "Urr-rah!" he cried, right after tossing his drink down in one gulp. It did not help his welcome aboard, though, that right after he had drunk, he threw the glass at the pierced metal grate door of the stove, where it shattered.

And no wonder everyone despises you! Lewrie thought, wincing at the mess, and the loss of one of his better glasses; *He keeps that up, he'll be drinkin' from cupped hands . . . we all will. I'd wager he has* hosts o' people lined up, waitin' t'slap him silly.

Count Levotchkin smirked at their reactions to his action, and tossed off a small shrug that was all they would get by way of apology. He rose to go to the wine-cabinet for a fresh glass, perhaps a taste of something else more pleasing, while his kinsman, Count Rybakov, looked at Lewrie and rolled his eyes as if to say "what may one do with these young-sters?" while nodding and blinking a silent apology for him. Whitsell, Lewrie's runty cabin boy, went for a broom and dust-pan.

"One of our customs, *Kapitan* Lewrie," Rybakov said. "Whenever an oath is pledged, or a toast of significance to us, we break the glasses in the hearth, or on the floor, to seal its importance . . . so that no one may re-use those glasses, and renege, later. That is how urgent our . . . peace mission is to us . . . to Anatoli, you must understand."

Lewrie looked over his shoulder to the young man in question to see him opening another decanter and sniffing it, and young Whitsell by his side, as if to deter him from causing any more mayhem.

Anatoli Levotchkin, were one not aware of his cruelty and perversity, really did appear as a handsome, well-set-up fellow; tall, slim and with the build of a courtier, or a light cavalryman. He had close-cropped dark blond hair, with the typical blue Slavic eyes in a lean scholar's face, framed by sideburns to below his earlobes, and brushed forward almost in Frenchified fashion. Lewrie imagined he was rich as Croesus, or the Walpoles, but Levotchkin was dressed in scholar's drab; a black doubled-breasted coat over a grey waist-coat, with the collars of his shirt turned up to his jaws, with a bright yellow neck-stock at his throat. Dark buff, snugly-cut trousers and top-boots completed his suiting. *Lawyers* dressed more colourfully.

Levotchkin *might* be taken for a well-off young student about to take his final exams, and Blues for brilliance, or an off-leave cavalry officer in a fashionable regiment; he *could* be mistaken for a typical "Merry Andrew," yet . . .

Cavalry, for certain, Lewrie decided to himself; *Only cavalry's that top-lofty, and dim. Lord, make this a short voyage!*

He turned back to look at Rybakov again, and stroked his cats, who had each taken a thigh on which to sprawl and knead his waist-coat for attention and comfort.

"Tea, sir," Pettus announced, returning from the galley with a large pewter pot held in folded towels. "Boiling hot as you requested."

"Ah, tea!" Count Rybakov exclaimed, clapping chilled hands.

"Capital!" Lewrie heartily agreed as Pettus set the pot on the stove top and went for a tray of cups and saucers.

"Urr-rah" was Levotchkin's sneer, back to the laconic sulker he'd been when he'd first come aboard.

I'll not *shove him overboard, th' first dark night,* Lewrie vowed; *I'll* not!

CHAPTER THIRTY

As if in answer to Lewrie's prayer for a short voyage, the wind came round more Sutherly by sunset, prompting him to send word ashore for a harbour pilot to attend *Thermopylae* at first light, in the expectation that the prevailing Westerlies would be in full force by dawn. He also directed Lt. Ballard to dismantle and stow away the stoves by Eight Bells of the Middle Watch, at 4 A.M., when the crew was roused out to swab decks, stow hammocks and bedding, and clear away.

"Sir . . . sir," a sleepy Pettus said, tapping the wood side of his hanging bed-cot. "Eight Bells, sir."

"Very well, Pettus," Lewrie said with a grunt. The quilts and furs really had made a pleasingly snug and warm cocoon, and coming up from it was like a dive into cold water. "Clothes . . . quick."

"Pot of coffee is on your side-board, sir," Pettus told him as he left the small partitioned-off sleeping space, closing the slat door. He'd left a lit lanthorn over which Lewrie warmed his fingers, once he had donned his thickest wool stockings, a set of underdrawers, a pair of slop-trousers, and his tasselled boots. Two shirts, his neck-stock, and waist-coat quickly followed, topped with his heaviest old uniform coat, hastily doubled over

and buttoned against the chill. Over that he threw a dressing robe to
hoard his body's warmth 'til the very last second before he would have to
appear on the quarterdeck.

Some hasty attention to Toulon and Chalky, who seemed glad that
they could nestle together on the furs once he'd gone, and he was out
with the lanthorn in his hand to light his way to the dining-coach for a
welcome cup of coffee, which Pettus had already sugared for him.

"Christ," Lewrie snapped, as one booted foot thumped against one
of his passengers' chests.

"First off'cah . . . SAH!" the Marine sentry by the outer door announced in a loud, thunderous *basso*, with the requisite thud of a musket
butt on the deck.

"Come," Lewrie bade, glad for at least one friendly face.

"Good morning, sir," Lt. Ballard said, hat in hand. "The wind is
come round to West-Sou'west. Once the hands have eat, the ship is
ready for sea, in all respects."

"Very good, Mister Ballard," Lewrie said. "Coffee?"

"Most welcome, sir," Ballard agreed. As Pettus poured him a cup,
Ballard gazed about the great-cabins. "May I say, sir, that your quarters
now more resemble the hold of a coasting brig."

"Barely enough room t'swing a cat, aye," Lewrie agreed, grumbling
over the rim of his cup, which he held between both hands. "How I am
expected *t'land* all this flotsam and jetsam with 'em, I don't know. Heard
from the pilot, have we, Arthur?"

"We have, sir," Ballard replied, all grim business, as was his wont
when on duty. For a moment, Lewrie could almost imagine that Lt.
Ballard's tone of voice held a note of reproof for the casual use of his
Christian name. "He assures us that his boat will be alongside at six,
and suggested, in his note of reply, that our best course would be to
depart through the Saint Nicholas Gat channel, which will lie to leeward of the winds . . . and is most-recently re-buoyed and marked,
sir."

"I'd *dig* a channel through the shoals and bars, does it get us on our
way soonest," Lewrie said back. "Lord, what a chore they are!"

"Our 'live-lumber,' I take it that you mean, sir," Ballard said with
only the faintest smirk.

"One a talkative wind-bag, t'other a gloomy, drunken 'sponge,'"
Lewrie griped. "Before Mister Mountjoy departed us, he told me it was

part of my 'diplomatic' duty to dine 'em proper . . . play the tactful host, hah! I'd rather have the other officers and Mids in, and get a feel for 'em, but I can't do that with our passengers at-table at the same time. I can have a few of 'em in each meal, but, only for *their* amusement," he said, jerking his head aft in the direction of his sleeping guests. He spoke low, as well, so as not to wake them. No matter, for the sounds of hundreds of sailors opening and slamming sea chests, their shoes thundering on the decks and companion-way ladders, and the thuds and squeaks of wash-deck pumps being set up and drawing sea water . . . followed by the rasp of holystones and "bibles" on those decks for the morning's scrub-down to pristine whiteness, which *could* be conjured as the wheezing breath of a great dragon at times, was sure to awaken them, sooner or later; even Levotchkin, who had been *poured* into his swaying bed-cot by his servant, Sasha, as drunk as a lord.

"The stoves stowed away?" Lewrie asked, pouring himself half a cup of coffee, to warm up the rest in his mug.

"No fuel added since the start of the Middle Watch, sir, and the embers are now in the process of being cast overside," Lt. Ballard replied. "They shall be dismantled and stowed away on the orlop directly."

"Very well," Lewrie said with a sigh, "Damned shame, really. I fear the people will be half-frozen, by the time we're under way."

"Top up your coffee, Mister Ballard?" Pettus offered.

"Aye, thank you, Pettus," Ballard agreed.

"Whaa?" came a strangled cry from aft, and the creak of a swaying cot as its occupant sat up too quickly. "Stop that noise at once! You disturb my . . . *chort! Yob tvoyemat!*" followed by *thud* as whichever of the nobles fell out and hit the deck. "God damn you!"

"They're *such* a joy, Mister Ballard," Lewrie said in a sarcastic drawl. "I will join you on deck. D'ye need your manservant, sir?" he called aft in a louder voice.

"*Da*, send Sasha to me, so . . . *Bulack!*" Count Levotchkin yelled, just before all the liquor and wine he'd taken aboard re-arose, and he "cast his accounts to Neptune." Lewrie *hoped* he had enough wit to find a handy bucket.

"Get a mop, sir?" Pettus asked with distaste and trepidation.

"No, get his bloody manservant," Lewrie said. "I expect his man has *bags* of experience, cleanin' up after him. I'll breakfast once we are through the Gat, and made our offing, Pettus. A stale roll, with some jam . . . and a lot more coffee . . . will serve 'til then."

"Aye, sir," Pettus replied with a relieved grin.

Once through St. Nicholas Gat, past the barely awash barrier isles and shallow belt of shoals and bars, ghosting along under jibs, tops'ls, and winged-out driver, and about four miles offshore, the harbour pilot's single-masted cutter came alongside, and their guide departed, leaving HMS *Thermopylae* free to make her own way.

"Make her fly, Mister Ballard," Lewrie bade with a broad grin, elated beyond all measure to be back at sea. "Show me what our ship's capable of. All but the fore course, t'keep her bow lifted."

"Aye aye, sir," Ballard was happy to agree, and began bawling out orders through a brass speaking-trumpet. Lieutenants Farley and Fox, with wolfish grins, cheered the hands on to lay aloft and trice up, with half the Midshipmen scampering up the rat-lines with the topmen to cast off harbour gaskets and brails, and loose canvas.

Half an hour later, at Seven Bells of the Morning Watch, "all plain sail" had been set, and *Thermopylae* was pounding roughly to the Nor'east over a fine-wrinkled steel-grey sea, flecked with rollers and "sea horses" topped with white spume.

"Eight and three-quarter knots, sir!" Midshipman Privette, the dull-ish one, cried from the taffrails where he and two men of the Afterguard had plied the minute glass and the chip-log.

"How does she steer, off the wind?" Lewrie asked the Quartermaster of the watch, who, with one of his Mates, manned the large helm.

"Sweet, Cap'm sir," Beasley replied, shifting his tobacco quid to the other side of his mouth, away from Lewrie. "She's a lady at any point o' sail, almost."

"Mister Lyle?" Lewrie asked the Sailing Master. "D'ye think we could free the last reef line of the t'gallants? Or does your experience with the weather in the North Sea suggest against it?"

" 'Tis a fine morning, sir, and no hint of storm," Mr. Lyle replied, looking as if he relished speed as well, after a long spell in harbour. "I see no problem with such."

"Full t'gallants, Mister Ballard," Lewrie ordered, strolling to the starboard bulwarks to take hold of the after-most mizen mast stays and the cap-rail of the bulwark with mittened hands. With the winds almost right up the stern, there was no windward side, at present, to be reserved for him alone. He leaned far out to look forward, beaming a foolish grin of pleasure to eye *Thermopylae*'s wake as it creamed along her hull; a great kerfuffle of white spray where her cutwater and forefoot sliced ocean, a churning, white-foamy waterfall curving back and upwards in a slight swell from the bows to almost amidships, where it sloughed downwards to bare a glittering peek at her coppered quick-work before rising and spreading further aft, where it grew out into a broad bridal train of pale green and white that pointed astern towards the coast as straight as an arrow, so disturbed that it lingered long after the frigate had created it. The ship thumped, thudded, and drummed as it met each oncoming roller, flinging short columns and curtains of spray as high as the anchor cat-heads and the forecastle bulwarks, misting aft in a shivery, cold rain that dappled the quarterdeck like the first, fat drops of a storm.

And it was glorious!

Eight Bells chimed from the forecastle belfry in four twin tings to end the Morning Watch and begin the Forenoon. Almost in unison to the last double-ding, Midshipman Privette's last cast of the log, and his last official act of his watch, was to call out "Nine and a quarter knots, sir! Nine and a quarter!"

"We'll reef t'gallants, should the wind come fresher, Mister Ballard," Lewrie called out over the loud bustle of the sea, and the sounds of creaking masts, timbers, and the groan of standing rigging. "But . . . does it ease, we'll go 'all to the royals'!"

"Very good, sir," Lt. Ballard soberly answered, though Lewrie's last thought seemed to please the officers and hands who manned the quarterdeck. They had a captain who was willing to press if weather allowed, and let their frigate, of which they were justifiably proud, run like a thoroughbred.

"Who's the lucky devil who'll stay here and freeze?" Lewrie asked with a merry smile on his face, and tongue in his cheek.

"Me, sir," Lt. Farley piped up. "I've the Forenoon."

"Stay warm, Mister Farley, God help ye," Lewrie japed. "I will be below. Is there need for a pot of coffee round Four Bells, do you send for it, t'keep the people of your watch thawed out. Practice on the guns at Two Bells, weather permitting, mind."

"Aye aye, sir!" Lt. Farley replied, looking eager and thankful for the kind offer.

Pettus helped him shed his hat, muffler, mittens, and heavy fur coat once he'd taken one last look about the decks with an experienced (if rusty) eye, before trooping down the starboard gangway ladder to the upper deck, then aft to the great-cabins.

He found one of his passengers, Count Rybakov, still seated at the dining table, sipping tea which, in the chilly cabins, was visibly steaming. He had been up on deck, once they'd gotten the anchors up and stowed, and had made their way into the St. Nicholas Gat, standing well aft by the taffrail lanthorns and flag lockers, out of the way of working sailors, to experience the departure. His servant, Fyodor, was fussing about him with some sweet biscuits from his personal stores.

"A good beginning, *Kapitan* Lewrie?" Rybakov jovially enquired.

"A splendid beginning, sir . . . my lord," Lewrie told him as he took a seat at the other end of the table. Another cup of coffee was set before him, along with a plate of scrambled eggs speckled with bacon crumbles, diced onion, and melted cheese. With it was a piping-hot heap of shredded fried potatoes, and a goodly slice of the roast beef on which they'd dined the night before. On a separate, smaller plate lay two thick slices of buttered toast, and the jam pot was close by.

Lewrie rubbed his hands together, to warm them as much as welcome his breakfast, before spreading jam on his bread. He took a first bite, tastebuds tingling in anticipation, and looked up at Rybakov for a second.

Dammit, this'll get tryin', Lewrie thought, feeling irked that anyone shared his table. Captains of His Majesty's warships were, by dint of authority, required to live apart from the rest of their crews and officers; inviting them in for a meal only so often, and spending the bulk of their time at sea in enforced isolation. Frankly, there were times that one could *relish* such isolation, and this was one of them. It was rare that Lewrie had anyone in for breakfast, and he was used to eating by himself as the ship's day began. Now, here was this interloper that Admiralty and Foreign Office had foisted off on him!

A sip of very hot coffee, a forkful of eggs, then a bite of the roast beef, sauced with a bit of potatoes, a second bite of bread, and he could almost dismiss the nobleman's presence, if he made it plain he was concentrating on his victuals, and wanted to be left in peace.

"I was just thinking, *Kapitan* Lewrie . . . ," Rybakov began to say.

Burn in Hell! Lewrie silently fumed.

"I am hungry," Count Levotchkin complained, emerging at last from his sleeping space, and stumbling towards the table. He looked like Death's Head on a Mop-Stick, and his elegant clothing was rumpled.

"*Bonjour, cher cousin*," Count Rybakov cheerily greeted him, reverting to a Russian aristocrat's preferred French.

"You ate without me?" Levotchkin petulantly groused as he reeled into a chair with a dizzy thump. "We are moving? At sea? Damn. You, boy," he said, snapping fingers at Pettus. "I will have what the *Kapitan* is having. First, fetch me tea."

Pettus got a squinty, clench-mouthed look, and Lewrie, recalling why he'd been sacked by his last employers, worried that the tea might end in Levotchkin's hair. He gave Pettus a warning look.

"You rose late, Anatoli," Rybakov gently chid him. "Yes, we are at sea . . . on our way, at last. You slept through it? Amazing."

"I'll send word to the galley," Lewrie offered, "though, I fear there'll be a delay, if the galley fires've been curbed. And you'll have to supply my cook with the makings. Whitsell, run tell Nettles he's another breakfast to prepare, and the goods are on the way."

"Aye, sir."

"My *tea*!" Levotchkin demanded, head in both hands. He looked round for his manservant. "Sasha, tea, *davai. Vite vite!*" he snapped.

The big, burly bald manservant went to the side-board, poured a cup, and placed it before his master. But . . . just before he did so, he peered long and hard at Lewrie, as if undergoing an epiphany; not a glad one, from the way he frowned. As Count Levotchkin was having his first restorative sip, Sasha bent down to whisper in his ear, all the while with his eyes glued on Lewrie, who was irked with such effrontery, and put down his utensils to glare back.

"Mumble mumble London . . . argey-bargey Panton *ooleetsa*," Lewrie could barely make out. "Hiss-hiss-whisper *chi magaʒeena* . . ."

Ooleetsa *that's 'street,'* chi, *that's 'tea,'* Lewrie translated from his thin stock of Russian words in his head; *but what the Hell's a* magazeena?

"Buzzle-muzzle Strand . . . ," Sasha imparted in a raspy whisper as Count Levotchkin stiffened and sat up straighter. "*Da, ya oovyerin*," the bruiser assured his master. Whatever the Devil that last meant, Count Levotchkin turned his head to glower at Lewrie, as well, eyes as wide as a first-saddled colt . . . just before his face turned to stone, and his eyes slitted. The sides of his fine nose pulsed in and out to each audible angry breath as his visage paled, his cheeks reddened.

Panton Street, the Strand, tea whatever . . . Oh, shit! Lewrie at last put together; *The little bastard's set his beast t'lurkin' after Tess, and put two and two t'gether. Saw us at the tea and pastry shop. Maybe* that's *what a* magazeena *is*.

Count Levotchkin set his cup down in the saucer, both rattling to the shaking of his hands.

"But, what is the matter, Anatoli?" Count Rybakov asked him in sudden concern. "You are ill? Should the ship's doctor . . . ?"

Levotchkin answered him in a babbling flood of furious Russian and French, mixed, neither of which Lewrie could follow. Rybakov had difficulty, too, so rushed did the younger man's plaint spew out.

"*Shto?*" Rybakov asked as Levotchkin paused for breath. "*Viy oovyeryeni? Tojeh sama-yeh dyevooshka?*"*

"*Da, ya oovyerin,*" Levotchkin replied, snarling this time, and glaring daggers at Lewrie. "Sasha is certain, for he *saw* them. *Him!*" Levotchkin accused, lifting his chin to point up the table to his host. "My honour has been insulted, and he must answer for it. I must kill him." He rose with a napkin in his right hand and began to advance on Lewrie, who shot his own chair back and stood ready to punch the fellow in the face if he dared issue a challenge with a napkin, not a glove.

"*Stoi!*" Rybakov barked. "I forbid this, Anatoli! Sit down! Do nothing. Remember our mission!" Rybakov then launched into a tirade in Russian—no French which might be shared with anyone else this time—and went so far as to lay a restraining hand on Levotchkin's right arm. "*Obey* me in this, Anatoli. *Obey* me!"

Levotchkin uttered a growl of frustration, shaking off his kinsman's hand. He threw the napkin at Lewrie, missing wide, then, to the astonishment of everyone, gave out a howl, an inarticulate bellow akin to the sound a hound might make over the corpse of its master.

"I refuse to share these rooms with the man," Levotchkin vowed. "I will not dine with him, drink with him, breathe the same air . . . !"

That'll save my spirit store, Lewrie inanely thought.

"Anatoli, that would be imposs—" Rybakov chid him.

"Damn him! Damn him to Hades!" Levotchkin cried, spinning on his heels and stomping aft to his partitioned-off bed-space, slamming the

---

*Da, ya oovyerin= Yes, I'm sure. *Shto?*= What? *Viy oovyereni? Tojeh sama-yeh dyevooshka?*= You are sure? The same young woman?

louvred slat door and making the flimsy deal and canvas partitions come nigh to collapsing like a tent.

"Well," Rybakov softly said in the immense silence. "*Kapitan,* I must apologise for my cousin's manners, but . . . he feels that you give him great insult, over a young lady."

"Not quite a lady, no, my lord," Lewrie said with a wry grin as he sat back down to resume his cooling breakfast. "The girl in question's adenizen of 'Mother' Batson's brothel, in Panton Street, for whom he took a fancy."

"A . . . prostitute?" Rybakov asked, looking appalled as he sat down in his own chair at the other end of the table. "A common whore?"

"Well, I wouldn't call her 'common,' no, my lord," Lewrie said, and laid out for Count Rybakov the entire scenario, from meeting Tess to the last morning in the Strand . . . perversions, included.

"He was not set upon by thieves?" Rybakov mused aloud, eyebrows up in wonder. "No wonder he explained his wounds differently. But . . . he really treated the poor girl so badly?"

"Afraid so, my lord," Lewrie told him, dabbing his lips with a napkin after he'd eaten his last morsel, and asked Pettus for another cup of coffee. "She was afraid for her life. Had she known . . . had I known, that his man, Sasha, was lurking to discover who else might be sporting with her, or meeting her outside the establishment, I doubt she'd have ever dared step out the door, 'til she was sure that Count Levotchkin had left England."

"But he's so *devout*!" Rybakov insisted. "Anatoli never misses a service, even in London, at the few Orthodox churches, no matter how mean the neighbourboods. He's a pure son of Mother Russia . . . or so I thought. Lord, what will his mother say, or the young lady to whom he is affianced in Saint Petersburg? A young lady of one of the finest families in our aristocracy. He has *such* a promising future . . . a colonelcy in one of the most distinguished cavalry regiments, assured of a place at the Tsar's court as soon as we return . . ."

Knew it! Lewrie told himself; *Devout,* and *a cavalryman. They're sure t'be secret bastards, every time.*

"Happens in the best of families," Lewrie commented. "Just look at our own aristocracy. The Earl of Sandwich, for instance . . . simply *brilliant* First Lord of the Admiralty, but a founding member of the Hell-Fire Club. Orgies in the old undercroft of his restored abbey at Medmenham, then preached in dominee clothes of a Sunday . . . to hundreds of cats his farm workers'd round up and herd into the chapel. Mostly against fornication," he added with a droll expression.

Lewrie knew all there was to know about the Hell-Fire Club; his father, Sir Hugo St. George Willoughby, had been a member, too.

"I will speak to him," Rybakov offered, as if that might mollify the
young hot-head. "Now I know the circumstances, I will point out to him
the ludicrous cause for his grudge. Even so . . . for a few days, arrangements can be made to limit your contact with him?"

"If he wishes to take the air on the quarterdeck, he'll have to wait 'til
I'm below," Lewrie said, calmly stirring sugar into his cup. "If he doesn't
wish to dine with me, he can take his meals aft, in his little sleeping-space.
I'll *not* give up my cabins, my table, my chart-space, or my desk or day-
cabin settee. Does he loathe me that much, he will just have to take pains
to avoid me, my lord."

"You will not duel him," Rybakov said; not a request.

"That . . . will be up to him, my lord," Lewrie evenly replied as he
laid aside his spoon and lifted his cup. "Does he not heed you and accost
me, issue a formal challenge, then . . . my *own* honour is put in question,
and there can be but one answer."

"Sadly, I understand, *Kapitan* Lewrie," Count Rybakov mournfully
said, his face twisted up as grievous as a hanged spaniel.

Outta the fryin' pan, into the fire, Lewrie queasily thought as he took
another sip of coffee, all outward calm to an impartial observer. *Mine
arse on a band-box, he'll challenge me before we reach Russia, sure as Fate.
Too damned proud an' arrogant t'do else. Christ, am I t'die over a* whore?

He allowed a wee grin to lift his mouth for a second.

Ev'rybody said *I'd come to a bad end,* he reminded himself.

"Midshipman o' th' watch, SAH!" the Marine sentry by the door
barked.

"Come," Lewrie bade.

"The Second Officer's duty, sir," Midshipman Furlow announced,
hat under his arm, "and I'm to tell you that the wind's come more Westerly, fine on our larboard quarter, and he requests permission to alter
course a point Northerly."

"My compliments to Mister Farley, and inform him to do so. I will
come to the quarterdeck . . . just for the air, Mister Furlow," he formally
replied, grinning as he uttered his last thought.

As he dressed for the cold, Lewrie could not help thinking that, could
Thermopylae fly with the wings of Hermes the Messenger, and get to
Russia by the next dawn, this voyage, this mission of his, would *still* feel
like an eternity!

CHAPTER THIRTY-ONE

*F*our days in blustery, grey weather, with the winds whipping cold and occasionally spitting rain, sleet, or fat flakes of snow, and HMS *Thermopylae* bowling along like a Cambridge coach, and they were shaving a low-lying coast to starboard, which emerged as ephemeral as mist, just round dawn.

"Quite good, for dead reckoning," Lewrie told Mr. Lyle, the Sailing Master, as the shore of the Danish island of Jutland appeared solid, at last. They had not been able to take sun-sights to determine their position, or their progress. "But . . . just how *far* along, Mister Lyle?"

"I do believe we are beyond the cape East of Thisted, sir," Lyle cautiously allowed, a mittened finger pointing along the chart pinned to the traverse board by the binnacle cabinet. "Do you concur, Captain Hardcastle?"

"Indeed I do, Mister Lyle . . . Captain Lewrie," the experienced merchant master said, bustling closer to the chart to employ his own finger. "That long coast, yonder, is called the Jammerbugt, and the port of Hirstals lies beyond our starboard bows, no more than fifty or sixty miles. Next day will see us off the Skaw, does the wind cooperate," he added, moving his finger on to the mouth of the Kattegat, and the entrance to the Baltic.

"Where we turn South," Lewrie said. "Beyond that, sirs? What is your estimate of the time it'll take to reach the narrows 'twixt Denmark and Sweden?"

"Well, that'll take much longer than the crossing, sir," Capt. Hard-castle was quick to say, perhaps to take temporary precedence over a *Navy* Sailing Master. "The Baltic has no tides, but the currents—"

"And when an outflowing current coincides with a Sutherly wind, sir"—Mr. Lyle was just as quick to trample his way back to dominance—"you face a 'dead muzzler,' and might as well anchor 'til one on the other changes."

"Not so bad in the Kattegat, sir," Hardcastle rejoined, "as we would be in open waters, but more noticeable as we close with the Narrows 'tween Helsingør . . . the Bard's Elsinore . . . and the Swedish side, and the forts at Helsingborg. That's where the outflowing current will be strongest."

"And the very worst place to be reduced to a crawl," Lewrie said with a grumble, rubbing a mittened hand on his unshaven chin, which rasped against the wool, "*or* come to anchor."

Damme, but that's really *narrow!* Lewrie thought. He borrowed a di-vider from the binnacle cabinet and set its needle-sharp points upon the chart's distance scale, then walked the divider from the Swedish side of the narrows to the Danish—he came up with a width of only two miles, plus eight hundred yards.

"This bloody shoal right in the middle, sirs," Lewrie asked his Sailing Master and civilian adviser, jabbing a finger at the long and skinny north-to-south shallows indicated smack-dab down the centre of the passage. "The, ah . . . Disken Shoal?" he made out from the smallish letters on the chart. "Might it force us to choose which side of the Narrows to take?"

"Oh no, sir," Capt. Hardcastle chuckled. "For though it *can* be a bother to the biggest, deepest-laden ships in the Baltic trade when the wind's been blowing for a week or longer, *stiff*, mind, outta the South, most times even a First Rate could sail right down the middle of the Nar-rows, right atop it. Ye only draw about seventeen or eighteen foot, so you should have no problem with it."

"Uhm . . . *perhaps*, sir," Mr. Lyle cautioned almost by reflex, or just to be contrary with a *civilian's* opinion. "As he says, sir, with a following wind, several *days* of Nor'westerlies, there should be more than suffi-cient depth cross the Disken Shoal."

"Uhum" was Lewrie's terse comment to that information; though he still fretted about the forts on the Swedish side, and the massive Kron-borg Castle on the Danish side of the Narrows, both built at the very narrowest points, designed to cooperate to close the strait with their artillery. It wouldn't do, Lewrie thought, to voice open concerns about how heavy were the cannon on each shore, not before any of his officers or men. "For now, we'll just have to hope for Northerly winds, and steer a . . . diplomatic . . . course right down the centre of the Narrows, gentlemen. Favouring neither side, hmm? Will both you men join me below in my cabins for a moment? Mister Fox, you have the deck."

"Aye aye, sir," the Third Officer replied.

"Now . . . about these damned forts," Lewrie said in the relative warmth of his cabins, all three of them crowded into the small chart-space to pore over his own recently purchased copy of the chart they'd studied on deck. "Have you ever had cause to visit Kronborg Castle, Captain Hardcastle? Seen their armaments?"

"Oh, I've anchored under its foot a time or two, sir, but I've never had a tour of the place," Hardcastle admitted, warming his hands round a china mug of hot coffee which Pettus had produced for them all. "Townfolk'll tell anyone who asks, though, that they've over eighty or ninety heavy guns. Right proud of them, they are. An odd measure of metal, though, sir. . . . I believe they said they were thirty-*six* pounders, not thirty-twos. P'raps the Danish pound is greater than anyone else's, or they just cast them to their own tastes."

"Let's assume they're roughly equal to a thirty-two pounder," Lewrie allowed, picking his own divider from its velvet-lined box of navigational tools. "Range-to-random-shot for a thirty-two is about a mile and a half . . . ," he muttered as he scribed two half-circles on the chart. "Assume the Swedes mount much the same calibre guns, too, so . . ."

Damme, that *ain't pretty*, he thought, for right in the middle of the Narrows, the overlap from Kronborg Castle and its Swedish equivalent formed a long, sharp-pointed oval where round-shot, perhaps even *heated* shot, could hammer *Thermopylae* from both sides, and no frigate ever launched was built to withstand a pummelling that massive; a lone frigate as good as opposed by an entire squadron of ships of the line!

Turning the dividers up-and-down the Narrows, instead of right-to-left, he stepped off the distance from the northern end of the overlapping fire to the southern; one and three-quarter miles, all told.

"Average speed of the outflowing current, Captain Hardcastle?" he asked.

"Uhm . . . anywhere from two to four knots, sir, depending on the winds from the South, or thereabouts," Hardcastle guessed.

"So, with a followin' wind, and two knots of current, say, we *could* make six knots 'over the ground,' " Lewrie puzzled out, stepping off that assumed crawl. "Which'd mean we'd be under fire for at least twenty minutes, do the Swedes and the Danes refuse us passage. Can't assume *more* than six knots, altogether, as anything more than whistlin' in the wind."

"Well, do the Swedes not cooperate with the Danes, sir," Mister Lyle contributed, "we could sidle over towards Helsingborg and limit our exposure to the Danish guns."

"Have to assume the worst, there, too, Mister Lyle, so . . . let's say we barge down the Narrows atop the Disken Shoal, equidistant from either shore, and endure the fire from both forts. Twenty minutes, or more, of it. Captain Hardcastle?" he suddenly asked.

"Sir?"

"The fort at Helsingborg looks much smaller than the Danes'," Lewrie said with a sly rise of a brow. "Ever anchor under *their* guns, or put in there to wait for a good wind home?"

"A time or two, aye, sir," Hardcastle told him. "And it is a smaller place, with fewer guns, I gathered. Never thought to ask how heavy they were, for the Swedes are a *peaceful* sort, mostly. Dull as ditchwater folk for the most part, too. Fair but sharp traders, when it come to dickering over stores and victuals. Why, the last war they had with Russia, I don't even think Helsingborg ever had to fire one shot. Most of the war took place much further East in the Baltic, on Sweden's eastern coast, poor bastards."

"And when you anchored close to Kronborg Castle," Lewrie eagerly pressed, "did you ever see them practicing with their artillery?"

"Why, I can't say that I have, Captain Lewrie," Hardcastle said with a hesitant smile and a shake of his head. "I been sailing the Baltic trade, man and boy, nigh on thirty years, and but for watching them fire *salutes* to passing warships, I can't recall them ever *practicing*. After all, the Danes've been at peace with the world for over eighty years."

"Slap down the middle, it'll, be, then, gentlemen," Lewrie said, amazing Lyle and Hardcastle by the broad smile that accompanied his decision, "and Devil take the hind-most! Eighty years, d'ye say, Captain Hardcastle? Why, they couldn't hit Westminster Cathedral if it was anchored in mid-stream between 'em! A frigate's a small, *moving* target to gunners who haven't fired anything more than *salutin'* charges since . . .

well, I can't rightly recall *which* historical event. And range-to-random-shot, with us in mid-channel, would be about sixteen hundred and fifty yards. Then, are you correct, Mister Lyle, and the Swedish forts don't chime in, we can edge over closer to their shores, making things even more difficult for Danish guns, at maximum elevation. Mine arse on a band-box, gentlemen! Things might get *noisy*, but I doubt if they score a single hit before we're past their reach."

Nobody shared his enthusiasm, of course; no one huzzahed, or, for that matter, looked inspired and relieved. Well, the cats did, as they leapt atop the chart on the angled desk, drawn by the sounds of people engaged in something useful, and determined to take part . . . or put a stop to it. The much spryer Chalky sprang to the middle of the chart in one go, and began sniffing about. Toulon, ever more awkward even as a kitten, took a couple of tries before he alit on the edge of the table, and sprawled to expose his belly for a petting, at once.

Mr. Lyle stepped back a pace, though Capt. Hardcastle reached out to stroke Toulon's fur with a fond smile. Lewrie put the dividers back into the box with the rest of his brass instruments, with Chalky pouncing on busy hands for a play-fight.

"Always been fond of ship's cats," Hardcastle told them.

"Keep the ship's rats in check," Mr. Lyle dourly allowed.

"Then what'd the Midshipmen eat?" Lewrie japed, rolling Chalky over to give him belly rubs, and engage in a contest to see which was faster, his hand, or sharp little teeth and half-sheathed claws.

Crash! went something made of glass from aft of the great-cabin.

"*Droogoy shampanska-yeh*, Sasha!" Count Levotchkin demanded. "*Ya hachoo bolsheh. Davai*, Sasha, *davai!*"*

"Christ," Lewrie swore under his breath. "By my reckonin', it's his third bottle since breakfast. Must *live* on champagne." Of a certainty, the number of crates scattered round the cabins had diminished noticeably since departing Yarmouth Roads, most of them filled with an assortment of bottles, from sherry to *schnapps* to vodka.

"Another for Mister Eades's Marines for target practice, sir," Mr. Lyle said with distaste. "And the wood's welcome in the galley." Lt. Eades had snapped up any bottle he could find, from their guests and the gun-room, to hang at the end of the tops'l yardarms, and let his Marines

---

*"*Droogoy shampanksa-yeh. Ya hachoo bolsheh. Davai!*" = "Another champagne, Sasha. I want another, quickly!"

try their eye at them with single shots, not volleys, at practice at small arms. Even with a smooth-bore Short Navy Pattern Tower musket, Lt. Eades had proved himself to be a fine shot, and expected every one of his Marines to be, as well. Or else.

"It's been my experience, sir, that Russians have a grand capacity for spirits," Capt. Hardcastle said, intent upon the pleasant chore of stroking Toulon, the bigger black-and-white tom, who was now purring loud enough to beat the band, and squirming in utter delight.

"It keeps 'em warm in winter, I'd imagine," Lewrie jested.

"Or, too addled to notice the cold," Mr. Lyle added, smirking.

"That young Count's man, that Sasha?" Capt. Hardcastle said. "I seen his sort before. A real Russian peasant . . . the sort who boasts he never buttons his coat to the throat, no matter how cold it gets. And, like all of 'em, meaner than a den full of bears when in drink. A run ashore in Russia during the trading season is done warily, Captain Lewrie, and polite smiles to one and all, else some raging drunk takes umbrage, and rips your liver out."

"Don't imagine we'll have that pleasure, this voyage," Lewrie said back, putting the box of navigation instruments away. "Hark. I think Lieutenant Eades is already at practice."

Sure enough, overhead on the quarterdeck, came a ragged volley; fired from the taffrails at something tossed overboard and bobbing in the frigate's wake, by the sound of it. "Second rank, level!" Eades cried, and they could hear the shuffling of booted feet as the front rank of ten fell back to re-load and re-prime, whilst the second rank of ten stepped forward to take aim. "Second rank . . . fire! *Dammit!*"

If their Russian guests' private quarters did not take up most of the after portions of the great-cabins, Lewrie might have been tempted to dash to the transom sash-windows to see how they were doing . . . evidently none too well by the exasperation in Lt. Eades's voice.

"Let's go on deck and watch the show," Lewrie suggested.

"Third rank, present . . . level . . . and don't shoot like you've emptied the bottle first . . . ready . . . fire!" Eades was snapping. Ten Brown Bess muskets barked, and a flurry of small waterspouts erupted within a couple of feet of the empty bottle, now slowly bobbing further astern, almost out of accurate range of a musket, which even on solid ground ashore could not attain much more surety of shot than fifty or sixty yards.

"Damn!" Lt. Eades spat again, brought up his own musket, took quick aim, and fired. The dog's jaws holding the flint snapped against the frizzen's raspy surface, the powder in the priming pan went *Pop!* and, an eyeblink later, the fire in the pan transmitted down the tiny hole to the barrel, where the main charge exploded with a louder *Bang!* Eades's lead ball plunked only inches to the right of the empty bottle. "Damn!" he muttered in frustration, though that sort of accuracy from a moving ship at a moving target so small would have allowed Lt. Eades to hit an enemy anywhere he wished, in chest, bowels, or the head, in "musket shot" range between ships.

"There'll be another bottle coming, Mister Eades," Lewrie drolly assured him. "Courtesy of our Russian gentlemen. Damned close shootin', by the by."

"Thankee, sir, though I *should've* made allowance for the wind," Lt. Eades said, pulling his lowered musket to half-cock to re-load for himself.

"Captain, sir?" Midshipman Tillyard said, doffing his hat as he approached them at the taffrails. "Mister Fox's duty, and he asks, may Count Rybakov come to the quarterdeck, sir?"

Lewrie turned to look forrud, and spotted the elegantly, warmly dressed Count Rybakov just peeking over the deck edge, a few steps up the larboard gangway ladder, with an expectant smile on his face, brows up in query . . . and a long firearm slung over one shoulder.

"My compliments to Mister Fox, and aye, Count Rybakov may mount the quarterdeck," Lewrie told him.

"Good morning, *Kapitan* Lewrie," Count Rybakov cheerfully said as he reached them, right-aft. "I hear the shooting, and I cannot resist the wish to practice. I may be allowed?"

"But of course, my lord," Lewrie agreed. "Lieutenant Eades is exercising his men, ten at a time, so I hope you don't mind firing as they re-load, 'tween volleys."

"Ah, but I must re-load myself, *Kapitan* . . . at leisure, for I am not drilled to speed, as are your Marines," Rybakov graciously admitted, "and my rifled piece takes more time. I would be delighted to observe the slight delay, ah ha!"

Lewrie and Eades marvelled over the rifled weapon that Rybakov took down from his shoulder, and let them paw over. It was based upon a German *jaeger* hunting rifle, though made by one of the most skilled gunsmiths in Paris. The barrel was a highly polished blue octagon of almost four feet length, with gilt inlays and a gold bead for aiming. The barrel bands, the ramrod, and the lock plate, the pan, frizzen, and dog's jaws were bright steel, also elaborately engraved and inlaid with gold, and all was set into a stock of highly polished and glossy burlwood, with a steel patch-box built into the right-hand side of the butt.

"A *most* handsome piece of work, sir," Lt. Eades said in awe, and with a hint of severe envy. "What calibre, may I ask?"

"Sixty-nine calibre, the same as a French musket," the merry count replied, beaming with pride of ownership. "Sadly, most of my hunting at home in Russia does not involve a rifle, except for bears. Wild boar is our main quarry, and that is done on horseback, with the lance. With the sword for the *coup de grâce* . . . and a pair of *large* pistols, does the boar un-horse me, ha ha! There are not as many of the great stags as there were before, in my youth, and with *them* I must use the rifled hunter."

"French-made, you say, sir?" Eades asked. "One hopes that they do not become enamoured of rifled weapons for general issue to their armies."

"There's not an army in the world can afford them," Lewrie said. "Slow to load, as the good Count says, might mean only one volley per minute, and, to rifle an hundred thousand barrels would make them too expensive, and slow their delivery to the troops in the field. Think of my own breech-loading Ferguson rifle-musket . . ."

"You *have* one, sir?" Lt. Eades openly gawped in wonder. "Why, I doubt there were a thousand ever made!"

"My late father-in-law in North Carolina, and Major Patrick Ferguson, were acquaintances, and Mr. Chiswick bought enough to equip a regiment . . . more like a half-battalion, really . . . of North Carolina Loyalist Volunteers. I got mine at Yorktown, during the siege," he told them.

"You have it here, aboard ship, sir?" Eades asked, in lust.

"Aye, I do," Lewrie said. "Mister Tillyard?" he called to the senior Midshipman of the Watch. "Pass word for my Cox'n, Desmond, for him to fetch up my Ferguson rifle, and all the necessaries. In the meantime, though, Lieutenant Eades . . . Count . . . do continue with target practice. I'll jump in when Desmond brings mine up."

Over the taffrails went another empty bottle of champagne, most-like Count Levotchkin's latest "dead soldier," along with a wee barrel not much larger than a mop-bucket, now drained of an ordinary wine.

"First rank . . . level," Lt. Eades ordered as the targets bobbed astern, to about thirty yards. "Take aim . . . fire! *Much* better!" he congratulated, as the small barrel was bracketed by balls, and set to spinning by two actual hits.

"Ahem," Count Rybakov announced as he raised his *jaeger* to his shoulder, took careful aim, and squeezed the surely-light trigger. A split second later, the flash in the pan, and the explosion of the powder charge went *Pop-Bang* almost together, and the wood barrel leaped as it was hit, one narrow stave driven completely in.

"Huzzah!" the Marines and onlookers could not help exclaiming at the old fellow's accuracy.

"Oh, it is no great thing," Rybakov modestly said as he lowered the rifle, and drew the lock back to half-cock. "At fourty yards, that is still an easy shot. Now, when the little barrel is further away . . . *that* is the challenge, *n'est-ce pas?* Not so?"

"Yer rifle an things, sor," Desmond announced, as the second rank of Marines tried their eye at the receding barrel.

"Carry on, Mister Eades," Lewrie urged, wishing them to continue whilst the bottle and barrel were still within range, and not waste any precious time gawking over his Ferguson. Lewrie pulled the lock back to half-cock and tore the top fold-over flap of a paper cartridge with his teeth, to sprinkle a small amount into the pan. One turn round went the trigger guard and hand-grip, rotating the large screw below the end of the barrel, into which he crammed the paper *cartouche,* the ball-end first. Another single turn to raise the screw upwards, and the barrel was sealed and ready for firing.

The second rank of Marines had fired at the barrel, now bobbing and rocking about sixty yards astern. Lewrie brought the Ferguson up to his cheek, pulled the lock to full-cock, took aim, drew one breath and slowly let it out, then gently squeezed the trigger, hoping for the best, in point of fact, for it had been months since he had fired a single shot at practice, and nigh a year since he had even *thought* of using the Ferguson. *Pop!-Bang!* and his shot was in the wind.

"Good'un, sir!" Eades enthused, for Lewrie had clipped the barrel right on the top, raising a tiny cloud of wood splinters.

Encouraged, and in a mood to show off, Lewrie went through the loading process again, showing how a breech-loader could get off at least three or four rounds a minute. Within fifteen seconds, his second shot went off, with the barrel over seventy-five yards astern this time. And he hit it again!

"Pardon!" Count Rybakov cried, stepping up to the taffrails for a shot of his own almost at once, and clipping the barrel's lid, driving a large, visible hole in the thin slab of wood. "Ah ha!"

"We're forgettin' the bottle, sir," Lewrie said, rapidly loading for a third shot. "It's what . . . an hundred yards, by now?"

"One of your guineas, *Kapitan*?" Rybakov teased, going red in the face as he primed his pan, poured powder down the barrel, and set a lead ball atop a paper-thin oiled leather patch at the muzzle of his *jaeger*, and strained to drive it down to rest against the powder.

Why the Devil not? Lewrie asked himself, ready to fire again; *I can afford a little flutter. And plead Navy-pay poverty, if he's as good as I think he is.*

"A guinea, d'ye say, my lord? Done, and done," Lewrie replied with a grin and a shrug. "First honours to you, when you're ready."

"Ha!" Count Rybakov laughed with glee for his wager to be accepted, as he stepped to the taffrails and brought his *jaeger* rifle up to his shoulder once more. "Over one hundred yards, now, so . . ." Count Rybakov seemed to mutter cautions to himself in French, taking his own sweet time before barely touching that over-sensitive trigger.

Pop!-Bang! and a tiny feather of spray arose, barely a foot or so short of the champagne bottle, grazing over the neck, and clipping the mouth of the bottle off!

"My *stars*, sir, what a shot!" Lt. Eades whooped.

"Your turn, *Kapitan*," Rybakov said, quite pleased with himself, and his moment of adulation.

"Well, all right then," Lewrie said, frowning in concentration as he stepped to the taffrails and took aim. Rybakov's shot had set the bottle rocking like a lunatic duck, and it was nigh 150 yards astern, by then. He held a touch high, loosening his knees, to spring with the motion of the ship and absorb all the uncertainties in his lower body. *Here goes my guinea* he told himself, firing at last.

"Dead *on*, my *word*!" Lt. Eades shouted. "Shot the neck, not the body, clean *off*, sir!"

"Well, I *was* aimin' for the biggest part," Lewrie said in seeming modesty, though secretly amazed that he'd hit it at all.

"Another bottle, my lord?" Lewrie asked the Count.

"No, *Kapitan* Lewrie!" Rybakov guffawed. "I cede the field to a sharper eye than mine," he said, digging into a waist-coat pocket for a coin, and handing over a golden guinea. "Did we continue, I imagine you would end up winning even my *jaeger* rifle, when I am reduced to a sad state of poverty! Urrah!" he cried, taking Lewrie in a bear hug and dancing him round the deck.

"Another bottle, *da!*" someone snarled. "I have it here. Will you match shots with *me, Angliski Kapitan?*" Count Levotchkin had come on deck, had mounted to the quarterdeck despite Lt. Fox's cautions to not do so without permission, and had shoulder-bludgeoned his way past the after-guard and the rear ranks of Marines. Instead of a rifle, he held a bottle of champagne in each hand, and his man, Sasha, behind him carried two polished wood boxes of pistols.

"Empty, are they?" Lewrie asked with one brow up in mockery.

"Does not matter," Lovotchkin snapped, swaying more than necessary to the motion of the ship. One bottle was open, and he raised it to his lips to drink from the neck.

"No one ever drinks spirits on *deck*, my lord," Lewrie told him with sternness. "And most especially never in front of the crew, when they're limited to their rum rations at set times. Count Rybakov, do oblige me to inform your compatriot that he is violating the discipline of my ship, and should take himself, and his champagne, below at once."

Whatever Count Rybakov urgently, angrily, said to his younger relative mattered no more than water to a duck's back, for Levotchkin just sneered, swayed, and took another deep drink. "Pistol, Sasha!" he demanded, reaching behind his back without looking. His manservant handed him a sleek duelling pistol, taking the off-hand champagne bottle in exchange, so Levotchkin could cock it with the back of his wrist, then throw the bottle from which he'd drunk high into the air. With a feral cry, the young Count rushed to the taffrails, shoving people out of his way, frankly making everyone scamper to avoid the cocked pistol which he handled so breezily and dangerously. He looked astern, then took a duellist's stance, feet wide apart, one hand on his hip, body turned sideways to make the slimmest target for an opponent, and fired. The bottle, about twenty yards astern, was hit, of course, and Count Levotchkin turned to look at Lewrie with triumph on his face, cruelly smiling, To make his drunken point, he raised the empty pistol to his mouth and blew across the muzzle, then pointed it directly at Lewrie, and barked "Pom!" to imitate the bark of a pistol.

"Now see here, you!" Lt. Eades shouted. "Put him in irons, sir? Threaten our Captain, will you?"

"A bottle, Sasha," Lewrie said, raising a hand to still the ire of his crew.

"And a pistol." He looked at the brute, who glared back 'neath heavy, beetled brows, snorting at the effrontery. Sasha looked to his master, matching Levotchkin's top-lofty sneer.

"*Seechas, yob tvoyemat!*" Lewrie barked in a fair approximation of Eudoxia's father; "*Now*, fuck your mother!" he added in English so everyone would know what he'd said in poor Russian.

Lewrie jerked his gaze from Sasha to Levotchkin, savouring the looks of utter surprise on their faces. The manservant looked again to his master for instruction; the Count shrugged and nodded, sure of himself . . . or, too drunk to care. With a growl of displeasure, the servant opened the box and handed Lewrie the mate to Levotchkin's pistol. It, too, was French, Lewrie took note as he quickly examined it; long-barreled and slim, and worth a fortune in its own right. The mouth of the barrel revealed the crisp-cut rifling. Lewrie drew the lock back to half-cock, freed the frizzen and pan cover, and saw that it was already primed. "You keep *loaded* weapons in my cabins, sir?" he asked in a voice loud enough to carry to every curious ear, from officer to cabin boy. "That is something *else* I will not tolerate from a *guest*, Count Levotchkin. Hear me plain, do ye, sir?" he demanded. That was met by yet another sneer. "Bottle, if you please," he said to Sasha. "No, don't hand it to me . . . toss it high and hard as you can. Understand? *Ponyimayu?*"

And for God's sake, don't fuck this up, Lewrie chid himself as the brute drew his arm back. He'd always been a better-than-average wing-shot, and when up the Mississippi to spy out Spanish New Orleans, he'd reaped his share of wild ducks with a musket; had even tried his eye at potting turtles resting on logs on the banks, and shooting off-hand at thrown bottles with that trading fellow with the Panton, Leslie and Company.

"Throw it!" Lewrie snapped. Sasha gave a great heave worthy of a weighted messenger line or a grapnel 'tween ships. The bottle soared aloft and astern, tumbling end-for-end. Lewrie raised his pistol and took aim, leading it as it fell, and . . .

Pa-Bang! as the pistol bucked in his hand, and the ball hit the bottle, shattering it ten feet above the ship's wake, and at least ten to twelve yards astern. *And just thankee Jesus!* Lewrie thought as the ship erupted in cheers; *So long as I don't have t'do that* twice *in the same day . . . or year!*

He brought the pistol to his face, blew across the muzzle, and smiled at Count Levotchkin, who had gone about cross-eyed in disappointment, then opened the pan and blew the last smoke and soot out of it, as well. Lewrie cocked one brow, then tossed the emptied pistol to the stunned young nobleman, who all but lost it overside before snagging a finger in the trigger guard.

"Lieutenant Eades . . . I'll thankee to discharge the rest of his pistols for me," Lewrie said, turning to his Marine officer. "And I must request, Count Rybakov, that any other firearms in my great-cabins are to be unloaded and locked away, my lord? I'd dislike for an accident to occur."

"But of course, *Kapitan* Lewrie," Count Rybakov gravely replied, taking a second to glare at his drunken young relation. "You have my utmost assurance that it will be done."

"Well, then," Lewrie said, clapping his hands together, "that'll do me for the day. Carry on with small arms practice, Mister Eades."

"Aye aye, sir!"

CHAPTER THIRTY-TWO

$\mathcal{H}$MS *Thermopylae* passed the long, narrow point of the Skaw in a
light snowstrom, and altered course for the Sound under reduced sail;
even so, with the wind blustering and shifting to the Nor-Nor'west she
still scudded along at a good eight knots, all that next day and night, with
the wind from out of the Arctic pressing her onwards into a grey,
swirling mystery, with the horizon blanketed out from view aloft from
the mast-top-lookouts, or the extra lookouts posted in the bows. Icy-cold
sailors manned the lead lines, casting from the foremast channels for the
shoaling water that would warn them of their nearness to the East-West
lying island of Laeso, which they hoped to pass well clear to the East'rd
of it. But . . . in the swirling snow as thick as a fog in the Thames Estu-
ary at times, then clearing for tantalising minutes before closing down
again like heavy window drapes, the best warning of anything ahead
was limited to mere hundreds of yards.

Thermopylae steered roughly Sou-Sou'east, by dead reckoning of
course, as if in a phantasmical Christmas village. A ship sailing off the
wind could rarely go any faster than the wind itself, so there was little of
the usual keening and rushing from the running and standing rigging. In
the smothering blanket of snow, even the usual sounds of the working
hull, or the hiss-roar of her passage through the sea was muffled, and . . .
the frigate was regularly dusted with fat and heavy wet flakes that softened

her warlike nature. Even her brute-iron artillery bore an inch or more piled atop the barrels and wood carriages.

"Best we don't let it pile up, Mister Ballard," Lewrie told his First Officer. "I'd admire did ye break out brooms and such, and sweep her down, every hour."

"I will see to it, directly, sir," Lt. Ballard replied, gravely sombre and formal, as usual.

A snowball came flying aft from the starboard gangway, near the foremast stays, and splatted Midshipman Pannabaker square in the chest. Midshipman Plumb, their cheekiest, whooped with glee over his aim.

"You may reply with one round, Mister Pannabaker," Lewrie said. "Mister Plumb, sir! Yes, you, sir! I saw that! Now stand still, and prepare to receive!"

Pannabaker quickly stooped to scoop up a heaping handful, packing and shaping it round and round in his mittened hands, much like a gun-captain would select the roundest and smoothest round-shot from the shot-racks or rope garlands for his first long-range broadside. This "shot" would be a tad slushy, Lewrie noted, as Pannabaker drew back to throw. He got his fourteen-year-old cater-cousin, Plumb, just beneath the chin, nigh staggering him, and knocking his hat off.

"The *next* throw'll put the thrower at the mast-top 'til I feel like lettin' him come down," Lewrie loudly warned. In a softer voice he said to Pannabaker, "Good shot, young sir," and tipped him a wink.

"No bottom t'this line!" the starboard leadsman cried out as he began to haul in his icy-wet coils of line, and the plumb weight.

As Lt. Ballard and the Bosun called for sweepers, Lewrie turned to walk to the large double-wheel, and the binnacle cabinet and chart pinned to the traverse board, where both Mr. Lyle, the Sailing Master, and Capt. Hardcastle fretted and "ahummed."

"No landfall yet, sirs," Lewrie prodded them.

"Nossir," Hardcastle commented, "and I'm not sure why. Even by both our dead reckonings, we should be close to Laeso, but . . ."

"It might be prudent, sir, to alter course to East, Sou'east," Mr. Lyle suggested. "The Kattegat is both wide and deep enough for us to have sea-room all the way to the Swedish coast, which has enough depth for a Third Rate, quite close to shore. In that way, we could skirt *well* clear of this island, in all this snow."

"Or, do like the Vikings did in their day," Hardcastle said as he pulled a large red calico handkerchief from a pocket and blew his nose quite loudly.

"And what was it that the Vikings did, Captain Hardcastle?" Mr. Lyle asked, a dubious brow up in case he was being twitted.

"Oh, they lowered their sail, slow-stroked the banks of oars, and put a fellow in the bows a'hollering 'Odin!' 'til they got an echo off the shore," Hardcastle told him with a grin.

"Mister Ballard," Lewrie said, "bring us round two points more to the East. And Mister Pannabaker? Go below and pass word for the Master Gunner, Mister Tunstall. He is to fetch up a swivel, and powder charges only, to mount up forrud."

"Aye aye, sir," Midshipman Pannabaker replied, eyes wide in wonder at what his captain might have in mind. As he dashed for the starboard gangway ladder to the main deck, he almost collided with Count Rybakov, swathed in his heaviest furs, scarf, gloves, and felt hat.

"Permission to take the air on the quarterdeck, *Kapitan* Lewrie?" he asked.

"Come up, my lord," Lewrie bade him with a grim smile, intent on peering forrud, as if he could squint hard enough to pierce the swirls of snow . . . and wondering who aboard had the stoutest lungs, should they be reduced to crying "God Bless King George!" from the bows before Mr. Tunstall was ready.

"A thick day, my lord," Lewrie commented to Rybakov.

"Oh, this is nothing, compared to a Russian winter, *Kapitan*," Count Rybakov said with a laugh and a deprecating shrug. "There, the winds howl days on end, and the snow comes down so quickly that a man who stands still for a minute or two can be buried in it, ha ha! Uhm, do you think it would permissible for me to smoke, *Kapitan*?" Rybakov asked, reaching deep into a side pocket of his sleek fur coat to pull out a cigar.

"Don't think there's much of a fire risk today, my lord. Do go ahead," Lewrie told him.

"You will join me, *Kapitan* Lewrie?" Rybakov offered.

"Never developed the habit, thankee," Lewrie replied, watching as Mr. Tunstall, with two more gunners and a powder monkey, emerged from the midships companionway ladder with a swivel, stanchion mount, and gun tools. Rybakov snapped bare fingers to summon his manservant, Fyodor, who produced a tinder-box, flashed the flint to raise sparks 'til the rag took light, then offered it to the tip of his master's cigar. Once it was afire, Fyodor bobbed a bow and scampered away.

"You will sound for the shore of Laeso Island, yes?" Rybakov enquired, happily puffing away and producing a flavourful cloud of to-bacco smoke that only slowly drifted forward towards the cross-deck quarterdeck nettings and hammock storage. "The Baltic is quite often foggy, in all seasons, so I recognise what you intend."

"Louder than shoutin' 'Odin,' as Captain Hardcastle tells me the Vikings of old did, my lord," Lewrie agreed.

"Who became the Russ, *Kapitan*," Rybakov breezily babbled on, "for it was Vikings who entered the rivers from the Baltic and founded my country, who brought the trade goods from all round the world which they sailed."

"Mister Tunstall's duty, sir, and he says he is ready to fire," Midshipman Pannabaker reported. "Uhm . . . at what, sir?"

"At the snow off the starboard bows, Mister Pannabaker," Lewrie told him. "Slow and steady, and he's to listen close for an echo off the land. A round every two minutes, tell him, with my compliments."

"Oh. Aye aye, sir," Pannabaker said, whirling away, still befuddled, to bear the order to the Master Gunner.

"Once Mister Tunstall is ready to fire, Mister Ballard," Lewrie further instructed, "have the Bosun pipe the 'Still' so there will be no extraneous noises."

"Very good, sir," Ballard answered, sounding even stiffer than normal; as if he wished to sniff at the oddness.

Damme, he's a good friend . . . was, Lewrie thought with a brief flush of irritation; *so what's bitin' him?*

"Ready, sir!" Tunstall cried aft.

"Bosun, pipe 'Still,'" Lt. Ballard snapped, and the crew froze in place, eyes turned aft in query as Mr. Dimmock tweetled the short call, which was a rarity aboard *Thermopylae*. Other ships in the Navy might be run by martinets who demanded utter silence during every evolution and manoeuvre, with twitched lines and single-note peeps from bosuns' calls to relay orders, but, so far, *Thermopylae* had not been one of them. Not under good old Capt. Speaks (God bless him) and not under their new captain, who was beginning to win them over.

"Carry on, Mister Tunstall," Lewrie ordered.

The swivel gun barked like a lap dog in the relative silence, huffing a thick cloud of yellow-grey powder smoke over the starboard cat-heads, the aftermath seeming to roll off into soft, steady snow like a departing spook. But there was no echo.

"I have taken charge of all our firearms, *Kapitan* Lewrie," the genial older aristocrat told him in a stage whisper, leaning close to wreathe both of them in cigar smoke for a second.

"Good" was Lewrie's muttered comment.

"My apologies . . . *rifled* duellings pistols," Count Rybakov went on, face twisted with a grimace of distaste, and an exaggerated shiver. "I did not know. Such is . . . pah!"

"Explains my lucky shot," Lewrie said, grimly shrugging, trying to make light of it, though appalled, as was Count Rybakov, Lt. Eades, and every other man aboard who aspired to the title "gentleman." The Code Duello of every civilised country (even the Irish) where honour was defended with swords or pistols, abhorred rifled weapons as a sign of a coward seeking unfair advantage. There *were* gunsmiths in England who would rifle the back three or four inches of an eight-inch barrel for a customer, deep enough so that even a man's seconds or the judges were fooled . . . usually only *one* of a matched pair, with the coward armed for accurate murder, and his unsuspecting foe reduced to the limited accuracy of a proper smooth-bore. It wasn't strictly against the law—*yet*—but it was the social ruin of any so-called gentleman who tried.

"I do not wish to admit my family produces a coward . . ."

"Then say no more of it, my lord," Lewrie whispered back. "Do recall the old British adage . . . 'The least said, the soonest mended.' "

"*Spassiba, Kapitan* Lewrie," Count Rybakov replied. "Thank you."

"Ready again, Cap'm sir!" Tunstall shouted.

"Fire away, Mister Tunstall, and everyone perk yer ears up!"

The 2-pounder swivel gun yapped again, wreathing Tunstall and his assistants in a slow-moving belch of sour, rotten-egg stench. The report rolled away, fading, fading like a hard-sought whisper, and . . .

Thum-umum came the faint reply.

"There, sir!" Lt. Farley said in a harsh, urgent whisper, one hand cupped behind his right ear, and pointing off about three points off the starboard bows. "Seemed to come from there."

"A point more Easterly, Mister Ballard," Lewrie snapped. "Fire another, Mister Tunstall, quickly!"

"Bottom at *twenny* fathom!" the starboard leadsman cried. "*Twenny* fathom t'this line, there!" which produced a brief scramble over the chart, Mr. Lyle and Capt. Hardcastle almost knocking their heads together to trace the fathom lines for the closest to "twenty."

Bark! from the swivel gun. A shorter pause this time, then the slightly louder *Thum-um* echoing back.

"More like *four* points off the starboard bows this time, sir!" Lt. Farley cheered. "Hark," he added, head cocked in confusion. "Do I hear . . . ?"

"*Seals*, Mister Farley!" Lewrie, face split in a broad grin even as an eldritch shiver went up and down his spine. "The barking of seals."

"Eastern-most tip of Laeso, then, sir," the Sailing Master was first to tumble out, "for most of the island's shore is steep-to, and the eastern tip is the onliest place where the twenty-five fathom line lies close ashore."

"Shallows to rock and sand beaches, it does, sir," Hardcastle was quick to add, "and with so few poor fisherman livin' on the isle, 'tis always been a haunt for seals."

"Haunt, indeed, sir," Lewrie said, snatching up a day glass from the binnacle cabinet and stepping to the starboard bulwarks. "Damme, but I *like* seals," he added, lifting the telescope to his right eye. As if on orders from on high, from Lir, the old Celtic sea god and the ancient pagan pantheon, the snow squall thinned of a sudden, revealing a rocky, low-lying shore, bleak and snow-dusted, with only a few dark green patches of pine and stunted bush. And a dark taupe beach filled by sleek dark-furred seals, ripple-running on fins into the sea.

"*Thir*-ty fath-om, there!" the leadsman hallooed, unmistakable relief in his voice. "*Thir*-ty fathom t'this line!"

"Secure, Mister Tunstall," Lewrie shouted forward, shuddering with secret delight, and laughing. "We've found our unknown island."

"Wouldn't have believed it, had I not just seen it," Lt. Farley could be heard to mutter, and shared a meaningful glance with the others on the quarterdeck, behind Lewrie's back. Small as his entourage was when he'd come aboard, as Irish and myth-ridden as Liam Desmond and Patrick Furfy were (and as inclined to talk about the new captain's exploits), the arcane details of Capt. "Ram-Cat" Lewrie had been passed in whispers belowdecks; first among the hands, then filtered aft among the Warrants and officers. Lewrie and seals, *selkies* and the blessing of his doings by their appearances, such as the time he stole all those Black slaves in the West Indies, and the seals had swum out alongside the liberated, and their liberators; the warnings that had come to Commander Lewrie about the Serbian pirates in the Adriatic; the *geas*, the good *cess* that West Country and Irish sailors said had been bestowed upon a lucky ship, a lucky captain, and his defence of the right.

"The *captain's* seals," Midshipman Pannabaker managed to squeak from a tight throat as the seals flooded like a dark brown carpet into the faint surf, and swam swiftly out towards *Thermopylae*, small heads bobbing up then diving under, uttering hound-like harks, some of them leaping clear of the water like flying fish, and it was so uncanny he felt like tearing up. *Were they* summoned *to us?* he had to wonder.

Lewrie lowered the telescope and compacted it back into itself, stuck it in a pocket of his fur coat, then leaned on the bulwarks most lubberly-like, as *Thermopylae* cleared Laeso by a wider and wider margin. And still the seals came on, off the starboard quarter, almost to amidships off the beam, with a stronger few swimming and leaping almost against the bows and the outer edge of the bow wave and wake. Sailors now released from the "Still" crowded the gangways to peer down at the seals, who now raised a chorus of barks that put everyone in mind of a pack of pups glad to see their owner return up the cottage lane, after a day's absence at his labours. Great brown eyes wetly ashine under long lashes peered up at the frigate, whiskers on muzzles twitched in what seemed like joy as they barked. And, most eerily, a few of them half-rolled onto their sides to wave flippers at them!

All eyes went to the new captain, who was smiling fit to bust as he waved *back* to them! A long moment more, and *Thermopylae* began to out-distance them and leave them behind to gambol and leap in their wake, and the seal pack turned away towards their rock beach. A gust of icy Arctic wind arose, keening in the rigging as the frigate, now on a broad reach instead of a "landsman's breeze" from right aft, like the shriek of fast flying spirits. The rising wind brought a blizzard of thicker, fatter, softer snowflakes that blotted out the decks for another long minute, and, when it thinned, and the gust faded, there were no seals to be seen! As if they'd never been. Their barks from the beach on Laeso could still be heard, but . . .

"Give it one turn of the half-hour glass, Mister Ballard, then come about to Sou-Sou'east again," Lewrie ordered, still half lost in reverie, and pleasure. "There's still the small isle of Anholt ahead, but we should be able to leave it well clear off our starboard. It is *much* smaller, is it not, Mister Lyle? Captain Hardcastle? Easier to miss, pray God?" Lewrie japed, in happy takings of a sudden after days of tension and reined-back strife. "The Sound, and the Narrows, round dawn tomorrow, do you gentlemen believe?"

"Aye, sir," Mr. Lyle said, while Capt. Hardcastle could only nod and gulp, still too awed to trust his voice, and Lewrie turned away to pace over to the larboard rails, now the windward side, and his alone for as long as he was on deck.

"Seals don't *do* that," Hardcastle muttered. "I been past Laeso hundreds of times, and whenever the seals are present, they usually go ashore, t'get *away* from a ship passing too close to them."

"This was a rare occurrence, gentlemen?" Count Rybakov enquired, having enjoyed the seals' appearance as only a pleasing happenstance.

"Oh, rare, aye!" Capt. Hardcastle quickly affirmed. "Drawn out by the Captain, and his good *cess*."

"By *Kapitan* Lewrie?" Rybakov said, puzzled, with his brow knitted. "And what is this . . . *cess*?"

"A good-luck blessing, so the tale goes," the Sailing Master began to relate, though sounding dubious. "A funeral at sea, aboard the Captain's first command, in '94 . . ."

"Hundreds of miles offshore in the Bay of Biscay, just after the Battle of the Glorious First of June," Capt. Hardcastle stuck in, more superstitious than Lyle. "Seals came alongside, from nowhere, 'tis told by his Cox'n, and . . . took back the soul of the only lad killed . . . a *selkie*, and one of theirs, cursed by Lir, the old Celtic sea god who turned folks into seals 'cause they denied him, and doomed to live in the sea 'til they scream t'be people, again, Swim ashore and shed their hides on stormy nights, then live as men, or women, 'til they scream for a return to the sea, 'til the end of time."

"Seals *seem* to turn up in Captain Lewrie's career, and *some* deem their appearances most fortunate," Mr. Lyle faintly scoffed. "Likely, it is only coincidence, sir. Coincidence, and myth-making about a man who has had extreme good fortune, by superstitious sailors."

"*Uncanny* luck," Hardcastle insisted. "One can't deny that. The hands . . . do they believe their captain is blessed, his ship, and his crew that serves him shares in the blessing, well . . . who's to talk 'em out of that, I ask you, Mister Lyle? Might as well say that Nelson is just having a string of dumb luck, and will let them down, soon as they put their trust in him, hah!"

"Hardly the same thing, sir," Mr. Lyle said with a sniff.

"Well, it is nice to imagine that the appearance of those seals, whatever the reason for it, harbingers a successful voyage for us," the bemused Count Rybakov said with a cheerful shrug.

"Pray God, indeed, sir," Capt. Hardcastle agreed.

"Ah, but to *which* god?" Mr. Lyle said with a mild snicker. "The Great Jehovah, or old Lir?"

Count Rybakov tipped his beaver hat to them and paced slowly aft to the taffrails, puffing away on his cigar and squinting against the snow that swirled around him. As urbane and cosmopolitan as he appeared to the world, as educated and refined, and trained from birth to fit easily into any royal court in the world, yet he was Russian, a child of the Orthodox Church, and still able to be mesmerised by the rituals, the incense, and the grandeur of its chants and hymns. Superstition in signs and omens lurked close under his polished, cynically witty skin, and the significance of the seals' uncanny eagerness to swim out to the frigate . . . to greet one of their own? . . . put a shiver up his spine.

He turned his back to the blowing snow, hunched deep in his furs and drawing on his cigar, finding himself *hoping* that the seals' omen meant a swift and safe return to Russia, and the Tsar's court.

"*Chort,*" he muttered, frowning of a sudden. If this Englishman Lewrie was *blessed* by seals, *protected* . . . ! What would these *Angliski* sailors' *selkies* do to anyone who threatened their favourite?

And what fur was Anatoli's overcoat and *shapka*?

Seal.

CHAPTER THIRTY-THREE

$\mathcal{T}$he ship is at Quarters, sir," Lt. Ballard reported, once the last noisy rumbles and thuds had died away. Decks were sanded, water butts between the guns were full; seamen's chests and stowage bags had been struck down to the orlop, along with all the deal and canvas partitions, captain's and officers' furniture. The Misdshipmen's mess on the orlop had been converted to a surgery.

The 18-pounders of both batteries had been run in, un-bowsed from the gun-port sills, and the ports ready to be lowered. Captains and quarter-gunners had selected the truest, roundest shot from among the balls stowed in the thick rope shot-garlands, or the shot-racks by the hatchways. Tompions had been removed from the muzzles, and powder charges had been rammed down to the breeches, followed by shot and wadding.

Gun tools had been fetched up from the racks over the tables in the mess, the tables swung up against the overheads, and flint-lock strikers fetched from the magazines. The arms chests had been opened, and muskets, pistols, and cutlasses were ready to hand. The boarding pike racks round the bases of the masts had been un-locked and un-chained, making them ready to grab.

Sailors serving the guns had bound their neckerchiefs over their ears to preserve their hearing, and most had stuffed oakum into their ears, as

well. Officers and Warrants had dressed, in the wee hours of the pre-
dawn, in their cleanest clothing, exchanging their usual linen or cotton
shirts and stockings for silk, which was easier to draw from wounds.

HMS *Thermopylae* was ready for battle, no matter how out-gunned
they might be by the monster cannon of Kronborg Castle; ready to sell
their lives dearly, should *Thermopylae* be dis-masted, crippled, and captured. She would not go down without a fight.

"Very well, Mister Ballard," Lewrie replied, fingers of his left hand
flexing on the hilt of his hanger.

"Sorry, sir . . . they don't care much for their basket," Pettus apologised as he emerged from the great-cabins with both cats "bagged" at
last, on his way to the orlop where he would assist the Surgeon, Mr. Harward, and his Mates, should it come to it.

"They'll get used to you, Pettus," Lewrie called down to him from
the cross-deck hammock nettings of the quarterdeck, "and let you shove
'em in, as meek as baa-lambs."

He thumped the top of the nettings to assure himself that they were
tight-packed with rolled-up sailors' hammocks and bedding, passed
through the ring-measure that required them to be as snug as sausages.
Cross the forrud edge of the quarterdeck, down the bulwarks from bow
to stern on each beam, the snugly packed iron stanchions and nettings
might stop lighter shot, grape, and langridge, or flesh-flaying clouds of
wood splinters from hits. The Marines, in full red kit for a rare once
unless posted as sentries, could shelter behind them and fire their muskets at enemy sea soldiers, not out in the open like the Army did, and
shoulder-to-shoulder.

The night before, *Thermopylae* had come to anchor in Swedish waters,
bows pointing Northerly to best and second bower, just a bit South of
the long, narrow peninsula that marked the deep inlet named the Koll,
for Lewrie had no wish to try to skulk through the Narrows in the dark.
And he wished to measure the rate of the outflow from the Baltic that
they would face in the morning, after nigh a week of Northerly winds to
slow it. He had pored over his charts once more, in private, without
Hardcastle or Lyle, and scribbling on a blank sheet of paper, estimating
the strength of the next day's winds, and *Thermopylae*'s possible speed
"over the ground" in varying circumstances . . . and, how long his
frigate would be under fire in that one-and-three-quarter-mile oval of

vulnerability. With the ship safely anchored, the chip-log streamed from the bow had shown only a two-knot current that night, and with any luck (and his fingers crossed) Lewrie estimated that they *might* make at least five or six knots South. The simple mathematics was stark, though; that meant seventeen to twenty minutes under fire, if the Danes were feeling particularly bellicose, if the Swedes decided to join in, as they had vowed to when the Armed Neutrality was formed . . . as they had so long ago when Denmark, Sweden, and Danish Norway had been referred to as "The Three Crowns."

The mood of the ship had been sombre, the crew on the gun-deck singing to the accompaniment of fiddle and fife, or the strains of Liam Desmond's *uilleann* lap-pipes; "Admiral Hosier's Ghost," "The False Young Sailor," "Spanish Ladies," "One Morning in May," all the lachry-mose and sad dirges they knew. Oh, Desmond had struck up some lively tunes, but it hadn't sounded as if they'd rise to them, not full-voiced and eager as they usually might. There was no rhythmic thud of dancing to the horn-pipes, chanteys, or "stamp and goes."

Wonder if there's any horn-pipes of gloom? Lewrie had wondered.

Supper with Count Rybakov had been a sullen affair, too; thankfully without Count Levotchkin's presence, for both of them had more on their minds than sparkling and witty conversation. Count Rybakov had pressed him for more lore about *selkies,* Lir, and the particular instances when seals had appeared to him, but that subject was simply too eerie a matter on the possible eve of battle. The highlight, if one could call it that, occurred when Rybakov had expressed curiosity about Lewrie's Kentucky Bourbon whisky, and Lewrie had, in turn, had to taste several varieties of vodka, including a Polish version flavoured with buffalo grass. Neither had come away with a favourable opinion of the other's "tipple."

"And do *you* believe in this . . . *cess* of yours, *Kapitan* Lewrie?" Count Rybakov had finally asked.

"Believe?" Lewrie had gloomed. "No, not really, my lord. That would make me a heathen, though I will admit that there've been times that the presence of seals made me wonder. Eerie as it is, whenever they've turned up, I've been . . . thankful for the warning. There's an host of mysteries that happen at sea, so . . . ," he had concluded with a shrug.

By the first bell of the Evening Watch, at 8:30 P.M., both of them were more than ready to turn in. Thankfully (again) Count Levotchkin had dined alone in his sleeping-space, had picked over the reconstituted "portable" vegetable soup, the roast chicken and boiled potatoes and the last of the fresh-baked bread, and had washed it all down with more wine, more champagne, and at least half a bottle of vodka, and had babbled, muttered, fumed, and fussed himself to an early slumber matching their own, sparing everyone but for his manservant, Sasha.

Two Bells of the Forenoon chimed from the foc's'le belfry, a terse *ding-ding*, as *Thermopylae* sailed along with a steady breeze from the East-Nor'east on her larboard quarters, the snow gales gone, and replaced by a mostly cloudy morning, with only a brief glimmer of sunlight now and then. She was under all plain sail, with two reefs in her forecourse to aid the fore tops'l in lifting her bows, so she did not "snuffle" too deeply, and slow her progress. Her main course was fully spread, a peaceful thing to an outside observer, for a main course sail would only be brailed up for combat, so it would not catch fire from the discharge of her own guns, if fully deployed. Not that it could not be fully reefed in a moment, should it prove necessary!

Lewrie looked up to assure himself that the anti-boarding nets were rigged, but not yet hauled aloft; and to assure himself that all yards had been re-enforced with chain slings to hold them aloft, should halliards and lifts be shot away, to keep them from plunging down to the deck and smothering the gun crews, cannon, and ports in canvas and rope rigging.

Looking forrud, then aft, he noted that their largest flags of the new Union pattern were flying; one from the truck of the foremast, and the largest aft from the spanker. The Danes could not mistake her nationality, nor accuse them of trying to sneak past Kronborg Castle by employing a dishonourable false flag.

"Eight knots, sir!" Midshipman Privette cried from the taffrail. "Eight knots and an eighth, really!"

"Six knots over the ground, then," Lt. Ballard commented as he rocked on the balls of his boots; more-like *mooed* in a grim-lipped way.

"Seventeen minutes," Lewrie muttered under his breath. "Very well, Mister Privette," he called out in a louder voice, to an unsuspecting world the epitome of calmness.

"There's Elsinore, sir," Capt. Hardcastle pointed out as the old royal residence of Danish kings loomed up on their starboard bows. "Beyond, that'll be Kronborg Castle."

"*That's* a fortress, by God?" Lewrie marvelled. "I expected . . . something grimmer."

Kronborg Castle, formidable though it must be, looked more like a fairy castle, the sort of thing illustrated in a children's book, or a large toy to spur the imagination of the kiddies in their playroom.

It had four large, square bastions, with stout walls spanning the distances between them, all of red brick, not granite or limestone. Lighter-coloured, window-like apertures below the bastions and along the walls revealed a lower-storey casemate. Yet Kronborg sprouted spires and towers more like those rising from Muslim mosques, like minarets, and every steep roof was of copper; mostly gone verdigris green, but here and there as bright as a new-minted penny!

It sat at the end of a long, low peninsula, atop a built-up earthen base, with shallow-angled embankments that led straight into the sea, to the beach, all covered in grass as green as the criquet pitch at Lord's, and, overall, looked more like the country mansion of some incredibly wealthy, and eccentric, viscount, earl, or duke!

"For what we're about to receive . . ." Mr. Simms, the senior-most Quartermaster at the double-helm, whispered the old saw for steeling oneself to stand manful under the enemy's first broadside.

"Receive, Hell, Mister Simms," Lewrie scoffed. "What, ye think it's Christmas?"

"*Ship* off the *star*-board bows, d'ye *hear* there?" a lookout in the main-mast cross-trees shouted down. "She be a *brig*! Anchored by the fort!"

Everyone with access to a telescope raised it to look the brig over, Lewrie included. She lay quite near the shore, about a quarter-mile off from a substantial stone quay and landing, anchored from the bows and a single kedge astern, and though there was a thin skein of smoke from her, it was a single source, not the general haze arising from burning slow-match.

"Galley smoke, I make it, sir," Lt. Ballard said.

"Ah ha!" Lewrie exclaimed as a fluke of wind close inshore at last swung round to match their own, baring the nature of the flag at her stern. "The 'Post-Boy,' by God! One of our mail packets!"

Sure enough, the brig flew a red flag with a Union insignia in the canton, and the bulk of the fly covered by a large white square, in which a post-boy with a long trumpet astride a galloping horse was depicted.

"We're still talkin' with the Danes, it seems," Lewrie explained to the quarterdeck. "Mister Fox, Mister Farley!" he shouted down to the waist over the hammock nettings. "Draw shot from the starboard battery, quick as you can! Mister Tunstall . . . prepare to fire a salute to the castle. How *many* guns . . . anyone?" he asked, in a quandary.

"Twenty-one for their king, sir?" Midshipman Sealey, their eldest, guessed with his fingers crossed.

"I doubt he's there in the castle," Lewrie chuckled. "And their Crown Prince ain't, either."

"There's a Colonel Stricker, in command of Kronborg Castle, sir," Capt. Hardcastle supplied. "What'd a Colonel rate?"

"Uhm . . . fifteen, sir?" Midshipman Privette meekly piped up.

"I do believe that a Colonel does merit fifteen guns in salute, sir," Lt. Ballard gravely intoned, though there was, at last, *some* merriment in his dark eyes.

"Fifteen it is, then," Lewrie agreed, hoping that was the right number. "Mister Tunstall . . . fifteen-gun salute to the Colonel of the bloody fort! Soon as we're abeam!"

"Aye aye, sir!" the Master Gunner cried back, beyond puzzled by then. To fire a salute with blank charges would be to cede the enemy first honours, the carefully aimed first broadside should the fortress open upon them.

"You will permit us to come to the quarterdeck, *Kapitan*?" Count Rybakov asked from the foot of the starboard gangway ladder. He had a *somewhat* sober Count Levotchkin with him, swaying like a scarecrow in a stiff breeze in a grain field, and looking pasty-sick.

"Safest place t'be, I'd imagine, my lord," Lewrie japed back. "As safe as any, should the Danes be surly this morning. If you will not go to the orlop, then, on your heads be it," he said, waving them up, too excited by what might come to pay them much mind.

"Forgive us our curiosity, should the Danes attempt to deny us passage, *Kapitan*, but . . . ," Count Rybakov said with a deprecating shrug as he extended an expensive-looking telescope of his own, one chased in gilt, and its tubes overlaid with ivory. "Look there, Anatoli. Is it not fascinating? Shall we be among the living an hour from now, ha ha?"

"Oh, the Danes," Count Levotchkin said with a sickly sneer upon his face. At least some colour was coming back to his cheeks, from his first exposure to fresh air and the chill in nigh two days. "As dull as Hamburg traders, with no spines. They would not dare."

Damme, what's his coat and hat made of? Lewrie took a moment to ponder; *Is that . . . seal skin? Dirty bastard. Must've taken four or more hides t'keep his skinny arse warm.*

"They most-like will not, my lord," Lewrie said, his attention on Rybakov, not the whey-faced irritation. "Do ye look close, you'll see one of our packet brigs at anchor under the fort. Were the Danes of a mind t'shoot at us, they'd have given her twenty-four hours to be gone . . . or taken her as good prize."

"So the diplomats still correspond," Count Rybakov said, looking bemused, "and the Danish court and your Foreign Office still attempt to find a mutually pleasing compromise?"

"It very well could be, my lord," Lewrie said with an impish grin.

"Ready, sir!" Mr. Tunstall announced.

"Carry on, Mister Tunstall!" Lewrie shouted back.

"Number one gun . . . fire!" the Master Gunner barked, and an 18-pounder far up forward bellowed and jerked back to the limit of the breeching ropes. "If I weren't a gunner, I wouldn't be here . . . number three gun . . . fire!" Tunstall intoned, pacing slowly aft from the first discharged cannon. *Boom!* went the second, and Tunstall jerked his right hand, jutting out his middle finger to go alongside his index finger. "I've left my wife, and all that's dear . . . number five gun . . . fire!" and ring finger joined its mates.

On down the deck he paced, chanting the old timing cadence lyrics over and over, with pinky, then thumb of his right hand extended. He clenched that fist and began on the left hand as he reached sixth through the tenth round of the salute, clenching the left fist at last and returning to the right, working his way right aft to the break of the quarterdeck, into that now-empty covered space where Lewrie's cabins usually stood. As soon as the fourteenth starboard-side cannon had discharged, Tunstall showed a remarkable turn of speed to dash forward to the re-loaded first gun of the salute. ". . . a gunner, I wouldn't be here . . . number one gun . . . fire!"

The final crash and bellow, the last gush of gunpowder, and the echo of salute faded away, ghosting with the haze of sickly yellow-white smoke that was whisked beyond the frigate's bows by the wind on their quarter.

"Re-load, Mister Tunstall!" Lewrie ordered in the sudden silence. "Powder *and* shot . . . just in case!"

More flags were flying from Kronborg Castle's towers, plain red flags with a white cross extending to all four edges, offset towards the seam closest to the poles from which they flew. Thankfully, there was no smoke rising from the fort's chimneys to indicate that round-shot was quickly being heated.

Boom! came a far off bellow from the nearest square bastion and a matching eruption of spent powder smoke. Ten seconds later, there came a second. Lewrie tucked his tongue in one side of his mouth and listened for the deep wail of approaching iron, but heard none. With a quick glance about, he could not see any feathery water spouts from rounds fired short, or the skip of First Graze, and certainly not the Second-Graze, as if gun-captains were dapping a flat stone 'til it hit their intended target. *Boom!* came a third, followed ten seconds later, steady as a metronome on a young miss's harpsichord, or the clapping of a dancing master's hands, by a fourth, a fifth, a sixth . . . !

"They're returning our *salute*!" the Sailing Master, Mr. Lyle, exclaimed. "Well, just damn my eyes!"

"Well of *course* they are, Mister Lyle," Lewrie hooted with glee. "The Danes're a civilised lot. Can't just begin a war does your breakfast not suit! Takes reams o' scribblin', stern diplomatic overtures and warnin's. Like postin' the Banns, 'stead o' runnin' off t'marry. It's the done thing."

"Eleven . . . and, twelve," Lt. Ballard counted, but there were no more shots fired from Kronborg Castle. "Twelve for a Post-Captain."

"They didn't know the dignity of our honoured guests, Mister Ballard," Lewrie replied, feeling like laughing out loud, snapping his fingers under Ballard's nose, and doing a little dance. "How long at this speed to Copenhagen, Mister Lyle?"

"Uhm . . . twenty more miles, sir," Lyle answered after a moment. "Say, uhm . . . does the wind stay out of the East-Nor'east . . . another three and a half hours. Four at the outermost, does it prove necessary to reduce sail, or work our way though any merchant traffic."

"Just about my dinnertime, then," Lewrie jested. "Desmond! A lively tune, there! Secure the hands from Quarters, Mister Ballard. I doubt we'll face anything to match us at sea . . . not 'til we near the Trekroner forts above Copenhagen. The Three Crowns' batteries. They'll know of our coming."

"No rider can gallop that fast," Anatoli Levotchkin scoffed, in better fiddle than when he first appeared on deck. Perhaps gunpowder agreed with him; he was back to a live-human pallor, and back to his usually

haughty self, evincing an air of part disinterested boredom about the activities of the frigate's operation, and the gun salutes, and part simmer-
ing resentment—most of it directed at Lewrie, in sidelong sneers and
slitted eyes.

"No galloper, no, my lord," Lewrie countered, pointing ashore.
"They've a semaphore tower, which this minute is whirlin' away like a
Dervish."

"Ah," Count Rybakov realised, chuckling, "the wonders of tech-
nology."

"Warnin' the Trekroner Fort above Copenhagen of our arrival,"
Lewrie told him, "which is reputed t'be even more formidable than the
Kronborg. We'll take the Holland Deep, of course . . . you're familiar
with Copenhagen, and the other narrows there? The Holland Deep lies
on the Swedish side, with a very shallow Middle Ground, where I'm told
many ships have gone aground, dividin' the narrows from the King's
Deep, which might as well be Copenhagen's main harbour. We'll even
sail to the East'rd of Saltholm Island, *very* far out of the reach of Danish
artillery. Do they not have any warships ready for sea yet, we *should* be
fairly safe."

Liam Desmond on his lap-pipes, with the ship's fiddler and the Marine fifer, struck up a jaunty reel, and, of a sudden *Thermopylae*'s crew
began to clap, cheer, and dance about the decks; from relief that Kronborg had not opened fire on them, perhaps; from "by Jingo" pride that
perhaps the Danes did not *dare* match their weight of metal *versus* a
British frigate . . . *their* frigate!

Some men, now freed from the secured guns, scampered atop the
starboard sail-tending gangway to mock and jeer the Kronborg, now
receding astern, to shake their fists and hoot belated bravery. And
some began to *bark*, to extend their arms stiffly out in front of them,
and clap their hands together, palms turned outward, in emulation of
the Laeso Island seals . . . along with those who hoisted index and middle fingers of their right hands in the age-old "Fuck you, mate!" gesture.

"Uhm, Mister Ballard," Lewrie called for his First Officer.

"Sir?" Ballard replied, looking a bit piqued by such a crude display.
Exuberant enthusiastic displays of emotion had never been to his taste;
there was no fear that Lt. Arthur Ballard would ever become a "Leaping
Methodist." He was a staid High Church man.

"Let's let 'em have about a minute more o' that, then rein 'em back to discipline," Lewrie ordered. "I will be below."

"Aye aye, sir."

"Good *cess*, indeed," Count Rybakov whispered to himself, shaking his head in genial wonder. Such an odd thing, he thought, that a single eerie incident could be the making of this mercurial *Angliski Kapitan*. So new to this ship, and its crew, which could have resented his arrival, and his new ways of doing things, yet . . . could it be that the Laeso seals *had* blessed him in command? For it appeared that the seals' fey actions, combined with the peaceful passing of Kronborg Castle and its gigantic cannon—so easily explainable to civilised, rational people who understood the diplomatic niceties and the mores of behaviour between nation-states—had won Lewrie the trust and affection of his men. "A good *cess*, indeed, ah ha!"

"What is . . . *cess*?" Count Anatoli Levotchkin asked, snapping in impatience with the foolish antics of peasants, and quietly approving of Lt. Ballard and the officers and Midshipmen as they called the men back to duty, and to stop all that noise.

"Something British, Anatoli," Rybakov told him. "Said of a man with more luck than usual . . . luck awarded by God, well . . . an ancient god . . . upon one of his champions, his blessed. *Kapitan* Lewrie here, his men believe, has received a good *cess* from the seals we encountered . . . who came at the bidding of an ancient Irish sea god, to welcome him. To bless his new ship, and his voyage. *Our* voyage."

"Superstitious nonsense!" Anatoli gravelled. "These *Angliski* sailors are as stupid as our serfs. Seeing signs and portents in the yolks of eggs, or imagining that their grandfathers live on in the body of a light-furred wolf! Before we leave this ship, that bastard will have no luck left. I must see to it," Levotchkin insisted with his chin lifted in long-simmering anger.

"Then, I think, Anatoli, that *you* will be the one to die, all for your lust for a whore," Rybakov warned him with sadness. "A whore whom anyone can have. As your elder kinsman, I stand for your father and mother, and warn you to let it *go*! Once our mission is finished, you will have a golden future ahead of you. Do not throw it away for so little. The world is *full* of pretty whores, if they are what you desire. Though I wish you aspired to better things.

"Think long and hard, Anatoli," Rybakov pressed, his pleasant and merry face grim, and inches from the younger's, "for I do believe that *Kapitan* Lewrie's *cess* will prevail."

"*Now* who is the superstitious one?" Count Levotchkin rejoined with a sneer of cold amusement, taking one step backwards and striking a noble stance. "He has wronged me, and insulted me, and I will not abide it. He must die. I have sworn it. If anything counts as a blessing, uncle, the Holy Mother of Kazan will uphold me against any *pagan* god. I am a loyal son of the *true* Church, while this Lewrie is of the degraded *Protestant* Church of England, which we both know is a joke even to the British, observed only once or twice a year, by rote. I doubt Lewrie even adheres to *that*! He is as faithless as the Tsar!"

"Anatoli . . . !" Rybakov barked, a hand raised in warning. "This must *not* be done. Before you try, I will ask the *Kapitan* to put you in irons and chain you below. I will keep the keys until we set foot ashore . . . all the way to Saint Petersburg, if I have to! . . . until you come to your senses, and obey me. Too much is riding on our arrival, and I will *not* allow anything to prevent our success! *Ya paneemayu?*"

"Uncle, I . . . !" Count Levotchkin stammered, looking strangled.

"Swear to me you will swallow your pride over such a trivial matter, and obey me in all things," Rybakov demanded, drawing attention from the quarterdeck officers and men of the after-guard, who did not understand their Russian, but thought the obvious argument odd. "You pledged your wholehearted aid to me in London. What, a gentleman of the aristocracy will go back on his word?" he sneered.

"Uncle, for the love of God, please . . . !"

"*Nyet!*"

"I will seek him after," Count Levotchkin stated. "You cannot deny me *that*."

"After?" Count Rybakov puzzled, head cocked to one side. "What do you mean, after?"

"Once all is done, and there is peace, I will return to London and confront him," Levotchkin vowed, in all seeming earnestness.

"After your marriage to the Countess Ludmilla Vissaroninova?" Count Rybakov enquired, a wry brow raised. "And how will you explain that to her, her family . . . or yours? Pah, Anatoli. Once ashore on our own holy soil, your little whore in London will mean nothing to you, nor will your grudge against *Kapitan* Lewrie. Once in command of a regiment of Guards cavalry, well-married and welcome in every rich house in Saint Petersburg or Moscow . . . and with a guaranteed place in the New Court, this will seem to you *nothing*. A quibble!"

"But . . . ," Levotchkin tried to explain, his imagination flooded with images of the delectable, the *biddable* Tess.

"Swear to uphold me in all things, and obey me in this matter."

And, after a long moment, Count Anatoli Levotchkin, mind still asquirm with fantasies of bloody revenge, acceded, and swore. Though he did cross the fingers of one hand behind his back.

BOOK 4

Quaeritor belli exitus, non causa.

"Of War men ask the outcome,
not the cause."
-LUCIUS ANNAEUS SENECA
HERCULES FURENS 407-9

CHAPTER THIRTY-FOUR

*B*lessed, HMS *Thermopylae* seemed indeed to be, for no Danish vessel larger than a fishing smack stood guard in the Holland Deep as she sailed tranquilly on past Saltholm Island, far beyond the range of the forts protecting Copenhagen; the Trekroner, the Castellet, the Amager, the Lynetten, or the bastions that anchored the city's walls.

Even so, *Thermopylae* could espy, from the very mast-tops, that the navy yard, girded by those walls, did not yet contain all that many warships with masts set up and yards crossed; those yards that were in place looked bare of sails, as well. Oh, on the Danish side, in the Copenhagen Roads, and in the King's Deep, officers and lookouts aloft could count the number of warships and odd-looking floating batteries—bulwarked rafts with stumpy masts meant for signalling, and to fly their national ensign, only—arrayed from the Trekroner Fort down to the city proper, to guard the northern entrance to the Roads, but . . . oddly . . . none of them stirred as *Thermopylae* passed, on the other side of the Middle Ground shoals.

As if they were bewitched and blinded, some fearfully whispered.

South of Copenhagen, 'tween the Danish town of Dragor on Amager Island, and the Swedish coast and the town of Malmö, lay the Grounds, where Captain Hardcastle and Sailing Master Lyle both cautioned that a steady wind for several days could reduce the depth by as much as three feet over the shallow throat of the Baltic, and the largest vessels of the deepest draught might have to anchor and lighten themselves of cargo, water butts, or guns to get over.

With several days of Northerly winds, though, the leadsmen swinging their leads from the fore-chains found sufficient depth for *Thermopylae*; even drawing eighteen feet, she passed over the Grounds with at least two fathom to spare, and did not even feel the brush of sand, silt, or mud under her false keel.

By twilight, the frigate, on a steady course of South by East, with perhaps only half a point of Southing, rounded the lattermost tip of Swedish territory at the point of Falsterbo, and stood out into the frigid Baltic itself, at last. It was only at midnight, and the beginning of the Middle Watch, that Lewrie ordered course altered to Due East . . . sail taken in and speed reduced to a scant four knots, and extra lookouts posted to spot any drifting fields of ice.

With the dawn came a shift in wind, at last, starting to back round 3 A.M., an hour before All Hands was piped to wake the ship for another day of seafaring, of stowing hammocks topside, sweeping and mopping decks, and going to Quarters to guard against any foe revealed by the dawning sun. It changed to Nor'westerly, then quickly Westerly, and by Four Bells of the Morning Watch, had swung round to Sou'westerly. By the time Lewrie came to the quarterdeck for the third time of a sleepless night, so swathed in fur and undergarments that he resembled an Greenland Eskimo, it was from South by West, sweeping over the coastal plains of Prussia that lay to the South . . . and it felt just a tad *warm*, though none too strong.

"We'll not be able to pass between Sweden and the Danish island of Bornholm, sir," Mr. Lyle reported as they pored over the chart upon the traverse board. "By my reckoning, we've made twenty-five nautical miles since weathering Falsterbo last night, and—"

"No chance of sun-sights, of course," Capt. Harcastle stuck in.

"No. Of course not, not in this eternal overcast," Mr. Lyle agreed, though through clenched teeth to be interrupted. "I'd suggest we alter course to the Sou'east, and leave Bornholm broad to larboard."

"Sheltered waters, 'twixt Sweden and Bornholm, d'ye see, sir?" Hardcastle continued between sips of hot tea from his battered old pewter mug. "Calmer waters, more chances for ice floes to form. No one chances that passage, past November. Ye've seen the drift ice that we encountered during the night, Captain Lewrie?"

"Not really," Lewrie replied. "It was reported to me, but . . ."

"Rotten," Capt. Hardcastle declared. "Thin, and looking as if rats had been gnawing at the few pieces I saw, close enough aboard for me to judge. Damned near soft as pie crust, I'd imagine. Do we espy more this morning, it might not be a bad idea to put down a boat, and row out to give it a closer look-see."

"The thaw's set in for certain, then," Lewrie said, wondering how soon it might be that *Thermopylae* encountered Swedish or Russian warships at sea . . . or Danish, had they despatched one or two in chase of them.

"Oh, 'tis still too early for Karlskrona or the other Swedish ports to have clear passage," Hardcastle assured him with a smile and a wink. "And the Russian ports up the Gulf of Finland, well . . . they're weeks behind the Swedes. But we're getting there, sir, believe you me. And with this warm wind outta the mainland . . . ," he said, turning his face to it for a second before shrugging his inability to give an exact estimate, "mayhap the thaw will come even earlier this season. Were I back in England, I'd be loaded and stowed, just waiting for a favourable wind to start the first trading voyage of the Spring."

"Oh joy," Lewrie griped, looking up from the chart to peer over the bows, and the hobby-horsing jib-boom and bow sprit for the island of Bornholm, still lost in the overcast and winter haze. By Mr. Lyle's reckoning, it lay perhaps twenty sea-miles East. He was tempted to go as close as he dared to the passage between the isle and Sweden, but there were his passengers, and their diplomatic mission, to consider. Hardcastle's assurance that the passage would not be usable for a few more weeks would have to do, for now.

"Very well," he reluctantly said, looking about for the officer of the watch, then trying to determine which of the swathed and muffled individuals that might be. "Mister Fox, sir?"

"Aye, sir?" the wool-covered figure in a bright red muffler and knit wool cap replied, lowering the scarf to bare all his face.

"We will alter course to Sou'east, and make more sail," Lewrie directed. "All plain sail, first, then 'all to the royals,' perhaps."

"Directly, Captain," Lt. Fox crisply replied. "Bosun, pipe 'All Hands,' then 'Stations To Come About.'"

By mid-day, as the last of Eight Bells chimed, they stood with sextants and slates ready, hoping for a peek at the sun, but that orb refused to appear clearly, veiling itself as a bright, vague smudge in a sky solidly clouded over. The best they could do was agree that the various chronometers still kept the same time, within half a minute of each other, and that it was Noon, indeed, when the day officially began aboard a ship at sea; not at Midnight, but at Noon Sights.

"At least we see Bornholm, sir," Lt. Farley said, lowering his telescope after a peek over the larboard beam, "and can reckon by its presence just where we are. Its southernmost tip, yonder, 'twixt . . . ah, Aakirkeby and, ah . . . Nekso? And who picks the names for foreign towns, I ask you? Can't pronounce the half of 'em," he muttered.

"Do you concur, Captain Hardcastle?" Lewrie asked the civilian merchant master.

"That it be, sir," Hardcastle told them, chuckling. "Bless me, sirs, but you think they're hard to say, you ought to see how they're *spelled* in Swedish or Danish! All sorts of *umlauts* and hyphen strokes through the odd vowels. In Russian waters, it's even worse, for they use the Cyrillic alphabet . . . the old Greek, and thank God for Anglicised British charts."

"Ice!" cried a main-mast lookout from the cross-trees. "Do ye *hear*, there? Broken ice, two points off the larboard bows! A mile or more off!"

"You still wish to examine the ice, Captain Hardcastle?" Lewrie asked him.

"We must, sir," Hardcastle assured him.

"Mister Fox, we'll fetch-to, and lower a boat for Captain Hardcastle. Pass word for my Cox'n and boat crew," Lewrie ordered.

Thermopylae had been able to post about six or seven knots on the Sutherly winds, but now it was tossed away as the helm was put over and the sails trimmed to turn the frigate's bows about, into the wind, with squares'ls backed to check her forward motion, and with fore-and-aft sails cupping and drawing wind to counter any sternward drive. A rowing boat, the cutter, was seized up, and, with the employment of the main course yard for a crane, hoisted off the cross-deck boat-tier beams and carefully lowered overside, then manned below the starboard entry-port. Captain Hardcastle and Midshipman Tillyard joined the boat crew and began to row off towards the ice floes, now clearly visible from the decks. Lewrie paced the quarterdeck, from taffrail to the hammock nettings, and back again, stopping now and then to peer out and drum impatient mittened fingers on the cap-rails, knowing that such was as slow as "church work," as the saying went.

"Pardons, sir," Midshipman Plumb said by his side.

"What?" Lewrie impatiently snapped.

"Uhm . . . your man, Pettus, begs tell you that your dinner is ready, sir," the boy reported, looking a tad daunted.

"*My* pardons, Mister Plumb," Lewrie apologised, "but the state of the ice in the Baltic matters a great deal for Admiral Parker, and Admiral Nelson, and I'm anxious t'know what they discover," he added, jutting an arm at the slowly moving cutter. "Dinner, d'ye say? Hmm."

Proper Post-Captains did *not fret*; not where people could see them, they didn't. They were to show the world glacial serenity, even in hurricanes, he chid himself.

"Mister Fox, you have the deck," Lewrie called out over his shoulder as he tramped for the larboard gangway. "I will be dining in my cabins, 'til the boat returns. Send word when it does."

"Aye aye, sir."

"A nice slab of last night's sea-pie, sir," Pettus told him as he helped him disrobe his winter garb. "Pity the Russian gentlemen didn't fancy it much, but more for you, there is. A *scalding*-hot soup . . . beef broth, diced onion, melted cheese and crumbled biscuit, and Nettles fried you some lovely potato patties, with lots of crumbled bacon. The cats have got their share of that, sir, no fear." Pettus cheerfully chattered away as Lewrie sat down at the table. A moment later, and there was a rum-laced, sweetened, and milked mug of coffee before him; even if it was goat's milk. "Wine, too, sir?"

"Think I'll wait 'til supper for wine, today, Pettus," Lewrie decided as he dug in with his fork. His hunger was alive, clawing at his innards, but he forced himself to go slow, as he'd forced himself to come below, and *pretend* to ignore the boat, and the ice. One very good reason to dally over his victuals was the absence of both of the Russian counts, and their servants; they had dined earlier, together, with Count Levotchkin coming out of his self-enforced exile aft, and thus avoiding having to dine with

Lewrie, in proper manner, for once. The brief spell of privacy, free of Rybakov's ever-cheerful prattle, was *splendid*!

"Did Nettles whip up anything for dessert, Pettus?" he asked, once the last morsel had gone down his gullet, and the last warm sip of rum-laced coffee had been drunk.

"Nought for dinner, sir," Pettus answered, removing his plate. "Said he's saving his best efforts for supper. But there's jam and extra-fine biscuit I could fetch out."

"Sounds fine," Lewrie told him, requesting a refill of coffee, minus the rum this time. All the while keeping one ear cocked for a call from the deck, the sound of the cutter bumping back alongside of the hull . . . and the ticking of the carriage clock that he kept on the side-board.

Fretting and frowning, now he was in private, Lewrie went over to his desk and pretended to immerse himself in the *minutiae* of ship's paperwork. Finally . . .

"Midshipman Plumb, SAH!" the sentry called.

"Enter!" Lewrie replied, a tad too eagerly and loudly, even to his ears.

"Mister Fox's respects, sir, and he says that the cutter is—" Plumb began.

"Tell Mister Fox I will come to the quarterdeck, Mister Plumb." Lewrie cut him off, going quickly for his furs.

He trotted up the gangway ladder to the starboard entry-port, where Capt. Hardcastle and Midshipman Tillyard stood over a large wooden bucket.

"Well, sirs?" Lewrie asked, striving for at least a *shred* of *idle* interest.

"It's rotten, sir," Hardcastle said, kneeling down to lift out a slab, about the size of a serving platter, and about eight inches thick. The edges crumbled at his touch. Lewrie reached out to touch it, giving it a squeeze. At first it *felt* solid enough, but even as he applied moderate pressure, he could feel it flaking away, as if he could compress it into a slushy snowball, did he try harder.

"Get a lot of it together, sir, and it'll slow a ship down," Hardcastle told him. "Where the floes are solid, not like these bits that've broken off, you'll still have unbroken ice, about three feet or more thick, though there'll be air bubbles underneath, where it'll be half the thickness. Where it'll first begin to break up, sir."

"I thought it would be flat and smooth, top to bottom," Lewrie speculated aloud, putting out both hands to take the slab from Captain

Hardcastle. It was still quite heavy; though, as he turned it over, he saw that the bottom of the slab was pebbly and pitted. Without warning the slab broke in half, split right down the middle, and shattered on the oak decks of the starboard gangway. "Well, damn," he muttered.

"Up north on the Swedish coast, sir," Hardcastle told him, "up at Karlskrona, it'll still be solid, and three or four feet thick, as I said, but . . . won't be long before it's half that, and breaking up."

"And Kronstadt, and Reval?" Lewrie asked of the Russian ports.

"Two or three weeks behind the Swedes, sir," Hardcastle speculated with a grim expression. "It's melting fast, even so."

"Mister Fox? Get way on her again. 'All to the royals,' and wring the last quarter-knot from this wind, long as it lasts," Lewrie told him. "Soon as the cutter's back on the tiers."

"Aye aye, sir."

Get these Russians ashore soonest, Lewrie grimly told himself as he kicked some larger chunks of ice down the gangway; *Reconnoiter Reval, for certain—don't think we can get all the way t'Kronstadt if it melts out last—then dash back to Karlskrona t'smoak* them *out and . . . report to the Fleet. . . . if we can get back past Copenhagen and the Narrows . . . if the Danes* let *us!*

Getting in was the easy part, he realised; getting out of the Baltic would be the really tricky part!

CHAPTER THIRTY-FIVE

What am I doin' *up here?* Lewrie asked himself for the tenth time in five minutes as he steadied his most powerful telescope on the rat-lines of the upper shrouds in the main-mast fighting top. Swaddled in his furs, he was certain he resembled a shaggy cocoon wherein a larva slept, glued to a sturdy twig; it was certainly cold enough for him to adhere to any metal, did he grasp any without his woolen mittens.

Going aloft had never been one of his favourite activities, not since his first terrors as a Midshipman, who was naturally expected to spend half his waking hours in the rigging, chearly "yo-ho-hoing" and scrambling about with the agility of an ape. Damn his dignity, but he had eschewed the backwards-leaning final ascent of the futtock shrouds, and taken the lubber's hole, instead of clinging upside down like a fly on the overhead. All to take a gander at Kronstadt.

He didn't know quite what he'd expected when first learning his destination; Arctic glaciers and the entire Gulfs of Bothnia and Finland completely covered with vast sheets of ice several yards thick; littered with upwellings of ice like a boulder field, or a plain full of Celtic dolmens, a titanic Stonehenge.

But the fact of the matter was that the Baltic Sea was fairly open, boisterous and rolling, as much an ocean as the Atlantic or the North Sea, with the ice confined to still, protected waters, harbours, and short friezes along the beaches.

Thermopylae had scouted quite close to Reval, within a league of the naval port and its breakwater batteries, two days before, and had spotted the Russian navy preparing for war. They had counted the number of line-of-battle ships and frigates still locked in the ice, seen how many already had their masts set up and yards crossed, and the smoke from forges, barracks, shipwrights' manufactures, and what both Count Rybakov and Capt. Hardcastle had identified as the bakeries and smokehouses where rations were being prepared.

Even more ominously, they had all seen the hundreds, *thousands* of peasant workers out on the ice sheets *afoot*, chopping and chipping a channel wide enough for two large warships abreast, seen and heard the explosions as kegs of gunpowder were used to blast the thickest of the ice—or at least blow deep-enough craters, which the men with axes and shovels could attack, after.

Now, here was the principal naval harbour of Russia's Baltic Fleet, not three miles away, and it was the same story. Every now and then, an explosion spurted a dirty cloud of powder smoke aloft, along with a shower of ice chips (sometimes a serf along with it) behind the breakwater mole, or in the roads near the harbour entrance, the sound coming seconds later as a soft pillow-thump, and a tremor in the sea that thrummed through the frigate's bones. But, just as at Reval, no one had tried a shot at them from those heavy 42-pounder cannon along the mole, or the harbour entrance bastions . . . no matter how infuriated the Russians might be by the sight of a British frigate, all flags flying, lying just beyond maximum range. It was uncanny, as if stiff final diplomatic letters declaring a state of belligerence had to be exchanged first. Or whenever the Russians could finally get those ships of the line to sea, sail West, and announce a state of war with their first broadsides.

Lewrie tugged a mitten off with his teeth, reached into a pocket of his furs for pencil and paper, and quickly made notes on all he could see, then steeled himself for the descent to the deck once more.

Why am I doin' this? he asked himself again as he went through the lubber's hole, with his booted heels fumbling for firm purchase on stiff, icy rat-lines.

"Many ships, sir?" Lt. Ballard enquired, once he was down.

"Rum, first," Lewrie demanded. "Nigh-boilin', if God's just. Settle for tea or coffee, 'long as it's *hot*!" His teeth chattered and his words slurred from the stiffness of his jaws.

"Ah, that's better . . . thankee, Pettus," he said after a welcome swig of coffee from the ever-present black iron kettle. "The Russians' main fleet is back at Reval, Mister Ballard," he said, reading from his notes. "Here, I saw two un-rigged 'liners' . . . Third Rates, I make 'em. But there's nine frigates with their masts and yards set up, and what looks t'be five or six bombs, along with God knows how many floating batteries for harbour defence . . . useless at sea. Oh, there's several more Third Rates and larger in the graving docks, or on the stocks under construction . . . or would be, if it weren't so bloody cold . . . but the real threat's back West of here."

"They are chopping and blasting lanes through the ice here, as well, sir," Lt. Ballard commented with a faint grunt of puzzlement and a frown. "Even though there is not much to get out to combine with the Reval ships? Odd."

"They most-like want those frigates out," Lewrie decided aloud, gulping down more hot coffee. "I would."

In Reval, they'd seen twelve Third Rate 74s, three 100-gunned vessels of the Second Rate, and one huge First Rate, which the Naval List had named the *Blagodat*, of 130 guns. There were also three more warships slightly smaller than Third Rates, more of the sort of vessel employed by Baltic powers and the Dutch, which might mount anywhere from sixty to seventy guns. Still, mercifully iced in so solidly that horse-drawn sledges and working-parties on foot had done the ferrying and stowing instead of barges, sheer hulks, and hoys.

"Not as dire as I thought, Arthur," Lewrie said with a relieved smile, and a quick glance upward to where he had clung in shuddery terror. He looked back just quick enough to see Lt. Ballard wince at the use of his Christian name, and purse his lips in distaste.

What is *his problem?* Lewrie thought, vexed, and that, too, was for the hundredth time, this voyage. *He keeps that up, I'll start considerin' him in the 'hate Lewrie' club.*

"Mister Lyle, sir," Lewrie said, turning away to consult with the Sailing Master. "Where might we land our 'live lumber' best?"

Soon be rid of 'em! Lewrie exulted inside; *Thankee, Jesus!*

"Well, it appears there's less than a half-mile to a quarter-mile of ice off the shores hereabouts, sir," Mr. Lyle opined as he and Lewrie bent over the smaller-scale chart of the Kronstadt and St. Petersburg approaches. "We could row them to the edge, have them send for a coach."

"Too close to Kronstadt," Lewrie objected, "and we've trailed our colours to 'em already. I expect their army's astir like an anthill. Uhm . . . what about here, on the north shore? This little port town of . . . Sestroretsk? I doubt it's ten miles from Saint Petersburg, by road," he said, pinching fingers together against the distance scale of the chart, and placing them against the map. "There's even a road from there to the capital . . . and if Peter the Great left anything behind, it's probably a good'un, too. Mister Ballard?"

"Sir?"

"Get us underway, course Nor'east, for this piddlin' wee town here on the chart," Lewrie ordered. "We'll land our diplomats there, and be shot of 'em."

Lewrie went below to his great-cabins and found that his guests had already packed up their essentials, and looked eager to leave his company, as well. Off Reval, Lewrie had considered dropping them off at another wee place on the coast called Paldiski, but Count Rybakov (damn his genial, urbane soul!) had demurred, saying that it would be more than a week before they could reach St. Petersburg by *troika* and that he must seek out someplace closer.

"Ah, *Kapitan*!" Count Rybakov exclaimed upon seeing him, "There is good news? You have chosen a place to land us?"

"Sestroretsk, cross the bay on the north shore, my lord," Lewrie told him, stripping his furs off for a while. They stank like badgers, and had begun to itch him something sinful. "Far away from any of your country's forts or garrisons, but within mere miles of your destination."

"I know of it, and the road to Saint Petersburg is quite good, even by *troika*" Rybakov replied, as pleased as if Lewrie had presented him with King George's keys to the Tower of London, and all of its treasures. "No wolves, either, ha ha!" he laughed, snapping fingers in glee. "We are within hours of home, Anatoli. Is it not splendid?"

"At last," Count Levotchkin agreed, with the first sign of any real enthusiasm he'd evinced since first coming aboard. He'd dressed for the occasion in a new bottle-green suit, top-boots, and a striped yellow waist-coat and amber-gold neck-stock. And, for the first time since he'd come aboard *Thermopylae*, he even looked *sober*!

"We must express our gratitude to *Kapitan* Lewrie for our swift, and safe, passage, Anatoli," Count Rybakov insisted, looking round the great-cabins at their separate piles of luggage and chests, over which their manservants, Fyodor and Sasha, still fussed. There were *three* piles,

Lewrie noticed, the third the largest by far, and mostly made up of crates and middling-sized kegs. "We bought far too much before sailing, *Kapitan* Lewrie, and . . . what is the sense of taking vodka or Russian brandy ashore with us? Like how you *Angliski* say, 'carrying coals to Newcastle,' ha ha?" the nobleman chortled most cheerfully. "Caviar, pickled delicacies . . . all so available in Saint Petersburg, and for much less. We leave it to you as our gift, *Kapitan*," he said with his arms wide, and a smile on his phyz worthy of a doting papa, "in recognition of the great service you do us, in the cause of peace for *all* our peoples."

"Well, don't know as I can rightly . . . ," Lewrie began to object, wondering how many jots and tittles in the Articles of War he would be violating did he accept; charging passage aboard a King's ship? Taking a bribe for services rendered? Breaking bulk cargo for his own use? Extortion? *What could an attorney make o' that?* he wondered.

"Do we take it with us, *Kapitan*, it would take hours longer to unload and row ashore," Count Rybakov reminded him, "putting you and your ship in greater danger. Really, we insist, don't we, Anatoli?"

"It is as Count Rybakov says, *Kapitan*," Count Levotchkin seconded, sporting a smile upon *his* phyz which put Lewrie in mind of the expression "shit-eating." "It is a small expression of gratitude."

"Well, if ye won't land it, and won't take it with you . . . ," Lewrie said at last, "then I accept, though it's hardly necessary."

"Then it is settled," Count Rybakov cheered, beaming.

It was mid-afternoon by the time HMS *Thermopylae* came to anchor off the small coastal town of Sestroretsk. The small harbour inlet was iced up solidly, of course, its larger fishing boats locked immobile, its smaller rowboats drawn up on the shingle, upside down, for the winter, and the floating stages of its pier resting on the ice. Off the beach and solid ground, there was at least two hundred yards of dingy white ice; the depth in which *Thermopylae* could swim restricted her to lay off another quarter-mile.

All three ship's boats were hoisted off the tiers and overside—the cutter, launch, and captain's gig—then manned with a Midshipman and six or eight oarsmen apiece, as the main course yard dipped, swung, and deposited stout rope nets of dunnage into the two larger boats. The gig was sent ashore immediately, right to the edge of the ice floe, with Count Rybakov's servant, Fyodor, and Capt. Hardcastle, who was the only other man aboard somewhat fluent in Russian, to arrange for transport, carriage and dray waggons, or sledges. The gig could not reach the pier, of course, and spent many minutes at the outermost edge of the ice, with two men in the bows using a boarding axe and a gaff pole to smash through the thinnest, rottenest parts 'til the boat could go no further, and there was enough thickness for a man to trust his life upon it. Lewrie watched Fyodor and Capt. Hardcastle gingerly step out of the gig and tap their way shoreward, pace by wary pace, pausing to see if the ice would hold their weight, and listening to the ominous creaks, groans, and crackles, most-likely.

Lewrie lifted his telescope to scan the town. Sestroretsk looked sleepy, filthy, and smoke-shrouded from its many chimneys. It was a place mostly of wood construction, half the residences made of logs, with shake-shingled steep rooves. Its one church looked more like a barn, with the grain silo replaced by a bell tower on one end, and an onion-domed second tower at the other, the dome, and its odd-shaped cross, the only spot of real colour in town. Evidently, Lewrie imagined, paint was at a premium in Russia. Tall drifts of snow lay hard against every building, driven by the prevailing winds, or their last blizzard. And the people . . . ! There were only a few civilians about who sported European-style suits or dresses; the bulk of them wore an assortment of *shapkas* or *ushankas* with huge ear-flaps, tall felt boots, (men and women, both) and extremely baggy pantaloons or pyjammy trousers . . . all smothered, of course, in rough hide coats lined with wool piling, mangy furs, or blankets and quilts for extra warmth. And, to Lewrie's continuing edginess, most of them stood gazing dull-eyed at the strange, foreign frigate, as if they were so many cattle or sheep with about as much curiosity!

"It is a great pity that what little you see of my country is a poor village," Count Rybakov said from Lewrie's side, come up to the quarter-deck unbidden amid all the shifting of cargo. "Our great Tsar Peter changed us in one generation from an Asian country to a European nation, and blessed Ekaterina . . . Catherine . . . contributed more to awakening us from barbarism to civilisation, but . . . so much remains to be done before we truly become as neat and pastoral as your rural shires, *Kapitan* Lewrie. As well ordered as villages in France, or our cities as impressive as London, Paris . . . or even Dover or Yarmouth!

"But we are patient," Rybakov mused, "and those things will come, in time. As long as we do not spend our blood and treasure on useless wars, yes? Ha! Look at it. So close to Saint Petersburg, yet no one tries to make it even a 'Potemkin village'! What a hovel!"

"Potemkin . . . ?" Lewrie asked.

"One of Catherine the Great's court . . . one of her lovers, in fact," Rybakov admitted with a worldly-wise shrug. "Whenever she wished to travel to see her people, by river or by coach, Potemkin made sure that good roads were laid out, if only a single day of travel before the Tsarina's entourage. Villages on the routes were re-made and painted just for her passing. . . . She always stayed overnight with great landowners at their country mansions, or palaces, you see. If Great Catherine went by river, Potemkin erected *false* villages, just the façades, back from the banks as her ship went by. We Russians . . . we are very capable of deluding ourselves, ha! To *seem*, but not quite to *be*."

Expect yer vodka helps ye, there, Lewrie smugly thought.

"Ah! Fyodor has reached the pier, at last!" Count Rybakov exclaimed, clapping gloved hands in glee. "And I believe I see horses and carriages at the inn . . . carriages and sledges, in their stables. *Atleetchna!* Excellent!"

"If the ice will bear the weight of horses and waggons, and if they can get up and down off the ice, ashore, aye," Lewrie said, wary of risking his ship's people at the thinnest, rottenest edge of that ice sheet to unload the boats and bear the cargo to the sledges.

"We shorten the trip, *Kapitan*," Count Rybakov assured him with an easy, wry grin. "After all, there are many peasants there, and for twenty *kopeks* each . . . perhaps five pence in your money . . . they will chop and saw a way for your boats to ice which will bear the weight. It is winter! They have nothing *better* to do. Fyodor has more than enough coin to arrange this, I saw to it."

Indeed, after a long palaver, perhaps a harangue from Fyodor, villagers came flooding off the shore, down the stairs to the landing stages, with axes and saws, and came out to the edge of the ice where the gig waited to begin their labours. Ashore, three sledges emerged from the stables on their runners, and horses were put into harness to pull them.

"Let's get the launch and cutter under way, Mister Ballard," Lewrie ordered. "Pass word for the gig to return, and stand ready to bear our passengers ashore, once the sleds are loaded. And warn the lookouts aloft to keep their eyes peeled for any sight of infantry or cavalry on the road."

Sestroretsk might *look* isolated and without a garrison of its own, but it was *damned* close to St. Petersburg, and God only knew *how* many regiments. It was surrounded by scrubby, winter-fallow fields, and a massive swath of pine forest, in which a *brigade* could lurk.

The serf labourers made quick work of cutting an inlet through the ice sheet, wide enough for a royal barge, and about thirty yards or so deep. Their breath steamed in the frigid air, but they grinned and stamped their booted feet and pounded or jabbed their tools on the ice to show that it was safe. Sure enough, by the time the first boat poled its way into the tiny man-made inlet, the first sledge was there, about fifteen yards back from the new edge, and the serf labourers, in a flurry of arms and legs and strong backs, toted the cargo from boat to *troika* as quickly as *Thermopylae*'s people could manhandle it out.

"Russia has so *many* strong backs and hands, *Kapitan* Lewrie," Count Rybakov told him as the last of his light luggage was fetched to the gangway and entry-port by two sailors. "*Millions* of them. That is why no one will ever begin a war with *us*. It may not be modern, nor is brute strength and numbers *elegant*, but . . . it will suffice."

"I s'pose, my lord," Lewrie pretended to agree, though thinking of what a modern army with muskets and artillery could do to medieval peasant levies, poorly trained and led. Or, what the British Navy could do to what he'd seen so far of Russia's best, at sea.

"Almost . . . almost," Count Levotchkin muttered to himself with rising anticipation as he joined them by the entry-port. "*Pachtee vryemya, Sasha. Pachtee vryemya, da?*"*

"*Da,*" his hulking manservant grunted back.

"Side-party to assemble for departing honours, Mister Ballard," Lewrie ordered. *Thermopylae* was at Quarters, with at least half the guns of the larboard battery, which faced the shore, and half of the starboard battery facing the sea, manned and ready. Marines were in full kit, and under arms, and all officers but Lewrie wore swords on their left hips. "And, there's the last of the second boat's cargo on the sledges, at last!" he exulted.

"I say *dosveedanya, Kapitan* Lewrie," Count Rybakov said offering his bared hand for a departing shake, "That is 'good-bye.' *Adieu,* and may God keep His eyes upon you, and grant you and your ship a safe and swift passage back to England. It is a grand thing you do for our countries, might I even say a *holy* thing, to keep peace between Russia and England!"

Before Lewrie could do a thing about it, Count Rybakov clasped his arms round him, bussed him on both cheeks, and danced Lewrie about the deck, jostling him like a child, with his boots in the air!

*Pachtee vryemya = almost time.

"Well, now, my lord . . . uhm!" Lewrie spluttered, to the amusement of his watching crew. Rybakov at last set him back down.

"A safe journey . . . short though it may be to Saint Petersburg, yourself, my lord," Lewrie offered, after he'd gotten *most* of his dignity back, and his hat re-settled on his head.

"Well, then . . . it is time," Count Rybakov said in conclusion as he stepped to the lip of the entry-port and looked down at the gig waiting at the bottom of the boarding-battens, and the main channels.

"Ship's comp'ny, off hats, and . . . salute!" Lt. Ballard barked in his surprisingly deep, carrying voice, doffing his own cocked hat by example, as the Marines stamped their boots and presented muskets, and the Bosun, Mr. Dimmock, and his Mate, Mr. Pulley, piped a departing call. The count turned inwards, back to the sea, and seized hold of the man-ropes to begin his cautious descent. Once Rybakov's hat was below the lip of the entry-port, Count Levotchkin went to the edge and turned to face inboard as the call continued, and the crew stood to attention, doffing their flat, tarred hats.

"*Dosveedanya, Kapitan*," Levotchkin said, giving Lewrie a final, mocking sneer, as pleased with himself, it seemed, as a cat who lapped the cream. "Enjoy your *journey*," Count Levotchkin added, his blue eyes alight.

What's he mean by that? Lewrie asked himself as he stood there, doffing his own hat. (though abhoring the required honour) and caught a faint shift in Levotchkin's gaze; over his shoulder at something.

"*Seechas*, Sasha!" Levotchkin snapped, his face going feral just as he began a spry descent down the frigate's side.

Seechas . . . "*now*"? Now, what? Lewrie wondered as he recognised the word, feeling an odd prickle up his spine that forced him to begin to turn to look behind him.

"Bloody Hell!" Marine Lt. Eades cried, the first, loudest voice of alarm, as the Bosuns' calls squealed to a sudden stop.

Midshipman Tillyard grasped Lewrie's left arm and pulled hard, sending him stumbling towards the nearest Marine private by the entry-port, who didn't try to catch his captain, but was busy bringing his musket down from Present Arms to Poise, lowering the muzzle in rough aim behind Lewrie. It was a second Marine who caught him before he stumbled *through* the open entry-port, to fall overside and drown, for, like most British tars, Lewrie could not swim.

"Ya bastard!" Lt. Eades snarled, swinging with his already drawn sword, from ceremony to combat, making *somebody* howl.

Sasha, the shave-pated burly manservant, was grasping his hand and roaring with both sudden pain and frustration. The dagger he had whipped out of his left overcoat sleeve was falling from his grip, its hilt bloodied from his thumb, half-severed by Lt. Eades's blade.

"Murder!" someone shouted in the din.

Not done yet, Sasha let out another bull-roar and shouldered his way forward, towards Lewrie, half-knocking Midshipman Tillyard off his feet, and taking hold of the young man's half-drawn dirk with his good hand!

"Weapon!" Lewrie demanded of the Marine who'd kept him from going overboard, ripping the Brown Bess musket from the fellow's shocked and nerveless grasp. It wasn't *loaded*, but the bayonet was fitted.

Marine Sgt. Crick and the first private met Sasha first, with readied bayonets, Sgt. Crick getting his blade in, though Sasha's pile-lined hide coat blunted Crick's thrust. Lt. Eades slashed at his back, but the coat acted like armour. It was the Marine private who jabbed at Sasha's eyes, then reversed his musket and delivered a forehead smash that finally brought the brute down to his knees, swinging wildly with Tillyard's dirk, and *still* trying to rise and finish his master's orders! Lt. Eades's next slash connected alongside the Russian's bald head, clipping off the top of his right ear, followed by a brass-bound musket butt right in the teeth from Sgt. Crick that sprawled Sasha on his back, spitting teeth and blood, half senseless, so he could be dis-armed.

"Get up, you son of a bitch!" Lewrie snarled, edging round inboard of the entry-port. He lowered the musket to level the bayonet at Sasha's chest as he groggily got back to his knees, half-crawling to face Lewrie, as if only death would dissuade him. "Sasha *failed*, Levotchkin!" Lewrie shouted to the boat alongside. "He let you down! Are you man enough t'come back up here and do your own dirty-work? Or are ye the same drunken *butt*-fucker ye were in London?"

Hmmm . . . bet that *needs some explainin'*, Lewrie thought, hearing the buzz of confusion among his ship's people.

"Ye just *couldn't* use a fetchin' whore like Tess the *right* way, could ye, Levotchkin?" Lewrie taunted. "*Your* sort likes t'terrify 'em, and make it *hurt*. Make it *vile*! What, ye get your first practice on *sheep*, or *pigs*, Levotchkin? Ye *prefer* the 'windward passage'?"

In the gig below, Count Levotchkin howled in rage, cursing back in Russian, French, and English so rapidly and heatedly that only a few choicer words could be made out.

"Get on your feet, ye murderin' scum," Lewrie urged Sasha with the glittering point of the bayonet.

"Put 'im in irons, sir?" Marine Sgt. Crick asked, bristling.

"No, not yet," Lewrie said. "I've something else in mind. Hoy! Levotchkin!" he shouted overside again. "Tess told me she damned near puked her guts out, ev'ry time ye showed up at the brothel. She hated ev'rything *about* you! Ye *frightened* her. Said for all she got out of it, ye might as well've stuck your puny prick down the neck of a *wine* bottle, all the way cross the *room* from her! So disgusted by ye, she couldn't even *feign* it with you. Come up here and *face* me, ye little poltroon!"

"Oh Lord, sir, you'll not . . . ," Lt. Ballard exclaimed, sounding primly appalled. "Not again. It isn't . . ."

"I said, get on your feet, you . . . *ya idysodar charochko*,"* he spat at Sasha, jerking the bayonet tip upwards.

There was another strangled cry from the gig, and a hissing argument 'twixt Rybakov and Levotchkin, along with threats from Lewrie's Cox'n, Liam Desmond, and Stroke Oar, his mate Patrick Furfy. Whether to sit where he was, or be a man and scale the ship's side to face the consequences, it was hard to tell in all the shouting.

Sasha shook his head to clear it, spitting a couple more teeth and blood, swiping his rough hide coat sleeve to clear his eyes from his freely bleeding head wound, and managed to stagger and sway to his feet, still defiant, with an arrogant, pugnacious sneer on his face, breathing heavily through his nose like a bull in a Spanish fighting arena, still game to charge the cape.

"Sir, you *cannot* intend to simply *kill* him!" Lt. Ballard protested. "It's not within our jurisdiction, not—"

"Just rid the ship of trash, Mister Ballard," Lewrie flippantly said with a shrug of his shoulders, though his eyes, usually a merry blue, had gone as grey and cold as ice. He took a step forward, with the bayonet levelled at Sasha's chest. "Not coming, Levotchkin?" he shouted. He stamped forward another pace driving Sasha backwards.

"Mister Rybakov won't *let* 'im, sor!" Cox'n Desmond shouted back. "We're t'hold 'im, 'fore ye kill 'im, sure, says he!"

---

*ya idysodar charochko = (roughly) you son of a whore mother.

"And so I would, were he man enough," Lewrie loudly responded. "After all, *he's* the one who's been talkin' so long about challengin' *me* to a duel . . . for his *own* putrid honour. But too much a coward to face me, direct, Had t'sic his pet dog on me, instead. Hoy, Anatoli! Tess *liked* bein' with me! Wanted t'be under *my* protection, in a wee place of her own, and never see or hear of you again!"

Lewrie stamped forward once more, jabbing with the bayonet, and making Sasha back up towards the entry-port.

"Well, if ye won't come up and pay the piper, ye spineless, backgammoning little souse, I s'pose ye won't," Lewrie shouted a final time, looking disappointed. "I'll send your brute back to ya."

Sasha understood *some* English, and a smattering of proper laws. The *Angliski Kapitan* would rid the ship of trash? That irked, but he was surrounded by levelled, bayonet-tipped muskets, and officers with drawn swords, and could only swallow his rage at being bested. Someday he would have a second chance. He sends him back to Count Anatoli, as well? Because what the other *Angliski* officer said, that they did not have the legal right? His shattered mouth would heal, the cut on his head would heal, to match the other scars on his body. It was good!

"Get off my ship, Sasha," Lewrie growled, jabbing the bayonet at the man's eyes, and swiping that smug look from his face at last, and putting anger and caution in its place. Lewrie forced him to the very lip of the entry-port, facing inwards as the others had done, for their descents. Sasha's hands groped back behind him for the edge of the opened bulwark, fumbling on the cap-rails in search of the upper knots of the man-ropes. "I said . . . *get* off my *ship!*"

Stamp forward with the left foot, reversing the musket to smash the brass butt plate into Sasha's broad nose, making him "spout claret" in a fresh, red stream, and go cross-eyed!

Before his hands could get a grip on the man-ropes, the stout rope stays of the main-mast shrouds, or the bulwarks, Sasha teetered on the lip of the entry-port, arms flailing backwards in circles for balance, one foot behind him *hoping* for something solid that was not there. He overbalanced and went over the side backwards, roaring like a bear that had lost its grip in a tall tree, and was crashing to earth through the branches. Head and shoulders down, boot heels brushing the hull, there was a meaty thud, then a great splash as Sasha hit the gig, then the icy sea.

"*Yob tvoyemat!*" Count Levotchkin shrieked.

"Oh, my Lord!" Lt. Eades croaked as he and many others dashed to the bulwarks to peer over. Lewrie took out his pocket handkerchief and swung the Marine's musket barrel-down. He dipped the handkerchief into a gun-tub of slushy, half-iced-over water, and thorougly cleaned Sasha's blood from the butt-plate and buttstock, then went to the Marine from who'd he'd taken it, and handed it back.

"Thankee for the loan, Private . . . Leggett, is it?" he said in much calmer takings, almost as casually as if he'd merely taken it to inspect it, and had found no fault.

"Uh, aye sir . . . Leggett, sir," the stunned Marine stammered. "Uhm . . . thankee fer cleanin' it, sir."

"Get him! There he is! Haul him in! Quick, there!" a babble of voices cried instructions and encouragements, to which Lewrie paid no heed as he rinsed his handkerchief in the frigid water butt. Once somewhat clean and wrung out, Lewrie looked up to see Lt. Ballard goggling at him, deeply frowning.

"*What*, Mister Ballard?" Lewrie asked. "The son of a bitch tried t'murder me, at his lily-livered master's orders. You've a problem with that?"

"Where might one *begin*, sir?" Arthur Ballard gravelled, almost too disgusted to speak, his normally placid features a'twist in a grimace, and untypical emotion in his voice; as if he gazed upon a rotting pile of entrails and offal, aswarm with fat flies. "It was murder on *your* part, sir, and I—"

"Arthur, he had it *coming*," Lewrie pointed out.

"Do not *presume* to . . . excuse me, sir," Ballard said, choking back whatever objections he had before he became openly insubordinate to a senior officer. His face turned stony, his eyes indifferent and hooded. "I'll say no more for now, Captain Lewrie," he said, turning away to return to the quarterdeck from the gangway.

"Bastard's a goner, sir," Lt. Farley came back from the bulwarks to report, with a hasty doff of his hat. "Bashed his head in when he struck the stempost of the gig, then went under. Drowned, it appears, sir. That, or the ice-cold water finished his business. Serves him right, might I say, sir. God only *knows* what treachery *foreigners* are capable of!"

"Get your dirk back, Mister Tillyard?" Lewrie enquired, looking about the deck to his saviours. "Stout lad, and quick thinkin', t'tug me out of his reach. Thankee."

"My pleasure, sir," Midshipman Tillyard said, trying to come over all modest, as befitted British heroes.

"Lieutenant Eades, sir . . . my commendations to Private Leggett, Sergeant Crick, and Private . . . him, there," Lewrie continued with his praise. "Private Degan? Aye, and *your* quick actions sir. Lopped off his thumb, was it?"

"Aye, sir," Lt. Eades replied, more prone to preening than Tillyard, and all but buffing his fingernails on his red coat. "Fellow was perspiring, as cold as it is. I *should* have twigged to that, but put it down to his efforts to carry the last of our passengers' dunnage."

"No matter, Lieutenant Eades . . . you did for him," Lewrie said with a grin. "Thankee. Mister Ballard?"

"Sir?" the First Officer replied from the quarterdeck, turning to face Lewrie with his hands behind his back.

"Soon as the gig's back alongside, we'll rig the boats for towing astern," Lewrie instructed. "We've spent enough time close ashore what might soon become a hostile country. Once everyone is inboard, haul us in to short stays and get the ship under way. I wish us t'be as far west of Kronstadt as possible by the end of the First Dog."

"Very good, sir," Lt. Ballard crisply replied, as though nought had passed between them.

Lewrie went to the shoreward bulwark to watch the gig pull for the town. Count Rybakov sat sullen and slumped on a thwart, looking deeply sad. Count Levotchkin sat on another, with Sasha's soggy body resting against his shins, and could have been weeping with his failure.

Wish it'd been him, not his man, Lewrie thought, feeling that the affair 'twixt him and that young fool would have to be finished, sometime in the future. Without Count Rybakov around the next time, or someone else as level-headed, and there would be no stopping that arrogant shit.

Lewrie raised his gaze. It was rapidly growing dark, as it did in such high latitudes; not even Five Bells of the Day Watch, and dusk was gathering, and with it, the cold and the wind. A wind from out of the Nor'east, a flesh-freezing wind from the North Pole, it felt like. An icy wind that perfectly matched Captain Lewrie's mood.

"Well, that was an exciting hour or so," Lt. Farley muttered as he and the other officers conferred forward of the binnacle cabinet as *Thermopylae* sprinted Westward from the Gulf of Finland in the darkness. Lt. Farley was about to conclude his stint of watch-standing, and his good friend Lt. Fox was about to take over at the end of the Second Dog

Watch. Lt. Eades was there, as well, for one of the gifts Count Rybakov had left behind was several boxes of cigars, which the Captain had passed on to the gun-room; though they couldn't smoke them below.

"Wonder who this Tess they spoke of is?" Lt. Fox said with a roll of his eyes. "A cut above your run-of-the-mill seaport doxy, I'm bound. One might say she comes highly recommended, what? A Russian aristocrat . . . *and* the Captain, hmm?"

"Is he not married, though?" Lt. Farley pointed out.

"When did that ever stop a fellow?" Lt. Fox chuckled back.

"Now you are being crude, sir," Lt. Ballard, standing with them, cautioned.

"One may only *hope*, Mister Ballard," the irrepressible Lt. Fox rejoined.

"To *be* crude, sir?" Ballard snapped.

"To wangle an introduction, sir," Fox cheekily explained.

"My word, but so far, this voyage has been *bags* more exciting than the whole past year, entire, under poor old Captain Speaks," Lt. Farley said, changing the subject to something less risky.

"Just going to say," Lt. Fox was quick to agree, puffing happily on his cigar.

"Uncanny, this," the Sailing Master, Mr. Lyle, said by way of greeting, after a peek at the compass, and a report from the chip-log aft. "She's clapping on seven and a half knots, even under reduced sail. By dawn, we should be well West of Reval, and exiting the Gulf of Finland. May we imagine that the Captain's seals whistled up this fortunate wind for us, gentlemen? For I cannot think of a better, and at just the right time, too."

"Uncanny, indeed, Mister Lyle," Marine Lieutenant Eades agreed. "So many things about this voyage have been."

"Just saying . . . ," Lt. Farley stuck in.

"Quick thinking, sir," Lyle said to Eades. "Thought you'd hack that Russian in half, for a moment."

"Not for want of trying, Mister Lyle," Lt. Eades was happy to explain, again. "That hide coat of his, though . . . might as well have been plate steel, like knights of old, else I *would've* laid his backbone open."

"All over a whore," Mr. Lyle sourly commented, "Well . . ." Lyle slyly added, quickly glancing between his fellow officers. "I believe Captain Lewrie's name of 'Ram-Cat' in the Fleet is *not* for his choice of pets, alone, hmm?"

"Must be *hellish*-fetching!" Lt. Fox most wistfully said.

"Ahem!" from the brooding Lt. Ballard.

"Your pardons, Mister Ballard," Lyle said, "but I was merely speculating that our new Captain is a man of many parts."

"Just so, Mister Lyle," Lt. Farley chimed in. "A man of many parts, indeed."

Lt. Arthur Ballard coughed into his mittened fist, and cleared his throat in a pointed way, to silence further speculations. Discussing rumours about senior officers was simply not done, not even in the privacy of the gun-room, for it led to insubordination and undermined a commanding officer's authority, dignity, and proper discipline.

"You served under him before, Mister Ballard?" Lyle continued, undaunted. "I thought you said you had. Dear God above, has he always been so . . . bold?"

That was a safer word than the one Lyle had first composed.

"Gentlemen," Ballard said in the darkness, turned away from the dim illumination in the compass binnacle, so they did not see how his face clouded. "I will say this and no more, and let there be an end to such." He paused for a long moment, carefully choosing his words, so he would not be guilty of the same violation. "Captain Lewrie has ever had a . . . *mercurial* streak. You, sirs, have no *idea* of how many parts is Captain Lewrie made."

CHAPTER THIRTY-SIX

*U*ncannily, the winds, perhaps the sea gods, turned perverse to *Thermopylae* once clear of the Gulf of Finland. A Sou'Westerly gale sprang up and blew for days of spitting snow, sleet, icy rains, and stinging spray, forcing the frigate to tack away Sutherly to claw off the maze of isles and shoals of southwest Finland; "short-boarding" to the West-Nor'west for a single watch, to gain enough sea-room for a "long Board" on the opposite tack round South by East for two watches, each leg bashed out "close-hauled" under reduced sail, with the coasts of the Russian-occupied provinces of Latvia, Lithuania, and Poland a dreaded risk before the bows. Even after the storm blew itself out, they still relied on Dead-Reckoning, with no clear idea of where they were, and the sun hidden behind a continual low overcast. Even Capt. Hardcastle, experienced as he was in the Baltic, could not even hazard a guess. And when all concurred that they *might* be near the 56th line of latitude, and could finally steer West, a Westerly wind arose that smacked them square in the face, forcing them to short-tack their way along the 56th Latitude (perhaps), with the rocky coast of Sweden off their starboard side . . . *somewhere* out there in the haze and morning fogs.

To everyone's amazement, the wind at last went round to the Nor'west and the skies cleared, so that, a little after dawn of the twenty-eighth of March, they found themselves within two leagues of a tiny archipelago of wee, barren islets off Sweden. Capt. Hardcastle was beside himself in joy, for he *recognised* them.

"We are at the Sou'east corner of Sweden, sir!" Capt. Hardcastle exclaimed, "just about to enter the Hanö-Bukten. That means we're not fifteen miles from the main channel to their naval port of Karlskrona!" he said with an urgent jab at the chart pinned to the traverse board.

"Let's stand in closer ashore, then, Mister Ballard, and 'smoak' 'em out," Lewrie exulted. "Do what we came for, by God!"

Which they did, fetching-to within two miles of the entrance to look the place over with their strongest telescopes, discovering that the Swedes, too, had readied their fleet for war, with masts set up and yards crossed, with sails bent on. Well, part of their fleet, for they could only espy *ten* ships of worth that appeared ready for sea, none of the powerful First or Second Rates, with all but one looking as short and bluff as older Third Rate 64s, and three of the readied ships were frigates!

"Don't seem to have their hearts in it, do they, sir?" Lewrie commented to Lt. Ballard after he'd come down from the fighting top of the main-mast. "The Swedes *could've* put over twenty-five ships to sea, were they of a mind. So I heard from earlier accounts of naval action in the Baltic."

"I'm sure I do not know why so few, sir," Ballard replied, his lips pursed. He showed a remarkable lack of curiosity in the matter. "I suppose we should be grateful."

"They're still iced in," Lewrie informed him.

"Good, sir," from Ballard.

"No one's blastin', burnin', or, choppin' them a channel out," Lewrie further said. "Must be a lack o' peasants, yonder."

Arthur Ballard nodded, feeling prompted to respond somehow.

"A lot of ice-skatin' bears in the entrance channel, though."

"Sir?" Lt. Ballard asked with a raised brow, as if he'd only been half-listening.

"Never mind, Mister Ballard," Lewrie said with a wave of his hand, though he was fuming inside. "Do you launch the cutter and send them to the edge of the ice, for samples. Perhaps Captain Hardcastle may employ his expertise with such, and tell us how much longer they will be cooped up in harbour."

"Very good, sir!" Ballard said, perking up with a clear order, and a duty to perform.

And damn yer eyes, Arthur Ballard! Lewrie thought, highly irked, and just about ready to call his conduct Mute Insubordination; *What's got into him?* he asked himself for the thousandth time.

From then on, the fickle weather and winds turned more benign. As they stood away from Karlskrona, the Westerlies backed Nor'westerly, so they could run with the wind on *Thermopylae*'s starboard quarter to sail South of Bornholm Island. And, once they had Bornholm abeam, the winds swung right round to the North, allowing them a long beam reach towards Denmark, even close-reaching at West by North, then "beating" to weather at West-Nor'west as they closed the coast, and the sun made its appearance just often enough over the next four days to give them a much more accurate position to plot, each Noon.

Towards sundown of that last evening, both Mr. Lyle and Capt. Hardcastle could agree that the land that smeared the forrud horizon was the point below Kioge Bay, a large anchorage below Copenhagen.

So now we'll see if the war's started while we were away, Lewrie grimly told himself, lowering his telescope and compacting it, segment by segment, with slow clicks; *and if we'll get out of the Baltic, back to the Fleet . . . wherever the Devil they are . . . in one piece!*

"Time to tack, sir?" the Sailing Master prompted.

"Aye," Lewrie decided aloud. "Though there's not much room for us to make a board over towards Sweden. We'll not weather the Holland Deep on short tacks. Might have to come to anchor and wait for a wind shift."

"Don't see us towing the ship up the Sound with our boats, aye, sir," Mr. Lyle said with a glimmer of dry humour, hands in the small of his back and rocking on his shoe heels. "Not if the Danes object to us tweaking their noses a second time. Perhaps Captain Hardcastle's two-knot current to carry us along, but against a Northerly—"

"Deck, there!" a lookout shouted down through cupped hands with a phlegmy rasp from too many days of foul weather, and evenings below decks in damp, sodden clothing, clammy bedding, and the close, airless fug of close quarters. "*Ships*, ahead! *War*-ships! *Three* points off the *starb'd* bows! *Anchored*, with ridin' lights an' taffrail lanthorns lit!"

"God help us, if the Danes have got their ships out," Mr. Lyle whispered, scrambling for a telescope.

"Mister Furlow?" Lewrie called for one of the Midshipmen of the watch. "Aloft with you, and report."

"Aye aye, sir!" Furlow replied, dashing for the weather shrouds of the main-mast. Lewrie extended his own glass and crossed over to the starboard side, to the mizen-mast stays, and clambered atop one of the quarterdeck carronades, then to the top of the bulwarks, with one arm lopped through the stays. Yes, there were ships to the North near what he took for the entrance to the King's Deep, East of Amager Island and perhaps sheltering under the Danish batteries there. One or two of them stood out like whales compared to the rest; big, towering three-deckers of the First or Second Rates; most *definitely* warships.

No, Lewrie told himself; *not under Amager Island. They're just off the lower tip of the Middle Ground, outside the reach of the guns ashore.* Whose, *dammit? Do the Danes* have *that many? Do they* own *any First Rate three-deckers?*

"Sir!" Midshipman Furlow shouted down from his perch atop the cross-trees, above the main mast fighting top. "*Our* flags, sir! Blue Ensign on the biggest, Red on another! They're *our* fleet, sir!"

"Very good, Mister Furlow!" Lewrie shouted upwards, collapsing his telescope again, and hopping down as spryly as he suddenly felt. "Mister Ballard, Stations to come about to the larboard tack, and we will short-tack to join our ships, yonder. Have my gig and boat crew ready, soon as we come to anchor. I'll row over to the flagship and report."

"Aye aye, sir."

CHAPTER THIRTY-SEVEN

*L*ewrie? Where the Devil have you sprung from?" Capt. Thomas Foley of HMS *Elephant,* the Third Rate 74 that flew Vice-Admiral Lord Nelson's flag, exclaimed in wonder as HMS *Thermopylae*'s captain gained the starboard gangway and took his salute. "Greenland, by the look of it," Foley wryly commented as he took in Lewrie's swaddling furs. "I was amazed, when you made your private signal and number . . . joining us from the South?"

"Captain Foley, sir," Lewrie replied with a sheepish smile, and doff of his cocked hat, which was one of the few items visible marking him as an officer of the Royal Navy; or an Englishman, for that matter. "Just returned from a reconnaisance of the Russian and Swedish harbours, sir. And, some diplomatic tosh. The Admiral is aboard *Elephant*? Last I heard at Yarmouth Roads, he was to have a First Rate."

"Shifted his flag to a vessel of lesser draught, for this Danish business, sir," Foley said, thankfully feeling not a whit insulted that Lewrie *might* be making a back-handed disparagement of his ship.

"I must report to him, Captain Foley. Is he busy?" Lewrie asked.

"Frightfully," Foley replied, "Lord Nelson even now is dictating the orders for our attack on the Danes."

"Then I don't s'pose what we'll face once we've settled *them* is done matters that much at the moment," Lewrie said, slumping with disappointment. He'd imagined a grand welcome, with hearty congratulations all round, a toast drunk in his honour, perhaps even some light applause upon his dashing entrance and his less-than-dire discoveries. "D'ye think I should call upon Sir Hyde?" he asked, wondering if he'd get a better reception there. After only getting a new active commission by "the skin of his teeth," Lewrie had *hoped* that his duties up the Baltic might turn at least a *few* heads, and restore his reputation with Admiralty.

"Oh, Lord, don't do *that*, Lewrie!" Capt. Foley cynically scoffed. "Admiral Parker has quite enough on his plate, at the moment, worrying about the Danes! I gather," Foley said, leaning closer to impart his inside information, "that whenever the subject of the Russians arises, Sir Hyde is like to come down with the ague, and the vapours."

"Hmm?" Lewrie gawped, his head cocked over in confusion.

"In any event, it would take you the better part of the night to reach HMS *London*," Foley breezed off, "for Admiral Parker, with eight ships of the line, is now anchored off the *Northern* end of the Middle Ground, *above* Copenhagen and the Three Crowns fortress. Lord Nelson, with Rear-Admiral Graves in *Defiance*, command here. We're to sail in against the Danes and take them on from the South, as soon as we get a favourable slant of wind. We've twelve of the line, altogether, with Captain Riou and the frigates and lesser ships. Best we forward your written report to Sir Hyde, and your frigate remain here, sir. Every warship is welcome, and, I am bound, that Captain Riou will find your Fifth Rate and its artillery doubly welcome."

"I have a copy for Admiral Parker with me," Lewrie told Foley, groping into the canvas despatch bag slung over his shoulder. "If you would be so kind as to have it sent on, Captain Foley. I've another for Lord Nelson, though none for Rear-Admiral Graves."

"You'll need your orders from Lord Nelson, in any event, sir," Capt. Foley decided, summoning a lieutenant to his side, and ordering that he should signal an officer from one of the lighter vessels to come aboard and bear the report to the Vice-Admiral. "Will you come aft with me to Lord Nelson's quarters for something warming, sir?" Foley kindly offered, once that business was done.

"Most thankfully, sir," Lewrie eagerly responded.

In HMS *Elephant*'s great-cabins under the poop deck, Lewrie was shown into "the presence" of Vice-Admiral of the Blue Lord Nelson who, at that moment, was lying in his bed-cot, propped up by several pillows and dictating to several clerks and lieutenants, all scribbling away as he spoke. A cabin servant with unruly black hair and pug-face features was scuttling round like a mother hen, offering another quilt to spread atop the other bed covers, and Nelson's chequered overcoat. Hot drink steamed on a brazier, for the side-board, and every stick of furniture but for the bed-cot and some portable writing desks had been struck to the orlop already. And, in contrast to Lewrie's frigate, where those Franklin stoves had been re-rigged and stoked, now she was securely at anchor, *Elephant*'s great-cabins were *perishing* cold, and but dimly lit.

"Captain Lewrie, of the *Thermopylae* frigate, is come, my lord," Foley said in a soft voice, unwilling to intrude too loudly.

"Lewrie? That scoundrel?" Lord Nelson exclaimed in his squeaky high voice, peering querulously at the new arrivals with his one good eye, and a slim, almost girlish hand over the blind one, as if it yet pained him. "Yours is the Fifth Rate that came to anchor just after full dark, sir?"

"It is, my lord," Lewrie replied. "Fresh come from the Baltic."

"The Russians?" Nelson snapped, looking ill and impatient. "*You* were the one Lord Saint Vincent ordered to scout them out? How many?"

"One First Rate, three Second Rates, and twelve Third Rates, at Reval, along with three more I took for Sixty-Fours or lesser, sir," Lewrie rattled off from memory. "Nine frigates, two Third Rates still stripped to a gantline, and bomb vessels at Kronstadt, my lord. And, as of a week ago, still iced in . . . though the Russians have thousands of people choppin', burnin', and blastin' a single channel. It's the same with the Swedes at Karlskrona, my lord. Three frigates, only one Third Rate, and six Sixty-Fours or Fifty-Eights with their masts set up and yards crossed . . . and they're still iced in, too."

"Ah!" Lord Nelson said with a long, pleased sigh, reclining on the pillows and looking up at the overhead with a smile.

If he ain't half-dead a'ready, he's doin' a hellish-good imitation, Lewrie thought as he undid his fur coat. In his brief experience with Nelson in the Mediterranean in '95 and '96, at the Battle of Cape St. Vincent in '97, the man had always struck him as a frail sort, as pale and wan as a consumptive most of the time; he was barely a couple of inches over five feet tall, damned near as short as the Reverend William Wilberforce, and it was only combat, or the prospect of coming action, that livened Nelson up like an old horse "feagued" with a plug of ginger up its fundament to fool an unwary buyer.

"Some more hot tea a'comin', sir," the ill-featured manservant fussed, all but lifting his master's shoulders and putting the mug to his lips like an invalid. He cast Lewrie a ferocious scowl, as if he had barged his way into the privacy of the sick-bed. "Nigh-boilin hot from the brazier, sir. Drink it down now, 'fore it cools."

Damme, it must be a midget reunion, Lewrie thought, figuring the cabin servant was not a quim-hair taller than Nelson.

"A copy of Captain Lewrie's written report has just this minute been sent along to Vice-Admiral Parker, my lord," Captain Foley said.

"Oh Lord, that'll put the wind up him," Nelson moaned between sips of his steaming-hot tea.

Don't I get any? Lewrie silently groused; *It's freezin' in here.*

"Sir Hyde simply *will* not contemplate their existence," Nelson petulantly griped. "Or, that meeting them in battle and defeating them is the principal aim of this expedition, of our *orders*! It was all I could do to convince the man to enter the Sound at all, and dare the guns of Kronborg Castle. For days, we dithered, Sir Hyde thinking we should come at Copenhagen through the Great Belt passage, which would have taken *weeks*. Most dilatory, when the main thing is to go right *at* them, before any of the Baltic powers get their entire fleets out to sea, and combined."

"Now, don't fret yourself, sir," the wee manservant gently chid him, "for we're here, and ready t'settle the Danes'is hash."

"Thomas, you cosset me like a mother cat with her kittens," the Vice-Admiral said with a fond smile, relenting from his brief rant; a rant that had put colour in his cheeks. "Thomas Allen, Lewrie, my long-time 'man,'" Nelson explained. "Tea for Captain Lewrie, Thomas."

"Aye, sir," Allen said, though he still kept a wary eye on the Eskimo-looking interloper.

"Your weight of metal, Lewrie," Nelson demanded, looking healthier than he had a couple of minutes before.

"*Thermopylae*'s an eighteen-pounder Thirty-Eight, my lord," Capt. Lewrie crisply responded. "Where do you wish us?"

"Under Captain Riou, to re-enforce his group of frigates," Lord Nelson replied. "His *Amazon* is also a Thirty-Eight. Simply one *Hell* of a fellow, is Riou, and a man after mine own heart! I've put *Blanche*, under Captain Hamond, Captain Sutton and *Alcmene*, Captain Bolton and his *Arrow*, and Captain Devonshire's *Dart* under Riou's command, along with the *Fox* and *Otter* cutters, to assist the 'liners' assigned to the van of the line. A brace of Thirties, a Thirty-Six and a

Thirty-Two . . . now a pair of Thirty-Eights, as well, adding your frigate to the *Amazon*.

"Might be best, before the evening's done, Lewrie," Nelson said as he awkwardly cradled his mug of tea with his one remaining hand, "to be rowed over to *Amazon* and speak with Captain Riou. He, Rear-Admiral Graves, and I formulated the general plan for taking on the Danes, so Riou will be able to explain the salient points. All that's wanting is word from Captain Hardy's reconnoiter into the King's Deep."

"We've had to survey and re-buoy the Holland Deep," Capt. Foley explained, "so that's sure, now. As for the King's Deep—"

"*Splendid* fellow, Hardy," Lord Nelson interrupted. "Demanded him as captain of the *Saint Joseph*, then the *Saint George*, when the first one wouldn't do. He, and several others, are out even now, in all this cold, charting and marking the deep-water passage into the King's Deep, and Copenhagen Roads. What charts we have are next to useless, and the civilian masters and pilots we brought along are . . . *asses*! They tell us that the deep channel is along the Middle Ground, yet we have noted *large* Danish warships anchored in deep water close to the city, on the *land* side." The nearest one, the *Provensteenen*, we *know* is a cut-down three-decker, not two miles off from us."

"Well, she might be sittin' in the mud, my lord," Lewrie said as the promised mug of tea at last arrived. "Even so, that'd mean at least four fathom and a bit, perhaps five fathoms close by in which the Danes moved her into position."

He took a sip, and it was nowhere near the "nigh-boilin' hot" that the steward, Thomas Allen, had promised; there was no sugar and no milk, either. Allen all but smirked at him with an affronted "so there" expression, and a "go away, instanter," to boot.

"Passed Kronborg Castle, did ye say, Captain Foley?" Lewrie said.

"The Danes didn't score a single hit, sir," Foley told him with a chuckle, "and the Swedish batteries cross the Sound did not join in either." His bright blue eyes were agleam with amusement. "It was but a short, *noisy* passage. 'Sound and fury, signifying nothing.' "

"We exchanged salutes when I sailed down," Lewrie told him with a matching grin. He had to look up slightly, for Capt. Thomas Foley was six feet tall; perhaps the only human-sized man in the cabins, besides Lewrie; an impressive-looking fellow with curly dark-brown hair.

"First thing, Lewrie," Lord Nelson piped up from his blankets and cot, "be sure to pass a cable out from a stern port and be ready to come to anchor by your stern, opposite the foe I choose for you. I intend, should the winds come Sutherly, to sail in in line-ahead, and match broadsides 'til the Danes have had enough."

"I shall, my lord," Lewrie answered, and took another big gulp of his tea; it was now tepid, so he drained it off completely. "Well, I'll be on my way, sir." Lewrie began re-fastening his furs.

"By the by, Lewrie," Nelson enquired. "Your *legal* troubles . . . they are *quite* behind you?"

"Completely exonerated, my lord," Lewrie replied, though taking note of the Vice-Admiral's dubious expression, and the top-lofty tone to his voice, as though he thought very little of naval officers stealing slaves, even to man their ships for England's vital service.

"Such passionate beliefs as Abolition, Captain Lewrie," Nelson sternly intoned, "are best left to civilians who argue the matters in Parliament, our sovereign's Privy Council, or the parlours of the 'do-gooders.' Sea Officers holding active commission may *espouse* opinions on such matters, but not *act* upon them."

Nelson relented, and Lewrie could breathe again, for the Vice-Admiral would not tear a strip of hide from his arse; Nelson's mouth cocked up in a wry little grin. "You were lucky. *Very* lucky."

"I was, indeed, my lord," Lewrie agreed, grinning himself. "As are you, the nation believes. My Irish tars even think you are possessed of a *beannacht*, a good *cess*."

"Superstitious tripe!" Nelson snapped, turning stern once more. "We make our own good fortune, through boldness and courage. Perhaps by dawn, tomorrow, we will prove fortunate 'gainst the Danes, without blindly depending on . . . 'mumbo-jumbo,' amulets and charms, or slivers of the True Cross like . . . Spaniards and Irishmen. Courage, boldness, and audacity will win the day. That, and the steadiness of our tars!"

Lewrie's little stab at toadying, of "pissing down his back," which Nelson found tedious, shut him up; he answered with a firm and determined nod.

"Spend your passion, and *your* . . . *cess* on the Danes, Lewrie," Nelson said with a piercing look.

"I shall, sir," Lewrie promised, bowing his way out of the after part of the cabins. In the forward part, Midshipmen were gathered round several lanthorns or candlesticks, painfully scribbling away at sheafs of paper, copying out Nelson's dictates as they came, page by halting page, from Nelson's mind, and lips.

". . . *Edgar* will anchor abreast of Number Five," a Lieutenant was slowly reading off the latest page to them, "a Sixty-Four gun ship or hulk. The *Ardent* . . . got that, all of you? Good. Ah . . . *Ardent* to pass *Edgar* and anchor abreast of Numbers Six and Seven . . ." Lewrie heard as he stepped out into the icy cold of a clear, moonless night.

Britain might love him, but Lord, *he can be a Tartar!* Lewrie thought as he stuffed his muffler higher round his throat. He'd been on the receiving end of Nelson's temper in the Mediterranean when in command of HMS *Jester*, and though Nelson might *look* like the most inoffensive minnikin ever born, a natural "Merry Andrew," when rowed beyond all temperance, mad enough to kick furniture, his tongue could peel paint and varnish, melt tar and ignite oakum! *S'pose I got off easy*, Lewrie imagined; *though, a man as much in love with glory and praise as he* should be *easier to 'kiss up.'*

"Wind's coming about," he heard one of HMS *Elephant*'s officers comment to his fellows, who were gathered by the larboard bulwarks in a small, shivering knot. "It's come more Westerly, perhaps with just a touch of Southing?"

"Stand in on a beam-reach, then," another muttered back.

"My pardons, sirs," Lewrie said, going to join them. "Might I enquire where Captain Riou's *Amazon* is anchored?"

"Uhm . . . yonder, sir." One of them pointed over to starboard, closer to the southwest tip of the Middle Ground. "Just past *Bellona*, sir . . . and a hand's breadth astern of her, from where we stand."

"Ah, yes," Lewrie said with a nod as he followed the officer's outstretched arm. "Thankee kindly. I'll have to row over to her, and speak with Riou before Midnight."

He turned back to grin his thanks to them, and noted the lights cross the way, off the larboard bows, that sparkled like faint amber glims against the darkness of Amager Island, and ran Northerly up the coast of Sjælland, the much larger island on which Copenhagen stood. Up to the city, then far beyond it, the line of sparkles ran.

"Mine arse," Lewrie said, realising that he was looking at the Danish fleet, anchored in a long, protective line. "They aren't *all* of 'em ships of the line, are they?"

"A great many floating rafts, sir," one officer replied with a chuckle. "Razeed and dis-masted old hulks, or just big rafts, turned into gun batteries."

"Aboukir Bay," snickered another, "just like the French at the Battle of the Nile . . . anchored close ashore."

"No more than a cable off the land, some of them," another of them opined. "So we mayn't sail round their off sides, as the Admiral did at the Nile, yet . . ."

"Yet not close enough together in line-ahead to be able to support each other, as were the French," a third chuckled. "Foolish."

"They aim and shoot as poorly as did the gunners at Kronborg, on our way here, well! Two hour's pounding should finish 'em," the first imagined.

Hellish lot of 'em, though, Lewrie thought, frowning; *This'un could be a real bugger. Twenty or more?* And it struck him just how *odd* it was for two navies to lie anchored just out of maximum range of each other— from the West edge of the Middle Ground shoal, where the British fleet sat, it wasn't over two miles to the closest of the Danish hulks. With the loan of one of the officers' telescopes, he could clearly see the scurry on the old cut-down three-decker as Danish sailors prepared their defences for the morning, should the wind come fair.

"Like ancient armies," he muttered, returning the glass. "Night before Julius Caesar took on the Gauls, or somebody. Two camps, fires lit t'keep warm, and eat . . . and the battlefield between."

"Very like, sir, indeed," one of *Elephant*'s Lieutenants agreed. "Seems rather eerie, don't it? It don't seem . . . *naval*, at all, sir."

Lewrie stamped his cold feet and shrugged deeper into his furs.

"Luck t'ye all, sirs," he said in parting, touching the brim of his cocked hat in casual salute before heading for the entry-port, and his shivering, waiting boat crew. "I'm off."

CHAPTER THIRTY-EIGHT

*M*aundy Thursday," *Thermopylae*'s Third Officer said half to himself as he blew on his gloved hands to warm them. "Second of April, in the Year of Our Lord Eighteen Oh-One."

"Hmm?" Marine Lt. Eades idly asked.

" 'Tis Maundy Thursday, Eades," Lt. Fox said, louder. "We came in on the first, and now it's Maundy Thursday. Grim."

Back home in England, churches would be stripping down all the decorations, draping crosses in mourning cloths, and Divine Services would be conducted without music or hymns, in sombre grief following the Crucifixion, and their Saviour's Death on Golgotha.

"Must we fight the Danes on a Holy Day, I'd much prefer one more hopeful, like tomorrow, Good Friday," Fox added, his voice cautious as he sidled closer to the immaculately turned-out Marine officer. "Even Easter Sunday would be, ah . . . well," he trailed off, looking aloft to the comissioning pendant atop the main-mast, which streamed towards the Danish fleet on a wind that had come Sou'easterly during the dawn. It could be deemed a lack of courage to express doubts or fears too openly.

"Ah," Lt. Eades replied with a wry bark. "Resurrection!"

"Just so," Lt. Fox said with a nod. "But here's the wind, and here we are, so I suppose we'll be going in."

"Get it over with," Lt. Eades said, chin up and determined; even if his mittened fingers continually flexed on the hilt of his sword in nervousness. "Waiting's the rum part. Though our captain seems to be coping."

They both looked aft to see Capt. Alan Lewrie, turned out in his best-dress uniform with both his medals, swaddling furs traded for his grogram boat-cloak, at last; Capt. Lewrie was sipping a last hot mug of tea, and chewing on a thick, fatty-bacon sandwich. Between bites, he was chatting with the Second Officer, Lt. Dick Farley, and looking as unperturbed as the Royal Navy wished of its officers.

"Mmm," Lt. Ballard, the First Officer, wryly commented, having caught part of Fox's and Eades's conversation, "perhaps the captain's *seals* will look after us, sirs," he seemed to scoff. It was such an odd departure from Ballard's usual taciturn nature that both officers gawped in surprise, unsure whether Ballard was making a subtle jape, or being slyly insubordinate.

"Boat ahoy!" Midshipman Tillyard called to the approaching gig, though all could see that it was their Sailing Master, Mr. Lyle, along with their civilian adviser, Capt. Hardcastle, returning. Midshipman Sealey, their eldest, and the Captain's Cox'n, Liam Desmond, could be seen in the stern-sheets as they conned the gig smartly alongside the ship's side.

Desmond and the boat crew had had a busy night, and an equally busy morning; at 7 A.M., the flagship had signalled "Captains of the Fleet are to come to the Admiral," requiring Lewrie to be rowed out to *Elephant* for final instructions. Barely had Lewrie returned when the flagship had hoisted a signal to summon all masters and pilots.

"All's in order, Mister Lyle?" Capt. Lewrie asked once the man was back on the quarterdeck.

"All's *not,* sir!" Lyle spat, "the spineless, puling lotta. . . . !"

"The merchant masters and pilots have refused to conn our ships in, Captain Lewrie," Capt. Hardcastle supplied. "*Demurred,* I think the kindest word would be."

"Should be flung in irons, flogged . . . *keel*-hauled!" Mr. Lyle fumed. "Were they Navy masters, they would be!"

"I don't know where Admiralty dredged *up* the fools, sir," Capt. Hardcastle stuck in. "They insist the deep channel's alongside of the Middle Ground, and the shore side of the King's Deep is too shoal, but we can *all* see that's wrong. Equidistant of the shoal, and the foe, and we'll have five, six fathom, sure, sir."

"Hoist from the flag, sir!" Midshipman Furlow shouted. "It's a special . . . Number Fourteen!" He looked quickly through his slim ledger book for the sheet of addendums of Nelson's own devising. " 'Prepare for battle, with springs on the anchors, and the end of the sheet cables taken in by a stern port,' sir!" he translated.

"Very well, Mister Furlow," Lewrie replied. "Mister Ballard . . . bring the ship to Quarters, if ye please."

Furniture, sea-chests and personal belongings, deal partitions, and temporary bulkheads had been struck to the orlop hours before, as had the Franklin stoves, once their fires had been staunched and their embers and ashes cast overside. Chain slings and anti-boarding nets had been rigged while Lewrie had been aboard the flag soon after the hands had stowed their hammocks and breakfasted. The galley fires had been extinguished half an hour before (with Lewrie's last mug of tea warmed in hot sand in the brick fire-boxes below the cauldrons), and the spring and kedge anchor cable had been laid out just after the hands had finished sweeping, sanding, and scrubbing the decks, so HMS *Thermopylae* had just been waiting for Vice Admiral Nelson's order.

Bosuns' calls piped "All Hands," and Dimmock and Pulley roared orders. The Marine drummer began the Long Roll, with the aid of the fifer, and *Thermopylae* shuddered as hundreds of men spilled up companionway ladders from the faint warmth of their berth-deck to the guns.

Bowsings were cast off cold barrels and truck-carriages; tackle was laid out for free running, and the guns run in to the extent of the breeching ropes. Rams, spongers, and worms appeared from stowage over the mess tables, which themselves were now hinged up and lashed out of the way. Crow-levers were laid out to help shift the carriages, and gun-captains were issued the removable flintlock strikers, the trigger lines, and priming wires used to puncture powder cartridges, once seated in the breeches, along with powder quills should the strikers fail.

Decks were sanded and wetted for traction, and the water tubs between the guns were topped up for sponging between shots, and slow-match was issued, to be coiled about the tubs with the lit end trapped in a notch, hanging over the water, to ignite the quills the old way.

Barefoot powder monkeys went below to queue up before the felt and leather screens at the door of the magazine, the screens properly wetted and weighted at the bottoms, to keep out sparks, which could send the tons of gunpowder stored within off in a titanic blast. Inside the magazine, the

Master Gunner, Mr. Tunstall, his Mate, Shallcross, and the Yeoman of the Powder, Bohanon, in list slippers and leather aprons, passed out the first sewn cartridge bags, which the powder monkeys put into their leather or wooden cylinders.

Tompions were removed from the muzzles, and gun-captains chose the roundest, truest shot from the rope garlands or hatchway racks for the first broadsides, turning them over and over in their hands until satisfied.

"Load!" and the powder monkeys darted forward from the centreline of the deck and handed cartridges to the loaders, then once more dashed below for another, while loaders shoved cartridge down the iron throats of the guns, and the rammer men thumped them home. Round-shot came next, to be thumped in place, too, followed by damp waddings.

"Up ports!" and the gun-port lids were lowered, their blood red inner faces making a chequerboard against the wide, pale yellow horizontal hull stripe.

"Run out!" and gun crews threw themselves on the tackles, heaving 'til the truck-carriages thudded against the bulwarks, the wooden wheels and their ungreased axles rumbling and sqealing. The run-out tackles, blocked to the ring bolts set into the deck, were overhauled, as were the recoil tackles, and gun-captains and senior quarter gunners stuck one hand in the air to show that they were ready, and which was first. The powder monkeys returned with their second cartridges and knelt amidships, where they would bide 'til the artillery fired, and a further supply of propellant charge was needed.

"Marines at Quarters, sir," Lt. Eades reported with a doff of his hat. Sharpshooters were in the fighting tops of each mast, a file of Marines were posted down both sail-tending gangways, and sea-soldiers with bayonetted muskets stood guard at each companionway hatch to make sure that, from that moment, only officers, powder monkeys, Midshipmen, or the Surgeon's loblolly boys, with their stretchers to fetch wounded to the orlop surgery, could go below, or come up. "Arms chests opened, and weapons ready to hand, as well."

"Very good, sir," Lewrie replied.

"The ship as at Quarters, sir," Lt. Ballard reported a moment later.

"Capital, Mister Ballard. Now, heave us in to short stays, and ready to up-anchor," Lewrie bade him, wiping his fingers of fatty-bacon and mustard smears, then his mouth, on his pocket handkerchief.

"Hoist from the flag, sir!" Midshipman Furlow piped up. "The 'Preparative,' sir!"

By God, we're really goin' t'do it! Lewrie marvelled, wondering why he was so calm, for a rare once; *Total lack o' sleep last night, I s'pose.* His cabin steward, Pettus, took away his tin plate and pewter mug, and headed below. "Take good care of the catlings, Pettus!"

"Aye, I will, sir!"

"Two reefs in the tops'ls, t'begin with, Mister Ballard," Lewrie said, off-handedly, scowling at the sky, the pendant, and the state of the waters of the King's Deep.

"New signal, sir!" Midshipman Furlow cried. "Number Sixty-Eight!"

"We're right *here*, Mister Furlow," Lewrie chid him with a laugh. "We're not gun-deaf yet, so there's no need t'shout. Save your lungs for later, when it's *really* noisy. Watch for the 'Preparative' to be struck down. Calmly does it. Else, you set a bad example for the men."

"Hmm," came from Lt. Ballard, almost a snort of disbelief.

"Mister Ballard's your model, Mister Furlow," Lewrie chuckled, "quite unlike *me*. But I'm a Post-Captain, and *allowed* my . . . eccentricities. Shout and cheer, do I feel like it. Do I not, Lieutenant Ballard?" he asked, sidling up to the First Officer.

"Oh, of *old*, sir," Ballard gruffly replied, staring forward.

"Always *have* been enthusiastic," Lewrie prosed on, pacing 'til he was before Ballard's vision, and peering at him. "Pretty-much like Lord Nelson, over yonder. It works for *him*. Right, sir?"

"With no experience serving under that worthy, sir, I cannot in good conscience say, one way or the other," Lt. Ballard intoned.

"The Preparative is down, sir!" Midshipman Furlow announced, in calmer takings; though he was up on his tip-toes with excitement. " 'Weigh, the outer or leeward ships, first,' sir."

"Weigh, Mister Ballard," Lewrie snapped. And in the din of the capstan clacking round, the stamp of sailors breasting to the bars, and the groan of the cable of the best bower coming in through the hawse-holes, Lewrie stepped even closer to Ballard's right ear. "I swear I don't know what your problem seems to be with me, Mister Ballard, but you come over mutely insubordinate, you sneer at me one more time, and I *will* see you below in *irons*, . . . sir!" he harshly whispered.

Lt. Arthur Ballard half-turned his head towards Lewrie, swallowing what bile had sprung to the base of his throat, what reply he would have made, then grimly nodded, his sun-darkened, sea-weathered face going red as he stamped to the hammock nettings to be about his duties.

Sails sprang aloft, even as the best bower was rung up, catted, and fished, and *Thermopylae* paid off the breeze from her anchorage, a faint wake beginning to form as she gained a bit of steerageway among the many warships preparing for battle, slowly threading her way to join up with Capt. Riou's HMS *Amazon.*

"A tune, there!" Lewrie yelled. "Desmond, gather the lads, and carry us in!"

A moment later, and the Marine drummer lad, the fifer, Desmond and his *uilleann* pipes, and the ship's fiddler began *One Misty, Moisty Morning,* a gay, uplifting tune. Sailors began to stamp their feet in time, and several bellowed out the brief repeating chorus, of *"And How D'ye Do, and how d'ye do, and how d'ye do, again!"* whenever it came round.

Flags flying from every mast-head, reefed tops'ls, forecourses, and jibs standing, the squadron of twelve line-of-battle ships stood on towards the King's Deep channel, and the waiting Danish guns, sorting themselves out into line-ahead formation, with bomb vessels falling in trail, their sea-mortars prepared to throw shells into the Quintus and Sixtus bastions either side of the entrance to Copenhagen's main naval harbour, and the Arsenal, with six frigates and several armed cutters accompanying them, with barges full of Army troops idling out of gun-range awaiting the call to land and assault Copenhagen itself.

"Uhm, Vice-Admiral Sir Hyde Parker's squadron, sir," Hardcastle said with a worried look on his face. "Last I heard from the civilian masters when we convened aboard the flagship, his part of the fleet was anchored *above* the Middle Ground . . . far above the Trekroner Fort."

"Aye, Captain Hardcastle?" Lewrie asked.

"Well, sir, it strikes me that a favourable wind for us will be a 'dead muzzler' for *him,* and the other eight ships of the line, so . . ."

"He was to sail, the same time as us, aye," Lewrie said with a faint grin, "though it'll take his ships *hours* to cover the distance before they can be brought to action. The Danes won't even pay him the *slightest* bit of attention. Somehow, I'd wager that Admiral Nelson had that in mind, sir. The greater the glory, the fewer to share it."

"God help us!" Capt. Hardcastle said with a shudder. He could have left the ship, his duty done, and been safely a witness aboard Sir Hyde's flagship, HMS *London*, as safe as houses, but he'd decided to stay and see a naval battle *once* in his life. Hardcastle had a pair of pistols in his overcoat pockets, and a borrowed cutlass slung on a baldric over his shoulder, but they felt, of a sudden, the frailest pretension, and he found himself suppressing an nigh-uncontrollable shudder in his lower limbs and stomach. "Ye really think . . . ?"

"Captain Riou told me that Parker and Nelson *despise* each other, by now," Lewrie told him with a wink. "And that Nelson is sure that Sir Hyde should've stayed in bed with his 'sheet-anchor,' his wee 'batter-pudding,' than be trusted with a battle fleet. Don't know, really . . . but I've seen Nelson in action before, and if anyone can pull this off, then he's your boy. Mad as a hatter, he is. As a March hare."

"God help us," Capt. Hardcastle muttered again.

As *Thermopylae* came level with HMS *Cruizer*, anchored off of the very end of the Middle Ground to act as a marker which all other ships would leave well to starboard, the frigate's *impromptu* band struck up an even livelier tune, *Staines Morris*, a village dancing song that most knew from the Spring maypole performances; incongruous, yet uplifting.

Aboard HMS *Glatton*, 56 guns, Capt. William Bligh, of the mutiny fame, scowled and snapped. "Who is in *command* over there?"

"Lewrie, sir," his First Officer replied. "The 'Ram-Cat.'"

"*Fie* on such false enthusiasms!" Bligh grumbled. "That's no way to take a ship into battle . . . or anywhere *else!*"

"Of course, sir," his First Lieutenant pretended to agree.

"And why the Devil are they *barking?*" Capt. Bligh fumed.

CHAPTER THIRTY-NINE

This could quickly go t'shit, Lewrie told himself. *Agamemnon* had gone aground on the Middle Ground shoal early on, requiring hasty signals from *Elephant* to re-order the line of battle. A moment after that, the nearest Danish ships, hulks, and floating batteries opened fire. Great belching clouds of powder smoke erupted to leeward from heavy pieces, upwards of 36-pounder guns, and the roar of the broadsides crashed as loud as a summer's lightning and thunder storm. Shot moaned past, and overhead, as deep-voiced as a chorus of *bassos* and baritones, and the shallow waters of the King's Deep were speckled with geysers and feather plumes as iron shot dapped across the surface in First and Second Graze.

Then, to make things even worse, both HMS *Bellona* and the HMS *Russell,* Third Rate 74s down for the task of hammering the Trekroner forts, took the ground on an uncharted spur of sand and mud shoal about halfway to their anchorages, and could not be got off, either!

"Signal from *Amazon,* sir!" Midshipman Furlow said with a gulp. "Our number, and 'Conform On Me,' sir."

"Half a point to starboard, Mister Ballard, and fall in trail of *Amazon,*" Lewrie snapped. At the early-morning conference aboard *Elephant,* Nelson had given Capt. Riou the liberty of acting as he saw fit with his small squadron of frigates, but . . .

What the Devil's he aimin' at? Lewrie wondered as *Thermopylae* closed on *Amazon*'s larboard quarter, about two cables astern of her.

"Our number again, sir, and the signal is 'Make More Sail.'"

"Shake one reef from the tops'ls, Mister Ballard," Lewrie ordered. As topmen scrambled aloft and out on the tops'l yards, he took a look to the West, where hundreds of guns, perhaps a thousand guns, were hammering away with a speed he'd never seen from the French or the Spanish. *Thermopylae* had sailed past eight Danish ships by then, coming level with the ninth, a corvette-sized 6th Rate blasting away with some impossibly heavy guns for such a small warship, and another even larger North of her, a hulked two-decker with only a stump mast amidships, yet flying an admiral's flag, hurriedly firing what looked to be 24-pounders and 18-pounders. It felt as if every shot was aimed at *Thermopylae*, for the continuous rumbles and howls of shot passing overhead, of splashes in the water between their frigate and the Danes. There was a crash aloft as the main t'gallant yard was smashed in two like a pencil, to come screeching and snarling down in pieces, and a shower of ropes, blocks, and ravelled sail.

"Not so bad, so far," Lewrie said with a grin he did not feel. "See to it, Mister Ballard."

He looked astern and found support in the form of two-deckers in rough line-ahead behind them; not all of them, for the sternmost were lost in a thick pall of spent gunsmoke, but he could make out the *Edgar* and *Ardent* just coming to anchor by the stern, as ordered, with Bligh's *Glatton* right-astern. Off the starboard quarter, *Bellona* and *Russell*, though still hard aground on the shoal's unseen spur, were firing deliberate broadsides at long range.

Back Westward, they were just coming level with *Elephant* and Capt. Hardy's *Ganges*, with Riou in *Amazon* leading the frigates round *Monarch*'s starboard quarters to pass them and go on further North.

"Shall we fire, sir?" Lt. Ballard asked.

"None of 'em are our 'pigeons,' sir," Lewrie told him, though he was impatient to let loose, not swan on by without responding. "Do we fire, I want the first broadside t'be a smasher, at a target that'll matter. A few minutes more . . . let the damned Danes *guess* which of 'em will feel our sting."

Lewrie wished he could fancy that *Thermopylae*'s aloof silence might un-nerve whichever Danish ship she took under fire, but . . . from the sound of it, the Danes were too busy to be un-nerved.

As in all sea-battles where over an hundred guns bellowed and roared, the shock of gunfire seemed to smash the very wind to nothing, and *Thermopylae* slowed as *Amazon* led them to the starboard side of the *Defiance*, now anchored and duelling it out with one of those floating gun-rafts, a two-decker, still ship-rigged with three masts, and yet another of those older two-decker hulks with a single stump mast.

"Almost all the others have come to anchor, sir," Mr. Lyle said. "All our two-deckers are now in action."

"Leaving us . . . Christ!" Lewrie spat as the Trekroner Fort, the "Three Crowns" behemoth, loomed up off their larboard bows.

Riou can't *be serious, surely!* he thought, appalled at the very idea of frigates engaging a stone fort belching fire and smoke from an hundred or more cannon, upon which their 18-pounder shot would merely bounce, or harmlessly shatter!

" 'Come to anchor by the stern,' sir!" Midshipman Furlow cried.

"We'll anchor three cables astern of *Amazon*, Mister Ballard," Lewrie said. "Ready to let go the kedge when I call."

"Aye aye, sir," Ballard said, his voice steady, stolid, and as stoic as ever.

The *Jolly Thresher* and *Hey, Johnny Cope* strained to rise above the ear-shattering din of gunfire as HMS *Thermopylae* eased to a stop at last, spare hands aloft to take in sail and bind it to the yards.

"Desmond! Thankee lads, but we're in business!" Lewrie called. "Take your posts! Range to the fort, Mister Ballard?"

"I would estimate it to be eight hundred yards, sir," Ballard decided, sounding emotionless, though his full lips were taut-pursed, and his left hand quivered on the scabbard of his sword.

"That stump-masted two-decker's much closer," Lewrie said with a grunt of how useless it would be to waste their fire on the fortress and its stonework. "We'll engage her. Hands to the springs, sir, and place her square abeam."

A long minute or so, and the Danish warship was on a line with *Thermopylae* that put her directly amidships.

"Mister Farley!" Lewrie shouted down to the waist, leaning over the hammock nettings at the break of the quarterdeck. "Broadsides on that *big* bastard, yonder!"

"Aye aye, sir!" Lt. Farley eagerly replied, ordering "Prime your pieces!" to quarter-gunners and gun-captains. Wire prickers were stuck down the touch-holes to pierce the cartridge bags; quills filled with fine priming powder were jammed down next; flintlock strikers were set at full cock, and the gun-captains raised their free fists in the air to show their readiness, the trigger lines of the strikers as taut as bowstrings in their other hands.

"By broadside . . . Fire!" Farley cried.

The larboard 12-pounder bow chaser and fourteen 18-pounders of the larboard battery lit off together, spewing quick yellow and amber sparks through sudden surges of powder smoke, wreathing the frigate in a spectral, reeking fog. Though the range was a bit too great for the 32-pounder carronades on the quarterdeck, they erupted, too, at their maximum safe elevation, if only to add great, threatening shot splashes *somewhere* close to the Danish hulk, and make them wonder. Fired with their muzzles lifted, the carronades' heavy shot behaved more like sea-mortars, arcing slightly up, then down, in shallow ballistic paths to crash into the waters of Copenhagen Roads to throw up great, towering plumes of silty water and foam that only slowly collapsed on themselves but about three hundred yards short of the Danish warship.

God help me but I do love the guns! Lewrie told himself, taking a deep whiff of powder smoke, his ears already ringing despite the wee wads of candle wax he'd stuffed in them after giving the order to open fire. Lt. Farley nigh amidships, and Lt. Fox nearer the bows, already had the gun crews at the tackles to run out their swabbed and re-loaded cannon for a second broadside. As the smoke cleared just enough to see their target, the Danish warship responded, her lower-deck 24-pounders lighting off first, and her upper-deck 18s scant seconds later.

"For what we're about to receive," Mr. Lyle muttered, "may the Good Lord make us grateful."

Heavy shot moaned overhead, close enough to the upper masts to set them thrumming, their shrouds quiver. Splashes between both ships showed where round-shot fired a bit too low skipped in First Graze, but dead in line with *Thermopylae,* to thud into her hull, travelling about 800 or 900 feet per second after the Grazes, with enough force to make the frigate stagger, and smash stout scantling planks. One fired but a bit higher crashed through the sail-tending gangway bulwarks with a loud parrot *Rwark!,* creating a cloud of broken oak splinters as big as a man's forearm, cutting a Marine on the gangway in half at the waist, and spraying a cloud of his blood over the gunners on the deck below. Two sailors on the gangway spun away shrieking as they were quilled by wood splinters. Surgeon Mr. Harward's team of loblolly boys carrying a mess-table for a stretcher mounted the gangway, bearing one man away to the midships companionway hatch, but shoving the ruin of the second over the side through the blown-open gap in the bulwarks. The dead . . . those horribly dismembered and splattered, or the ones who seemed to be sleeping and whole . . . were to be gotten out of sight quickly. Was a hand too grievously wounded for the surgeon and his mates to waste time dealing with him, it was considered a mercy to deliver a skull-smashing blow with a maul, and pass the unconscious sufferer out a gun-port to drown and sink out of sight, before the pain of his wounds set in . . . and his screams un-nerved his mates. Mourning was for later.

"This'll be hot work, today," Lewrie said, watching the wounded man disappear down the companionway ladders, then returned his attention to their foe, straining to see what damage, if any, their fire had caused. He raised a telescope to peer at the Danish ship.

"Soaks it up like a bloody sponge," Lewrie griped, finding but little damage to cheer him, so far.

"That frigate of theirs," Mr. Lyle pointed out, jutting an arm over the larboard bows to the last Northerly ship in the Danish line, "is getting a drubbing, sir. As is our target. *Amazon, Blanche,* and the rest of the frigates share their fire 'twixt her and this one."

Before *Thermopylae* could fire another broadside, shot from the other frigates did splash round the stump-masted two-decker off their beam, and flay her scantlings and upper works with iron.

"By broadside . . . Fire!" Lt. Farley howled, and HMS *Thermopylae* belched out another great gush of smoke and thunder.

As the smoke from that fresh broadside slowly thinned, Mr. Lyle lifted an arm to point at the fortress beyond the embattled ships. "I do believe the Trekroner . . . the Three Crowns . . . has opened upon us, sir."

Indeed, the middle and southern faces of the great stone works were alive with gushes of powder, reddish flashes as heavy guns upwards of 36-pounder weight fired.

"Know why the Danes call it the Three Crowns?" Mr. Lyle asked, as phlegmatically as if they were on a day-tour in search of "quaint" sights.

"Recall the Bard of Avon," Capt. Hardcastle piped up, sounding squeakier. "At the end of *Hamlet,* the last of the tragedy is the seizure of Denmark by the Prince of Norway . . . wasn't it Norway? Way back then, Denmark, Sweden, and—"

He stopped his gob briefly, ducking as a heavy round-shot hummed close over the quarterdeck.

"Sweden, Denmark, and Norway were allies, with three kings, so they named it the Three Crowns," Mr. Lyle completed for him, unwilling to let the civilian get the last word on anything.

"And it's a bugger," Capt. Hardcastle said, straightening up.

"We're well within her greatest range," Lewrie noted, lifting his telescope once more. "Same as the guns of Kronborg Castle, up the Narrows. Their ramparts are, what . . .'bout a thousand yards or so to loo'rd? They've at least five hundred yards range over us."

"The fortress's gunners don't seem that well drilled, though, sirs," Lt. Ballard contributed to the conversation, his demeanour the required cool and unruffled *sang-froid* that British Sea Officers were to display. "And no more accurate than the gunners of the Kronborg were, when the fleet passed them without a single hit."

" 'Sound and fury, signifying nothing,' hey, Mister Ballrd?" Mr. Lyle japed. "To quote Shakespeare."

"Wrong play," Capt. Hardcastle quipped. "The First Lieutenant is correct, Captain Lewrie. The fortresses are manned by the Danish *army*, and I cannot recall seeing them practice with live powder and shot in all my years passing through the Narrows."

"Well, they're getting some practice today," Lewrie said with a smirk. "Hello! Well shot, Mister Farley! Hammer the bitch again!" he cheered as iron shot pummeled the Danish two-decker, smashing scantling planks and stoving in her bulwarks in showers of splinters. For good measure, there was an explosion aboard her, fire stabbing upward, and powder smoke jutting skyward . . . a sure sign of a burst gun!

A second later, though, the Danish gunners responded, their side erupting in a staggering, stuttering series of explosions as her guns went off, no longer in controlled broadsides, but as quickly as gunners could swab out, re-load, and run out.

Balls shrieked overhead, passing close-aboard their frigate's bow and stern. The roundhouse atop the forecastle was blown open with a round-shot that went clean through it; the larboard anchor cat-head was shattered with another parroty screech, and the best bower anchor, its cat and fish lines shot away, dropped free to splash into the harbour, lost forever, most likely. Yet a third ball, perhaps an 18-pounder, buried itself in the trunk of the foremast below the fighting top and made the mast, and the ship, sway to starboard, so that sailors and Marines in the tops had to hold on for dear life.

"Well, the Danish army may be half-blind dodderers, but it seems their *navy* knows their business," Lewrie said. "See to it, Mister Ballard."

"Aye, sir."

"By broadside . . . Fire!" Lt. Farley in the waist was yelling, his voice gone hoarse and raspy on smoke and excitement, and *Thermopylae* rocked to starboard a few degrees, settling an inch or two in the water to the massive recoil as the guns slammed backwards from the ports, the truck-carriages squealing and the breeching ropes and recoil tackle and ring bolts groaning. The guns were hot now, and 18-pounders weighing nearly two tons altogether were *leaping* from the deck as they lit off, thundering back down at the full extent of the breeching ropes at odd angles. Sure enough, there came a howl from a tackle man struck in the shins by an erratically recoiling carriage, and a scream as the heavy wood carriage and sizzling-hot gun rolled over one of his ankles.

"Loblolly boys, here!" Lt. Fox yelled. "Spare man from starboard, take his place. Quick now, lad! Overhaul *tackle!* Swab *out!*"

"Oh, poor fellow," Lt. Ballard calmly said, returning from up forward.

"The foremast sound, Mister Ballard?" Lewrie asked him.

"I would not trust it with more than forecourse and the fore tops'l, sir," Lt. Ballard gloomily replied. "The ball is half-buried in the trunk, fourty feet above the deck. It will need fishing, and banding, do we get the chance."

"Cold shot, I take it?" Lewrie asked with a wry grin. "Not sizzlin'?"

"Cold shot, aye, sir, not heated shot," Lt. Ballard replied with almost an impatient expression, as though he found Lewrie's attempt at humour disagreeable. "We've no fear of bursting aflame, sir."

"By broadside . . . Fire!" Lt. Farley yelled, and the guns roared and thundered yet again, re-wreathing the frigate in a dense cloud of spent powder smoke, adding to the acrid, rotten-egg cumulus that stood above and to leeward from their first broadsides, muffling *Thermopylae* in a white-yellow mist that made it hard to see the forecastle from the quarter-deck.

Lewrie paced aft to the taffrails, past the larboard carronades to the taffrail lanthorn, to see how the rest of the battle was going. But even his telescope could not pierce the palls of smoke towering over the British and Danish lines. He could make out the Lynetten, a smaller version of the Trekroner to the West–Sou'west, and only the nearest warships in the opposing lines of battle. Now and again, as the guns fired or the smoke pall cleared, he could espy a few Danish gunboats anchored with their bows pointing East behind the larger Danish vessels, great bow-mounted pairs of guns erupting, and sea-mortars huffing upwards with even more massive shot.

Dead astern lay HMS *Defiance*, Rear-Admiral Graves's flagship, belching broadsides at the furious rate of three rounds per gun every two minutes, the desired standard of the Royal Navy, with Graves's Red Ensign flying, along with Signal Number 16—"Engage the Enemy More Closely."

There came yet another broadside from the Danish two-decker as Lewrie turned to pace back forward. This one was even more irregular than the last, not quite as ordered and regimented, and . . . was it his imagination, or was it not quite as powerful as the ones that had come before? "Fool!" Lewrie spat, grinning as he realised that the Danish captain had split his fire, his upper-deck guns directed at his ship, his lower-deck 24-pounders angled in the ports to engage *Amazon* and *Blanche*, which were pummelling her hard.

"*Over*-haul *tackle!*" Lt. Farley cried, almost wheezing on smoke. "*Swa*-ab *out!*" From Lt. Fox came "We're *latherin'*'em, lads!"

Lewrie paused to dig into his waist-coat pocket for his watch, and flipped open the lid. Amazingly, the action had been going on for an hour and a half; they'd weighed a little after 10 A.M., and here it was nigh 11:45!

Crash! came a ball right through the larboard bulwarks of the quarterdeck, just forrud of the first carronade, and a chorus of yells of alarm. Splinters the size of pigeons, the size of bed-slats, flew in a whirling, vicious cloud! The ball continued cross the deck, then exited by clanging off an idle starboard-side carronade barrel, darting skyward as a jagged blur of dark metal!

"Good Christ!" the civilian Capt. Hardcastle cried aloud, struck dumb by the sudden carnage that had, like the plague of Egypt that had taken the first-born and spared the Israelites, sprung up all about him. "Oh, my Good God!" he yelped, just before staggering away to heave his stomach's contents.

The captain of the Afterguard and two men of the mizen mast crew were down, gobbling fear and pain over their hurts, or lying dazed in sudden shock. Midshipman Privette was sprawled on the deck, his head and face completely covered in blood.

And the First Officer, Lt. Ballard, was down, his head and his chest propped up on the Sailing Master's lap.

"What are his—?" Lewrie began to ask, then clamped his mouth shut as he saw that Arthur Ballard no longer had a left leg; the heavy 24-pounder ball had taken it off at mid-thigh!

"Loblolly boys to the quarterdeck, *now*, damn yer eyes!" Lewrie bellowed. "Mister Tillyard . . . do you go below and warn the Surgeon the First Officer is comin' down to him."

"Aye, sir," Tillyard said with a gulp, his face as pale as new laundry. He staggered to his feet, recovered his hat, and headed for the larboard gangway ladder; rapidly, at first, then more slowly as he recalled that his actions could cause panic and despair.

Christ, why him? Lewrie asked the aether.

"Pass word for Lieutenant Farley," Lewrie snapped, forced by grim duty to continue as before. "My compliments to him, and he is to assume the duties of First Officer. Pass word to Midshipman Sealey, and inform him he is to replace Lieutenant Fox up forrud, and consider himself an Acting-Lieutenant, for the time being."

"Aye, sir!" Marine Corporal Frye replied, heading off quickly.

"Help's coming, Arthur," Lewrie said more gently as he took time to kneel beside Ballard, who was rolling his head back and forth, his agony already clawing at him, his weathered face gone whitish-grey as he bit his lips to keep from howling and jibbering. Lewrie took his hand as Mr. Lyle whipped out a length of small-stuff rope to bind about Ballard's leg near his groin to staunch the heavy bleeding. "Help's on the way. Stay with us, Arthur." Lewrie repeated, feeling helpless and holding out but the slimmest hope that his old friend would survive his horrid wound.

"*Damn* you!" Lt. Ballard hissed, "You lucky bastard, you always *were* . . . ah-*ah*!" he had to pause as a wave of pain hit him. "Dumb *blind* luck, *always* get what you want, not . . . ! Aahh! Walk through shit with nought stickin' to . . . *Christ*!" Ballard loudly howled as the loblolly boys arrived with a mess-table stretcher to fetch him to the surgery on the orlop.

And what's all that *about?* Lewrie helplessly wondered as he let go Ballard's hand, the hand *snatched* from his grasp, more-like by Ballard himself, not from a need to writhe in pain, or . . .

Lewrie got back to his feet, dusting the knees of his breeches, and his fingers came away bloody with Ballard's gore, which had spread in a wide pool.

"Very well, then, gentlemen . . . carry on," he ordered, reaching out to help the Sailing Master to his feet.

"Here, sir," Lt. Farley reported himself, dashing two finger to the brim of his hat in a casual salute. "Mister Fox has taken over my place, and Midshipman Sealey now commands the foredeck."

"The Dane, yonder, is mistakenly dividing his fire 'tween us and *Amazon* and *Blanche,* Mister Farley," Lewrie icily told him, his eyes gone Arctic grey. " 'Twixt the three of us, we should give her a *hellish*-good pounding. Keep up the rate of fire, sir."

"I shall, sir," Farley firmly declared, though his eyes rolled in horror of the bodies being borne off, and all the blood soaking in the snow-white plankings and the tarred oakum between.

Lewrie forced himself to pace to the larboard bulwarks by the head of the larboard gangway ladder, quite near the place the Danish 24-pounder shot had entered, and took out his pocket-watch, again. It was almost Noon of Maundy Thursday, and the day showed no sign of ending.

"Run-*out* your guns!" Lt. Fox was bellowing in Farley's stead. "Prime! Take *aim*! By broadside . . . Fire!"

And the chief of the loblolly gang paused, snapped his fingers as if remembering something, then bent over to lift Lt. Ballard's leg, shoe, and what was left of his silk stocking and breeches, and tossed them over the starboard side.

CHAPTER FORTY

Pace . . . fret . . . set a brave example, Lewrie chid himself as the hours crawled by, for there was little for a captain to do once his ship was engaged at such long range; it was all up to the skill and the speed of his gunners, the steadiness of his crew. *Look at your watch,* he reminded himself, finding that it was now half past one in the afternoon, which made him shake his head in wonder. Not too strongly, for the continual roar of the guns had given him a headache and rendered him half-deaf despite the candle wax in his ears.

"We seem to be gaining the upper hand, sir," Lt. Farley said as Lewrie paced near his post at the forrud edge of the quarterdeck. "The Danish fire is slackening . . . has been for some time now. Even that Three Crowns fort is firing slow."

"Umphf" was Lewrie's comment on that, not quite sure if he had heard the Acting First Officer correctly. He returned to the bulwarks with his telescope, laid it through the stays and rat-lines of the larboard shrouds to steady it, and looked about.

The old two-decker on which they'd directed their fire was now mostly silent, only a gun here and there still firing, with most of her gun-ports devoid of black-iron barrels. The frigate anchored North of her—! "She's struck her colours!" Lewrie shouted. "Look, there!" he insisted, jabbing his arm at her. "They're abandonin' her, see?"

The frigate *was* surrendered, the Danish flag meekly draped over her transom, and a white bed-sheet hoisted aloft in her damaged rigging. Rowboats were departing her unengaged side, heading for the shore.

Lewrie spun about to look South, eyes wide in wonder to note how much the dense pall of gunpowder smoke had thinned, to see several of the Danish warships nigh-dismasted, and slowly drifting into the mud-flats without controlling hands on their helms. They, too, were being abandoned. The rowboats that had fetched out a continous supply of powder and shot and fresh volunteers were now busy bearing away survivors, coming out to the silent warships empty but for their oarsmen. Almost all of those pesky little gunboats to leeward of the Danish main line had drifted away, too. Smoke billowed from a couple of larger Danish "liners" and older 60s and 64s, and while they had not yet struck their national colours or hoisted white flags of surrender, their guns were silent. For the most part, it was the forts, the Lynetten and Three Crowns, that continued the fight.

"Damned if it don't look as if we're beatin' 'em, Mister Farley," Lewrie exulted as he lowered his glass. "Beatin' 'em like a rug!"

"By broadside . . . Fire!" Lt. Fox yelled yet again, and the 18-pounders barked and roared, recoiling in-board. It was ragged, and it was slower than desired practice after all this time, but *Thermopylae*'s "teeth" could still bite, and were just as sharp as they had been hours before.

Lewrie looked down into the waist at his gunners. Despite a cold day, men were now stripped bare-chested, streams of sweat coursing pale as winter creeks through a coal-dust grime of blackpowder and gunsmoke, and their white duck slop-trousers had gone grey and grimy. Some shook their heads to clear their hearing, vainly protected by neckerchiefs bound round their heads to cover their ears; they served their guns by weary rote, by then. Idle gunners from the silent starboard battery spelled their larboard mates long enough for weary hands to go to the scuttle-butts for water, and to lean on their knees and gasp for air for a precious minute or two. The powder monkey lads no longer dashed up from the magazine with their cylinders, but seemed to belly-crawl up the steep companionway ladders, mouths agape and panting.

"Oh, *lovely* shootin', there!" Lewrie shouted for all to hear as their latest broadside smashed into the stump-masted Danish two-decker, their main target all morning. Chunks of wood flew fighting-top high, as bulwarks and sides were struck, more shot-holes punched through her hull planking, some low on her weed-fouled waterline.

And there was no reply!

"By God, I think we've *done* it!" Lewrie cried again.

Now the smoke was thinned, Lewrie could ascertain that she was not a Third Rate 74 gunner, but an older 60 or 64 . . . with not a gun firing!

"Yes!" he exulted, rising on his boot toes as the Danish flag, which had been shot away at least three times, fluttered down a halliard to disappear behind what was left of her poop deck bulwarks And a minute later, as *Thermopylae* drilled yet another broadside into her, a white flag took its place!

"About time, too," the Sailing Master muttered.

"Well, the Danes are a stubborn lot, Mister Lyle," Marine Lt. Eades quipped.

"Oh, not them, sir," Lyle countered. "I mean *them*, yonder. Sir Hyde's squadron . . . here at last."

"Cease fire on the two-decker, Mister Fox!" Lewrie shouted to the waist. "Quoins out, and be ready to engage the fortress. Parker's come, did ye say, Mister Lyle?"

"Aye, sir. Yonder. Still about four miles North'rd."

Sure enough, Lewrie could espy at least three British "liners" ever so slowly creeping to the mouth of the harbour entrances, short-tacking ponderously and most-like making no more than a mile per hour, but they were making their presence known, at long last.

"*Damn* my eyes!" Capt. Hardcastle yelped as a 36-pounder shot from the Trekroner fortress howled close overhead. "Isn't it over and done yet?" He sounded more affronted than frightened.

Captain Riou's frigate, *Amazon*, and the other ships under his command, were shifting their fire onto the Three Crowns fortress, as futile as that seemed to be. Though the army gunners over there had begun the day un-practiced and raw, they had learned a few lessons in gunnery over the hours, and though firing very slowly, were becoming more accurate.

"Signal from *London*, sir!" Midshipman Tillyard barked in a professional manner, the excitement drubbed out of him by then. "It's . . . Number Thirty-Nine. 'Discontinue the Action.' *Can't* be!" he gawped as he re-read the signal through his telescope, comparing it to his illustrated signals book.

"Discontinue, mine arse!" Lewrie snapped, lifting and extending the tubes of his own glass to confirm it. "Dammit. Dammit to Hell!" He spun about to look astern to *Defiance*, to *Monarch*, *Ganges*, and Lord

Nelson's flagship, the *Elephant*. Number Sixteen was still flying at *their* signal halliards' peaks.

"Number Thirty-Nine with two guns, sir . . . the 'General' for all ships," Midshipman Tillyard reported.

"We've *won* this battle, what's that man yonder *thinking*?" Is he *blind*?" Lewrie blustered. "Well, I'll be damned if we will. Not 'til I see Nelson repeat the signal, we won't!" Open fire on the fortress, Mister Farley. Pin their ears back."

"*Elephant* has hoisted 'Acknowledged,' sir, but still has Number Sixteen aloft," Tillyard reported, mystified by this turn of events. "*Defiance* still flies Number Sixteen, too."

"The signal *is* 'General,' though, sir," Lt. Farley pointed out.

It was not directed to Nelson in *Elephant*; Sir Hyde Parker's signal was speaking to every ship under his command, his own squadron up to the North, and Nelson's, and Graves's, and Capt. Riou's, too. For any ship, any captain, to disobey would mean a court-martial!

"The signal is *dog* shite, sir!" Lewrie snapped back. "A steamin' pile o' *horse* turds!" Sir Hyde *can't* see we've got the Danes beaten."

"Uhm, sir . . . signal from *Defiance*," Midshipman Tillyard called out, sounding nervous. "Now *she's* hoisted Number Thirty-Nine to her main tops'l yardarm . . . but, she's still Number Sixteen aloft at the mainmast head!"

"By broadside . . . Fire!" Lt. Fox rasped behind the guns, even as shot from the Lynetten and Three Crowns forts still howled overhead, and a fresh squadron of Danish warships, anchored in the merchantman channel behind the forts, began to fire.

Lewrie turned his back on *Defiance* and her contradictory flags, looking to *Amazon*, and the sturdy Capt. Riou. "Mine arse on a band-box!" he said with a groan to see HMS *Alcmene*, then the *Blanche* frigate, acknowledge HMS *London*'s signal and hoist Number Thirty-Nine as well!

"*Alcmene* and *Blanche* appear to be cutting their kedge anchor cables, sir," Lt. Farley gravelled. "Really isn't much we could hope to do against stone forts, I suppose, so . . ."

Lewrie stood and stared, hands on his hips and *glaring* at the *Amazon*, waiting to see what Riou would do. Did he not acknowlege the damned signal and continue the action, his mind was made up that he, and *Thermopylae*, would stand by him to the last.

Oh, for the love o' . . . ! Lewrie despaired, his heart sinking at the sight of *Amazon* suddenly ceasing fire, and almost shame-facedly hoisting Number Thirty-Nine. Even Riou was daunted.

"Cease fire, Mister Farley," he spat in anger. "Hands aloft to make sail, and just *cut* the damned kedge cable. Mister Tillyard, I'll thankee t'find that *bloody* Number Thirty-Nine in the flag lockers, and hoist it."

"Very well, sir," Lt. Farley said with a weary sigh. "Hoy, Fox! Cease fire, and secure your guns! Cease fire, d'ye hear, there! Bosun, pipe hands aloft to make sail. Mister Pulley, do you fetch boarding axes and cut the stern cable. Save the spring, mind."

Within ten minutes, HMS *Thermopylae* was once more under way for the North end of the Middle Ground shoals, the Southerly wind on her starboard quarters, fine, bound to join Vice-Admiral Sir Hyde Parker and his squadron . . . as *ordered*. It was galling, especially given the fact that the line-of-battle ships anchored astern of her still *fought*, despite their commander-in-chief's signal, and the Danish line was now a ragged string of silenced warships, grounded and dis-masted hulks, or half sunk, with one of them spectacularly ablaze!

"The foremast trunk won't take much sail, sir," Lt. Farley cautioned. "I expect we'll have need of a yard re-fit to replace it. For now, there's a spare main course yard we can use to 'splint' it, sir."

"As you say, Mister Farley," Lewrie glumly agreed, massaging his aching forehead, and clawing the wax plugs from his ears. "Perhaps Sir Hyde thought to bring along spare masts and spars, and will give us one."

No matter how disputatious and insubordinate it was, Lt. Farley heaved a loud, sarcastic snort of derision concerning Sir Hyde Parker.

Even though Riou's small squadron had cut and made sail, both the Lynetten and the Trekroner forts, and the un-damaged Danish ships in the far-off merchant's channel—which showed absolutely no indication that they would up-anchor, make sail, or sally out from their protected positions—still conducted a desultory fire, *drumming* the frigates out of the battle. They were now smaller targets, with their sterns pointed at the forts, but their fragile transoms *were* exposed to long-range raking fire.

Thermopylae slowly gained on *Amazon*, coming up to within two hundred yards of her starboard quarters. Lewrie went to his larboard side, looking for Capt. Riou. He saw him, the same instant that Riou spotted him, and they both shrugged at each other, shaking their heads at the futility of it all. Riou lifted a brass speaking-trumpet as if to shout something across, just as a fresh salvo from the Trekroner Fort arrived, raising great shot splashes round both frigates, howling overhead like baritone harpies.

"No!" Lewrie cried as one of those heavy 36-pounder shot struck *Amazon* on the quarterdeck, snatching Capt. Riou from sight. Was Riou slain? A long minute later as *Thermopylae* slowly crawled abeam of *Amazon*, a lieutenant appeared with the speaking-trumpet.

"Hoy, *Thermopylae*, Captain Lewrie?"

"Aye!" Lewrie shouted back through cupped hands.

"What is the date of your 'posting,' sir?"

"April, of Ninety-Seven!" Lewrie shouted back, mystified. "Why?"

"Lieutenant Quilliam here, sir! Captain Riou has fallen! I am to pass squadron command to the next senior officer present. Perhaps to Captain Sutton in *Alcmene*, then."

"Riou's fallen?" Lewrie shouted, shocked and suddenly saddened.

"Cut in half by a round-shot, sir!" Lt. Quilliam shouted back, his voice shaky with emotion. "Said . . . 'Let us all die together, my brave lads,' and . . . not a quarter-hour later, sir . . . !"

"A *damned* good man, sir!" Lewrie told him, with a speaking-trumpet of his own, this time. "My condolences to you and all your Amazons. And, by God, may he not have fallen in vain!"

The next salvo from the Danes fell short by two cables as they finally stood out of range, still creeping slowly ahead of HMS *Amazon*.

"Secure from Quarters, Mister Farley," Lewrie ordered, slumped wearily, un-captain-like, on the hammock nettings. "Fresh water butts are t'be fetched up for our people."

"Aye, sir."

Lewrie plodded back towards the binnacle cabinet and double-helm, but the Ship's Surgeon, Mr. Harward, was slowly dragging himself up to the quarterdeck by the starboard gangway ladder, his breeches and his shirt cuffs still stained with gore despite the long leather apron he wore when at his grim trade.

"Beg to report, sir," Harward wearily said, "we've seven killed and eighteen wounded . . . four seriously. Midshipman Privette's regained consciousness, but he's taken a hard knock, and must be counted on light duties for a few days, may you spare him."

"And Mister Ballard?" Lewrie had to ask.

"Passed over, sir, sorry," Harward replied, idly wiping hands on a damp towel that thankfully did not bear too many blots of blood. "We succeeded in seizing his femoral artery, the great artery found in a man's leg, and cauterised it, staunching the loss of blood, and we managed to neaten up his thigh bone for a stump, with enough flesh as a covering, for later . . ."

Lewrie held up a hand to shush him, damning surgeons for being so enamoured of their learning that they just *had* to prose on about the *arcana* of their trade.

"Well, the loss of blood was too massive, in the end, sir. He is gone. Sorry. I know he was an old friend and shipmate of yours," Harward told him. He reached into an inside pocket of his unbuttoned waist-coat and produced a letter. "He surely must have had a premonition, sir, for he pressed me to deliver this to you."

"Thankee, Mister Harward," Lewrie said, taking it and turning it over and over, for wont of something better to do. "I know you did your best for him . . for all our brave lads."

"Thankee for saying so, sir," Harward said, bowing himself away to the starboard side for a breath of fresh air, after hours cooped up in the foetid horror of the cockpit surgery.

Lewrie looked up at the signal halliards on the main-mast, and saw Number Thirty-Nine still flying. "Mister Tillyard? Now we've ack-knowledged it, haul that shameful thing *down*, sir!"

CHAPTER FORTY-ONE

*F*ull darkness, at last, after an eerily red and gold sunset that silhouetted Copenhagen's spires, castle towers, and bastioned walls in war-like colours, as if a battle still raged, though by mid-afternoon, the guns had fallen silent. The mild winds had long before blown away the last wisps of gunsmoke arisen in impenetrable thunderheads from ships and shore batteries, and now only a few faint mists from burning or sunken Danish floating batteries or warships remained.

HMS *Thermopylae* lay peacefully at anchor among her sister ships by the North end of the Middle Ground shoal, near HMS *London* and her consorts, about three miles off the Trekroner Fort, and well out of range of its cannon, though there was little expectation that the Danes would resume the contest.

They were beaten, after all; seventeen of the eighteen warships, anchored hulks, or floating batteries had been taken, burned, or sunk in action, and the enemy commander's ship, *Dannebrog*, had taken fire and blown up with stupendous loss of life well after the artillery duel had ended. Nelson and his squadron had persisted despite the "General" signal to discontinue the action, and had won, though at great cost in men.

The rest of *Thermopylae*'s day had been spent repairing; re-roving and splicing cut-up rigging, replacing shattered yards and upper masts. The entire ship needed scouring to erase the stains of gunpowder

THE BALTIC GAMBIT 331

residue . . . and blood. Vinegar had been used to ease the odours of rotten eggs from the guns' discharges, the coppery reek of splattered gore, and the foetid stench from Mr. Harward's surgery on the orlop.

When the foremast had been "fished" and banded, the weather decks had had to be re-sanded with bears and bibles. After that, the cannon had to be thoroughly swabbed out and washed down from muzzles to breeching rope cascabels, the truck-carriages touched up with a little paint, and the recoil and run-out tackles replaced in some cases after all the strain and fraying placed upon them.

On top of that, all the ship's boats had been led round from being towed astern, and had spent the entire time since the cease-fire at rescuing Danish sailors from the wrecks of their vessels, taking prisoners, then cooperating with the crews of Danish rowboats in transferring their dead and wounded ashore to the hospitals in the city.

Alan Lewrie had been busy, too, visiting aboard HMS *Amazon* to attend Capt. Riou's brief funeral, then conduct his own rites for the seven officers and men who had died from *Thermopylae*'s complement, then see to his wounded, some of them in a bad way after amputations, and sure to join the Great Majority, and their slain shipmates, in a few days.

In his gig, he had had to report to Lord Nelson aboard, *Elephant,* then to Sir Hyde Parker aboard *London,* and there had been no time for food or drink, or a chance to catch his breath, it seemed, since they had dropped anchors. Finally . . . *finally,* the sun was down, and there were no more demands upon him or his crew. A harbour watch was set on deck, with the usual lookouts posted at bow, stern, and both gangways. Marines in full, freshly cleaned kit stood sentry posts to prevent desertion, though it made no sense given a three-mile swim to a hostile shore. It was simply what the Royal Navy did when anchored.

Captain Alan Lewrie touched the brim of his hat in casual salute and nodded with a grin to Marine Private Leggett, who stood guard by the door to his great-cabins, receiving a musket salute, and a shy hint of a grin in reply as he entered his quarters.

"Thank God," he breathed in relief as he shut the door on care and worry and grief, and the demands of Duty. He hung up his own hat and sword belt, not waiting for Pettus to serve him, and almost limped on weary legs and slightly sore feet to the starboard side settee.

"A glass of something, sir?" Pettus asked, looking as clean and natty as if the day had never been, as well-turned-out as a civilian servant in a London club.

"God, yes!" Lewrie enthused. "It's been a long, dry day." And, as Pettus fetched him a refreshing glass of white wine, as Toulon and Chalky, happily resettled amid their familiar environs with the terrifying din of battle long over, leaped into his lap and made glad mews of joy to be stroked and cossetted in peace, Lewrie could relish the homeyness of his cabins returned to normalcy, with every piece of furniture, every chest, chair, and framed picture put back in the right places.

And after a long, dry-mouthed sip of the light white wine, he could even allow himself a long, happy sigh of near bliss. Pettus had the bottle, and topped him back up for a slower, more meditative drink.

"Galley's up, and Nettles will be fetching your supper in half an hour, sir," Pettus told him. "No hope of fresh vegetables or bread from shore, I'd suppose, sir, but he's putting together a celebratory meal, he said to say. Anything I may do in the meantime, sir?"

"I'd admire did you help me get my boots off, Pettus, and fetch out that old, sloppy pair o' shoes," Lewrie decided. "And a fresh pair of cotton stockings. I fear the silk ones I've worn nigh two days in a row are quite ruined, by now."

"Of course, sir," Pettus said, and went to hunt up the shoes and stockings. Once back, he straddled Lewrie's calves and tugged off the boots; sure enough, the silk stockings were laddered with tears. They were fine for formal occasions, and for battle; silk shirts and stockings could be drawn from wounds more cleanly than linen or wool, limiting the risk of anything left in ravaged flesh to fester or go gangrenous, but such protection was too delicate to wear with boots, and too costly.

Once in fresh, clean stockings, and comfortable old loosely buckled shoes, Lewrie slumped into one corner of the settee, throw pillows and cushions rearranged for comfort. He threw one leg up atop the seat, the other resting on the low brass tray-table he'd brought back from Calcutta so many years before, and let out another blissful sigh. On the smaller side tray-table stood the wine bottle, and Lewrie poured himself a third glass, all but smacking his lips in anticipation. Yet . . .

As he reached over, then leaned back, something crinkled in his coat's inside chest pocket. *Oh,* Lewrie sadly thought; *Arthur's letter.*

He withdrew it and broke the wax seal, thinking that the letter was just like Arthur Ballard; folded evenly, meticulously, and the seal forming a perfectly circular blob of wax covering all four corners of the folds which met at almost mathematical exactitude.

> *Sir* (it began) *I would beg that you keep this in the strictest of Confidences. I find myself in the very worst sort of personal* Contretemps, *and, for want of a better Solution, and at the considerable Risk to my career, must inform you that I find it impossible to serve under you as First Lieutenant. It is my intention to request of Admiralty to be relieved of my Position.*

Lewrie furrowed his brows in surprise, wondering just what the fellow might have gotten into; gambling debts, the risk of debtors' prison by over-spending? He'd gotten some young woman in trouble? None of these even remotely seemed likely, not with such a straight-laced prig as Arthur Ballard, he could quickly dismiss.

> *Though we established a somewhat compatible Cooperation aboard* Alacrity *in the Bahamas, as Time went by, I found myself loath to call it true Friendship, and, by the end of our joint Commission, felt quite relieved to go our separate Ways.*
> *Truthfully, Sir, I hold that you are Reprehensible, and wish most devoutly to have as little to do with you and your Character as naval Service will admit in . . .*

"Bloody *Hell*?" Lewrie gawped in a very small voice.

Arthur Ballard laid it all out in precise terms; he *despised* Captain Alan Lewrie, just as he had come to despise Lieutenant Alan Lewrie in the late '80s. Ballard cited his many reasons; recklessness being one of them; a lewd, lascivious, and adulterous nature, another. He blasphemed freely; he'd shot that captured, kneeling pirate in the head at close range with a pistol in front of the cave on Middle Caicos to urge the rest, and that foul Billy "Bones" Doyle, out and free their captives—just as he'd all but murdered Count Levotchkin's servant not a fortnight before! The theft of a dozen Black slaves to man his ship; Ballard knew it was a crime, despite what the court, and all the newspapers and tracts in praise of him, said.

He got that pretty-much right, Lewrie admitted to himself.

But it was Lewrie's rakehellish, adulterous streak that Ballard found the most despicable. Why, he even recalled the name of the Free

Black woman Lewrie had rutted with at Clarence Town on Long Island one sultry and boring afternoon, after all these years—even if Lewrie didn't.

Wyannie Slocum, of course! Lewrie thought, surprised; and, just for a bit, remembering rather fondly . . .

The rumours of Lewrie quickening a bastard son on a rich Greek widow in the currant trade, the rumour of a mistress in the Mediterranean earlier in the war; the scandal of associating with a "painted circus wench," and how shamefully Lewrie had ignored and abused, and been unfaithful to his wife, Caroline, lo these many years, betraying the . . . "Betraying the Trust of one of the finest women it has ever been my honour to know . . . ," Ballard wrote.

Damme, it could've been Ballard, *wrote those bloody letters, not Theoni, if I didn't* know *better,* Lewrie thought, re-reading what Ballard had penned about Caroline one more time, then leaning back on the settee and taking another long sip of his wine.

He never wed, Lewrie recalled; *Turned up his nose at every promisin' lass we introduced to him. Betsy . . . whats'ername? He thought her . . . all of 'em . . . too "fly" and "flibberty-gibbet." The way Arthur writes of Caroline, though . . . Mine arse on a* band-box, *he was in* love *with her, all these years!* he realised with a start.

Lewrie had always fancied that Caroline could coax Ballard out of his grave and aloof manner, and for several hours loosen up in her, and his own, presence ashore. . . . Arthur would even laugh and *smile!*

At a subscription ball or party at Nassau, Ballard would actually dance with Caroline—no more than two in an evening, Lewrie recalled; and, oh, he'd be gracious enough to ask other women and girls to dance as well in the course of the night; the *dutiful* sort of thing one did with the older ladies, with fellow officers' wives, or the unmarried damsels and daughters, yet . . . he'd never followed through.

Do I go through his sea-chests, do I find a shrine to Caroline? Lewrie wondered; *The unattainable, the unrequited . . . paragon of womanhood, t'his lights. The poor, sad, unloved bastard!*

Yes, there was his affair with Tess cited as the last straw for Ballard; that Lewrie would stoop to associating with common trollops, no matter their feminine charms, and imagine such a sordid item reason for a duel of *honour,* well! And why was he not home in Anglesgreen in his wife's company, anyway? How could he be so dismissive and beastly towards such a splendid lady? Ballard had demanded.

No, Arthur Ballard hadn't had a premonition, as Surgeon Mister Harward had imagined; he'd expected to survive the action, request a posting aboard another ship (perhaps after a brief spell of leave, for medical reasons?) and put Lewrie in his place for good and all.

Coach to Anglesgreen, and place his heart in Caroline's hands, as he always wished he could? Lewrie mused; *Surely, in fiften bloody years, he* must've *met somebody else . . . given* some *proper girl a go! Poor, sad, lonely . . . deluded . . . prig.*

Lewrie finished his glass of wine and stuffed Ballard's letter into a side pocket of his coat, wondering what to do with it now that he had read it. Toulon butted his head against Lewrie's thigh, while Chalky came trotting from back aft with his tail up to rejoin them and mewing for more pets, too, from the litter-box of dry sand stowed in the larboard-side quarter gallery. With a firm nod, Lewrie rose and headed for the quarter gallery himself, in need of relief after three glasses of wine.

He shut the door, lifted the lid of the "jakes," and undid his breeches buttons for a long, easing piss down the metal tube that led past the tuck of the transom directly to the sea. With his buttons re-fastened, he turned to stare out the window panes at the riding lights of the anchored fleet, and the lanthorn-glades upon the waters dancing and sparkling in the dark.

Meditatively, Lewrie withdrew the letter once again and shredded it into tiny bits, letting the fingernail-sized pieces drop into the cat's litter-box. With the small, long-handled fireplace shovel, he stirred the pieces in deep, as if turning grass under a fallow field before Spring planting. Hoping that no "seeds" would ever sprout from *that* epistle.

Best leave Lt. Arthur Ballard, RN, a brave and honourable memory to his family, his associates . . . . and everyone else. Courageously lost in the King's Name . . . and not a jealous, love-sick, and ascetic fool.

"Ah, there you be, sir," Pettus gaily said as Lewrie came back to the cabins. "Your supper is here, sir. Can't speak for the quality of the boiled carrots, but the potato hash with bacon is fresher, and there's half one of the gun-room's chickens, with some of your good Cheshire cheese rolled in biscuit crumbles, and toasted. Claret with it, sir?"

"Capital, Pettus," Lewrie said with genuine eagerness for food, though feeling a pang of conscience to sound too eager, after the death and ravaging of some of his men . . . of Ballard's passing. He sat down at his solitary place at the head of his dining table and scooted up to his place setting, whipping the napkin cross his lap.

Just as a bowl of portable soup was put before him, he caught a strain of music from up forward on the gun-deck. "They sound in decent spirits, considerin'," Lewrie commented.

"Oh, aye sir," Pettus agreed, pouring a new glass of good aged claret for him. "Earlier, well . . . you can't keep our tars gloomy for very long, after all, sir. Once they're done grieving, that is."

Earlier, Desmond had played the dirge-like *Johnny Faa* while the funeral service had been read, and the corpses—those that had not been slipped out a gun-port during combat—were slid overside from beneath the Union Flag, wrapped in canvas and weighted with shot for sea-burial. As Lewrie had come back aboard round dusk, and the labours to repair the ship had ended, and the crew gathered idle during what was left of the Second Dog, it had been *Admiral Hosier's Ghost*, an old American air, *Katy Cruel*, and other gloomy tunes.

Now, though . . . once the hands had eat, and the mess-tables had been cleared away, Lewrie could recognise a gayer minuet tune called *Constancy*, the livelier *Flannagan's Favourite*, and the tune played as they'd stood into action in the morning, *The Jolly Thresher*.

And by the time that Lewrie finished his soup and started in on his *entrée*—with two smaller saucers of everything for the famished cats, the crewmen had launched into *One Misty, Moisty Morning* again.

> *One Misty, Moisty Morning, when cloudy was the weather*
> *I met up with an old man, he was cloth-ed all in leather.*
> *He wore no shirt unto his back, but wool upon his skin,*
> *singing Howdye-do and Howdye-do, and Howdye-do, again!*
> *I went a little farther, and there I met a maid . . .*

As it had been in the morning, perhaps only three or four hands took the main verses, whilst everyone else roared out the short refrain, pounding their fists on the mess-tables, stamping their feet on the oak decks, hard enough to make the frigate's timbers shudder.

> *This maid her name was Dolly, 'twas in a gown of grey.*
> *I was feeling somewhat jolly and persuaded her to stay.*
> *And many kind embraces there, I stroked her little chin,*
> *singing Howdye-do, and Howdye-do . . . !*

"Amazin', really," Lewrie mused aloud after dabbing his lips and taking a sip of wine. "After all they've gone through today, the mates they've lost . . . ."

"Like I said, sir," Pettus reminded him, "the life of a sailor, or so I've learned in my short time aboard, is hard misery, and short commons, most of the time. They'll take what joy they can, when there's a reason for it . . . and time enough. After all, sir, it isn't every day they're in a real battle, and win it." They'll *miss* their shipmates but . . . not for all *that* long . . . not so long as *they're* still alive, sir, and able to brag about it."

"Amen," Lewrie agreed, perking up at the notion; and how apt it was when applied to the late Arthur Ballard. "Amen to that."

EPILOGUE

Sir Valentine: These banish'd men that I have kept withal,

Are men endu'd with worthy qualities.
Forgive them what they have committed here
and let them be recalled from their exile.
They are reformed, civil, full of good.
And fit for great employment, worthy lord.

–WILLIAM SHAKESPEARE,
THE TWO GENTLEMEN OF VERONA,
ACT V, SCENE IV

CHAPTER FORTY-TWO

*T*he Danes had thrown in the towel, withdrawing from the League of Armed Neutrality. For a day or two, the British fleet had lain at anchor in Kioge Bay below Copenhagen, then departed for the Baltic to confront the Swedes, but that was anti-climactic. They had gotten to sea with their small squadron, but, as soon as they'd learned how the Danes had been beaten, they returned to port at Karlskrona, pointedly warned by Lord Nelson that it would be better did they *remain* there, if they knew what was good for them!

That left only the Russian fleet to deal with, and there were signs that the confrontation would be at sea, for the amount of drift ice had been greatly reduced by the arrival of Spring. Surely the thaw had reached Reval and Kronstadt, and the Tsar's warships were now free.

A swift frigate had caught up with the fleet, fresh from Great Yarmouth, bearing orders and mail to the flagship HMS *London*. Just as soon as the signal flags had been hoisted, every ship had sent a boat to her to collect it. Midshipman Furlow returned in the launch with a large canvas bag, and scampered up the side with it, holding it aloft like a fresh-killed fox at the end of a thrilling hunt as the officers gathered round him and cheered, as happy as the pack of hounds would round the Master of the

Hunt. Lewrie's clerk, the unfortunately named Mr. George Georges, the Purser Mr. Pridemore, and his Yeoman took hold of it and quickly sorted it out for distribution at Seven Bells of the Forenoon; when gunnery practice had ended, just before "Clear Decks & Up Spirits" was piped for the rum ration.

Aft, Lewrie quickly pawed through his own small pile of correspondence, the official letters first. "Victualling Board . . . Sick & Hurt Board . . . general bumf to all ships," Lewrie muttered as he tore them open and quickly scanned them, laying them flat in a shallow wood box on his desk once read, not in any particular order, to be dealt with later. There was nothing of urgent import regarding him, just the ship; no orders direct from Admiralty. He could turn to the rest.

"Ooh, shit!" he hissed inward through his teeth. There was actually a letter from his wife, Caroline! She had broken her bitter and aloof silence, wonder of wonders, and written him! Naturally, he would leave that one for the very last, sure it was yet another of her acidic screeds . . . the sort sure to curdle his mid-day meal, whether he read it before or after dinner. Tentatively holding it at two of its corners, Lewrie laid it back down on his desk-top.

The rest of his personal mail . . . there was one from his eldest son, Sewallis, and one from the younger, Hugh. There was a bill from a Yarmouth chandler and one from a London tailor. Eudoxia Durschenko had written him—"Leave that'un for the *very* last," he muttered—and one from his solicitor, Mr. Matthew Muntjoy. He was about to open it when he caught sight of the senders of a pair of others.

Christopher Cashman, his old friend who'd moved to Wilmington, North Carolina, and had become an American, who'd provided a thoroughly false affidavit for his trial, had sent him a letter! He was about to pounce on that one, when the last *really* caught his eye.

His barrister, Mr. Andrew MacDougall, Esquire, had written him!

"Oh, shit," Lewrie muttered again, sure that the combination of letters from his solicitor, and his attorney, portended another dreadful stint in a courtroom. With a grimace on his phyz, he opened it.

In neat Spencerian "copper-plate" calligraphy, MacDougall told him glad tidings.

Sir, I take pen in hand to deliver unto you the most amazing turn of events, of which I but lately heard; events sure to elicit within you

*the greatest Joy and sense of Relief, for, your former Accuser, Mr.
Hugh Beauman, is no more. The packet in which he and his Wife
and Coterie embarked for Portugal to escape the Folly of their Suit
against you missed the landmarks when attempting to enter the
Tagus River and the port of Lisbon in a great Gale in late January,
just weeks after your Acquittal, and was driven aground not half a
mile from shore, with great loss of Life, principal of whom was Mr,
Hugh Beauman himself.*

"And it couldn't happen to a better person!" Lewrie whispered, feeling like leaping to his feet and dancing a little jig of mourning; barely
containing a whoop and a guffaw of laughter.

*Perishing along with him were several of his perjurious Witnesses
among his followers, though his Wife was rescued.*

And, as MacDougall had heard it, that icily imperious beauty, now
sole heir to the lion's share of the Beauman riches—rivalling the wealth
of the famous Walpoles, or so it was said—beyond what profits that
went to the elder Mr. Beauman and his wife, now retired in the English
countryside, was of no mind to bother with trifles like her late husband's
pursuit of Capt. Alan Lewrie's life and honour, no!

*Mrs. Beauman is reputed to delight in her Widowhood, and the salu-
brious Clime of Lisbon in particular and in the Society of the English
colony in Portugal in general, Purchasing a substantial House in Lisbon, as well as a country Retreat, rather than leasing, and I have it on
the best, first-hand Authority from one of our senior Benchers, K.C.,
of my Lodge, Grey's Inn, who now represents her interests in London,
that all Beauman holdings on Jamaica are now put on the market,
Mrs. Beauman having absolutely no Desire to return to the Fever
Isles, nor (so it is rumoured) any Desire to have any further Association with the quality of Society found there.*
    *My Bencher also informs me that she hopes to invest in the wine
and spirits trade in Portugal . . .*

Lewrie *did* let out a whoop of glee at that point, slapping his desk-top
for good measure, loud enough to startle the cats awake from their nap

on the settee cushions, and make Whitsell, his little cabin boy, jump and gawk and gulp.

"Good news from home, sir, pardon for asking?" Pettus enquired from the dining-coach, where he was setting out dinner things.

"The very absolute best, Pettus!" Lewrie exclaimed, imagining that, someday, he could drink a toast to his freedom and continued life without fear of further litigation in a fine Madeira from a *Beauman* vineyard, and savour its taste *doubly* well! And, why wait? "Pettus, I'd admire did ye fetch me a wee glass o' port while I go through the rest of my mail."

"Aye, sir."

The last half-page of MacDougall's letter was chatty folderol about London doings, the Spring Season, and hints that the Addington government was seriously considering negotiating a treaty of peace with Republican France, and its First Consul, Napoleon Bonaparte, of all the insane things! Just as Adm. Duckworth had taken Guadeloupe! Lastly . . .

> *By the by, your Solicitor, Mr. Matthew Mountjoy, has told me that you may find News regarding a certain Lady in the currant trade of Interest. He tells me he shall write you with all the Particulars, but it seems that her recent Scandal, the details of which escape me, has found it necessary to Remove herself, her children, and household to Dublin to avoid the Acrimony.*
>
> *Allow me, last of all, to congratulate you on the complete Ending of your legal problems anent the Beaumans, et al. If I may ever be of service in the future, do consider me, your most obdt. Srvt. . . .*

"Well, well, well!" Lewrie chortled, wondering if Dame Fortune could be *any* kinder to him! He was about to request a larger glass of port, but before Pettus could even pour the first, two faint thumps in the distance could be heard, which thumps caused a stir on the quarterdeck overhead, which he could hear through the partly-open windows of the coach-top. A moment later and his Marine sentry was bellowing the arrival of Midshipman Plumb.

"Lieutenant Fox's duty, sir, and he bids me inform you that the flagship has made general signal for all ships of the fleet to send a boat to her again," Plumb announced.

"Very well, Mister Plumb," Lewrie replied, "my compliments to

Mister Fox, and he's to despatch a fresh crew of his choosing. Keep me informed, what it's all about."

"Aye aye, sir!"

Just after his dinner, and with all but Caroline's letter left to read—he was still fearful of that'un!—the launch returned alongside. Not a minute later, Lewrie could hear another excited stir on the quarterdeck, the scamper of feet on one of the gangway ladders, and the sharp rap of his Marine sentry's musket-butt on the deck as he called, "Midshipman Privette t'see th' Cap'm, SAH!"

"A note for you from the flag, sir," Privette began, coming to the dining table to hand it over, puppy-eager. "George, who conned the launch . . . Midshipman Pannabaker, sir, sorry . . . heard a lieutenant on *London* say it was something about the Tsar, sir!"

Lewrie cocked a wry brow at the lad. With his hat under his arm Midshipman Privette's head still sported a gauze bandage where he had been struck unconscious at Copenhagen. The lad was all but panting in excited curiousity.

"Calm as does it, Mister Privette," Lewrie chid him, "you aren't to over-exert yourself, our Surgeon tells me, not quite yet. Fluster over this surely can't be good for . . . Holy fuckin' shit!" Lewrie cried after he'd broken the soft wax seal and read the single-page note, and rose so quickly from his chair that he up-ended it. "Tell the officer of the watch . . . who's on?"

"Acting-Lieutenant Sealey, sir," Privette supplied.

". . . that I'll come up," Lewrie ended, going for his hat. Once on the quarterdeck, he could see that Midshipman Pannabaker, fresh from the flagship, had already imparted his rumour to one and all, for he could see a sea of expectant, wolfish smiles.

"Summon all hands, sir?" Acting-Lieutenant Sealey asked.

"Not just yet, Mister Sealey," Lewrie countered, "for we don't know if the situation has changed all that much. What we *do* know is, gentlemen, that early this morning, one of our scouting cutters spoke a Prussian trading brig, which gave them a copy of a German newspaper . . . in which it was reported that the Tsar . . . the mad, despotic bugger . . . has been assassinated."

He had to hold up a cautioning hand to still the officers' glee.

"The new Emperor of All the Russias is Crown Prince Alexander, a lad not much older than Mister Furlow, here," Lewrie went on. "And, we know what a fire-eater is Furlow, so the new Tsar may be even worse. God only knows will he continue his late father's nonsense of an Armed League of the North, now we've thrashed the Danes, and run the Swedes back to port with their tails 'tween their legs. I assume he's heard o' those events by now, same as we've had news of his father's demise."

"*How,* sir?" Lt. Farley pressed. "When?"

"Accordin' t'this, he was strangled in his bed-chambers," Lewrie told him, "in the grand palace at Saint Petersburg, the night of . . ." he referred to the note, "the night of the twenty-fourth of March."

"Not two days after we landed those Russian emissaries, by God!" Lt. Fox marvelled. "My word, what a turn of events!"

"Deuced *favourable* turn of events, for us, sirs," the Sailing Master, Mr. Lyle, chortled.

Damme, it was! Lewrie realised, stunned; *Oh Christ, have we . . . have I, been part of regicide? Rybakov, Levotchkin, and . . . Twigg!*

Why else had it been so important for Count Rybakov, that shit Levotchkin, to hasten to Yarmouth in such a tear, escorted down from London by Thomas Mountjoy, his old clerk, sent by the Foreign Office? Mountjoy, whose mentor in Secret Branch was, who had been recruited and trained by, Zachariah Twigg, who'd once said that to spare Europe of Russian imperial ambitions would ignite class warfare and terror, civil war and peasant serf rebellion, no matter how many millions of people died.

And, how best *t'force the Russians out of the League of Armed Neutrality but t'scrag the insane bastard behind it all, the Tsar!* he furiously thought . . . furious at himself for being fooled into a role in it, if it indeed *was* an English scheme. *A "peace mission," mine arse! Ye wish peace? Kill the leader who* wants *a war,* Lewrie thought.

He shook his head in mute anger as he paced the deck. He had *always* been Zachariah Twigg's gun-dog, for bloody years, and in all of his dealings with the bloody-handed schemer, had *never* been told *all* the truth. There *was* the possibility that it was the Russians who had approached the Foreign Office, not the other way round, and asked for help, . . . which would explain why it was that Thomas Mountjoy had been so eager to foist his emissaries off on Lewrie, and wash Government's hands, not even taking the risk of "un-official presence" in the Baltic.

A simple task, oh, and drop these people off, why don't you, on yer way?

Countin' me too simple t'puzzle it out 'til much too late, the arrogant old schemin' bastard! And I didn't! he ruefully thought.

He couldn't imagine the new Prime Minister, Addington, hatching such a plan; not if he was so hen-headed as to contemplate negotiating a peace treaty with France right after smashing Denmark and capturing the last French-held outpost in the Caribbean! No, it smacked more of the former Prime Minister, William Pitt, the Younger, or Henry Dundas, the former Secretary of State for War.

Once set in motion, though, and if Addington didn't know *about it . . . !* Lewrie realised. The current crop of buffoons, the Earl of Elgin, the Duke of Portland, Lord Hawkesbury at the Foreign Office itself, or Lord Hobart would never have had the *nerve . . .* so perhaps England *hadn't* had a hand in it!

Who's t'say the old Tsar was such an insane terror, the Russians *did him in,* Lewrie further speculated; *It's happened to Tsars before, and it's not like he didn't give 'em* hellish-good *cause t'be rid of him. Like the old sayin' . . . 'Uneasy rests the head that wears the crown'?*

"Pipe 'All Hands,' then, sir?" Lt. Farley prompted.

"My pardons, Mister Farley, but I was just composin' my thoughts on how best to phrase it," Lewrie lied, forcing himself to perk up and sound eager. "Pipe 'All Hands,' aye."

Capt. Alan Lewrie, RN, took himself a contemplative pace about the deck, head down and his hands in the small of his back as the Bosun, Mr. Dimmock, and his Mate, Pulley, fweeped away on their silver calls, and *Thermopylae*'s people not on watch came boiling up from below in a thunderous roar of feet, both shod and bare, on companionway ladders.

Lewrie hitched his shoulders before turning to go forward to the break of the quarterdeck to overlook his men in the frigate's waist, the hands assembled on the sail-tending gangways. The sun was shining in a mostly clear blue sky, and the Baltic glistened and heaved slowly and peacefully, a glittering steel-blue, with only here and there any specks of rotting ice. The wind stood in the Sou'west and, for once, actually felt almost temperate! There would be no more need for his reeky furs, except as a place for his cats to romp, and nap.

"Ship's comp'ny . . . off hats, and stand easy!" Lt. Farley bellowed. "All hands assembled, sir."

"Thankee, Mister Farley. Lads!" Lewrie began, with expectant faces looking back at him from HMS *Thermopylae*'s 250 sailors, petty officers, Warrants, and boys. "We've gotten a bit of good news . . ."

AFTERWORD

*A*s one may see, we've come a long way in the conduct of trials since Alan Lewrie's appearance in court. As his barrister, Andrew MacDougall, Esq., told him in *Troubled Waters,* before his first court appearance, the first trial that lasted more than a single day didn't occur 'til 1794!—and yes, there was no such thing as cross-examination allowed; nor were there *government* prosecutors. A barrister could go both ways, depending on the wishes of his "brief," not client; Defence Counsel for one trial, then be hired as Prosecutor for another. People back then had about as much distrust of a too-powerful government as we do today. And for good reason! Both systems hang too many.

The identity of Alan and Caroline's anonymous tormentor; it was a retired NYPD detective, living in Florida, who was the only one who nailed Theoni Kavares Connor as the culprit, years ago, for which I congratulate him, and I hope when he reads this, he'll enjoy a drink, *with his friends buying,* to reward his shrewdness, and insight into human nature. He's so sharp, they ought to throw in appetisers, too!

⚓

The Baltic Gambit depended heavily on three sources of research, two of which my friend Bob Enrione at CBS sent me: *The Great Gamble: Nelson at Copenhagen* by Dudley Pope, and, to a lesser extent, *Naval Wars in The Baltic, 1522–1850* by R. C. Anderson, both of which, unfortunately, are long out of print, and it's a trusting soul who loaned them to me for over a year, once I'd mentioned that Lewrie might be going to the Baltic in the winter of 1801. The third, providing all the "Dirt" on the King of Denmark, his queen the unfortunate Caroline Matilda, the daughter of King George III, and that earnest nut-job, her lover, and father of her bastard daughter, Johann Struensee. Oh, I know, people now prefer "love child," but they took bastardy and illegitimacy very seriously in those days, so bastard it'll be. As I said before, I'd rather be Historically Accurate than Politically Correct. I bought *Royal Affair: George III and His Scandalous Siblings* by Stella Tillyard locally. It's a very fun read, the prissiness of Jane Austen's novels bedamned; the eighteenth century and the first part of the nineteenth was "warts and all," "balls to the wall," and pretty randy, right through the Regency, before all of Wilberforce's moralising, and the influence of Jeremy Bentham, Hannah More, Priestley, and all the other "Do Good" reformers led to the reigns of King William IV and Queen Victoria . . . even Jane Austen commented on how radically morals and mores had changed in her own life; what was tacitly accepted without a roll of anyone's eyes in her youth had become Crude, Lewd, and Common in her adulthood.

Vice-Admiral Sir Hyde Parker, and that infamous Signal Number 39; all newspaper quotes I cited were real, culled from Dudley Pope's *The Great Gamble*. What Lewrie did not witness, since he did not stay in Yarmouth Roads with the rest of the gathering fleet, was Sir Hyde's *complete* lack of urgency. The allotment of warships to Lord Nelson or Rear-Admiral Graves, and the Order of Sailing, had to be *wrung* out of him bare hours before the expedition set sail. Indeed, it took a *very* stiff note, what Harry Potter would call a "howler," from the Earl St. Vincent ("Old Jarvy") at Admiralty in London, to get the man to board his flagship, HMS *London*, leave his bride, Frances, his "little batter pudding," at the Wrestler's Arms, and "pull his bloody finger out!"

The voyage from Yarmouth Roads to the Skaw, the top of Denmark, took longer than Lewrie's voyage, with a few odd, un-necessary jogs at Sir Hyde Parker's orders, with *no* communication between Nelson,

Graves, or Sir Hyde about how they'd go at the Danes, or what was to be done with the fleet, did they get into the Baltic! It was only after they anchored in the Koll, on the Swedish coast above the Narrows, that all three commanders of the Van, Main Body, and Rear divisions even "clapped top-lights" on each other, and both Nelson and Graves came away with not a *clue* to Sir Hyde's intentions. Then came the dithering as to whether they could sail down the Narrows past Kronborg Castle with both Danes and Swedes firing at them, as Lewrie dreaded, or whether it would be safer to take the long way round through the Great Belt, and come at Copenhagen from the South, which might delay the *decision* for battle a *week* or more! They tacked back and forth for at least a day before Nelson got the man to commit to the Narrows.

Vice-Admiral Sir Hyde Parker's favourite colour could safely be called "Plaid," and, if asked whether he ever had trouble making a decision, his likely answer would have been "Well, yes . . . and no."! Sir Hyde was surely in dread of the Russian Fleet, big as it was reputed to be, and even if he successfully engaged the Danes, feared that his ships would be so cut-up and damaged that they could never risk a *fresh* battle. He was certainly one of those historical figures who could snatch defeat from the jaws of victory, and, if left on his own, could screw up a two-car funeral.

It seems certain that Lord Nelson finagled Sir Hyde out of the way, with the winds of April 2, 1801, dead against him, as Captain Hardcastle realised; his squadron could have no effect on the battle, and it was Nelson's alone to manage as he wished with no interference.

Ah, but Sir Hyde *did* interfere, didn't he? His signal to "Discontinue the Action," Number 39, made absolutely *no* sense; he couldn't see, from his distant vantage point, through the pall of gunsmoke, that most of the Danish ships below the Trekroner Fort were surrendering, fallen silent, afire, or drifting out of the battle already.

Horatio Nelson, upon seeing Sir Hyde's signal, put his telescope to his blind right eye and told Capt. Foley that he really *couldn't see* it—"I have a right to be blind, sometimes," he said. He *acknowledged* it, since Number 39 *with two guns* was General to all ships, but he kept his own Number 16 aloft to "Engage the Enemy More Closely," knowing that he was winning. Nelson arranged the terms of the truce on his own, too.

There was a bit of a scandal within the Fleet after the battle, too, when Sir Hyde heaped praise on his favourites from his own distant squadron, which had hardly fired a gun in anger the whole day, his old favourite swashbuckling, prize-money reaping Capt. Otway, in particular, and ignoring the accomplishments of those of Nelson's, and Graves's, squadron. It is unlikely that Capt. Alan Lewrie will be "Mentioned In Despatches" in the *Gazette!* No medals were awarded for Copenhagen.

To Sir Hyde Parker, Horatio Nelson was a "whipper-snapper," too famous for his own good, too young, promoted over the heads of stolid, conventional men—perhaps too infamous for his scandalous dismissal of his wife, Fanny, and his affair with Emma Hamilton, which, by the by, resulted in *another* bastard daughter, Horatia, just as Nelson went down to Plymouth to board his first flagship. To the "Respectable," solid Sir Hyde, Nelson might have seemed such a little "pip-squeak" of a man, so prone to flattery, so in love with fame, glory, and honours, that he was quite put off. Which made things even worse for Adm. Parker, later in the Spring, when he was relieved of command and ordered home, whilst Vice-Admiral Lord Nelson was given command of the British fleet in the Baltic, where it would cruise for the rest of the Summer.

Did Great Britain, Zachariah Twigg at Foreign Office, and Alan Lewrie *really* have a hand in the assassination of Tsar Paul?

For all you conspiracy nuts, there were no black helicopters in those days, so . . . *stifle* yourselves! Take a deep breath and remind yourselves, "It's only a novel, it's only a novel." Though it was "a thing devoutly to be wished," an act that *did* destroy the League of Armed Neutrality, and its prime sponsor, it appears that it was home-grown. How else could one explain how all the devoted Cossack guards were somewhere else at the moment, the night of March 24, and how the conspirators gained such easy access to the Tsar's bed-chambers? The Tsarina's apartments were cross the passageway, and, from her own open doors, she witnessed the deed done through the open doors of the Tsar's apartment! Without too much in the way of complaint, it seems.

Later on that summer, once Tsar Alexander had taken the throne, peace and free commerce was returned to the Baltic and all of those British merchant ships and their crews had been freed, Capt. Thomas Fremantle of HMS *Ganges*, one of Nelson's old stalwarts and a fellow whom Lewrie knew from 1796 in the Mediterranean (buy *A King's Commander*—please!) made an official visit to St. Petersburg and the Russian Court. He wrote his wife, Betsy, that at several official *soirées* he was introduced to many of the conspirators, who were as gay as so many mag-pies, none suffering *any* recriminations, and prospering nicely!

This may be bad news for Lewrie, if Count Rybakov, and Count Anatoli Levotchkin, *were* part of the home-grown conspiracy, and had finagled HM Government and the Foreign Office to find a swift way home in time to participate, and benefit from the deed.

Though it's long odds that he and that arrogant, murderous lad, Anatoli Levotchkin, will cross hawses, there are some who keep grudges a whole lot better than most, and one can never tell. . . . Russia, after Napoleon Bonaparte's invasion in 1812, will become a British ally once again, and should Alan Lewrie ever have to go *back* to the Baltic . . . !

So, here's Capt. Alan Lewrie, RN, once more secure in command of a hellish-fine frigate. Sooner or later, though, he'll have to return to England . . . and Caroline. What *was* it she wrote in that letter he dreaded to open? Had Twigg's visit, and explanations, mollified her to yet another wary reconciliation?

Come to think on't, what was it that Eudoxia Durschenko wrote him? Has she become one more of "Florizel's"—the Prince of Wales's—passing fancies? Or did she rebuff his advances and precious gifts? More to the point, did her papa, Arslan Artimovich, take umbrage and a hopeful dagger-slash at the idiot?

And what of the delectable Tess? Has she become the mistress of Peter Rushton, Viscount Draywick, or does she pine for Lewrie? And, with his new fame, glory, and the possibility of "Respectable" renewed congress with his wife, would Alan Lewrie be so *huge* a fool as to . . . ?

Hmmm . . . faithful readers by now should have a clue as to what idiocy Alan Lewrie can get up to, if ever allowed idleness ashore. I promise that all shall be unveiled soon, in *King, Ship, and Sword*.

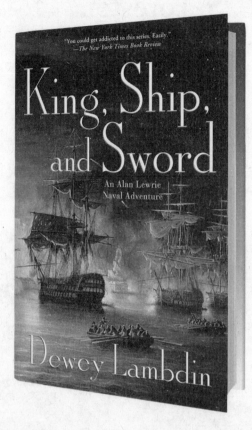

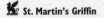